DREAMS AND SECRETS BOOK ONE

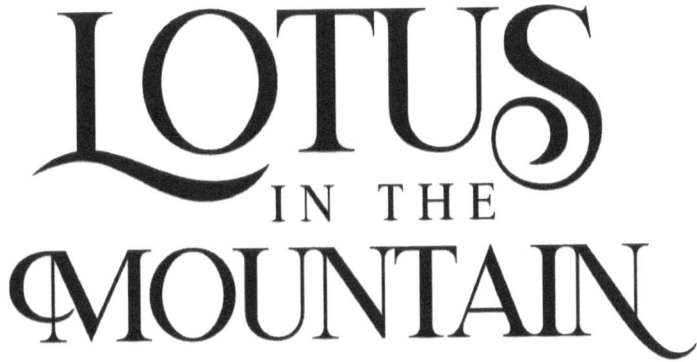

LOTUS
IN THE
MOUNTAIN

LINN COLDIRON

Cover Design by Jules Designs
(www. coversbyjules.crd.co)
Book Layout by Linn Coldiron

Lotus in the Mountain / Linn Coldiron ~ Second Edition 2024
ISBN: 978-1-955200-27-1

10 9 8 7 6 5 4 3 2

To Jen and Nani. After all the half-finished drafts I shoved in your faces in China, I hope you can enjoy the finished version.

The Dreams and Secrets Series

To Jen and Nani. After all the half-finished drafts I shoved in your faces in China, I hope you can enjoy the finished version.

The Dreams and Secrets Series

A Note from the Author

In the process of creating this story, world, and characters, I've spent hundreds of hours researching the cultures involved, including learning Mandarin and living in China for a period of about a year. However, research does not replace lived experience and I, in no way, claim that the experiences of my characters represent the entirety of the Asian American community. The same goes for the indigenous tribe I created for the sake of the story and clans. I created the culture based on my own readings and understandings of Native American tribes, particularly the Shoshone tribe which much inspiration was taken. For lived experience representation, please seek out books by authors of any culture you wish to read about. There is a list of some of my favorites on my website, linncoldiron.com.

Content Warnings

While a work of fiction intended for entertainment, there are darker elements and themes in *Lotus in the Mountain*. This book contains the following content warnings: violence using fantasy magic, swears and curses, and psychological abuse (non-familial).

Chapter One

If it had at all occurred to Mia that her best friend would be having a panic attack in a closet, she would have thought twice about begging her to wear a dress. But there she was, ankles sore, foot tapping, fist banging on the door as her worry grew. Worry for her friend. Worry for the night. Worry for her parents.

Mia had a lot to worry about.

"Blair," she said in a tight voice. "I know you hate dressing up, but please. It's going to start soon."

"I'm fine in here."

Mia groaned and banged her forehead against the door. Dull pain radiated through her head. On any other day she would have been more compassionate, but Blair had *insisted* she would be fine. Yes, this all made her uncomfortable. Yes, being in a dress made her feel like a doll, but it would be okay, because this was important to Mia.

She could handle it.

But they were running out of time.

"Do you need to go out and get some air?" Mia asked. "My

parents are going to speak soon. We promised we'd be there."

Her plea generated no response.

"Goddammit," Mia muttered. She reached up to her tight bun and pulled out one of the dozens of bobby-pins her mom had shoved into her hair a few hours ago. Crouching, her short satin dress threatening to slip up her thighs, she bent the bobby-pin and jammed it into the old-fashioned lock. She, of course, had no idea what she was doing, but it was worth a try.

Down the dimly lit hall, conversations rumbled through the half open door by which Blair had escaped—and Mia had followed— three minutes before. Laughter followed. Mia glanced at the door, frowning.

It was the party of her parents' dream. For the past five years, they'd traveled between Colorado and Thailand, spent hundreds of hours commuting through the Colorado mountains, missed basketball games, cello recitals, and parent-teacher conferences. They'd lived on a crazy schedule for so long, Mia couldn't remember what life had been like before.

And tonight they got their reward. The soul of the fights, of the frustrated tears lived on in their beautiful South East Asian Art exhibit.

Mia had been waiting for this night for five years. She couldn't wait for it to be over.

But first, she had to get Blair calm and out of the closet. And, as she attempted to do something she was pretty sure was impossible, she vowed to never force Blair into a dress again. The girl would go through great lengths to help Mia out, but this was, apparently, where she drew the line.

A dress.

Over a dress.

"Since when do you know how to pick locks?" Footsteps clacked across the hallway, coming to a stop beside her.

Mia didn't bother to turn.

"I don't," she admitted. "But they do it on TV all the time. How hard can it be?"

Derek, her twin, crouched next to her. She spared him a glance. It was odd, seeing him in a suit. Like Blair, he wasn't one for dressing up, but at least he didn't feel vulnerable. Uncomfortable, but not anxiety attack worthy.

He kept his green eyes glued to her hand, brow raised. "You suck at this." He nudged her and held out his hand. "*Gěi wǒ.*"

Mia scoffed. "Excuse me?"

He rolled his eyes and jerked his head toward the party door. "Keep watch."

Before Mia could protest, he nudged her out of the way and took the bobby pin from her, stared at its crushed self, and quickly snatched another one from Mia's hair.

"Hey!" she protested, but he pressed a finger to his lips.

Grumbling, she moved out of the way and stood, leaning against the door to do as he said. She doubted Derek would be able to do what she couldn't, though he did have a knack for getting them out of trouble. If anyone could get Blair back to the party, it would be him.

After a moment, the door opened again. Mia nudged Derek with the side of her leg. He cursed, but didn't stand or stop his mission. Mia nudged him again, and he swatted at her leg.

"Stop that," he said.

"Hurry up."

"I'm doing my best."

"Someone's coming, idiot." She kicked him one more time, and he muttered something incomprehensible in Chinese under his breath.

She tensed, preparing to explain why they were looking so sketchy in front of a broom closet, but when the person appeared,

Mia relaxed. It wasn't a security guard, or a janitor, or even an adult at the party. It was, instead, the only other teenager at the exhibit opening.

"Cody." She waved at him, keeping her voice hushed. He looked over at them, brow furrowed. He glanced behind him, closed the door, and hurried their way, walking much more softly than Derek had managed. Also unlike her twin, Cody looked far more comfortable in the suit Mia's mom had picked out for him. His auburn hair was long and shaggy, untamed, while his gray eyes darted from the twins to the door.

"What are you guys doing?" Cody asked. "Your parents are looking for you."

Mia gestured toward the door, which Derek hadn't taken his eyes off of once. "Blair's having an anxiety attack."

Cody rolled his eyes and let out an annoyed sigh. "Seriously?"

"No one asked you!" Blair snapped from inside. Her voice was higher than normal.

"Come on, Cody, you promised not tonight," Mia said. She didn't have the energy to deal with her parents, her parents' friends, *and* Cody and Blair fighting. All she wanted was to go back into the party and listen to her parents speak about all the amazing work they'd done. The cataloguing, the connections between historical artifacts in Southeast Asia that no one had noticed before. And of course, the reason all of this was happening.

The Queen.

"I won't if she won't," Cody muttered.

"Just go in without me." There was a thump, and then cursing, and then the lock clicked.

Mia pushed away from the door, heart racing while Derek slammed down on the handle before Blair could lock it again, and the door opened.

In the doorway stood a shaking, crossed armed girl in a knee length, simple dress. The whites of her brown eyes were tinted red, the only sign that she'd been crying, and Mia grimaced. She really hadn't thought it would be a big deal. And Blair had been fine the entire ride down. Something must have changed.

"Are you okay?" Derek asked.

"Peachy," Blair muttered. She reached up and tugged one of her short braids, refusing to look at any of them. "Just needed a moment."

"A dramatic moment," Cody said, too quiet for Blair to hear. Mia sighed. This night was not going to go as planned.

But that was fine. It was all okay as long as it wasn't a major disaster. She could handle a few things going wrong.

Like Blair locking herself in a closet. Or Cody making snide remarks about her, even though *he* of all people should understand her anxiety.

"All right," Mia said. "The closet is open, Blair's peachy, my parents are about to speak, let's go."

Blair hesitated for a moment, then made eye contact with Derek, and stepped out of the closet. "Okay. Okay. Sorry. I'm good. Yeah, let's go." She headed back, ahead of all of them with her head held high. Mia knew they wouldn't be talking about this. Blair wasn't the most open person in the world, and she definitely didn't like talking about her weaknesses.

Mia tried to follow her, but an arm caught her before she could. She glanced back at her brother, while Cody followed Blair back to the door, and Derek held up the bobby pin.

"Mom'll kill you if your hair isn't perfect," he said, switching to Chinese. She rolled her eyes and twisted her head so he could replace the perfect bobby pin back in her hair. Almost like it had never left. Almost like he hadn't used it at all. Once it was done, her hands reached up to the back of her head, to the tight bun and flower ornament sticking out of it. She'd wanted to wear her hair down:

curled with these gorgeous pins cascading down the front. She'd spent hours researching, but her mom had said no. She'd wanted it tight and perfect. Mia and Blair wore dresses. Derek and Cody in a suit. Not a hair out of place.

This was Intira Sòng's night. It belonged to her. It belonged to Mia's father, Liang, and it belonged to no one else. It was supposed to be perfect.

At least, their vision of perfect.

With her hair once more flawless, Mia and Derek hurried after their friends. In the quiet of the hallway, Mia had forgotten just how many people had shown up to support their parents. Accomplished, well educated, prolific adults filled this room. People who could be her parents. People who could be her grandparents. For a moment, it took her breath away. The idea that she and her friends were the only ones under thirty in the entire room, that they really didn't belong here, overwhelmed her.

Her heart raced. Tonight had to go well. Not perfectly, but well. Because she wasn't sure what was coming after, and if this didn't go well....

Derek placed a hand on her shoulder. "Tonight's going to be great."

Her negative emotions dispersed. Calm washed over her, like it always did when Derek reassured her. And he was right. Tonight was going to be great. Her two best friends were here. Her parents were getting everything they wanted. Mia breathed out, then leaned her head against Derek's shoulder, still watching everyone. The adults. Blair and Cody wandering off to find wine somewhere.

"Tonight is going to be amazing," she said.

"I don't know if I'd go that far," Derek said. "We still have to pretend like we enjoy being around these people."

Mia laughed and straightened. "Oh come on, we like some of them."

He thought for a moment. "No, we really don't."

Mia's eyes scanned the room again until they landed on their parents. "We like Mom and Dad."

"Do we?"

She laughed again at his joking tone, when she spotted a familiar face talking to them. Her laughter faltered, and she frowned. The man standing with them was someone who'd been in her life as long as *The Queen* had been. The sculpture Liang had discovered buried near the Mekong River in Thailand five years prior. He'd funded the trip and had popped in and out of their lives ever since. A young man. Mid-twenties, maybe. It was hard to tell.

"Hey look," she said. "Dorian came."

That wasn't his real name. But the twins had been calling him 'Dorian' for so long now that they couldn't remember what it actually was.

"Looking the same as always," he said.

"Never changing."

"I wonder if he really does have a picture in his attic."

A laugh from both of them. Out of the corner of her eye, she noticed Blair returning with drinks, but no sign of Cody. Another jolt of concern, but she didn't have time to think about it because a woman she didn't know spoke, microphone blasting through the entire room.

"And now, ladies and gentlemen, it's my pleasure to introduce the couple who have worked tirelessly to put this exhibit together. Please, welcome Dr. and Dr. Sòng!"

That was their cue. Neither of them were going to speak, but they had to be there for their parents. Standing behind them as Intira gave her speech. A unified family. A picture for the Sunday paper.

Mia didn't want to do it.

Derek didn't want to either.

They exchanged a glance. One that shared a million annoyances at the life their parents had picked for them without so much a question. But it would be all right. Because tomorrow their lives would go back to the way it had been before *The Queen*. They'd have their parents back. This was a small price to pay for that.

Besides, this is what one did for their family.

Chapter Two

Derek didn't normally drink wine. In fact, he was certain that wine was the most disgusting form of alcohol out there, and he'd tried báijiǔ before. But tonight he needed something to take the edge off. A little bit of something to relax. To numb his skin to the overwhelming emotions pricking at them. He wouldn't get drunk. That wasn't his style. But…well…something.

It wasn't just the emotions, though. It was them mixed with everything else. The questions from his parents' friends. Where was he planning to go to university? What did he want to major in? How was high school? Did he miss Beijing? Did he have a girlfriend?

Honestly, it was too much. Which is why he'd hidden away. Right after Intira had given her speech, Derek had slipped away, leaving an annoyed Mia to deal with all of the family friends. He knew she'd get back at him later for that. He had no idea how, and he wasn't looking forward to it, but at the moment he didn't care. Mia was better at talking to their parents' friends. She had answers for all the questions they wanted to ask. And he'd do something to appease her annoyance. Buy her chocolate or something.

"Since when can you pick a lock?"

There were only so many people in the world who could add that much sass to a single sentence. A smile flickered onto Derek's lips. He took a sip of his wine and glanced over in time to see Blair lean against the wall next to him. It was kind of amazing to see her in a dress. Even if it caused her anxiety to shoot out in sharp spikes, threatening to draw imaginary blood from his body, she looked amazing. He wished he could somehow convince her of that. Quell her panic enough so she could enjoy the night.

So *they* could enjoy the night. Because, really, this night could not be enjoyable without her. Or any night, really.

"I'm a master at it," he continued. "Didn't I tell you? It's my crowning moment."

"Uh huh." Blair always tried to remain neutral around him. She tried to remain calm and unassuming. But it never worked. Even without her anxiety flying all over the place because of the party, Blair's emotions were too loud to keep from him.

Besides, it didn't matter who it was. He always felt them. Emotions. Textures snaking between the hairs on his arms. He always had.

He always would.

"You don't believe me?" He asked. He turned to face her, leaning his shoulder against the wall.

She snorted. "You couldn't unlock a door with a hairpin if you'd actually tried."

Derek grinned. He glanced around, searching for any possible eavesdroppers. "Then how'd I do it?"

No one paid attention to them. Mia was off talking to people, looking at art with Cody somewhere on the other side of the exhibit. The adults wouldn't care what they were talking about. To them, Derek and Blair were just two teenagers chatting. Flirting.

He definitely considered it flirting.

Her emotions fluttered. Impressed mixed with concern mixed with gentle curiosity. Butterflies against his skin. "You're getting better at controlling it."

A large grin spread across his face. It hadn't been easy. Fighting with her for control of the lock. Honestly, he had an advantage. Blair wasn't great at controlling her magic when she was upset about something.

Magic. It'd been years since Blair's mom, Mrs. Arbour, had sat with him at the park and explained what he was. What he could do. Still, he wasn't sure he'd ever get used to that word mixed in every day conversation.

He'd read plenty of fantasy novels over the years. Dragons, witches, warlocks, elves, and dwarves. From the western novels his classmates read, to the Chinese fables and poems his cousins sent him.

His parents thought it was because he liked the escape. But magic wasn't an escape. Magic was his reality.

"I've been practicing," he said. Hiding away in his room at night trying to let the energy flow through his veins. The warmth that was different than any emotion. He couldn't do much, but he was trying to learn.

"I can tell." Blair reached over and took the wine glass from his hands before taking a sip. Derek didn't argue. "But you have to be more careful when you use it. It's not like your empathy. People might notice. People you don't want to notice."

Her concern enveloped her other emotions. Oil against water. A shudder ran up Derek's spine, and he closed his eyes, feeling out for his sister. For her emotions. The ones he could always feel, no matter how far apart they were. All it took was a moment to focus.

He wasn't sure when he first realized he'd had these powers. A tickle of pain whenever Mia cried when they were toddlers. The burning fire of anger when his parents fought. The crinkled excitement at the Spring Festival celebration when he was five. For the longest time, he'd thought everyone could read emotions. He wasn't unique or special. It was just another sense that everyone had.

But it wasn't. People couldn't feel emotions. People could manipulate emotions. And until Mrs. Arbour had come to talk to him that day, explaining about the magic world hidden underneath the surface, he hadn't told a single soul what he could do.

Mia's emotions shifted. All of her anxieties washed away into excitement. A special kind of excitement she only got when she was talking about ancient art. No one doubted that Mia would follow her parents into their chosen field. She was intelligent. Academic. Curious about ancient arts and cultures. This stuff interested her way more than it did him, and it was nice to feel her happy. Really, truly happy.

He wondered if he'd ever tell her about all of this. His powers. The magic world.

"No one is going to notice." He realized it'd been a hot minute since he'd spoken, but Blair glanced over at him anyway. "We're careful. And it's not like anyone here is a mage."

Blair's eyes narrowed. "Seriously, you don't know who is who. It's not just…." Her voice dropped in volume. "It's not just mages who know about magic. You know this."

Unlike Derek, who spontaneously got his powers after generations of non-magic family, Blair had grown up in a clan. Her mother and grandmother had taught her all about their customs and their secrets, instilling paranoia in her from day one of her life. He tried to understand, but he didn't. No one said anything about their powers. But, he didn't want to push. He hated the negative emotions bleeding off of her.

So, instead of pushing, he nudged her shoulder with his.

"All right, fine. No more talk of…," he glanced at her never ending glare. "…things." She rolled her eyes. "How about we go do something fun? Like…I dunno, go make out or something." His tone was light and teasing, though he wasn't entirely joking. That would be much more fun than standing around waiting for the night to end. And it wasn't like they hadn't kissed before. A couple of times. Once or twice when drunk. Once or twice when sober. Just two magical teens trying not to let anyone know the feelings they had for each other.

Blair's anxiety shifted, fluctuating between annoyance and curiosity. He grinned at her, and she scowled.

"Seriously?"

"Sure. Why not?"

She rolled her eyes. "Let's go see the thing we drove three hours to come see. You haven't seen *The Queen* yet, have you?"

Derek groaned. *The Queen* was the last thing he wanted to see tonight. When his father had discovered her, it'd destroyed everything. Their once close family drifted apart. His father grew more and more obsessed, trying to suss out the secrets of this beautiful, amazing, life-sized sculpture of a woman. Where did she come from? How did they sculpt something so intricate and life-like in an artistic time period that show-cased nothing else like it? And more than that, what was the sculpture crafted from? It looked like marble, but preliminary tests said no.

Derek protested seeing *The Queen*. Her picture was enough.

"You really want to see that thing?" he asked, unable to mask the bitterness in his voice. Blair reached out and slipped her hand in his. Tingles shimmied up his arm. Not from her emotions, but from the warmth of her skin.

"God no," she said. "It gives me the creeps. But it is important to your parents. I think it'll hurt your dad if you avoid it."

Derek wanted to say 'screw that,' but he held his tongue. In his mind, Mia explained that he shouldn't be passive aggressive and purposefully hurt their father just because he was butt-hurt about a few years of absence. Things would go back to normal after this. It would be all right. Why make things worse?

Mia's imaginary lecture won out, and Derek groaned out an elongated, "Fine."

Blair let go of his hand, and the two headed into the crowd. Derek itched with anxiety, but not his own. Or was it? His mind struggled to find the unique signature all emotions held. The one that indicated who the emotion belonged to, but there was nothing.

The two wove their way through the people, stopping every now and then, in silence, to look at the pieces of art his parents had collected for the exhibit. None of them were new to Derek. He'd seen them in photographs, or tucked away in his parents' office at the museum. Each one came with a specific lecture, one he could almost recall.

Dates.

Materials.

Cultural significance.

It was what his parents did.

It was everything he couldn't care less about.

"So, why does *The Queen* freak you out?" Derek asked as they made their way to the centerpiece. The grand finale. The pièce de résistance.

Blair shrugged. "I just get a weird feeling around it."

"You've never been around it."

She rolled her eyes. "Fine. Every picture I've ever seen has this vibe to it. I don't know what it is. Maybe she's too realistic. Maybe there's something off about her. I dunno. But every time I've seen a picture of her, I get this sinking feeling. Like something...like something bad is going to happen."

Derek did say anything, unsure of how to react. It wasn't that he didn't believe her. It was that he did.

"Ugh, it doesn't matter," Blair said. Frustration emanated from her body, clinging to his skin. "Let's just go see the damn thing."

She charged on, and he chased after her. Each step grew heavy, like someone had dropped lead into his shoes.

His breath shortened.

He blinked, shaking his head to get rid of the dizziness. Blair came in and out of view. His ears rang like Notre Dame.

Please.

A voice broke through the bells. A voice much like a bell itself. Quiet, yet commanding. Unrealistic. Imaginary.

Help me. Please.

He tried his best to ignore the voice. He wanted it to be imaginary, but like with the rest of the world, with the people standing around him in the crowded museum, it had something he couldn't ignore. The plea, the simple words, radiated emotion. No, emotions. A million bursting, bright emotions consuming his every sense. His skin erupted with sensations. Emotions danced in front of his eyes, dancing and twirling like a bad acid trip. He could even hear them, whispering in different tones. It wasn't like this. It wasn't supposed to be like this. Emotions didn't talk to him.

Please.

Attempting—and failing—to take a deep breath, he pressed forward. His sluggish legs drew him to the ground, and he fought against the gravity. He couldn't see. Through it all, in the distance, he felt Mia. Her happiness.

Help.

He tried to focus on his sister. To keep her in his sights. To hold on to the one grounded thing in his life.

It all became too much.

Please.

Mia spotted him standing in front of a tapestry with his hands in his pockets, staring up at the piece of art with a blank expression. She breathed out, relieved. After having been alone, fending off her parents' friends for the past twenty minutes—as her jerk of an antisocial brother disappeared immediately after the speech—she was grateful for the sight of a friend.

"Cody!"

The adults surrounding her glanced in her direction before returning to their conversations. She ignored them. Who cared what they thought? Her excitement bled through every pore in her body. This was it. Her parents had given their speech. Everyone was at the exhibit. Tonight, a chapter in her life was coming to an end, and tomorrow she'd have her family back. Nothing else mattered.

Cody twisted his head to look at her, tearing his eyes away from the tapestry. He smiled and she strode over to him, tempted to take off her heels and run barefoot across the tile floor. Mia couldn't believe he'd actually come. If you looked up the word, "homebody" in the dictionary, not only would it have Cody's picture, but his birth certificate and life's story. She was pretty certain he'd left Willow Creek, their tiny mountain town, a total of five times in his entire life. And none of them by choice.

"Thank god I found you," she said. The tapestry hanging above them depicted two women dancing, stitched onto the cloth with golden silk thread.

"Is it wrong to thank a deity you don't believe in?" he asked. His tone was light and teasing, but Mia knew better. Cody had mastered the art of masking his emotions from a young age. It'd taken a while for her to pick out the small things. The shiver in his voice. The tremble behind every word. The anxiety behind the joke.

She had to keep from frowning. If she showed her concern, he'd only get more anxious, and then he would most likely disappear for the rest of the night.

Instead, she said, "Probably. But I don't believe in him, so I doubt he cares."

Cody chuckled. "All right. Fair."

She glanced around, wondering where Blair and Derek had disappeared off to. Probably together somewhere acting like total idiots. There was no point in trying to find them, especially not if she wanted to see the exhibit. Neither of them had any interest, unlike Cody and herself.

She turned her attention back to the tapestry. "Beautiful, isn't it?"

"Yeah," Cody said. "It's a great collection. It's clear they love their work."

"Oh, they do," Mia said, a hint of bitterness to her voice. Cody glanced at her, and she shook her head, forcing a smile.

Cody coughed, before changing the subject. "Where did Derek and Blair go?"

"Who knows," she said, tone light. "Let's walk around. We might find them actually showing an interest in my parents' work."

"That would be a miracle." Cody laughed. "Come on. I've mapped out the best way to look at everything without having to double back."

Mia gazed up at the tapestry one more time, taking in the twining golden threads. Her entire life she'd grown up with art like this in her house. Art from Thailand, from Vietnam, from Laos, from Cambodia—countries her parents studied. The ones from Thailand spoke to her. Well, more like a whisper. A sense of her history. Of her mom's culture that she'd only been allowed to study.

"Okay," she eventually said. "But I'm pretty sure it was my mom who made that map."

Cody shrugged. "Her attention to detail might have helped me do all the work, sure."

The two of them laughed and headed around the exhibit,

following Intira's layout to a T. The art, arranged by region and time period, was beautiful. Red and gold dominated the art, depicting people and animals and scenery that one would never find in the United States, much less Colorado. Now and then, they came across little statues of people and gods, some drawing influence from Hinduism, some from Buddhism—Chinese and Indian—and some from the stories and history of the individual areas. A mix and match of culture, of religion, of thoughts through an ancient and beautiful part of the world.

Mia explained the art she knew to Cody, delving into all things she'd picked up living with her parents. And he listened with barely a word, nodding and saying, "yeah," or "that's cool" now and then to show he was listening.

She wanted more out of him. For him to engage and ask questions, but at the same time, she knew he wouldn't. Not here. Not with all these people. Even now, with the two of them ignoring all the adults around them, without Blair or Derek to overtake the conversation, he was tense. Shaking.

How Mia had ended up with two friends with anxiety, she wasn't sure. Especially since the two of them tolerated each other at best. Still, she was grateful that they had put aside their own struggles to come be here for her and Derek.

After winding their way through the exhibit, Mia sucked in a deep breath. There was only one more thing to see.

Nerves trickled up her throat. She'd spent five years preparing herself to see the sculpture that had changed the entire dynamic of her family. She'd seen pictures, and she'd spent many dinners listening to her father chatter about all the new things he'd learned about the sculpture during his research. But she'd never seen it in person.

"I guess it's time to see *The Queen*," she said.

Cody glanced at her. "Are you okay?"

"Yeah," she lied.

"Conflicted?"

She reached out and slipped her hand into his, seeking comfort. "It's just…what if I don't get it? What if I look at her and I don't see what my dad sees and he expects me to be excited about something when I just don't care?"

Cody gripped her hand and showed his gentle smile. "It'll be fine."

But he didn't sound certain, and she didn't feel certain. Still, they pressed on, heading the piece of art that everyone was really here to see. Yes, the tapestries and small sculptures were beautiful, but they were the leaves on a California redwood. Beautiful, rustling, adding to the atmosphere, but not what took your breath away.

Mia had expected everyone to surround *The Queen*. To have to push to get close enough to see her. But the crowds thinned as they closed in. Mia's heart raced. She couldn't tell if it was her hand shaking, or Cody's. A weight settled on her chest, pressing down on her lungs. On her heart.

But when *The Queen* came into view, it all vanished.

Mia stared at the sculpture, eyes taking in everything at once: the woman's smooth cheeks, her frozen strands of wild hair framing her face, the lashes pressed together from closed eyes. Her hands, one pressed against her chest in a tight fist, the other wrapped around her body, pushed against the belt of her robes which billowed out over her legs in a flowing skirt. Beneath it all, one bare foot revealed itself, caked in mud.

A calm washed over Mia. Her muscles relaxed. Her heart slowed. Her hand slipped out of Cody's, falling to her side as she stared up at the woman. No, the sculpture. It was a sculpture.

But…was it?

"Wow," Mia breathed. There were no other words. No explanation for the feeling of content that overtook her body. Her

19

mind. She turned to Cody, ready to tell him that he was right. It was all right.

But the moment she looked away from *The Queen*, the moment she laid eyes on him, concern overtook her. Cody stared at *The Queen*, but unlike her, there was no tranquility in his expression. His eyes were wide, body shaking, and he stepped back from her.

"Cody?" she asked.

He continued to back away, stumbling over his own feet, but his eyes never left *The Queen*. She grabbed his wrist to stop him.

"Cody, what's wrong?"

He wasn't listening. He pulled his arm out of her grasp and turned, finally breaking eye contact with the sculpture. Mia tried to stop him, to keep him from running into someone and causing a scene, but it was too late.

Cody crashed into a figure. A man. Mia braced for Cody's anxiety to overtake him, for him to run off like he used to when they were kids in an assembly. Her instinct was to grab him again, to try and talk him down, but she knew better than to touch him. Instead she faced the man with a whole speech and apology prepared, only to falter.

The man cocked his head. Dorian. It was the man Mia and Derek called Dorian. Someone she knew.

Cody's chest heaved. He stumbled away and Mia tried to find the right words to calm him down and appease the strange, never aging man.

But Dorian didn't yell. He didn't chastise or even ask what was wrong. Instead, he smiled, his eyes alive with curiosity.

"Oh, hello," he said. "Are you enjoying your evening, Cody?"

There was a moment of relief. Dorian wasn't a bad guy. Even Cody was calming down from his gentle words.

But the relief didn't last long. Mia had no time to think. No time to react when Blair's terrified voice rose above the murmur of the crowd.

Blair was loud. Blair was brash. Blair didn't care what anyone thought of her. But she'd never screamed like that. Mia turned, heart racing. The crowd parted, as if knowing she needed to see Derek laying on the ground, Blair crouching over him, shaking his shoulders.

Everything happened so fast.

Her mind went blank. One second, she was pulling away from Cody and Dorian. Running to the other side of *The Queen*. Toward her unconscious brother.

The next, a wave of dizziness halted her progression. The world blurred. Her mind spun. She stumbled, trying to catch her balance.

And then a loud crack eclipsed every other sound in the room.

Mia's vision cleared, but her chest tightened. She couldn't breathe. She could barely think. She turned her head, not wanting to witness the tragedy. She knew. Just like with her brother, she knew without having to see.

And yet she had to look. She stared up, heart sinking into her chest. Because Derek was unconscious on the floor, and the sculpture, *The Queen*, fell to the ground in two pieces, split down the middle by a thin, sinister fissure.

Chapter Three

Her voice tickled his ear. Tracing the outline until it wormed into his blood, traveling like flaming ice through his body, into his muscles. Contracting until every bit of oxygen fled from his lungs. Her plea haunted him. He knew it. He knew the voice. And yet, he didn't. He recalled her name. Her face. Her everything. They wouldn't stay still; droplets of water slipping through shaking fingers.

His chest moved. Up and down. As if he were breathing. As if the voice wasn't suffocating him. The ground, rough and hard, jabbed into his back. Through the suit. Piercing his skin until droplets of blood soaked the ground. Had he any oxygen, he would have screamed.

Then, without warning, the pain vanished. His memories of her turned to acid and dissolved his torture.

He fell.

Air tickled the back of his neck. It washed through his hair, and encased his limbs. His clothes, tight and uncomfortable, melted into loose robes that fluttered around him, folding into themselves like a cocoon. Strong memories picked at his mind. Strong emotions picked at his skin.

Fear.

Confusion.

Desperation.

A kitten's nails clawing an unsuspecting toy.

He gasped.

"Please."

A gust of wind caught him. His eyes opened, revealing a world of inky darkness. Like guiding hands, the wind repositioned him upright and he drifted downward until he hovered inches above a reflective surface. His eyes adjusted to the darkness, guided by a single light shining in front of him.

He tilted his head, unable to tear his eyes away from the light. Chilled water rippled under his toes as they touched the pool. And he stepped forward. One. Two. Three. Disturbing the smooth glass in his quest to embrace the warmth of the light.

It called to him.

As he drew closer, he realized the light was not alone. It floated, an ethereal ball of energy, above a stone pedestal. He halted. A modern memory rushed forward. One of him and his mother, sitting in her office while she showed him and his sister pictures of Greek architecture. Pedestals, similar to the one in front of him. Marble. Rising tall with an intricate design of leaves and vines.

He blinked, and the memory was gone. He blinked, and his feet drew him forward, step by step, second by second, until he reached the pedestal. The light. And he held out a hand.

The light lowered, twisting and turning. Unfolding into a small, pink flower. It landed in his palm, petals thin as tracing paper, center yellow as the sun on a four-year-old's drawing. A warm shudder tingled up his arm, spreading through his entire body and he breathed out.

A lotus.

"Méilián?"

He spoke his sister's Chinese name. For as long as he could remember, the lotus flower was a long standing symbol in his family. They floated lazily in his grandparents' pond. They told him and his sister the tale of Chengxiang and the Lotus Lantern. He'd known about the meaning of the lotus since he was a child.

It was the flower his sister was named after.

Light spread through the veins of the petals. He stepped back, away from the pedestal, as one by one, the petals dropped to the ground. As each one caressed the surface of the water, it chimed a different pitch. Their echoes enveloped him in warmth. Bliss. Happiness. He smiled as the gentle emotions enveloped him.

And then there was pain.

A punch to the stomach, removing all oxygen from his lungs once more. He tried to gasp. He could not. He tried to remain on his feet. He could not. He collapsed to the ground, core of the flower creating a ring of ripples in front of him. He stared at it, choking on nothing, until his lungs expanded.

He screamed.

Make it stop!

"Niran?"

He didn't understand. Everlasting? Was she asking to live forever? Or maybe…she was calling out a name?

Tears streamed down his face. A clap of thunder broke the sky with lightning.

"Niran."

"That's not me." His voice was hoarse.

"Please let me be free," the voice replied.

He coughed. Shuddered. Another clap of thunder and the pain vanished. The ringing vanished. Everything vanished but him and the light. The center of the flower floating on invisible water.

"I want to be free."

"I'm not the one you should be asking," he said. "I can't set you free."

"*Please.*"

The flower's light dimmed. His eyes burned from the tears, breath ragged and unpredictable. He held out a hand to touch the flower, only to find he lacked the strength.

She was begging him. The flower. The voice. They were begging him and he didn't understand why. Asking permission from him when he had no idea who she even was.

"Please."

But she kept asking. And he found he couldn't say no to her.

"If you want, you can be free."

Her voice remained in his ears. Different than before. Not harsh. Not demanding. A gentle echo pleading with him for help he couldn't give. He wished he could. To appease the voice, to appease her, would bring him unbridled joy. He understood wanting to be free. To let go of all the secrets he'd been sworn to keep and just *be*.

Softness enveloped him. No more stones. No more ripples. A bed?

The echo morphed into something different. A rhythm thumping alongside his blood. His pulse. His heartbeat. He tried to shift, to open his eyes, but found he couldn't. The blankets weighed him down, trapping him to a bed he didn't recognize. On his eyelids, the image of the lotus remained burned in the darkness. Sad and weak with wilted petals dropping one-by-one to the ground.

The lotus.

He recalled the final moments before meeting the lotus. His

hand in Blair's. No. Further forward. Chasing after *The Queen*. A piece of art they only visited out of obligation. Then he was in the darkness.

Was it a dream?

Derek had never been one for vivid dreams. But even with his knowledge of magic, none of that had made sense. None of *this* made sense. The thumping in his ears quickened. His chest rose and fell as if commanded to a higher tempo by an invisible conductor.

What had it all meant? What had he done? Why couldn't he move?

His eyelids fluttered. The image of the lotus flickered until finally it vanished and his eyes snapped open. Darkness greeted him, but a different kind than the possible dream. In there, the only light source came from the flower. It cast across nothing, leaving only himself, the pedestal, and the ripples bathing in light. In here, moonlight outlined an entire room.

He scanned the room. Cabinets. Monitors. A door. He pushed himself into a sitting position. Something tugged at his left arm. He glanced down. An IV.

I'm in a hospital?

He rubbed his eyes and gazed toward the window when a figure in the corner caught his attention.

"Mia?"

His voice came out hoarse and he coughed once. She was curled up in the corner, shoulders rising and falling in a gentle rhythm. Bare feet poked out beneath a thin blanket. She didn't stir at the sound of her name. He'd been too quiet. He pushed himself further into a sitting position, head spinning, and tried again.

"Méilián?"

This time, she did stir, but she didn't wake. He closed his eyes, breathing heavily. Instead of pushing his voice, he tried to reach out to her emotions. It wasn't easy to do without touching her, but sometimes he could convince her emotions—anyone's emotions—to change texture.

Only he couldn't.

Because there were no textures.

He collapsed against the bed, panting. No textures. He'd never not been able to feel the textures before. Especially not with Mia. Her emotions had always stood out to him, stronger and more tactile than anyone else in the world. They were bonded. Twins. Two halves of the same coin. Different, but always connected.

His heart pounded.

"Méilián!"

She jerked. The blanket fell to the ground and she looked around, blinking rapidly. For a moment, as she woke, she stared at him. She was awake. Alive. But...still no emotions.

"Démíng?"

He did his best to smile. "Hey."

Her eyes widened and she stood, nearly tripping over the blanket. "Oh my god, you're awake," she said, switching between English and Chinese. She was by his side in an instant, going off in rapid-fire Mandarin. "Are you okay? What happened? Blair said you collapsed? You have a fever and they have you on oxygen. They said something about a possible seizure? But we've seen Blair have seizures before and I don't think it was the same—"

"Can you like...slow down?" Derek asked with a groan. His head pounded. Body burning.

Mia laughed, quick and breathy. "I'm so glad you're okay."

Tears. Normally there was something before the tears. A patter along his arms. This time, they caught him off guard. All he could think to do was reach out and grab her hand.

"Yeah, I'm fine."

She nodded, wiping away the tears with her other hand. "Good. I...I should go get Mom and Dad. I think they're getting coffee."

"Where are we?" Derek asked. "Besides a hospital. Are we home?"

Mia shook her head. "The ambulance took you to a hospital in Denver. Anschutz, I think. I wasn't paying that much attention."

"Oh." He'd never ridden in an ambulance before. "Where are Blair and Cody?"

"Cody took Blair home," Mia said. "They wanted to stay, but Blair's mom insisted she come home. The phone call was very loud and very angry."

Derek grimaced. Something was going on. "Why? I just got sick. Not like anything crazy happened."

Mia hesitated. "Um...about that."

No. No. No. He already had the dream. He already couldn't feel Mia's emotions. He was already sick. He didn't need anything else going on. There didn't need to be another problem in his life. Voice sharp, he asked, "What?"

"Well...." She bit her lip. "I just...when you collapsed, something happened to the sculpture. No one understands it, but Mom and Dad are in a lot of trouble, and the entire party was in an uproar."

He closed his eyes. "What happened to it?"

In a quiet whisper, she said, "It broke."

Silence fell over the room. Or maybe Derek's ears had stopped working. A wave of dizziness washed over him. He tried to think. To understand. To get a grasp on what was going on, but nothing came to him. He let himself sink back in the hospital bed, closing his eyes.

The lotus appeared on his eyelids.

Petals falling one-by-one.

The sculpture broke.

The Queen.

His parents' dream.

It had broken.

"Derek?"

Mia's voice grew in volume. He opened his eyes and looked at her, trying to understand. Something was going on. All those bad things that Mrs. Arbour had warned him about: they were happening. He didn't know what it was. He didn't know how he was involved, just that something, *something* was going to go wrong sometime soon.

"Are you okay?" she asked.

No. He wasn't okay. Mrs. Arbour had called Blair home after the sculpture, the one that gave Blair the creeps, broke, and he'd had the most vivid dream he'd ever had in his life. "No. I need to tell you something."

Enough was enough. Everyone had told him he needed to keep his magic a secret. *He'd* convinced himself he needed to keep it a secret. But that wasn't fair to Mia. Not if something was coming. Not if he was about to get wrapped up in something insane.

But what if I'm not?

It didn't matter.

"What's up?" she asked.

"I–"

"You're awake!"

Derek jumped, shaking. He hadn't realized how tense he'd become until he heard his mother's voice. His head whipped around as his parents hurried into the room, coming to his side.

"We were so worried," Intira said in Chinese. To her husband, she said, "Go get the doctor. I'm sure he'll want to know."

Liang nodded. Before he left, he placed a hand on Derek's shoulder. "I'm happy you are awake."

All Derek could do was nod. He glanced at Mia, who glanced at him. She mouthed, "Tell me later," before the fussing began. He would have to tell her later. When their parents weren't in the room. When Intira wasn't asking him all the same questions Mia had moments before. When his head had stopped spinning and he stopped seeing the lotus on every surface in the room.

Mia sat alone in the living room, staring at the ticking grandfather clock. It was an heirloom. From her grandparents. They'd purchased it when they were young from a British merchant trying to make it in Hong Kong. It stood old and tall, made of pearwood with a gold face and pendulum. The ticking relaxed her. It was the sound of her childhood, a reminder of her grandparents' living room in Beijing. Of sitting with tea and oranges after playing soccer with Derek at the park, both exhausted.

Her grandparents had gifted it to Liang when they moved to America. It was a Western artifact, they'd said. It should belong in a Western home. When she was young, Mia believed that lie. But that was seven years ago, and she'd come to understand a lot more about their move from China to America. Still, despite the complicated history of why the clock was in the living room, she loved the sound of the ticking.

Or, on a normal night she did.

Tonight it mocked her. Each tick was another second her parents had holed themselves in Derek's room. She'd wanted to go with, but they'd told her it was best if she went to sleep. It was late. Almost three in the morning, if the clock read accurately. Which it did. She'd planned to sleep, but the hassle of getting ready for bed, she'd found she was unable to.

She sat alone, phone lighting up with a ding every now and then as Cody texted her to check in.

<<Derek is still asleep?>> he asked.

Mia breathed out through her nose. Derek had said he needed to tell her something, but ever since they left the hospital, he'd been in and out of sleep. It had proven difficult to get him inside and to his room. It wasn't unlike him to need a lot of sleep. She'd spent most mornings over the past year or two trying to get him up on time for school, but this felt different.

<<Yeah,>> she replied. <<His fever is still high. I'm surprised they let us leave the hospital.>>

<<AMA?>>

<<What?>>

<<Against medical advice. Did your parents take him home and sign one?>>

Mia had no idea. She hadn't been in the room when the discharge papers were signed. She'd stayed with Derek and Liang while her mom spoke to the doctors about their options. Next thing she knew, they were getting Derek ready to leave, and he was asleep the entire three hour drive back to Willow Creek.

<<Maybe.>>

<<It'll be okay. Your parents know what they're doing.>>

She wished she believed that. Tonight was supposed to make everything go back to normal. Now *The Queen* was broken, her parents and their careers were in trouble, her brother was sick, and she had a sinking feeling in her stomach that something had shifted.

<<I hope so.>>

Cody took a moment to reply. <<I know it will. I have to sleep though. Got work in a couple of hours. I'll check in tomorrow.>>

Mia nodded in response, and was about to put her phone down when it rang. She fumbled with it as a picture of Blair and her hugging and laughing popped up with the name, "That Bitch"—a name Blair had insisted on—in big letters. Mia answered quickly, hoping it wouldn't alert her parents. She didn't want them telling her to go to sleep before she got news on Derek.

"Why are you up?" Mia asked in a hushed voice.

"Hello to you too," Blair said. Whenever Mia and Blair spoke on the phone, Mia could either hear Blair's younger brother screaming in the background, or hear one of her parents trying to talk to her, but tonight it was eerily silent. "How's it going?"

"Oh, you know," Mia said. She glanced over her shoulder, at Derek's door, and frowned. "Things are crazy right now. Mom and Dad are super worried about Derek, but they also have the Thai government on their ass about the sculpture. They won't tell me much, but I heard my mom talking to someone on the phone and she sounded stressed. They have to go back to Denver tomorrow."

She'd wanted to take the phone from her mom and scream at the person on the other end. Derek rarely got sick, but when he did, it wasn't good. It was hospital worthy sickness, just like now. He needed his parents. More than the Thai government needed to find out what happened to a stupid piece of art.

"That sucks," Blair said. "I know my mom's gonna come over tomorrow and help out. She might stay with you while your parents are in Denver."

Mia smiled. Mrs. Arbour was the most motherly person Mia had ever met. With four kids, three boys and Blair, she spent most of her life *being* a mother, and she adopted everyone else she knew. Whenever Mia or Derek saw her, she asked them about their health, their grades, their social lives, and what they'd eaten that day. Besides her own parents, she couldn't think of anyone better to take care of Derek.

"Thanks," Mia said.

"No problem."

The door to Derek's room opened. Mia jumped up from the couch, eyes wide. Her parents exited, muttering to each other in hushed Chinese. Mia strained to listen, but they were too quiet.

"I gotta go," she said quickly into the phone. "I'll talk to you later."

"Okay."

Mia hung up and hurried over to Intira. Her slippers slapped against the wooden floor, catching her parents' attention. They frowned at the sight of her, but she didn't care. "How is he?"

"Sleeping," her mom said. "You should be sleeping too."

"I wanted to know how he's doing," Mia said.

Her parents exchanged a glance. One that said a million words Mia would never be able to decipher. And then Intira placed a gentle hand on Mia's shoulder, smile soft and sad. "Things will be better in the morning."

"But you won't be here," Mia muttered.

Her mother sighed. "I know, I know. Things are complicated. It isn't ideal for us to leave, but Derek is doing all right, and the sooner we can investigate, the stronger our evidence will be. You understand, right?"

Mia nodded, but internally she wanted to scream. She didn't want to understand. She didn't want to have to understand. She didn't want her parents to leave them alone to go work. Again.

Her mom reached out and pulled Mia into a tight hug. "Everything will be all right. We'll get through this. You know how Derek can be when he's sick, but he always comes out of it happier and healthier than ever." She pulled away, holding Mia at arm's length. "You should sleep now. We'll say goodbye in the morning, all right?"

"Okay." Mia muttered the word in English. "I'm going to check on Derek first."

Her mom kissed Mia on the forehead. Without another word, her parents disappeared upstairs, leaving Mia alone in the hallway. Mia closed her eyes for a moment, trying to wrap her mind around the past day and a half. The party, the illness, the sculpture…it was a lot at once, but her mother had been right. They would get through this.

The blinds were open in Derek's room, moonlight casting an eerie glow across the room. Deep breathing rose from the bed. He was asleep. That was nothing new.

The smell of ginger tea wafted through the air, annoying Mia's nose with its harsh scent. She shook her head, and stepped into the room, making her way through piles of clothes until she could sit on the wooden desk chair next to his bed.

"Démíng?" she whispered. Seeing him lay there, a bag of ice on his forehead, cheeks flushed with fever, created a niggling feeling in her gut. Something wasn't right about any of this. She didn't want to wake him, but maybe he knew something. He'd said he'd wanted to tell her something.

What was that something?

When sleep threatened to claim her, dragging her eyelids down with a vengeance, she yawned and stood. Sitting with him would do him no good. He needed to sleep undisturbed, and she needed rest. She'd check on him in the morning and spend some time making easy to eat vegetarian dishes that she knew he liked when he did get sick.

She turned to close the blinds, ready to sleep, when something outside the window caught her eye.

At first, she thought nothing of it. A shadow underneath the street lamp. But on second inspection, Mia realized it wasn't a shadow; it was a person. A woman, standing on the sidewalk, staring into Derek's bedroom.

The street lamp lit her up, casting a glow around her body. Her bleached blond hair was pulled into a side pony tail that reached down to her waist, and her skin seemed to glow as if it were a piece of the moon. She wore simple clothes—a t-shirt and jeans—and on her face was a smile. A smile that sent shivers up Mia's spine.

They made eye contact. The woman cocked her head.

Mia gasped and stepped back, hand flying to her mouth. Her heart thumped in her chest. Jumping into action, she scrambled for the drawstring to close the blinds, taking her eyes off the woman for one second to see where it was. When her gaze landed on the sidewalk again, she froze.

The woman was gone.

For a long moment, Mia continued to stare at the spot on the sidewalk.

Did…did I imagine her?

It had to be her imagination. Exhaustion had turned her brain into mush. She needed sleep. Once she got sleep, everything would make more sense.

With haste, she closed the blinds and placed a hand over her heart, feeling the thump against her chest.

I imagined her. I imagined her. I imagined her.

Yet, as she left the room, ready to sleep and forget this day, she couldn't shake the feeling that someone—possibly the woman— was watching her.

Chapter Four

Mia's legs burned. Her lungs ached, desperate for oxygen. The ball touched her fingertips and then dropped to the floor with an echoing thump. It touched her fingers again. Sweat dripped down the temples of the girl in front of her. She charged to take the ball. Mia pivoted around her, the ball coming to both hands, and she jumped, simultaneously aiming and throwing.

The ball flew through the air.

It hit the rim and bounced out of bounds.

A whistle screeched across the gym and all ten girls on the court froze. Mia's heart raced, blood pounding in her ears as she relaxed, turning to see Coach Smith head toward them, arms crossed. The girls moved, almost in unison, to meet their coach in the middle of court.

"Excellent practice, ladies." Coach Smith was a tall woman who looked no more than twenty-five. Her dirty blond hair was, as always, pulled up in a high ponytail and she kept her clothes athletic and comfortable. "If we keep this up, we'll be taking home that championship trophy for sure this year."

The girls cheered, but Mia remained quiet. She'd come to practice today, despite Blair telling her to take the day off, because she needed a distraction from everything in her life. Sunday, the day after the opening, had been quiet, but stressful. Mrs. Arbour had spent the day taking care of them, as well as the night, but Derek hadn't spent much time awake.

It was draining. She needed to be here, even if she was struggling to focus.

"We have a few weeks until the championship game," Coach Smith continued. "Just because we're doing well now, doesn't mean we can get lazy at practice until then. But I know how hard you work, and we're going to kick some ass!"

Mia wanted to cheer with them, but jubilation didn't come. She hadn't been able to stop thinking about Derek, no matter how hard she'd tried during practice. His empty seat in their shared classes mocked her. She'd hoped he would get better after a day of rest, but if anything, he seemed to be getting worse.

Maybe he'll be better when I get home.

"All right! Let's hit those showers and head home!" Coach Smith said. Everyone cheered again, and the huddle broke up. Chatter spread among the girls as they hurried out of the gym, gossip and complaints about homework. Mia, however, hung back. Coach Smith didn't need to say anything. Mia knew a conversation was coming after the disaster of a practice she'd just caused.

"So," Coach Smith said when the rest of the girls had left the gym.

"I know," Mia said. "I wasn't focused today."

"Are you doing all right?" she asked.

Mia kept her gaze on the ground. "Things are crazy right now. It's no big deal."

"Your parents aren't home and your brother is sick. That is a big deal." She reached out and placed a hand on Mia's shoulder. Mia finally looked up, coming face to face with a concerned expression. "Everyone will understand if you need to take a few days off. I'm sure the school would understand if you need to skip class too. We're all here for you if you need us."

As grateful as Mia was for the support, she didn't want that. School and practice were the only things that'd kept her sane since coming to America, and she wasn't about to give them up because things were a little rough at home. Other people had it much worse, and still managed to come to school. Mia would be fine.

"I'm the captain. I should be here for my teammates," she said.

Coach Smith examined her. Mia squirmed under her scrutiny. She hated it when Coach Smith got this way. Most of the time, the coach didn't get too involved in the girls' drama. As long as it didn't affect the court, it didn't matter what was going on in their personal lives. But she was worried. Mia could tell. The entire team was worried, though not about her.

They were worried about Derek.

News about Derek's illness had spread, like it always did at Willow Creek High: like a wildfire after a drought. From the moment Mia got to school this morning, she'd been bombarded with questions and concerns from her classmates about Derek, about her parents. None about her.

"All right," Coach Smith eventually said. "Go shower and get home. Word around the teacher's lounge is that homework is piling up, and I'm not about to let poor grades take down my star team."

"Yes, Coach," Mia said, and then she scooted out of the gym. She dashed down the hall, mentally preparing herself for the onslaught of questions she knew was waiting for her. She'd come late to practice, so the girls hadn't had a chance to bombard her with questions about Derek beforehand. And all during practice, they shot each other glances, like they wanted to say something, but drills kept them breathing too heavily to chat.

38

Once she got to the locker room, she paused in the entryway. Gossiping voices echoed through the brick hallway, a few voices rising above the others. Mia closed her eyes and listened to the piercing voices, placing names to them.

"Brad asked out Ariel this morning," Kaylee, one of the freshmen on the team, said.

"Seriously? She is way out of his league," Miranda, her senior friend, responded.

"Yeah, but she said—"

"I don't want to do the math homework tonight," another voice said, this time belonging to Eloise, a small girl who had only joined the team because it looked good on a college application.

Mia opened her eyes. The minute she entered the room, all attention would be on her.

With a deep breath, she entered the locker room, keeping her head high. The minute the girls saw her, a hush overcame the room. She did her best not to examine the room, knowing full well that any eye contact would lead to the barrage of questions.

Instead, she made her way to her locker, doing her best to smile.

The minute she opened her locker, the girls crowded around her and the questioning began.

"What did Coach want?"

"Is Derek okay?"

"Are your parents really in trouble with the Thai government?"

"Are you guys going to have to move back to Asia?"

"Can you give Derek this card we all signed?"

Mia held up a hand to shut them up. All the girls fell silent, and Mia worked on figuring out which question to answer first.

"Derek's okay," she lied. "He's not doing well, but he'll be fine after some rest and medicine. Coach just wanted to talk. My parents are not in trouble with the Thai government. No, we aren't moving. Yes, I will give Derek your card."

There were hushed whispers among her teammates before Eloise asked, "What happened?"

Mia really didn't know how to explain it. "I…Derek collapsed at the opening. We don't know why."

"And the sculpture?"

At any other school, the kids wouldn't care about some random sculpture from Thailand, but everyone's favorite teacher, Mr. Becker, had taken an interest in it and talked about it in all of his history classes, whether they were focused on Southeast Asian history or not.

Mia shrugged. "It broke. My parents are dealing with it."

It must have been clear from her tone that Mia didn't want to answer any more questions, because the girls nodded and slowly went back to their lockers. Hallie, however, stayed behind.

"If there's anything we can do, let us know, okay?" she asked, all smiles.

"Thanks," Mia said. She turned back to her locker and closed her eyes again, wishing that all of this would go away.

He couldn't feel his body. Each time he tried to twitch his fingers, they refused to move. Or, maybe they did move and he couldn't feel the motion. He blinked. Where was he? What was he doing here? Was this the same place as the lotus flower? Was he back there? To finish the business someone else had started?

There were no answers.

He couldn't see. The world wasn't black, it wasn't white. It was filled with nothingness. An expanse of an empty world waiting to be filled. He blinked again. Darkness. Nothingness. He tried to breathe. If he succeeded, he couldn't tell.

Then, his fingers twitched. He glanced down and there they were, tingling as they waited for blood to bring oxygen to individual digits. Something streamed down his face. He reached up with his phantom fingers and touched water. He blinked.

The rain appeared out of nowhere, vivid and slow. Each droplet fell from the sky as if in a vacuum: falling at the same speed as a goose's feather. He managed to breathe this time as his newly appeared lungs screamed for oxygen. Musk swirled deliciously through his nose. He blinked again. The world came into view. Dark. Foreboding. Through the rain, thick trees burst from the mossy ground. They ran alongside him, winding, lining a path of stones.

A rush of heat filled his body. He gasped and his arms wrapped around his body as if they had a mind of their own. Bare skin met bare skin, and he realized he was naked. Rain pounded against his body. Little bullets incapable of penetrating skin. His gaze fell to the ground.

Bare feet twitched against the chilled path beneath them. Each stone was smooth and slick, damp from the falling rain. He wiggled his toes. They tingled, like his fingers, before matching the temperature of the ground beneath them.

With as much caution as he could muster, he stepped forward. A light stretched from his foot, lighting the path with glowing, blue, intricate vines. He gasped. The rain returned to a normal speed, pounding against his body. With one hand, he wiped his hair out of his face. With the other, he shielded his eyes.

Another step.

A chime sounded this time, light rippling out across the ground. Up the trees.

Another step.

More light.

More sound.

He continued, pushing through the worsening storm. But each

step drained him. Each step claimed more of his soul until he could no longer move. He collapsed to his knees, letting the water cleanse his body of impurity. Of his sins.

What sins?

He gasped for air.

All of them, a whisper on the wind said.

A hoarse scream split from his lips, tearing at his ears while simultaneously muted by the rain. He couldn't tell if the water streaming down his cheeks came from the sky, or from his eyes. None of this was real, he tried to tell himself. All of this was a dream. An elaborate and vivid dream.

"Rise. Continue." A new voice spoke to him. One he knew. One he didn't recognize. It dripped down with the rain—a gentle lullaby tempting him from within the liquid beads.

"I can't," he tried to say. *I can't.*

"You can. You will. Rise."

He lifted his head, panting, body like lead. Through the drops of rain appeared a shadow. Large, looming, and alone. All alone. He blinked water out of his eyes. A building rose from the ground, stone walls glowing as blue as his footsteps. It was magnificent yet simple. Grand yet plain. Power radiated from it, washing him with a wave of energy. It burned his veins, encouraging them to speak to his muscles. To speak to his bones. To get up and move.

"Go in. She waits for you," the voice hissed in his ear.

He climbed to his feet. Light flashed. He shielded his face with a hand until the light dimmed again, leaving him in a room lit only by candles. The symbols from outside were etched into the walls of the temple. He tried to read them. He knew the words, but couldn't bring them to his tongue.

"Come forward and see Her Highness. Her Majesty. The Queen."

Without his permission, his feet moved. Sandals slapped against the stone, and he realized he dressed, wearing beautiful, old robes spun from the finest silk. As he moved, he listened for the bells, the ones that had accompanied his footsteps outside. There was nothing but the sound of wood against stone. He reached a staircase, energy returning with each step. By the time he reached the top, he stood tall.

Confident.

Sure.

As if he'd become another man entirely.

His gaze fell on the front of the temple, and his heart caught in his throat. A woman dressed in beautiful cloth, her black hair wild and reaching down to her mid back, hunched over a table, hands gripping the edges. Eight candles surrounded her. Lights flickering. Wax melting as if someone was fast forwarding reality.

He stepped. A million emotions touched the tips of his fingers. His. Hers. His throat tightened, words escaping him. She tensed. Still, he stepped forward. She flinched. *Still* he stepped forward. She spun around, hair flying like leaves in a windstorm. *Still he stepped forward.*

He stepped forward, limbs melting at his side.

Her eyes pierced through the night.

Irises the color of rubies.

They stared at each other, and then she moved. She crossed the rest of the room, charging at him. His body pleaded with him to run, but his feet remained chained to the ground. Her hand caught his arm. Fire exploded at her touch. He did not move. The pain begged him to run. He did not move.

She whispered something. A quiet voice drowned out by bells.

One-by-one, the eight candles blew out until one remained in the center.

A lotus.

It blew out.

And the darkness returned.

"Mia!"

Mia halted. The brisk fall air stung her cheeks, and she breathed out a cloud of steam. She turned, slipping her chilled hands into her coat pockets. Blair, with no backpack and a grin on her face, ran toward Mia. An odd sight. Mia was the athletic one in the group. Cody studied all the time, Derek at least used to love music, and Blair...Blair spent a lot of time obsessing over memes on the internet.

Mia didn't get it, but it made Blair happy.

"Hey, how's it going?" Mia said with her best smile. Blair came to a stop next to her, panting. Mia resisted giving her a lecture about being in shape. She'd given it before, and it never amused Blair. She said life was too short to waste on running every morning, like Mia did in the summer.

Once she'd caught her breath, Blair stood upright and placed her hands on her hips. "Don't give me that. I'm not everyone else."

The smile faded and Mia nodded. "Right. Sorry. Got into a rhythm."

"You don't have to apologize. I get it. Sucks being the center of attention."

Mia grimaced. Of course Blair would understand. It was hard not to when she'd had three seizures at school over the years. People loved to obsess whenever it happened. They would ask questions. Bother her. Ask her what kind of medication she was on. Just overall being completely nosey.

"Yeah, it does," she said. At least, this kind of attention. Mia looked to the ground, and before she knew it, Blair had pulled Mia into a hug.

"It's okay," she said before stepping back. "It could be worse." Mia responded with a smile before the two of them headed to the other side of Willow Creek. To Mia's house.

Off highway 34, in the middle of the mountains, Willow Creek was no one's first stop during a road trip. Once a tourist town, it had become a place where people were from, not where they went. So, it didn't matter that school was on one side of Willow Creek and Mia's house on the other. The girls would be home in fifteen minutes. Less if the gray clouds in the sky didn't indicate snow like Mia predicted.

To be honest, Mia wasn't sure how she felt about Willow Creek. Sure, it had its good things, like her friends, but most days she missed Beijing. There, her parents didn't have to travel three hours for work. They didn't trade off being home every two weeks. And more than that, Beijing had her grandparents. Her aunt and uncle. And she'd had friends there too, though they'd long since lost touch.

Beijing was her home. Willow Creek had always been a place of discomfort for her. The place where she never quite fit in, no matter how hard she tried.

"When do you think Derek will get better?" Blair asked about five minutes into the walk.

Mia blinked, coming out of her thoughts. "Soon. Probably. It was likely just an infection or something. He's on antibiotics, and my mom picked up some weird tea from an Asian store in Denver. Guess which one she thinks will work first?"

"The antibiotics," Blair said. "Obviously."

Mia laughed. It felt good to laugh. "I'm supposed to give him three cups of tea a day."

"That won't be hard."

"It wouldn't be, except he's having trouble staying awake."

"Right."

They fell silent again, walking through the small downtown.

People milled about. Some went in and out of shops, while a group of their classmates hung out near the coffee shop they all loved, and others had on work out pants and were getting in their daily power walk. And as the two of them walked, Mia thought back to the night in the hospital. Derek had needed to say something to her. A secret? It wasn't like the two of them to keep secrets. But if he was going to have one....

She glanced at Blair, who had pulled out her phone. Mia wasn't blind to Blair and Derek's flirtations. She kept her mouth shut because she didn't feel like it was her place to say anything, but it certainly bothered her. Dating in friend groups never went well, and she wasn't about to have to pick between her best friend and her brother.

Still, if he was going to tell anyone a secret he hadn't told Mia, it would be Blair.

"Hey," she said.

"Hm?" Blair looked up from her phone.

"Derek said he wanted to tell me something." Mia figured she should hear it from Derek, but they'd had no time alone. "Back in the hospital. He seemed really serious. Do you know anything about it?"

Blair shook her head. "No. You think he's keeping a secret from you?"

Mia shrugged. "Dunno. He never has before."

She stared up at the sky, tracing pictures in the clouds blocking out the sun. It was always weird when they couldn't see the sun. Colorado was known for its sunny days, even if the light only lasted for a few hours. Today, though, it'd been gray and dreary, the temperature dropping, wind picking up. A storm was coming.

She shuddered.

"Oh well," she said. "He'll tell me eventually. Just thought you might know something."

"Nope. Sorry."

That was a dead end. But it didn't matter. Like Mia had said, Derek would tell her eventually. He wasn't great at keeping secrets. They'd based a large part of their sibling relationship on their honesty with one another. From the time they were kids, struggling to adjust to a new country, fighting to help keep their family together, they'd always told each other everything.

A flake of snow drifted from the sky. Mia held out a hand and caught it, watching it melt on her warm hand. The girls exchanged a glance.

"Time to get home," Mia said.

"Agreed."

They sped up as more flakes drifted down, eager to get out of the cold.

Derek gasped, eyes flying open. Air filled his lungs, expanding them as though they'd never experienced oxygen before. He burned, her fingers still wrapped around his arm. With shaking hands, he grabbed at them, fighting to escape her grip. His hands found nothing. No woman. No fingers.

He lay there, taking in the dim room, body enveloped in softness, and gasped. Heart thumping in his ears, he turned his head, blinking as he examined his room.

He was in his room.

Not a temple. There was no rain. Candles didn't illuminate his desk. His walls didn't glow with blue text. His hand touched his arm as the pressure disappeared, and he pushed himself up. Everything spun. His head burned with fever.

What the hell was that?

He placed a hand on his chest, feeling his heart flutter. It was like before. The night of the opening. So vivid. So alive. But this one was different. It hadn't been so surreal. Not as mystical. It wasn't really like a dream. More like...like a memory.

A sharp knock at the door interrupted his thoughts. He coughed, unable to get any words out. The door opened, revealing not his mom. With dark skin, high cheekbones, and long, braided black hair, Mrs. Arbour stood out from most of the residents in Willow Creek. On her face, at all times, was a gentle smile. Everything about her was soft. Even her negative emotions didn't have the sharp sting that others did.

Derek recalled a moment, hours ago, when she'd come into his room to let him know she'd be helping him and Mia while their parents were in Denver.

"Oh, you're awake." She glided into his room, scooping up dirty laundry as she did so, and sat on the bed next to him. "How are you feeling?"

His heart rate had returned to normal, and he breathed out, shrugging. Physically, he felt like crap, and mentally he couldn't stop thinking about the dream. The reality of it all. The niggling feeling in the back of his mind that said he should pay attention to what his conscience was trying to tell him.

"A shrug is not an answer," she chastised. "Your mom called about an hour ago. She's very worried. Is there anything you want me to text her? Let her know that you're doing all right?"

"Just that...." And then he noticed it. Just like in the hospital. The drive back. He'd thought sleep would help, but they were still gone.

Mrs. Arbour had never been the easiest person to read. If Mia's emotions were a flash flood, Mrs. Arbour's were a trickling stream. Quiet and gentle, but still there. Always there. Derek had always been able to be feel something from here.

But there was nothing.

He wracked his memory, trying to remember the last time he'd felt an emotion from someone else. The rush of anxiety. The silk of embarrassment. The sting of fear. Anything.

"Derek? Honey, what's wrong?"

His chest tightened, eyes wide. He held out a hand, begging the energy to flow from his heart to his fingertips. Normally, warmth would rush into his hand, swirling and forming until a ball of light floated above his palm. It wasn't difficult. Besides reading emotions, it was one of the first things he'd ever been able to do with his magic.

Nothing happened.

"I can't do it," he muttered, anxiety rising to the back of his throat. "Magic. I can't…it's not working."

Mrs. Arbour placed a cool hand on his forehead. "Your fever is better."

"But my magic…."

"Sometimes," she said, pulling her hand away, "our powers diminish when we're ill. Our body searches for any way to heal itself, and it will draw on the energy within our bodies. On our magic."

Derek wanted to believe her. Mrs. Arbour had grown up in one of the mage clans. And not just any, one of the main five. It was a community that built their culture around the idea of magic. She grew up hearing the history of mages, about magical theory, reading books designed for young mage children. If there was anyone who would understand what was going on, it was her.

And yet…yet he didn't know if he could believe her. Something felt different this time. A heavy rock settled on his chest.

"I don't like this," he said. "I…I think something is coming. Everything is just so weird with my dreams and…." He recalled the feeling he had in the hospital. "I think I need to tell Mia."

He stared up at Mrs. Arbour, seeking her permission. This was her world. She'd grown up in it. She was raising four children in it. She was the one who sought him out and explained to him what he could do. Who he was. Where he belonged. She was the one who told him it needed to be secret.

He couldn't read her expression. He'd never had to before. Her eyes were soft, lips turned down slightly at the corners. The rock on his chest grew heavier.

"Oh, honey," Mrs. Arbour said.

"I have to," Derek said. "If something is wrong, if she's in danger—"

"She's not a mage." Mrs. Arbour placed a hand on his shoulder. His breathing shortened. "We have rules. And…yes, I reacted strongly to *The Queen* breaking, but that doesn't mean anyone's in danger. And until she is, we aren't allowed to tell her about magic."

"But why not?"

"Because it's not safe for her." She smiled, but Derek had a feeling it wasn't a happy one. "We can't evade the risk of danger because we are caught in this world. But she can. If she's unaware of what's going on, she's much safer. You can't tell her yet."

He wasn't going to get permission, and he had no grounds to argue. He didn't know this. Mrs. Arbour grew up with the warnings and the rules. The fact that she shared them with him at all was a gift he wasn't about to turn his nose up.

She'd said no.

The doorbell rang, shattering his thoughts. Mrs. Arbour glanced at his door.

"I believe Cody's here. Mia said he was coming." She stood. "Your mom left me tea to make you, as well as some recipes. Once you eat and drink, your strength will come back along with your magic."

He bowed his head and said nothing. She sighed.

"I know this is hard. But it's for the best."

She headed out of the room and Derek watched her leave, wondering about the validity of her statement. This whole thing felt off. When he focused on the energy inside of him, on the idea of magic, it felt like something was draining it. As though something was taking away his magic. That's why he was sick. Not the other way around.

And if that was the case, if someone was attacking him, then Mia was in danger, right? He had no proof, and without proof he couldn't justify bringing her into this world. Yet it felt wrong. All of this felt wrong.

Frustration taking over him, he held out his hand again and focused. At first there was nothing. No spark. Just dullness. He bit his lip and held his breath, eyes narrowing in on his hand. After a minute, a trickle of warmth spread to his fingers. Energy traveled from his heart to his hands. His vision clouded, ears ringing. He blinked, trying to keep his body from giving up on him.

He needed to do this.

Needed to….

The energy lifted from his skin, spinning into a tight little ball of light.

A gasp from the doorway distracted him. The ball of light vanished into a cloud of smoke, and Derek collapsed, catching himself barely with his cold hands. Everything spun, and he shook his head in an attempt to orient himself. When strength returned to his arms, he pushed himself up, fearful of whoever stood in the doorway.

To his credit, Cody didn't move or say anything. As Derek rested, his vision cleared, and he could make out Cody's expression. His eyes were wide, one hand on the doorway, the other clenched by his side. Desperate to know what Cody was feeling, Derek reached out, hoping it would work. He felt nothing.

"Um…." Derek ran a shaking hand through his greasy hair and

tried his best not to let out nervous laughter. "Hi."

"What were you doing?" Cody asked. The thing about Cody was that he was always quiet. Even when frustrated or angry, his voice rarely rose above a quiet mutter, something that often drove Derek nuts.

"I...uh...." Derek didn't know what to say. Cody had seen the light. "It's...a magic trick. I was practicing a magic trick." He laughed, hoping Cody would buy it. He didn't.

"That wasn't a trick," Cody said. "That was magic."

"What?" Derek squeaked. He cleared his throat and tried again. "What? Magic isn't real."

He silently begged Mrs. Arbour to come back in the room. Cody wouldn't talk about this if she was around, right? As far as he knew, Mrs. Arbour was a normal mom who went to PTA meetings and didn't know the deepest secrets of the universe.

Cody glanced over his shoulder, then stepped into the room, closing the door behind him. Derek's stomach turned. He desperately wanted to know what Cody was feeling. He reached out again. Nothing. Why was there nothing?

"Look," Cody said, then paused. Cody had these nervous habits, like taking long pauses between sentences, or rubbing his hands together. It got worse when people asked about his life, or when he was in crowds of people. There were so days that these habits were so bad, Derek wondered if Cody was going to make it through a sentence. "I...know...about...magic."

His voice got quieter with each word. Derek's heart leapt into his throat. First Blair, and now Cody?

When Derek said nothing, Cody continued, rambling on incoherently about his knowledge of magic. His knowledge of a world that most people didn't know existed. Derek waited, hoping maybe he would say something clearly and Derek could get a good sense of how he knew. It never came.

"How do you know about magic?" Derek asked.

Cody pressed against the door, looking to the ground. "Because…," he murmured, "I can use magic too."

Chapter Five

Mia and Blair ran the rest of the way to Mia's house. Well, 'ran.' The increasing layer of snow on the sidewalks made it difficult to go fast without slipping. By the time they reached the house, a full blizzard raged around them. Mia shivered, using a bare hand to cover her eyes. The forecast hadn't said anything about a blizzard.

Heat washed over them when they finally made it into the house. Mia shuddered from the warmth and stripped herself of her coat and shoes. Shivering, Mia dashed into the living room, Blair close behind her, and headed for the fireplace.

"I'm glad to see you two made it," Mrs. Arbour said from the kitchen.

Mia waved at her, too cold to speak. The fire, already lit, blasted heat onto her shivering hands, and she settled in front of it. Blair appeared next to her, wrapping a blanket around the two of them. Mia had lived here for years, but she'd never get used to the cold.

She glanced out the sliding doors that led to the back porch. Past the wooden awning, the blizzard raged. On a normal day, Mia would have been able to see into the forest behind her house. At the moment, all she saw was a blanket of white.

Mia scooted closer to Blair. The girls tightened the blanket around them.

"Would you two icicles like some tea?" Mrs. Arbour asked.

"Yes, please," Mia and Blair said between chattering teeth.

Mrs. Arbour laughed. "You should have called. I would have picked you up."

"It's a fifteen minute walk, Mom," Blair said with a roll of her eyes.

"In a mountain blizzard."

"We're fine."

"All right, all right." She appeared with two mugs of steaming tea, bags still steeping in the water.

Mia released the blanket and touched the burning mug. She hissed and retracted her hand back against her chest. Blair and her mom exchanged a few more words, but Mia wasn't paying attention to what they were saying. Instead, she twisted, facing her brother's room, and wondered if she should go check on him. She'd noticed Cody's red truck outside and figured he was keeping Derek company. Which meant Derek was awake. Which meant she should go check on him.

The thought brought a wave of exhaustion over her. As much as she wanted to make sure her brother was okay, she also wanted to warm up enough to drink her tea. She wanted to sit with her best friend for a moment and not think about the fact that he was sick.

He wasn't alone.

Mrs. Arbour had been taking care of him all day.

Cody was with him now.

He was fine.

She reached out to take the mug again. This time it only burned a little bit, and she smiled against the lip as hot liquid slid down her throat. Into her stomach. Warming her very core.

"I'm going to go finish dinner," Mrs. Arbour said. "Cody said he would get Derek, but they're taking a while. Blair, do you mind going to get them? Mia, I could use some help in the kitchen."

Mia blinked, staring up at the woman. "Oh. I'll help you in a minute. Once my hands warm up."

Mrs. Arbour smiled. "Sounds good, dear."

She disappeared back into the kitchen, leaving Mia and Blair huddled in front of the fireplace, both with their tea, the blanket over their shoulders.

After a moment of silence, Blair said, "I hate weather."

"Agreed." Mia nodded.

"Think the boys are doing something stupid?" Blair asked.

Mia rolled her eyes. "They're probably talking or playing video games."

"So doing something stupid."

Mia laughed. "You're so judgmental."

"Am not."

"Are so."

Blair sipped her tea, then stood, letting the blanket fall from her shoulder. "Well, I'm going to go tell them to stop being stupid and come get dinner. See you in a minute."

"Yeah." Mia didn't move at first. She continued to sip her tea and stared at the flames dancing to the beat of the howling wind. She closed her eyes and allowed the heat to wash over her. When she'd first moved to Willow Creek, she hadn't been used to the winters. Beijing got cold, but it was different here. The air was thinner. The snow was harsher. The weather was unpredictable. It'd taken years to just accept it for what it was. To learn the ways of mountain winters.

Still, staring down at her unhappy fingers, she wasn't sure how much she would ever fully adjust.

After consuming a bit more tea, she stood as well and headed into the kitchen to help Mrs. Arbour with the potatoes.

"I appreciate your help," Mrs. Arbour said. "I'm not used to this kitchen."

"I'm happy to help," Mia said. It gave her something to do. To take her mind off everything.

Mrs. Arbour smiled and went back to chopping. Mia turned on the sink to wash her hands, both to clean them and to help them warm up. When she looked up from the sink, out the window leading to the side yard with wonders of how much snow they would have in the morning, she froze. A woman stood in the yard, staring into the house.

Just like she had the night before.

Mia jolted back. They made eye contact, Mia's dark brown against the woman's hazel, and the woman smiled. And then she waved.

Mia gasped. The water running into the sink grew louder and louder until Mia had to tear her eyes away from the strange woman outside the window. She shut it off, wet hands the only source of water dripping into the sink, and looked back up.

The woman was gone.

"Mia, can you grab the potatoes?" Mrs. Arbour asked.

Mia blinked and stared down at her hands. They tingled, warmth slowly returning to them, and she closed her eyes.

She wasn't real. I imagined her.

"Mia?" Mrs. Arbour walked over to her and glanced out the window. "Are you all right? Did you see something?"

"N-no." Mia's nervous laugh didn't seem to persuade Mrs. Arbour of Mia's conviction. She cleared her throat. "I'm just still shocked by all the snow, you know? Not used to this still."

Mrs. Arbour watched her for a moment, then looked out the window one more time. Mia did the same. The woman wasn't there.

Finally, Mrs. Arbour moved away from the sink, back to where she was chopping vegetables for a salad. "It is a lot of snow, isn't it?"

Mia nodded but didn't say anything. Instead she stared out the window again, unable to stop thinking about the woman. That was two nights in a row. Both outside a window. Both in situations where there shouldn't have been a woman.

And both times, Mia had been able to see her. In the dark of night. In the middle of a blizzard. She'd been able to make out her bleached blond hair or her hazel eyes.

She closed her eyes again and shook her head.

I imagined her.

She went to work, helping Mrs. Arbour while Blair took forever to get the boys.

I imagined her.

And she tried to put the woman out of her mind. She had other things to worry about. Things that didn't involve Mia suddenly hallucinating a woman in a blizzard.

I imagined her.

With a deep breath, she went to peeling potatoes and put on a smile. Because it was fine. Everything was fine.

Derek had to take a moment. It wasn't a long moment. Maybe thirty seconds. Less than a minute. But he needed it to process what he'd just heard. Cody. Cody Velt. The anti-social, highly intellectual, guy who followed after Mia like a baby duck, who'd never shown any interest in anything related to fantasy and preferred to stick to science and math, had *magic*.

"Excuse me?" Derek said when the moment passed. "You what?"

Cody grimaced. He glanced behind him, out of the room. A couple of voices joined Mrs. Arbour. Mia and Blair. Derek tensed while Cody stepped inside and closed the door with a deafening *click*.

"I…can use magic," Cody said again, voice even quieter.

Derek relaxed against his headboard, mind a jumbled mess of questions. He went through them all, trying to understand. Trying to reorient his world.

"Your family are mages?" He tried to imagine Cody's mom and dad using magic. His mom, a cold, quiet woman who always seemed just a little out of place, and his dad, a warm and friendly accountant who was known for helping people pro-bono too many times to make a good living.

Cody shook his head. "N-no. It's just me. But I don't think I'm a mage. Mrs. Arbour said I felt different."

Derek sighed and placed his face in his hands. "I'm gonna need more. Mrs. Arbour knows? Does Blair know? Does *Mia* know?"

"Mia doesn't know," he said quickly.

Derek waited for the lingering affection that always slithered along his skin when Cody said Mia's name. There was nothing. He clenched his fists, waiting for the warmth to return, but the exhaustion was too much. He was going to have to get used to this for the time being. He just hoped it wasn't permanent.

"Blair knows. We kinda…had a run in when we were kids. But no one else knows. Not even my parents." Cody examined Derek, looking him up and down. "What about you?"

"It's just me," Derek said. "Mrs. Arbour says I'm a lone mage, or whatever. Skipped some generations. Mia doesn't know, but Blair does."

Cody's eyes widened. He stepped further into the room, sinking into Derek's wooden desk chair. "Mia doesn't know you have magic?"

Derek shook his head. "I…wanted to tell her, but…."

"Mrs. Arbour told you to keep it a secret?"

"Said she'd be safer without knowing."

"Yeah, that's why my parents don't know."

Derek wanted to say it was ridiculous, but he also didn't want to disrespect Mrs. Arbour. She was the authority on this. Not him. He had to respect at least that.

"I don't do it anymore," Cody said.

Derek blinked. "What?"

"Magic." He breathed out. "There was an accident and... whatever. I just don't use my magic anymore if I can help it. The only thing I can't control is seeing the mists."

"Mists?" Derek's brow furrowed. He'd never heard of that before. Mrs. Arbour had told him about people who had gifts like him—since apparently even in the mage world, empathy was incredibly rare—but she'd never mentioned anything about a mist.

Cody waved his hand around his head. "It's like...I dunno. Maybe they're auras or something. But it's different than that. Everyone has a color that can shift sometimes. Just a little. Depends on their intentions. It can be a lot when I'm in a crowd."

Derek had no idea a person could speak so quickly. He had trouble keeping up with the words tumbling out of Cody's mouth. But one thing he did catch clearer than anything else was his last sentence. About the crowds. Derek had always assumed he hated to be around people because of anxiety, and that was still an option, but it made so much sense that he got overwhelmed because of these...mists.

And the other thing that stuck out was the fact that everyone had a different color.

"What color am I?" Derek asked.

Cody sighed. "Gold."

"Mia?"

"White."

"Blair?"

"Blue."

"You?"

Cody glanced at his hands. "I…I don't know. I can't see mine."

"What about—"

"Look," Cody said, once again with that quick tone, "I don't know how to explain it. I don't have answers. No one seems to. I even confuse Mrs. Arbour. So I don't like talking about it. What I can do…it's almost intrusive and I hate it. The problem is I can't stop it. So I try to ignore it as best as I can."

They were opposites. The two of them. They both had powers they couldn't control. Feeling or seeing something that belonged solely to someone else. But where Cody tried to run from it, Derek was more than eager to learn more about his powers and what he could do with them. He couldn't imagine ignoring the emotions.

He relied on them.

"I can feel emotions," Derek said.

Cody looked up from his hands. Derek, once again, longed to know what he was feeling because it could have been anything. Shock. Betrayal. Confusion. Maybe all three. People and their emotions were complex as hell.

"What?" Cody asked.

Derek recalled the moment when he first told Blair and Mrs. Arbour. The hesitation they'd had. How long it'd taken them to get used to the idea that everything they felt, he knew.

"I can't right now," he clarified. "I guess I'm too sick. But normally—"

"You can feel everything?"

Derek thought about the very secret feelings Cody harbored for Mia. He could lie, but he already felt like shit about having to hide all this from Mia. "Yeah."

"Oh."

"I won't tell her," Derek said quickly.

A sharp look entered Cody's eyes. "I don't know what you're talking about."

"Okay," Derek said. The two fell silent in time for the door to burst open. Both jumped, Derek's heart thumping in his chest. He expected Mia but instead found a yawning Blair.

"Hey, what are you idiots up to? Dinner's gonna be ready soon." Blair glanced between them, but when neither of them said a word, she crossed her arms. "What? Are you planning a bank job or something? Because I so want in. Should I get Mia?"

"No!" both Derek and Cody shouted.

Blair glanced between them before closing the door. "You two are talking about magic, aren't you?"

"Well," Cody tried to say but then faltered. He looked at Derek, who shrugged. Blair was right. They had been talking about magic. He just didn't know if that was a bad thing or not. People kept closing the door. To keep this from Mia. To protect her from something she knew nothing about.

Blair sighed. "You two have got to be more careful. If Mia found out—"

"Why don't we just tell her?" Cody asked. "We all know. I was just staying quiet because I didn't think Derek knew."

"Hey."

"What? You haven't told Mia about your powers," Cody said. "But if all three of us know, she should know. She has a right to know what's going on around her."

Derek agreed. One hundred percent. If all three of them took the blame for bringing Mia into the world, then Mrs. Arbour couldn't get too angry, right? And Derek had agreed not to tell her because he thought Cody was also out of this world. If all three of them were in it....

Except Blair's face told a different story. A hesitation. Maybe...

he couldn't really tell, but maybe fear?

"Oh come on," Cody said. Derek shrunk back. Mia was the one who got them to stop fighting, not him. "You cannot seriously be suggesting that we keep Mia in the dark? We're her best friends."

"I don't like it either," Blair said. "But the clans have rules."

"Derek and I aren't part of the clans."

"That won't stop them from coming after you if you start shit by telling someone without magic."

"Based on the way your mom reacted to *The Queen* breaking, I'd say shit has already started."

"There's no proof of that. She just overreacted."

"But–"

"Guys!" Derek couldn't take them arguing. Mia always had a much more diplomatic way of getting them to shut up. He didn't have the time or patience. It worked, at least. They both fell quiet, glaring at each other. "Okay, look. Mrs. Arbour said no. I don't like it, neither of you like it, but right now we don't know that anything is a problem so let's just pretend like everything is fine. All right?"

He hated saying this. But it was putting it off in someone else's hands. Mrs. Arbour's.

"Okay," Blair said as Cody muttered, "Fine."

Derek relaxed. His stomach grumbled. His face burned. Exhaustion picked at all of his limbs. This was so stupid. Magic was supposed to be fun. Not an argument.

"We've been in here a while," Blair said. "Mia might be wondering what's going on. We should go help with dinner."

"Fine," Cody said again. Blair glared at him. He glared at Blair. Then she stormed out of the room to go help her mom and Mia in the kitchen. Derek watched her go, as did Cody, until Derek found the energy to push himself off his bed.

Then it hit him.

An emotion.

He halted, gaze landing on the window. The shade was open, which caught him off guard. He remembered his mom closing it before she left in the morning. When she wished him well and kissed him on his forehead. A rare gesture from his workaholic mom.

Outside, a storm raged on, unrelenting and powerful. And standing in the middle of it, black hair whipping around her face, was a woman. Derek frowned. In a second, she'd vanished as if she hadn't existed in the first place.

"Derek?" Cody asked. "You all right?"

Slowly, he nodded. Slowly, he stood upright, despite his spinning head. And slowly, he followed his friends out of the room where his secret had come out. And where he'd made a decision he still wasn't sure was right.

Chapter Six

The snow on the grass rose up to Mia's waist, taunting her with its sheer mass. She tried to keep her eyes off it, focusing instead on the sidewalk. People had come out to shovel, but the snow had started up again around the time Mia and Blair had left for school.

With every breath, Mia watched the steam from her mouth rise to the sky. She wanted nothing more than to shove her numb hands in her coat pockets, but seven winters of experience had taught her she might fall flat on her ass if she did. Neither girl spoke. They were spending too much energy trying to stay warm.

The night before had gone as well as possible. Derek had been quiet, but that was nothing new when he was sick. Blair and Cody had seemed on edge, but again, nothing new. It wasn't until after Cody had braved the blizzard home and Derek had retreated to his room to sleep, that Blair had relaxed a bit. She and Mia had hung out in front of the fire doing homework and gossiping about people at school.

When their fifteen minutes of walking were up, Mia and Blair came around the bend to the edge of town where their school loomed, and both hesitated. High school—and middle school in the case of this building—wasn't the most enjoyable place to be on a normal day. But after a massive blizzard, the energy changed. No one cared about class. Their attention was always outside, to the beautiful fields of white that called their names. It didn't help that the forest backed the school's soccer/football field, enticingly forbidden to all students during school hours.

"Ready?" Blair asked.

Mia shrugged. "No."

Blair let out a bitter laugh and the two of them headed into the two story building. The warmth of the building was the only welcoming part of the morning, and they shook the snow off their hats and stomped it off their boots before heading down the carpeted hall. Up the stairs. Toward their lockers.

"I can't believe it's so cold," Blair muttered as they climbed. A bunch of students greeted Mia, and she waved at them with a smile. "Why is it so cold, dammit? This is ridiculous."

Mia rolled her eyes. "You're the one who's lived here her whole life. You tell me."

Blair grumbled. "Global warming my ass."

"You know as well as I do that's not how climate change works," Mia said with another roll of her eyes. Blair liked to pretend she wasn't good with science or math, but when she actually sat down long enough to read the material, she picked it up faster than she liked to admit in polite company.

"Yeah, yeah." Blair waved a hand before yanking off her glove to open her locker. "Whatever. It's cold. I hate it. Let's move on."

Luckily for both of them, a very loud, very bouncy voice called out their names, interrupting whatever conversation neither of them knew how to start. They glanced at each other, then at Kaylee, a girl from Mia's team, who strode over to them wearing a cute sweater and a mini-skirt with leggings. Not the most weather inappropriate clothing Mia had ever seen on a Colorado girl, but it was up there.

"You're chipper," Blair muttered.

"And based on the fact that you're acting like a sourpuss, I take it you two haven't heard." Kaylee grinned at the two of them.

Mia frowned. When Kaylee got this excited about something, it was never good. "Heard about what?"

Kaylee clapped her hands. "Oh good. I get to tell you."

"Out with it," Blair said.

Mia sighed and Kaylee scowled. Blair had never been great in the mornings. Everyone in their class, and about ninety-five percent of the rest of the school, knew better than to take her annoyance seriously unless it was after third period.

"You need to eat a cupcake or something," Kaylee said before turning fully toward Mia. "Anyway, there's a new student."

The words washed over Mia like Niagara Falls. A new student? There hadn't been a new student in years. No one moved to Willow Creek. No one *knew* about Willow Creek. It was the town that cartographers literally forgot to add to the map. The place with so few tourists, they didn't even have shot glasses with the town name on them. The place Mia had thought was made up when her mom had first told her Liang had bought a house there.

"A new student?" Blair's foul, morning mood vanished. "Boy? Girl? Neither? Name? Age? Grade?"

"Give her a chance to answer," Mia chastised. She was just as eager to learn this information, but Kaylee needed a chance to actually breathe between questions if they wanted to know more about them.

"I know almost none of that information," Kaylee admitted. "I think he's in our grade. No idea what his name is, but I've seen him and oh man. Just...oh man."

Mia had to keep from rolling her eyes. There were plenty of attractive guys in their grade, and based on the way Blair turned toward her locker, Mia had a feeling she was thinking of one in particular. A thought Mia immediately pushed out of her mind.

"All right, well thanks for the news," Mia said. "See you at practice?"

"Yeah, see you then." She waved and headed out down the hallway to her first class.

Mia watched her go, thinking of her own first day of school. They were much younger, of course, but they definitely hadn't talked about her like that. It'd taken her forever to get people to say hi to her every morning. For them to stop teasing her about the way she looked. About her accent. About her struggles speaking English. The only two kids in the entire school who hadn't treated her like crap at first had been Cody and Blair.

"New kid, huh," she said, lost in thought.

Blair glanced at her. "Maybe he'll be an asshole."

"Maybe."

The two girls closed their lockers and split off to their separate classes. Mia kept her head down, trying to block the memories of her first day. Of the fear. Of the way Derek had held her hand the entire walk home while she cried and tried to calm her down.

How much she'd wanted to just go home.

And she hoped the rest of the school had learned their lesson since then and treated this new kid—this new guy—much better than they'd treated her.

Derek sprawled out on his bed, hand on his forehead, phone to his ear. Some part of him figured he should actually listen to what they had to say, but he'd learned over the years that when they started going off about some topic, as long as he responded every minute or so, they didn't ask him if he was disrespecting them.

And he wasn't. Or, he didn't mean to. He'd just heard it all before. This wasn't the first time both of them had been stuck out of town, and it wouldn't be the last.

"They're having issues clearing the road," Intira said. "Something about a narrow road. I swear, this happens every year. You'd think that they'd be used to it by now. But that means we're stuck in Denver for the time being."

"That sucks," he said without thinking.

"Derek, language."

"Sorry." He rolled his eyes. "That's absolutely terrible, dear mother of mine. Whatever shall we do about this unfortunate circumstance?"

She exhaled, breath rustling the earpiece. He pulled his phone away to see how long they'd been talking. Only ten minutes. There was one point in his life when he couldn't wait to get more time with his parents. But that was years ago. Before *The Queen*. Before Colorado. Back when things were a lot simpler, and he relied on them for a lot more than a warm house and a fridge full of food. He missed them. He did. But he missed them here. A phone call didn't make up for that.

"We're going to get up as soon as we can."

"Kay."

"How's your fever? Has your stomach been upset at all? Mrs. Arbour says you've been sleeping a lot. Has that helped?"

He mentally went through all the questions before answering with a catch all. "I'm fine, *Mā*. Fever is low. Stomach is fine. Sleep is good. This is going to go away before we know it."

She sighed. "I know. I know. But I still worry. If your fever gets—"

"Above 102, go to the hospital."

"And if you run out of food—"

"There's extra money upstairs in the safe."

"You know–"

"The combination? By heart."

"Intira, darling, I think Derek and Mia will be all right for a few days." Derek's dad came on, voice quieter than his mom's.

His mom groaned. "All right, all right. I'll call again later. But don't be afraid to call me if anything goes wrong. Mrs. Arbour said she'll spend the next few nights with you, and Mr. Smith is going to check on you when Mrs. Arbour can't. You remember him, right? Coach Smith's husband?"

Of course he remembered Mr. Smith. With a name as common as that, Cody and Derek used to pretend that he was a secret agent working for the government, stationed in Willow Creek because there were aliens trying to infiltrate small town America. Plus, they knew everyone in town. If not by name, then by face. It wasn't like new people showed up.

He thought of the woman in black.

I imagined her.

He shook his head. "Of course I remember him."

"And–"

"Mom, I'm getting tired." He faked a yawn. "Can we talk later? I think I need a nap."

"Of course." Intira's voice faded into a gentle hum. Any other day, Derek wouldn't have noticed the lack of emotion through the phone. But today, he was eager for something. Any kind of emotion. He longed for it. "Please, get some sleep and make sure to drink that tea I got you. It has yarrow and elderflower to help with your fever."

"Will do."

"I love you, *lôok*."

The familiar Thai pet name brought a small smile to his face. While he loved speaking Chinese, his native language, it was his mother's tongue that called to him. When he was little, his

70

grandparents wanted his mom to speak English to him and Mia, make sure they knew it well enough for school, but he would always beg her to sing him Thai lullabies. To tell him common Western fables in Thai.

"Love you too," he said.

They hung up, and Derek sighed. He let the phone drop to the bed, and then rolled to his feet, wanting to see how much snow had piled up overnight. Mrs. Arbour had left early, along with Blair and Mia, but she'd left a note for Derek reminding him to eat and letting him know she'd be back later.

He'd stayed in bed until his mom called, and with a burst of energy, he decided he wanted to get up.

But when he looked out the window, it wasn't just piles upon piles of snow that he saw. No. Standing there, black hair whipping in the wind, was the woman he'd sworn he'd imagined.

Derek shut his eyes, begging his brain to not play tricks on him again. But when he opened them again, she was still there, head tilted back so she could look at the sky. Expecting something. His skin tingled with activity. Like the night before. Pins. Needles. Oil. Fire. Ice. Liquid Mercury.

Head spinning, chest tight, he bolted from his room. His legs, like lead, fought him the entire time, but he pushed forward. Shoving on boots. Yanking on his coat. Ripping open the front door. He bolted out into the front yard, head twisting to find her.

The woman was gone, as were her emotions, but she'd left footprints in her wake.

She's real?

Excited, he sucked in a breath and followed the footprints. He wasn't one hundred percent sure, but somewhere deep in his gut, he knew. She was the woman from his dreams.

She's real.

He made it to the forest behind his house when the footprints disappeared. His lungs screamed at him to get out of the cold. Panting, he glanced around, hoping he would be able to find another set. The snow was fresh around him, untouched by humans. Untouched by animals. He leaned over, panting. A gust of wind blew past, rustling his coat, his hair, and bringing with it, voices.

Gentle, mysterious voices.

They spoke in a tongue he didn't recognize. He closed his eyes, trying to make out what they were saying.

This isn't my imagination. It's not a dream. Is it?

Then, it all went silent.

He opened his eyes again, lungs tight and painful. His head burned from the fever. He needed to get out of the cold. Irritated, he kicked some snow and headed back inside, desperate for a warm shower, a blanket, and some of the new tea his mother had insisted that he try.

Mia was the first person to her calculus class. It wasn't anything new, of course. Mia had second period off, as did Mrs. Kirkling, and she liked to go in and discuss the homework, just in case there was something she didn't understand. Being the only junior in a senior level course, she felt a level of pressure to perform well and to prove she actually belonged there.

Today, though, she hadn't arrived ten minutes early. She'd only arrived two minutes early. Barely enough time to talk about half a problem from the homework set. She'd meant to arrive before this, but all during her off period, she hadn't been able to stop thinking about the new student.

The apparently very attractive new student.

She hadn't seen him yet, but he was the topic of gossip around school. Just like she had been. Except this time, everyone was excited whereas with her…well, she didn't want to think about all of that anymore.

"Mia, you're late today," Mrs. Kirkling said, voice jovial.

"Sorry," Mia said. "Got distracted."

Her teacher chuckled. She was a tall woman. Thin with heavy earrings and enough wrinkles for a retirement home. For a math teacher, she was always so upbeat and excited for the day, even if her students wanted to be anywhere else. She kept insisting this year was the year she was going to retire, and then came up with some excuse to stay and "teach the silly children math".

Mia didn't mind. She liked Mrs. Kirkling.

"Well," Mrs. Kirkling said, "I can imagine you would be. It's not every day we get a new student."

Of course she knew about it. Mia retreated to her desk and pulled out her homework. "Yeah. I haven't met him yet. But I've heard…." That he was attractive. Polite. Smart. A lot of things. "…good things."

"Well, you're going to meet him in a minute here."

"He's in this class?"

"Yes."

Mia didn't know if she should smile or frown. On the one hand, she was curious about this new student. On the other, all morning she'd been bombarded with memories she'd rather forget. Blair had texted her saying she was all for shit talking him if Mia needed. Mia had smiled at that, but it wasn't the new kid's fault the other students had been awful to her. Besides, maybe she'd like him.

"What's his name?" Mia asked.

"Hm…." Mrs. Kirkling looked through some papers. "Looks like it's Steven Lourdes."

"That's me."

Mia's head spun toward the door. And blinked.

Kaylee hadn't been lying when she said he was hot. His hair was thick and brown, wavy, but not quite curly, and he stood tall. Not lanky, but not well built either. He ran a hand through his hair and stepped inside, heading for Mrs. Kirkling's desk. Mia watched him and cursed herself for the heat rising to her face. Everyone always told her she was too easy to read.

She hoped, in that moment, that they were lying.

"Oh, Steven." Mrs. Kirkling stood and held out a hand. "It's such a pleasure to meet you. Welcome to Willow Creek High. I hope your morning has gone well."

He took it, not paying any attention to Mia. "Same. This is...this is calculus, right?"

"Yes."

"I think your curriculum is a little ahead of where we were back in Los Angeles. Is it okay if I come in to catch up during my free period?"

Mrs. Kirkling nodded. "That would be perfect. Or...." She waved at Mia, who swallowed thickly, trying to get the blush out of her cheeks. They made eye contact, his eyes like a crystal ocean, and his smile made her melt a little. "This is Mia Sòng. She's my best student, and always looking for ways to pad her college applications. I'm sure she wouldn't mind tutoring you."

She definitely wouldn't mind. If she could get her voice to work.

"That would work," Steven said. A few other students trailed in behind him, chatting. He glanced at them right as the five minute bell rang. "I have to talk to Mrs. Kirkling about some stuff, but I'll get your number after class, yeah?"

"Uh...yeah." She internally smacked herself. She was more composed than this!

As class began, Mrs. Kirkling let Steven introduce himself, probably not for the first time that day. He spoke as if on a script. He was from Los Angeles. His parents moved here to get away from the big city and try ranching life. He liked to read.

Mia had tried to say something similar back in the day.

It hadn't gone nearly as well.

Instead of bored students nodding and muttering muted greetings, she got giggles and a teacher telling her it was okay. All she'd wanted was Derek, but he'd been put into another class.

The rest of class went without incident. Mia only paid half attention to Mrs. Kirkling's lecture, instead forcing herself not to look at Steven. At one point, she wrote her email and number on a piece of paper to make the exchange easier. And when the bell rang, signaling the end of class, Steven beelined to her, all smiles.

She did her best not to gulp.

"Mia, right?" he asked.

"Yeah." She stood and held out the piece of paper. "My... number. Just let me know when you have some time. I'm kinda busy right now but when my brother gets better–"

"You have a brother?" Steven asked. He had a gentle voice. Smooth. A brook rumbling down the side of a gentle slope.

Mia nodded. "He's sick right now. Just helping out."

"Oh, I'm sorry to hear that." Steven glanced over his shoulder at the mass of seniors disappearing out the door. "Hopefully he gets better soon."

"Yeah."

He turned to her again, still smiling. "All right. I'll text you after school with more info, cool?"

"Yeah."

"You on lunch right now?"

"Yeah."

Yeah? Who just says yeah over and over again?

She prepared herself to ask him to join her, since he was a new student and all, when Blair popped up almost out of thin air and linked her arm with Mia.

75

"Hey, let's go! The line is going to get longer if we aren't careful."

Mia had no idea where Blair had come from. She avoided Mrs. Kirkling's room like it was a rotten egg. Sometimes even her own class. It didn't matter, though. Because Mia barely had time to wave goodbye to Steven before Blair yanked her out of the room. The last she saw of Steven was him holding up his hand, the same one with the paper, and wave back.

Once they were down the hallway, Mia yanked her arm out of Blair's. "What was that about?"

Blair shrugged. "I dunno. I saw you with the new kid. Something about him gives me the creeps."

Mia rolled her eyes. "I think he's nice. Mrs. Kirkling asked me to tutor him in calc."

"Just be careful, okay?"

Mia didn't know how to respond. What she did know was that Steven definitely didn't deserve to be treated like a pariah because of her welcome to Willow Creek seven years ago. He wasn't an ass. He was as kind and respectful as his baby-reputation deemed him. And when she thought of him, she glanced back over her shoulder and smiled.

Chapter Seven

Soft grass tickled his bare feet. A light breeze rustled his hair, bringing with it a myriad of smells: ponds of rice, the musk of the river, smoke from the fires preparing the midday meal, gutted fish from the market down the way.

It was a collection of normal. A sense of familiarity that drew him into the world.

His world.

A world with soft grass tickling his feet. With his brothers shouting down the way, screaming at each other over a game they were forbidden to play. With his sisters annoyed and angry that he'd run off.

He didn't blame them. There was work to be done. Work for them. And work for him.

He smiled and crouched, running his small hands through the blades of grass, searching. Searching. Searching for the perfect stone. A scream caught his attention.

His mother.

His heart raced. The sun beat against his exposed back, the wrap tied around his waist half falling off in his desperate search for a magnificent specimen for his experiment.

His family, farmers, would notice him gone, but it would be worth it. All he needed to do....

When his fingers closed on a stone smooth as the un-spun silk he saw at markets with his mother, his heart fluttered like the moths confused by their nightly fires. The stone rested in his palm, a gray oval with flecks of white peering out from beneath the dirt. He brushed it off and stood, glancing behind him.

No sign of his mother. Just his brothers. But she was coming.

He slipped the rock into a makeshift pocket he'd crafted out of his waist wrap. It nestled against his concave belly, cool and wet. And he took off, running through the rice fields away from his family home.

The small cluster of wooden shacks wasn't safe for his experiment. The jungle his family's land bordered, however, was isolated. No one would find him there.

Breath heavy, he dashed through the forest to his favorite spot in the whole world. The large river, which fed their rice fields and produced fish all year round, met a patch of trees at a bend. It was the closest point near his home to the other side of the river.

The forbidden side.

The side where the *nạk māyākl*—mysterious humans who were rumored to mix with magic—lived. Where the *phūtphī pişāc*, human by shape but inhuman by nature, tortured anyone they deemed too normal.

The side he'd always been just a little too curious about.

His parents would never know of his escapades to the bend in the river. He was too clever. Too sly. He was always able to sneak off. They were never able to follow him. They didn't enter the jungle. They didn't venture from the family home unless it was to the market to trade grains for fish. For cloth. For exotic wares from the north. The west.

Away from the river. Away from his secret.

Which is why when he arrived, he was shocked to discover someone lounging on the bank of the river.

At first glance, she appeared like any other human. Black hair was pinned into an intricate braided bun, while her clothes spoke of someone from the royal family. Her colorful, silk *phānùng* spread across her legs, revealing more than he was used to seeing. Her shoulders remained bare, torso only half covered by another silk wrap. Not a farmer. Not a commoner. But human.

At second glance, he noticed something abnormal. Her skin frightened him. It was the first time in his life he'd seen someone with skin the color of a leelawadee flower—white with just a tinge of pink.

She didn't hold herself like anyone he'd met. There was a softness about her. A gentle wave of calm that didn't exist when you were poor and hungry. When the sun beat down on your back day after day.

His skin crawled, toes digging into the earth. Something was… off.

He pulled out the stone from his makeshift pocket.

Did she come from across the river? Was she one of the *nạk māyākl?* Or one of the *phūtphī piṣāc?*

Was she like him?

Warmth flooded his body. He didn't have to push. He didn't struggle. It came as naturally as breathing, lifting out of his skin and encasing the stone. The energy chipped away at the stone, carving it until it was left as a tiny flower. One that reminded him of her.

Smiling, he returned his gaze to the majestic woman.

Only to find her staring back.

It wasn't the frightened expression on her face that startled him into dropping the flower. It wasn't her sudden change of position, from relaxed to guarded. Nor was it the shift in her aura to fascinated fear.

It was the eyes locked with his, waiting, watching, shimmering the same color as a king's ruby.

The energy didn't come. Derek sat at the table, house vacant and quiet, with his hand extended. Next to him, the nauseating tea waited for him to drink it, but he found he really didn't want to. What he wanted was for the energy to return. To rise through his fingertips. He wanted to feel the emotions of people around him. He'd wanted to know how worried Mrs. Arbour was when her husband called saying her youngest son had a fever. He'd wanted to feel her concern when she told him she'd called Mr. Smith and that he was coming over.

He wanted to be able to hold out his hand and create a ball of energy, just like he'd practiced.

Instead his life was dull. He'd never considered how empty the world was without his ability. He'd never thought about how alone he was only feeling his own emotions. It was chilling. Disturbing in a way he'd never considered. In all of his seventeen years, he'd never wondered what it'd be like to live without one of his major senses.

He despised it.

With a loud groan, he took a sip of the foul, bitter tea, and grimaced. This was nothing like the other medicinal teas his parents had forced on him and Mia over the years. Bitter, yes, but there was something lingering beneath the surface. A hint of something reminding him of spoiled mint.

Another grimace and he lay his head on the table, trying not to let his distraught frustration overtake him.

It was fine.

Mrs. Arbour had said it would come back.

He just needed to....

He closed his eyes and thought of the dream. The warm, welcoming dream with the emerald waves of grass, the concerned shouts of a mother with too many children, and a face he'd never forget. The woman with the red eyes. The woman lounging by the river, dressed as royalty. The woman with a gentle, but startled, expression on her pale face.

It was easy to picture himself back there. Standing in the jungle at the edge of the Mekong River. A place he recognized from his own travels as a child. Visiting his father during one of his trips.

It was the first time he'd ever felt at home.

The food. The language. The culture. The people. The suffocating humid heat. Wandering around with his mother, he'd felt alive. Like his soul had found the place it was always meant to be. Something about Thailand called to him.

Something felt so real about this dream. A memory.

A gentle knock at the door startled Derek to his feet. Too fast. His head spun. His stomach turned. He lowered himself back into the chair and let his body catch up with his actions.

Shit.

He glared at the tea, half convinced it was making him feel worse, not better, then he stood—slowly this time—and lumbered toward the door. The bell rang, and he grumbled about impatient people and "why didn't Mrs. Arbour give Mr. Smith a key" and "shouldn't the man know he was sick? What if he'd been sleeping?". Things along those lines.

When he finally got to the door, he rested his forehead against it for a second. Just a brief second, letting the cool wood chill his fever enough that he could at least try and smile when Mr. Smith entered with food for lunch. If he could get anything down for lunch. After another ring of the bell, he opened the door.

Derek had spent little time with Mr. Smith. Besides the occasional neighborhood BBQ, the two of them had exchanged very few words. He was a stoic man. Tall. Brown hair and green eyes, though a different shade than Derek's. More like a cucumber than jade. Derek and Cody had had many entertaining moments coming up with different back stories for Tom Smith, the most boring man in Willow Creek. Because, seriously, who was that boring?

"Hi," Derek said, letting the man in.

"Mrs. Arbour said her son is sick. She asked me to bring food to you." He held out a container of chicken noodle soup. Derek took it, trying not to grimace. He didn't have the heart to tell the man, and through him, Coach Smith, that he was a vegetarian.

But, he figured Mia would be grateful for the food later.

"Thanks." He let Mr. Smith in and headed to the kitchen to put the soup in the fridge. He'd have to make himself some rice when Mr. Smith left. Assuming his stomach settled enough for him to eat at all. "I'm not that hungry. But I'll eat some later."

Mr. Smith nodded. "Are you doing all right? Esther…Mrs. Arbour, gave me a list of questions to ask."

He fumbled with his coat pocket before pulling out a piece of paper and handing it to Derek. It contained a list of questions, the same barrage he always got from his parents or Mrs. Arbour.

Temperature?

Stomach?

Sleep?

Eating enough?

Drinking enough?

And then, scribbled at the very bottom was a note from Mrs. Arbour to Mr. Smith telling him to try and engage in a social activity. Play a board game. Ask him about his day. The homework Mia had been bringing home for him. Simple things like that.

Derek held in his laugh.

"Everything's fine." Derek handed him back the list. It wasn't true. Beyond not true, but he was tired of the questions, and Mr. Smith didn't seem like the kind of guy to press. It was okay to lie here.

Mr. Smith nodded. "I suppose I'll leave. Make sure to eat."

Derek noticed he didn't mention eating the soup. "Thanks."

He prepared for Mr. Smith to leave. Head back out the front door and leave Derek to the quiet of his house, but the man didn't move. Instead, he stared at the cup of tea on the table, brow furrowed. Derek reached out, trying to get a sense of his emotions.

Still nothing.

Had Mr. Smith not been there, and had he not been so exhausted himself, he might have thrown the tea against the wall, frustration growing to overwhelming levels.

"Everything okay?" Derek asked.

"That tea you were drinking…."

"What about it?" Derek asked.

"It smells bad."

Well, at least he wasn't alone in that opinion. "I know. But it never smells good."

"I see." He chuckled. "I'll be going now."

"All right."

Derek led him to the front door and the man waved, not saying another word. And once he was alone, the exhaustion returned. He pressed his back against the door and slid to the tile floor. Dirty snow water soaked his pants, but he didn't care. He could change them in a moment.

When he regained his strength.

In that moment, all he wanted to do was close his eyes. So he did.

He closed his eyes and pictured himself back among the emerald waves, desperate to understand why he felt more at home in his nightmares than he did in his waking one.

Steven hadn't texted her. Mia had spent most last night trying not to check her phone every few minutes. But there hadn't been any texts from the new kid. There were some from Blair. A few from Cody. Her parents. Some girls from practice, but none from Steven. And Mia…she knew it was stupid, but she'd gotten her hopes up that maybe he'd wanted to talk to her, and not just to study.

Or maybe he'd found another study partner.

Regardless, when she'd left in the morning, Mrs. Arbour scolding Blair and her for skipping breakfast, and Derek still passed out from his fever, she'd found herself disappointed.

"You okay?"

The voice was gentle at first. It took a moment, as she sat at lunch staring at her untouched food, for her to realize that Cody had actually asked the question. That it wasn't just an echo in her mind from people asking her for the past few days if she was, in fact, okay.

Her head jerked up.

Cody, with his books out, pencil in one hand, chin in the other, stared at her. It was just the two of them today. She, Cody, Derek, and Blair always sat together, but other people joined them sometimes at random. Today, though, everyone had other engagements, and Blair's mom had called, taking her away from the table possibly for the rest of lunch.

Her mind went blank. He'd asked a question. If she was okay. For most people, she smiled and nodded. Said a few words. But with Cody, he knew she wasn't all right. He was one of the few people who hadn't asked her about that at all since Derek collapsed.

"What?" she asked.

Cody cocked his head. "You look like you're thinking about something. Is everything all right?"

"Oh. Yeah." She broke eye contact and stared around the cafeteria. She'd never seen Steven in here. He seemed to be incredibly busy getting caught up. They hadn't spoken since she gave him her contact information, but she'd seen him around. In class. Heading to the library. Just…existing.

She hadn't realized she'd spaced out again until Cody poked her in the arm. She jumped.

"Are you sure you're okay?" Cody asked. "I thought Derek was doing better."

"He is," Mia said. "Or, he says he is. You know."

Cody chuckled. "Yeah, he's blowing up the group chat. I don't think I've ever seen him this bored."

"That's because you don't live with him," Mia said with a roll of her eyes. Getting him to do homework was a chore in itself, but once he got it done, he did it quickly and efficiently, often leaving Mia to finish hers while he sat and bugged her to play video games with him or go explore the woods.

"True." Cody scribbled something in his notebook. "But you're okay?"

"Yeah." Mia sighed. "I'm just thinking about Steven."

"The new kid?"

"Yeah." She didn't know how to explain this to him. This wasn't exactly a topic the two had ever talked about before. Everything else? Sure. Cody was her best friend. There wasn't anything the two didn't feel comfortable talking about. Except, apparently, an attractive new student. "I'm supposed to be tutoring him in calc, but he hasn't contacted me."

Cody nodded. "That'll look good on a college application."

"Right?" Mia tried to sound enthusiastic, but she wasn't sure if it worked or not. Because it was a little more than just her college applications.

"Well," Cody said, "I'm sure he'll text you. He's in a couple of my classes and he seems a little lost. He could use a good tutor."

"What about you?"

He grimaced. "No. I...I'm good."

"Right." They didn't exchange any more words about Steven after that. Instead Mia went back to her food and Cody back to his books.

Silent.

Just like before. And Mia's mind wandered to Steven. To Derek. And finally to Blair who appeared in the cafeteria and stormed over to them. She thought of how uncomfortable Blair had seemed yesterday when she'd appeared in Mia's calc class and dragged her away from Steven. Blair was usually a good judge of character. In fact, both of her friends were. But she hoped Blair was wrong about this. Because Steven had been...kind.

Stop it. You barely know him.

She shook her head, catching Cody's attention. He opened his mouth, but before he could say anything, Blair collapsed back in her normal chair, groaning.

"My mom. Is so. Frustrating."

"Really? I find her quite kind," Cody muttered.

Blair glared at him.

"What's going on?" Mia asked. She didn't want them to fight. It was better to cut Blair off before she could snap a comeback to Cody.

Blair huffed, then crossed her arms. "Nothing. I guess. She's just...she...ugh, I don't know how to explain it."

Mia frowned. That wasn't the first time Blair had changed the subject when it came to her family. Whether it was her immediate family here in Willow Creek, or her family in Wyoming. The ones she only got to see for a few weeks every summer. It wasn't anything new for Blair to not give up information about herself, but this time she seemed less…smooth about it. Almost as if Mia's question caught her off guard.

"Okay, well I'm here if you want to talk," Mia said.

"Yeah. Oh." Blair leaned forward, knocking Cody's notebook in the process. He grumbled and erased the line he'd accidentally drawn. Mia flinched. "Can I come over again tonight? Mom can't. She has to take care of James and his fever. But she said I was free to hang out."

Mia nodded. "Yeah. Cody, do you want to come too?"

Blair grimaced. Mia ignored her. Cody looked up from his papers. Mia smiled at him.

"I wish I could," he said, "but I have work tonight and tomorrow."

"Oh. Right." Mia shifted. "Well, maybe after work tomorrow."

"Yeah," he said. But there was a distance there, especially when Mia's phone dinged. A text message.

She didn't recognize the number, but that made her heart soar. She didn't get spam. No one gave out her number accidentally to get away from creepy guys. There was only one person it could be.

<<Do you want to meet up tonight for a bit and study? This is Steven, btw.>>

"Is it Derek?" Blair asked.

"Um…no, Steven." Mia didn't like the look that crossed Blair's face. "What? He asked me to help him study."

"You're not going to say yes, are you?" Blair asked. "You have way too much on your plate."

Of course she was going to say yes. "It'll be fine."

"Yeah, it'll look good on her college applications," Cody said.

Blair rolled her eyes. "Whatever. I'm still coming over tonight."

"I'll be home by then."

Mia quickly texted back that that would work and they should meet up at the library when she was done with practice. When she returned to the table, to her friends, she found them staring at each other, communicating silently. Mia watched them for a moment. Watching Blair's forehead bunch up. Watching Cody's eyes narrow. Were they fighting?

"Um...?"

They looked away from each other, faces going back to normal right as the bell signaling the end of fourth period rang.

"Shit. Class." Blair sighed as Cody packed up his books, not saying a word.

Mia didn't know if she should say anything. It was clear the two of them were having a moment. Something was going on, but she wasn't sure she felt comfortable prying into their lives. Not when it was so clear they didn't want her knowing what they were doing there.

They left the cafeteria, and Mia tried to focus instead on school. Not on her study session with Steven tonight. Not on her sick brother. Not on her best friends—who hated each other—apparently keeping something from her. And definitely not on the bleached blond woman she kept imagining.

Nope. Just school.

Just. School.

Chapter Eight

Everything burned. His body ached, water dripping down his temple. He didn't want to think about it. The way his chest struggled to rise and fall. But it was all he could think about. The pain. The exhaustion. He couldn't sleep. The warm bank of the Mekong River was so far out of his grasp that he couldn't even imagine it anymore.

The only thing on his mind was the fever.

Through it all, he remembered a conversation with his parents. If his fever was too high, he needed to go to the hospital. There was banging out in the kitchen. Mia? Mrs. Arbour? He tried to call out, but his voice caught in his throat. He tried to move, but his limbs went numb. He tried to breathe, but his lungs tightened.

Was he dying? Was this what it felt like?

-You aren't dying. -Get up.

The voice appeared beneath his thoughts. One almost matching his own. One just different enough that he noticed it wasn't his. Or was it? Was it his own?

A splurge of energy rolled through him. He gasped, air filling his lungs like the first day he was born. Painful and sudden. Sparking a hint of tears. The world around him spun. His body swayed, and yet he stayed upright. And yet he managed to twist. Swing his legs over the edge of the bed. His feet touched the cool wooden floor of his bedroom. A chill ran up his spine.

He needed to get to the kitchen. Tell Mia he needed…he needed…what did he need?

-A hospital.

He needed a hospital. He needed to eat. He needed to drink. He needed his tea.

-Don't trust the tea.

He hesitated, leaning against the wall next to his door. Why shouldn't he trust the tea? As disgusting as it was, his mom had never steered him wrong before. He may have hated the tea, but it couldn't hurt him. It was tea.

-Don't trust the tea.

The tea didn't matter. He yanked open the door and stumbled out of his room into the bright hallway. Across from him, the kitchen. Mia standing with her back to him, cleaning something in the sink. Sitting next to her the tea. It blurred in and out of focus, like his thoughts.

He didn't trust the tea. He'd never finished a cup. He always tossed the rest in the sink when Mia or Mrs. Arbour wasn't looking and pretended like he wasn't thirsty anymore. Because he didn't trust the tea. Something was wrong with it. He knew the medicinal teas Intira forced on them. They all had a similar taste and this was different. Like she'd grabbed the wrong one.

-Like someone switched it.

"Derek?" Mia must have heard him because she turned around. He leaned against the wall again, exhausted. Burning. Throat parched. "Holy shit." She rushed over to him and placed a refreshingly cool hand against his forehead. "You're burning up. Let me call Mrs.

Arbour."

Mrs. Arbour would tell her to give him the tea.

He grabbed her arm before she could go far, gripping hard. If she'd wanted to, she could absolutely get out of his grasp. He was weak. She'd always been much stronger than him. But she didn't pull away. She placed her hand on his shoulder.

"What's wrong?" she asked.

"Water," he said.

-Don't trust the tea.

"You mean tea?"

"Water." His throat scratched with the word. It was all he could think about. Not tea. Nothing flavored. Nothing tainting the purity of fresh, clean, water. An image of the Mekong River flashed through his mind. Water was everything. Water was life.

"Okay," Mia said. She pulled out of his grasp and hurried to the counter where she poured a cup of warm water for him. He stumbled to the table, collapsing in the nearest chair. He couldn't trust the tea. He couldn't trust the tea. He couldn't–

Mia returned with a glass and Derek took it from her a little too roughly. He lifted it to his lips, spilling droplets on his hands as they shook. And once the water slithered down his throat, quenching the fire burning down to his stomach, his hands settled. He drank more. Barely breathing. Just drinking. And as he did, an energy rushed through his body.

When it was empty, he let the cup drop to the table, gasping. Gasping, but not struggling. It was still there. Whatever poison had been stealing his magic. Stealing his emotions. Stealing his life. Mia filled his cup again and he drank more, Slowly this time. Relishing in the way his body cooled. The shivering stopped. One last droplet of sweat streaked down his cheek.

He wiped it away with a steady hand.

And then, like it was never gone, he felt it.

Concern.

Not his.

Mia's.

She sat next to him, curled into a ball on her chair. It was faint. A shimmer of lace against his skin, but it was there. And the more he drank, the stronger it became. The stronger the energy flowing through his veins became.

His magic.

-I told you. -Don't trust the tea.

"Are you okay?" Mia asked.

Was he? He finished the last drops of water and placed the glass on the table. Soundlessly. At some point, while he'd chugged the water, the world had stopped spinning. And for the first time since he'd collapsed at the feet of The Queen, Derek felt a little bit like himself.

"Yeah," he said. "I'm okay. Don't call Mrs. Arbour."

Mia frowned. The concern must have been a one-time thing, because he felt nothing else from her. "Can I at least take your temperature?"

Yes. He wanted to see what it was himself. He nodded and she stood to go get it from the counter. And while she did, he glanced around the kitchen, energy returning to him at an increasing pace until his gaze landed on the tin of tea.

He narrowed his eyes. It looked like something Intira might buy for her family at an Asian Store in Denver, and yet…there was something off about it. Something so wrong.

-Don't trust it.

He tried to figure out if the voice belonged to him or not. It was distinct, but clearly one that belonged to him. A voice that he'd known all of his life.

And he knew that he needed to get rid of the tea.

Without much thought, he stood up and went to the container.

92

Mia watched him, holding the thermometer in one hand as he grabbed it, went to the sink, and dumped the entire thing into the trash.

Mia watched, horror struck, while Derek dumped the contents of the tea into the trashcan. She didn't blame him, honestly. She'd tried a sip of his tea this morning before delivering it to his room and it'd almost made her want to run to the bathroom and vomit. But still. The fact that he'd actually done it?

"I don't care what Mom says," Derek said, slamming the empty tin on the counter, "I'm not drinking that shit."

She didn't argue. He demanded water, looking much less like death than he had a few moments ago. The thermometer felt useless between her fingers. Still, she held it out to him.

"You get to tell her," she decided to say.

He waved a hand before taking the thermometer and shoving it in his mouth and returning to his seat. Mia thought, briefly, that they should wait a bit because he'd just drank some water, but she also wanted to know if it was at least in a normal range. Not over one hundred and four, like it had been when he collapsed at the opening. They'd take it again before she left to meet with Steven.

It beeped and she snatched it from his mouth, much to his protests.

One hundred even.

It made no sense, but that was all right. Technology didn't lie.

With a heavy breath, she sank into her chair and let her body relax a little. It wasn't over. He was still sick. But they wouldn't have to call Mrs. Arbour. They wouldn't have to go to the hospital. She wouldn't have to deal with this alone.

He was fine.

"You okay?" He reached over and poked her forehead.

She smiled at him. "Just glad you're okay. You looked like death."

"I felt like death." He gave a toothy grin. "But I'm feeling a lot better. I think...." He hesitated.

"You think?"

"I was probably dehydrated," Derek said. "Can't tea do that?"

Mia shrugged. "You'd have to ask someone who knows anything about tea."

"So, Năinai?"

A giggle escaped Mia. Their grandmother knew everything about tea. The two of them had grown up with her talking about it. It was most likely why Derek had fallen in love with drinking tea, though Mia had found the lectures more annoying than anything.

"Yeah," she said. "Năinai would know."

They fell silent while the rice cooker steamed. It wasn't until Mia's phone chimed that she moved at all, looking to see who it was.

<<Can we meet a bit early? My parents want me home for dinner at seven and I have a lot to cover.>>

Steven's text sent a gentle butterfly roaming around her stomach. She couldn't stop the smile from spreading across her face.

<<Yeah, sure. My brother just woke up and he's feeling better. I don't think I have to finish making dinner for him.>>

<<Okay. I'll meet you at the library in a few?>>

Oh, he meant now. Mia checked the time. It was almost five-thirty. She hadn't been home for very long, and she felt a little odd leaving Derek here alone, since Blair hadn't shown up yet, but he was feeling better.

<<Sure.>>

"Who are you texting?" Derek asked. "You have a stupid grin on your face."

Mia forced her lips into a frown. "Do not."

"Do too. Who is it?"

She sighed. "It's a new kid. I meant to tell you about him but–"

"I've barely been awake, I get it." He leaned back in his seat, staring at the ceiling. "New kid, huh?"

"Yeah."

"Weird."

"That's what Blair said."

"Blair is smart."

Mia rolled her eyes. "I'm helping tutor him since he's behind. He wants to meet up now. You okay to wait for Blair by yourself?"

"Yup."

"The rice is almost done."

"Cool"

"Don't forget to eat protein. You're terrible at that."

"Okay."

She frowned and crossed her arms. "You speak three languages. Can't you muster up a complete sentence in at least one of them?"

Derek grinned at her. He was absolutely feeling better. "Nope."

"Whatever." She stood and stretched. "I'll be back in an hour or so. Please don't burn the house down."

"Will do."

She decided not to clarify that he *shouldn't* burn the house down. They were seventeen, not seven. He didn't need to be told not to destroy the dwelling that kept them warm, especially not with the four feet of snow outside. Instead, she headed to the front door and slipped on her coat and boots, staring at her phone. At Steven's name. A hint of excitement blossomed in her chest.

Then she grabbed her backpack and headed out the front door.

The moment she entered the warmth of the library, she searched for him. It was a small building. One large room connected to the high school with a collection of tables and a desk where the librarian sat, making sure people didn't steal books or talk too loudly. Mia had spent quite a bit of time in here, whether it be studying with her friends or passing her off periods reading a book from her cousin in Beijing.

It was the place she felt most comfortable. Where no one could bother her if she didn't want them to.

Sitting at a table in the corner, she spotted Steven with his face buried in a book. She paused for a moment to examine him. Try to figure him out. He'd seemed so confident when he had spoken to her that day in calc, but after that he came off as so shy. He barely spoke in class, other than his introduction. Never raised his hand. Didn't seem to speak to anyone at all.

Maybe he'd open up in a few days, when he got used to the culture of Willow Creek High.

With a deep breath, and practicing a few phrases so she said more than "fine" this time, she headed over to her study partner.

"Steven."

He looked up from his book, and for a moment Mia's breath caught. She'd forgotten how intense his gaze could be.

"Mia, hey." Steven grinned and closed his book. Modern European History. A class she'd opted not to take. "Sorry, just catching up on some reading. I hate that schools don't all have the same curriculum. Makes it hard to move."

Mia nodded and sat. She'd felt very much the same when they'd moved here, though that was a little more complicated. Different curriculum. Different speeds in topics. Different language entirely.

"Well, hopefully you'll catch up soon," she said.

"Yeah. It's only been a week, and I'm getting there." He laughed, moving his books around to pull out his calc one. "I'm going to need a couple study sessions though. Maybe just the rest of the semester. I mean, if you want."

His words were so earnest, Mia flushed. She pulled her own books out of her bag and placed them with a thump on the table, hoping it would cause him to stop looking at her with such wide eyes. He was like a puppy, waiting on any words that might come out of her mouth.

"I can," she said. "But you might want to find someone better at teaching. I can't promise I'm any good."

"I'm sure you're great."

Her lips flickered up into a smile. "Um...thanks. Um...why don't we start with calc, since we have that first thing on Monday."

She was aware that he was watching her, even as she pulled out her books and flipped to the page she guessed he needed to be on based on what she knew about him. Which, granted, wasn't much. "Where do you want to start?"

"Where are you from?" Steven's question came so out of nowhere that Mia actually flinched. Memories of back then, of girls asking over and over where Mia was from and why she couldn't speak English flashed through her mind. Memories she'd done her best to block.

He did not just ask me that.

"Excuse me?" she asked, irritation rising.

Steven jolted away from her, eyes widening. "Wait. No. I just...I mean...you have an accent. So I–"

Horror rushed through Mia. She and Derek had spent months practicing their accents. Trying to get rid of any signs that they might not be from Colorado. Or, at least the US. "I don't have an accent."

"Hang on," Steven leaned forward. "I didn't...no that wasn't supposed to upset you."

"I'm not upset." The lie of the century. "Let's just get this over with."

He groaned and placed his face in his hands. "Dammit. Okay. Wait. Just…let me explain."

She crossed her arms and tried her best not to glare. He'd seemed so kind. So polite. Coming from LA, surely he should have known what that question meant. And she did not have an accent.

He breathed in, then out. And then said in a language Mia didn't even recognize, *"Jeg er norsk."*

Mia blinked. "What?"

He looked down at his book, wringing his hands together. "I just…I'm not from America. I'm Norwegian. I heard your accent and thought maybe someone would understand what it was like to be an immigrant."

Mia's anger dipped from one hundred to the low twenties. He hadn't meant what she'd thought, but she still hated how bluntly he'd asked the question. "I might not be an immigrant. My parents might be and they don't speak English."

"Oh." He paled. "I didn't think of that."

"But…." She sighed. "I lived in Beijing until I was ten."

"Beijing!" His voice rose to too high a level, and the few people who were in the library glanced over at them. Mia shrunk in her seat. "Oh. Sorry. Um…Beijing. That's so cool. I've always wanted to go there. Is it as crowded as they say?"

"Compared to Willow Creek?" Mia asked.

Steven chuckled. "Okay, good point."

The conversation lulled as Mia tried to think of something to say in response. She wasn't here to talk about her heritage. She was here to help the new kid study. And yet, she found him interesting. And he was interested in her. Not because she'd had to fight her way for him to see her as worth being liked, but because he just…was.

"We should study," Steven said. "I have to get home soon."

"Yeah, same." Mia gestured at her calc book. "Guess you should tell me what exactly you *need* help with?"

Steven grinned. "Yeah. Guess I should."

And while they worked, Mia's heart refused to return to a normal rate. Especially as he asked more questions about her life. Especially as he pushed to know more about her. Especially as she found herself really enjoying his company. Blair had said to be careful around him, but Mia found she really didn't want to.

It was almost seven.

Derek stared at his phone, obsessing about the time while picked at his lightly sauced rice, tofu, and bok choy. He'd never been the greatest cook in the world, having no interest at all in cooking or food, but he at least knew how to throw something together that wouldn't piss off his upset stomach.

Except, his stomach wasn't exactly upset anymore. In the time since Mia had left, he'd downed at least eight cups of water, had to run to the bathroom more times than he wanted to admit, but he felt almost completely back to normal. But the only problem was, he was alone. Completely alone in his house and he couldn't test if the one thing he absolutely wanted back had returned or not.

Which is why he was staring at his phone. Counting down the minutes until either his sister or his crush showed up and he could finally, finally, feel some emotions.

But his phone said nothing. No text from Mia telling him she was on her way home, and nothing from Blair making a stupid joke about her being a lady and that he should be a gentleman when she arrived. Groaning, he leaned back in his seat and tried to find some kind of distraction from the waiting.

What he landed on was the new kid that Mia had mentioned.

A new kid. At Willow Creek high.

He grimaced. He did not remember his first few months in Willow Creek fondly. They'd spent the first couple of weeks in America visiting his grandparents in the Midwest while his parents figured out what they were going to do with their jobs. With their marriage.

Those weeks had been fun. Stressful, but fun. They traveled a lot. Spent time with their grandparents. With their Aunt Malee, who they didn't know very well. But then they'd moved to Willow Creek. The bullying began. Mia's emotions had been all over the place. Derek had tried to figure out how to keep her calm, but some days it was too much for her. It was too much for him.

All he'd wanted to do was make her feel better, but the only thing that worked was time. Time and a lot of hard work on Mia's part. Derek had felt so useless.

And now there was a new kid. A kid who probably wouldn't be bullied the way Mia had been. He couldn't imagine that this was easy for Mia. He wondered if, possibly, Mia would be too upset to do more than eat dinner and go to bed. And then he wondered if maybe he should try and make her something for dinner. She'd already half started something with chicken and broccoli. It wouldn't be hard to finish.

Right?

But before he could stand, before he could help his sister out, he felt something.

A tingle on his skin.

An emotion wafting through the air, enticing him back into reality. His reality. The reality he'd craved for days now.

He stood. It was light. Not Mia. But Blair.

When he reached the door, he opened it before Blair could knock. Cold air blasted him as a gust of wind forced its way into the house. But he didn't care. He didn't care that Blair stared at him like he was insane. He didn't care that she was bundled up. That he was in his pajamas and his feet and arms were protesting the chilly weather.

All he cared about were the textures grating against his skin. The nuanced balance of confusion and excitement. Of happiness.

Blair's emotions.

Derek couldn't help himself. He reached out and pulled Blair into the house, ignoring her yelp. The door closed behind her, blocking out the cold.

"You're energetic," Blair said.

Yes. He was. He reached out and placed his hands on her cheeks for a brief moment, waiting for her to push him away. When she didn't, he leaned in. Her emotions shifted from confusion to a hint of lust, trailing like silk along his entire body. And when their lips touched, it turned to fire.

He didn't kiss her for long. But when he pulled away, grinning like a damn idiot, the look in her eyes mixed with the disappointment on his skin gave him all the information he needed to know.

"I take it you're feeling better." She muttered this time, eyes trailing to the ground.

"Yup." Derek moved away from her, not wanting to push, even though all he wanted to do was pull her into the tightest hug ever.

Because he could feel them.

Her emotions.

Blair slowly stripped of her clothes, cheeks filled with a deeper color. "According to Mia you were still passed out when she got home. What changed?"

What had changed?

Derek led Blair into the fragrant kitchen. His half eaten dinner waited for him on the table, and Mia's uncooked food in the fridge. Blair walked over to the wok with the rest of his meal and sniffed.

Meanwhile, Derek's eyes drifted toward the trashcan under the sink. He could tell her his theory. It was a stupid one, but it made sense. He listened to the voice—which he wasn't about to tell her about—and stopped trusting the tea. Someone must have switched it somehow. At some point. He didn't know who, but his biggest guess was the woman in black he kept imagining.

Because he was starting to really doubt that he'd imagined her.

"You're going to think I'm crazy," Derek said.

Blair rolled her eyes. "You greeted me by kissing me in a doorway. I already think you're crazy."

He grinned. "Sorry. Just…I got excited."

"To see me?"

"Well, that."

"And?"

"I can feel emotions again."

Blair halted, brow furrowed. The confusion returned, encasing him like crinkled wrapping paper. "What happened?"

And so, Derek explained. Not everything. He didn't talk about the woman in black or the voice, but he explained how he felt worse with the tea, and that when he drank water instead, it was like life returned to his body. He was no longer being drowned, but instead breathing.

She listened, eventually settling in a seat with a bowl of Derek's dinner. When he finished, she tapped her chin.

"I mean, I guess," she said. "But it's kinda weird. Who would want to poison you?"

The woman in black. "I'm not sure. Still working on that."

Blair opened her mouth to respond, but another feeling hit Derek. Something much stronger. He held up a hand to stop her from speaking and focused. His powers were back, but they weren't perfect yet, so it took a moment to pick out Mia's flustered happiness from behind the door.

"She's home," he said.

Blair dropped the subject immediately and dug into her food

the moment the key turned the lock. There was some mild cursing, stomping of boots, and then shuffling of clothes before Mia appeared in the kitchen, rubbing her hands together.

"Man, it got cold," she said. Her eyes landed on Blair. "Hey, did you just get here?"

"Yeah," Blair said. "Sorry. Got caught up doing homework."

Surprise hit Derek like a brick. He placed a hand on his chest and shook his head.

"Oh, that's good." Mia looked between the two of them. "Um… I'm going to finish dinner, but then do you want to watch a movie or something? Since Derek is apparently fine now."

He smiled at her. "Fit as a fiddle."

Relief. He loved relief. It didn't matter who it came from or why. It was one of the most gentle emotions someone could feel. And he absolutely loved it from Mia. She was always so tense. Even if he hadn't been able to sense her emotions the past few days, he'd known it had gotten worse, and it made him happy to see her shoulders relax.

"I'm glad."

Mia went about getting to finishing her dinner, with Blair standing to help, and Derek closed his eyes.

He focused, relishing the feel of their emotions dancing on his skin. And then, when he opened his eyes again, for a moment he was back at the Mekong River. No snow. Just humidity. No Mia or Blair. Just the woman in black. The woman with the red eyes.

He blinked and the scene was gone. He blinked and his smile dipped into a frown. He blinked and realized that the woman in black had tried to kill him. With tea. And he had a feeling she wasn't done.

Chapter Nine

Mia stared out the cafeteria doors, waiting for her friends to arrive. For Derek to arrive. The weekend had passed without another spike in his fever. When their parents had returned home yesterday, he'd gotten the parental seal of approval to go back to school. Turn in all of his homework. Finally attend class. Be social.

She was happy for him. She really was. The moment they'd gotten to school, pretty much the entire student body had swarmed him, asking if he was okay. In a moment of evil siblingness, she'd taken off without him, leaving him to curse after her. And indeed, at lunch he'd pouted the entire time, clearly exhausted from the sudden attention. Which left her, Blair, and Cody to chat.

Again, Mia hadn't known where Steven was, but she'd tried to keep her mind off of him. They'd agreed to meet up today after class—since Coach was out sick and she'd cancelled practice—to study, so she'd see him then. And that was enough.

Sort of.

Regardless, she'd gone through lunch with Derek eventually speaking to her, which made Cody ten bucks after a silent bet with

Blair, enjoying the full company of all of her group. And now, standing by the copier in the teacher's office, she listened to her favorite teacher, whom she TA'd for during seventh period, rant about the changing curriculum notices from the state of Colorado.

She adored Mr. Becker. A teacher of history, Mr. Becker came across as crass and rude when students first met him, but there was something so intriguing about him. For one thing, his eyes were different colors: one green, one blue. For another, he always, always, knew when someone was passing notes in class. But lastly, he had this way of talking about history that made it come to life. He wasn't just repeating what the documents said. He told a story. He talked about the people like he'd known them personally. And he didn't cut things out because someone somewhere was embarrassed about it. If it had happened in history, no matter how good or evil, he knew about it. And he talked about it.

It never took long for him to capture the attention of every class. Each year, students fought over who got to be in his classes, and who took classes from Mrs. Garrison.

Mia had gotten lucky every year. And she loved being his TA. Sometimes he kept the best stories for when he was rambling in his office, grading essays and textbook outlines.

Today, though, he wasn't spouting off about some random soldier during the Northern Crusades. Instead he was focused on the modern day.

"So tell me," Mr. Becker said, "what hot gossip is going around the school today?"

Mia looked away from the copier for a moment, lips tight with second-hand embarrassment. "Hot gossip?"

"Yeah!" Mr. Becker sat back in his seat and stared up at the ceiling. "I like to know what's going on with you kids. You have such interesting interpersonal relationships and circles. I never hear enough about the drama going on. So tell me. What's happening in your lives?"

Mia rolled her eyes. "There's no drama."

"Now that's a lie. This is high school. Drama is a staple of life here."

He had a point. And there was drama. Stupid stuff about who was dating who, and what friend groups were having a falling out. She was sure Mr. Becker would be interested in some of it to keep his students on their toes, but there was nothing actually interesting.

"It's just the new kid," Mia said. The copier stopped and she collected the papers. "But that's dying down. Today people are excited that Derek's back in school. But I don't think that's hot gossip."

"Hm, I suppose not." He sighed. "But the new kid. That's an interesting development." He didn't say more than that. He never did, but Mia could tell he had a lot on his mind about Steven. She pressed sometimes, but he never relented. As much as he liked hearing about drama, he was true to his calling as a teacher and kept his mouth shut.

"He's nice," Mia ventured. "I'm tutoring him in some classes."

Mia returned to his desk, papers in hand while Mr. Becker thought about what she'd said. As she handed him the copies, something out the window caught her eye. She looked up, then froze.

The woman was back. The one from last week. With the blond hair and the clothes that didn't seem to match the weather. She sat in the tree outside of Mr. Becker's window, smiling.

"Be careful not to fall for that boy," Mr. Becker said. "You've got too much potential to waste your time with a boy in high school."

"Mr. Becker," Mia said, voice quavering. The woman waved at her.

She's not real.

She's not real.

"Probably not my place to lecture you," Mr. Becker continued, "but I've seen lots of girls throw away their lives for a guy. 'Oh, I'll just wait a bit to go to school,' they say while they support their man through college. 'No big deal. I'll focus on me after we're married,' and then next thing you know they have four kids and spend their time at PTA meetings."

"Mr. Becker…." She was too frightened to move.

"Not that there's anything wrong with being a homemaker, or a stay at home mom going to PTA meetings, but they didn't do it because they wanted to. They did it because some guy stepped all over them, and I hate to see it happen."

The woman reached into her coat pocket, and pulled out a piece of paper.

"So just be careful."

In red writing, the words, "Hello, Mia," were spelled out in cursive.

"Mr. Becker!" Mia's voice rose to a scream and she stepped back away from the desk.

Mr. Becker jumped out of his seat, eyes wide. "Mia?"

Mia pointed to the window, desperate to get him to turn around. When he didn't, brow furrowing. She glanced away. It was only for a second. To look for something to get him to do what she wanted. But by the time she looked at the window again, it was empty.

No woman.

No note.

Mr. Becker turned around, finally, finding nothing but a snow covered tree

Her heart sunk. Tears pricked her eyes. She tried to blink them away, but they streamed down her cheeks instead.

Mr. Becker turned back around. Mia couldn't look at him. Couldn't face him. Not after screaming at him. She bowed her head and stepped back, chest tightening.

There was the scraping of a chair. She stayed still. A hand

touched her shoulder. She let it push her into the chair, head still bowed, unable to breathe.

"Mia, what's wrong?" Mr. Becker asked. But she had no words for him.

No words for anyone.

"I think someone poisoned me."

Cody didn't respond at first. Derek had him practically cornered, since he locker was at the end of the hall. It was eighth period. The first time all day that Cody and Derek had a moment to be alone. Derek had already told Blair his theory, but he couldn't risk trying to tell Cody over text.

The information was too sensitive.

When Cody closed his locker, lips a frown, uncertainty filling the gaps the curiosity left, Derek expected his response.

"That sounds farfetched."

Derek groaned. "I know. Blair said that too. But seriously. Think about it. I collapsed at the opening. Fine. That happened. We don't know why. But it set some weird shit off, and whenever I drank that tea, I got worse."

"You think a tea your mom, *your mom*, bought you was poisoned?" Cody leaned against his locker. This was not going the way Derek had planned. All day he'd been overwhelmed with people bombarding him with questions. Welcoming him back. Pretending like they were friends when really they couldn't care less about him outside of the fact that he'd caused an excitement in the school. Sure, they liked him well enough, but they weren't his friends.

His friends were the ones he needed to believe that he'd been poisoned.

"I think someone switched the tea," Derek explained.

"Who?" Cody asked. "Mia? Mrs. Arbour?"

"No." Derek shook his head. "Of course not. If they wanted me dead they would have done it a long time ago."

Annoyance laced Cody's emotions. "Derek, come on. We're going to get in trouble for hanging around the hallways. Let's go meet up with Blair and do some homework. You're fine now. There's no reason to suspect someone wants to kill you."

Except there was. "You don't get it."

Cody sighed and stepped around Derek, heading down the hall. Derek stumbled after him.

"I'm serious," Derek continued. He lowered his voice as they passed another group of students who were hanging out in the halls, laughing quietly together. "Look, there's some shit I haven't told you guys. About…about stuff. But I'm serious when I say that something is going on and I don't think it was just some fever."

"Derek," Cody said. The two of them stopped halfway down the stairs. Cody's emotions shifted. Confusion. Fear. Just a mess of sandpaper rubbing up and down his skin. "There's a reason I don't talk about anything related to magic. I don't like talking about it. I don't want anything to do with it. I know it's something we have in common, but you aren't the only one with magic around here. If the tea was suspicious, why didn't Mrs. Arbour do something about it?"

Because…he didn't know why. He didn't know why some part of him refused to trust the tea. He didn't know why he kept seeing the woman in black. He didn't know why he kept having the dreams about ancient Thailand. He didn't know. He didn't know.

He didn't know.

But he did know it wasn't a coincidence.

"I got sick for a reason," Derek said. "I know you want to pretend like it's nothing, and I know Blair wants to pretend like it's nothing, but it's not nothing."

Laughter interrupted him. The group of students from earlier appeared in the stairwell and Derek grimaced. Once they'd passed, saying hi to both Derek and Cody, Cody spoke again.

"You said there's stuff you haven't been saying?" he asked.

Derek nodded.

Cody glanced around. Like before, his emotions shifted, too quickly for Derek to pick up on any of them. Then, after a quick moment, he said in a low voice, "But not right here. Let's go to the library and study. You can tell me what's going on then, okay?"

Derek nodded and breathed out. Cody might not believe him about the poisoning. Maybe Derek was completely wrong. Maybe Blair had been right and it was far-fetched. But even if he hadn't been poisoned by the tea, something had happened. Something strange. Unnatural. His dreams. The woman. Collapsing. None of it was normal.

Between homework, texts from Blair complaining about having to do this group project with three people she couldn't stand, and people walking past their table, it took all fifty minutes of their off period for Derek to explain everything about what had *really* been going on with him the past week. From the dreams, to seeing the woman, to the voice in his head.

He didn't want to actually admit most of this. It was a little embarrassing to admit that he might be hallucinating, but it was all part of his theory that for some reason, a woman with black hair, black clothes, and red eyes was stalking him, and that someone, possibly her, was trying to kill him.

Cody listened, mostly silent. Every now and then he asked a clarifying question, but went silent again. It wasn't until the bell releasing them from the hell that was high school rang that he spoke.

"So, all of this has been going on, and you think it's related to you being sick?" The two boys stood, collecting their things.

"That's what I said." Derek had no time for this. Mia didn't have practice today, which meant she was going to go home with them. They were meeting up in front of the school in probably less than two minutes.

Cody sighed. "I…I don't know. It's a lot."

"Trust me, I know it's a lot. I've lived it."

"Maybe I'm missing something," Cody continued. "I'm not the best with this stuff. I've avoided magic for years. My parents aren't mages. I'm not exactly close with Blair. And I hate that I have these powers to begin with. Maybe we should talk to Blair about this."

Derek had wanted to talk to Blair about it, but the opportunity hadn't arisen. Either Mia had been there, or his parents had been there, or he hadn't had enough time. Something had stopped him each time. But Cody was right. He needed to talk to Blair about this. And if it got bad, maybe Mrs. Arbour.

"Maybe tonight after Mia leaves," Derek said. "She's going to help that new kid study, right?"

He didn't know what to think of the new kid. His emotions were…off. But Derek hadn't thought too much of it, since everyone's emotions were off at the moment. It was just jarring from someone he'd never met before. But he seemed kind enough. Maybe a little too interested in Mia, but not in a way that worried Derek.

"Yeah, he is," Cody muttered. A hint of jealousy pricked at Derek's skin.

He sighed. "Whatever, let's go meet Mia and Blair."

They continued through the school in silence, Derek wondering how he was going to explain all of this to Blair. Cody liked to listen. Blair liked to interrupt. It would take a lot longer to explain his theory to her, and he wasn't even sure she'd believe him. He wasn't even sure Cody believed him fully. It seemed almost like he was brushing Derek off, not wanting to say anything one way or the other to avoid hurting Derek's feelings.

Which was just like Cody.

As they walked, however, Derek noticed something off about the air around him. A tingle on his skin. Different than anything he'd felt in a long time. It was lower down. Sometimes, when a suppressed emotion was strong enough, it bled out among all the others, but it felt different. Deeper. Thicker. Like a double layer of whatever texture it was taking on.

And this had that. But not only did it have it, it belonged to Mia.

Derek halted, stopping Cody in his tracks.

"Derek?" Cody asked.

Derek focused. He focused until he pinpointed the place where the fear was coming from, and then he darted through the hallway. Straight toward the front door. The moment he exited the building, he spotted Mia standing with Blair, smiling like normal.

Except she wasn't normal. She was shaking. Her emotions fluctuated, trying to pretend like she wasn't absolutely terrified.

"Derek!" Cody called after him.

Derek ignored him and headed toward his sister.

She turned to him at the sound of his footsteps. Blair did as well. They'd been chatting, pretending like nothing was wrong. And Derek didn't want to bring up whatever was upsetting Mia to such a degree. Instead, he did what he tried not to do too often. He did what he always did when she was so upset that it was causing her physical pain.

He placed a hand on her shoulder and he pushed something positive into her.

The pain eased. Her hand stopped shaking. Her smile relaxed.

"Hey," she said. "How was your first day back?"

He removed his hand from her shoulder and grinned. Blair,

meanwhile, glanced at Derek, then at Mia, and she narrowed her eyes at Derek. He didn't acknowledge it.

"It was exhausting," he said. "Let's just head home." He could ask her at home. When she could melt down and no one would judge her. Where the whispers wouldn't start again.

"Sure, but I won't be home for long," Mia said. "Gotta grab something and come back. Mom and Dad said they'd be home later."

"Kay." Derek watched her walk away, Blair at her side, though she kept glancing back at Derek with a raised brow. He didn't care. He didn't care about where his parents were, or when they'd be home. He just wanted to make sure Mia was all right. And for now, she was. His power didn't last forever, but it lasted long enough to get them home, at least.

"What was that all about?" Cody asked.

Derek shrugged. "She seemed upset."

He said nothing else and the two boys hurried to catch up to Mia and Blair. Derek figured that once Mia was gone, he'd get a ton of questions about it. Even as they caught up to the girls, walking down the sidewalk toward his house, he could feel the emotions of his two friends. The confused questioning emotions that twirled together and stuck to his clothes like a vacuum.

But then there was something else. A feeling. Like the one he'd felt before.

His head swiveled, tearing away from the path in front of him. Across the street. To where she was. The woman from his dreams. The one who'd called out to him. The one who'd grabbed him. The red eyed woman lounging by the river.

Cody and Blair didn't seem to notice her. Could they not sense her?

She watched him. He watched her. The emotion, the feeling, it grew until it consumed everything. He didn't feel anyone else. He didn't hear anyone else. The only thing in the world was her.

Derek's feet disobeyed him. They stepped off the sidewalk. Onto the street. Toward her. Needing to be near her.

Until someone screamed his name.

Everything had happened so fast, he couldn't catch his breath. A hand caught his backpack. Pulled him back. He fell onto the sidewalk, hands catching himself. Scraping against the frozen ground. Pain exploded in his wrists. He flinched. But his eyes never left the space where she'd been. He didn't care about the speeding car. He barely noticed his terrified sister crouching next to him.

He didn't have the energy to quell her fear this time.

Time returned to normal and he breathed out. The woman vanished. He didn't blink. He didn't look away. She. Just. Vanished.

"Oh my god, Derek," Blair exclaimed, crouching next to him. She was shaking, grabbing his shoulders. Mia was crying, breath short and shaky. "Are you okay? Are you hurt?"

He didn't respond. All he could do was stare at the place where the woman had been. She'd been there. Waiting for him. Enticing him to cross without looking. When a car sped past.

And he knew then he hadn't been wrong about the tea.

The woman with the red eyes really was trying to kill him.

Chapter Ten

It happened so fast.

One second, he was on the ground, palms and wrists in pain from catching his fall. The next, with their classmates whispering and pointing, Mia had him on his feet and was dragging him home. Within ten minutes the two of them, along with Blair and Cody, were inside the house, Derek at the table and Mia off to find their first aid kit.

During all of this, he couldn't think. The woman in black. A car. An emotion. He'd never…he couldn't….

"Derek!"

He jumped, blinking. Time returned to normal. He and his friends in the kitchen. Mia cursing from the bathroom. He glanced down at his bleeding hands, stomach turning.

"Are you okay?" Cody asked.

Okay?

Was he…?

He breathed in, focusing. Deep down, in the pit of his belly, an emotion he didn't often feel boiled. He'd never been prone to anger outbursts, even as a kid. His grandparents would always brag that he never had temper tantrums and was the sweetest little boy in the world. His parents called him a gentle soul. A vegetarian. A calm in the storm. A pacifist.

He didn't often feel pure, uncontrollable rage.

But it was there. Bubbling up. Waiting for him to act. To do something.

"Of course he's not okay." Mia appeared in the kitchen again. She pulled up a chair and roughly grabbed his hands.

Her own anger oozed from her fingertips. It mixed with his, amplifying both. His anger. Hers.

Oh shit.

"Mia, come on," Blair said. "He almost got hit by a car."

Focus. Focus. Focus.

He breathed in. Then out. Trying to contain his emotions. He didn't care about the pain while Mia cleaned his palms. He didn't care about Blair's hand on his shoulder. He didn't care that Cody was glancing between him and his sister.

All that mattered was stopping their emotions from clashing.

Except, he didn't know how to do that. Because he had never lost control of his emotions before.

"He ran out into the street without bothering to look!" Mia exclaimed.

Shit.

He said nothing. Mia's anger thickened, encasing his hands. His arms. Pushing onto him. His heart raced, and he couldn't tell if it was from the anger or the fear. Nothing like this had ever happened before. White crept from the outskirts of his vision. He wanted to get out. Away.

"Okay but getting angry at him doesn't help."

"I'm not angry."

"You're yelling."

"I'm not."

She doesn't know why.

He couldn't tell who was talking. They were just empty voices. And he couldn't do it anymore.

Without warning, he stood, yanking his hands out of Mia's grip. Stumbling over the chair, with the entire room watching him, he backed up until he hit the counter, panting. The white receded. Mia's screwed up face came into view, her anger trailing after him like a demon obsessed with taking over his body.

Except, it was the other way around. It was his emotions manipulating hers. He'd done this to her.

He'd never pushed negative emotions onto her before.

As her face relaxed, the emotions lessening in intensity, his stomach turned, threatening to expel its contents into the kitchen sink.

She hadn't finished bandaging up his hands. With her emotions calming, the pain of him gripping the edge of the counter made him flinch. He relaxed, but stayed away from his sister. She glanced around. He followed her gaze. Both Blair and Cody were standing, shock electrifying his skin.

"I…." Panic washed over Derek like a spring flash flood. Mia's panic. "I have to go."

She ran out of the room, embarrassment trailing behind her, licking at his toes. No one moved to stop her. Instead, Derek recalled Mrs. Arbour's warning to him. The warning Blair had echoed. The one he'd known his entire life and had to fight against.

This is dangerous for her.

The door slammed, leaving Derek and his friends in silence in the kitchen.

"Derek?" Blair asked in a quiet voice.

But the adrenaline had worn off. From the woman. The car. The fall. The pure rage. It shriveled and died in his veins and fear replaced it. Fear of Mia finding out what he'd just done. Fear *of* what he'd just done.

He gagged, then spun around and vomited into the sink.

"Derek!"

Blair's hand touched his back but he jerked away. If he could do it to Mia, what was to say he couldn't do it to Blair? To Cody? To a random person he bumped into on the street?

It was too much. Today was too much.

He sunk to his knees, panting.

"What just happened?" Cody asked. "Why was Mia so angry? I've never seen her like that."

"Her twin almost got run over by a car after being sick for a week," Blair said. She touched Derek's shoulder again, and this time he let her wrap her arms around him. "I'd be pissed too."

Derek shook his head. "No. No. That was...I did that."

The other two fell silent. Blair pulled away from him a fraction of an inch. All concern was replaced with confusion and a little fear. Derek shuddered. He stood, moving away from Blair.

"I did that." His stomach rolled. "I didn't mean to. I was just... I was so angry, and then she was angry and I...."

"Hey." Blair placed a hand on his cheek, but he couldn't look at her. "It's okay. We know you didn't mean to...do whatever you did."

Cody nodded. The air in the room softened and Derek looked at the first aid kit on the table. Then toward the front door. He wanted to make sure Mia was all right. He thought of texting her, but he wasn't sure she'd answer yet. Not until she'd fully calmed down. Besides, he didn't know what to say. Apologize for running into the street? Ask her if she was all right? He knew she wasn't. The confused look on her face when the connection broken had haunted him.

And then he thought of the woman across the street. The one enticing him to do something so stupid. To do something that would make him angry. That would make Mia seethe with rage. That would cause something like this to happen.

"Blair?" he asked.

"Yeah?"

"You know a lot about magical lore, right?"

Her hand withdrew from his cheek and she backed away. Hesitance. Guarded concern. He had no time for either emotion.

"Of course I do," she muttered.

He looked at Cody, as realization dawned on his face.

"Oh," he said.

Derek nodded and Blair furrowed her brow. Derek took a deep breath. "In any of the lore, is there a woman with red eyes and black hair?"

The change in Blair was instant. From guarded to wide eyed. From tense to loose. From concerned to shocked. His body tingled.

She shook her head. Not a no. Disbelief. "What…how… where…did you read about her somewhere?"

No. He hadn't read anything about someone who appears and disappears. Who stands outside windows barefoot in the snow. Who encourages people to run into the street when a car is coming. Who switches someone's tea. That wasn't like anything he'd read.

"I keep seeing her," Derek said. "Who is she?"

Blair swallowed thickly. "I…she's…."

He hadn't imagined her. The woman in his dreams was someone special.

"She was killed," Blair whispered. "Thousands of years ago. The Gray Spirits…they disappeared after she was gone."

"The what?" Cody asked.

Blair sank into the nearest chair, shaking. "The Gray Spirits. They're a group of immortal creatures who have done nothing but cause havoc for the mage clans."

It was Derek's turn to sit. To try and comprehend what Blair had just told him. Immortal creatures. Immortality. Was anything possible here?

"Explain," Derek demanded.

"I...."

"This woman is in my dreams," Derek said. "She's showing up all around my life. She was there today. I saw her. I *felt* her. I need you to explain."

Blair picked at her fingers. This was not the Blair that Derek had known for the past seven years. She was different. Afraid.

"It's a story." She closed her eyes. "One we tell every summer at the solstice. The day of power for mages in my clan. I...I can tell you, but it's...it's a lot."

"Can you try?" Cody had never sounded so gentle with Blair. Derek watched her, trying to understand what he'd gotten himself into.

She nodded. "I guess to start, I should introduce them. The eight Gray Spirits who, at one point, ruled the world."

There are eight. Sitting together with a fire crackling between them. Five women of all colors. Three men of all builds. Dressed in clothes from all eras. From all parts of the world. They sit. They laugh. They eat. They drink. They look like a collection of friends telling ghost stories under a galaxy of stars.

And yet they are different. They are too perfect. Too beautiful. Features too immaculate. Even amongst each other they stand out, one more beautiful than the last.

There is a woman. She stands, hair long and beautiful, flowing in the wind like a rolling field of straw. She holds out a hand to the man standing next to her. A man of bronze beauty who holds himself like a stone in a rushing river.

"Eran," she whispers.

He takes her hand. "Adelia."

They are a couple. Lovers going about their life with unassuming invisibility. Centuries ago, the Inyoni Mage Clan, cried to the skies for help during a never ending drought and she appeared. They hail her as a hero. A brave woman who led them through the dried up earth and to Lake Turkana, saving their lives. However, she is not seen as innocent to all the clans. Some claim it was a trap. A trick. A way to save her lover from punishment, as he was the one who caused the drought. A man of evil means. Quiet. Unassuming. Invisible.

Dangerous.

They say he has powers over the mind. That she has powers over time. That together they are the root of evil itself.

And then there is another. Two women bound at the hip. One with eyes as dark as night, the other with a laugh of gold. With their powers of wood and water, they tormented the Kyeema Mage Clan, turning their once cultivated and gorgeous rainforest into an outback of desert. As they laugh, walking away from the campfire, they leave a trail of dying foliage in their wake. Their names, nothing more than a whisper on the wind, echo through the night.

Nina. Tori.

Which leaves us four. Half of a collection. But only growing in power.

Lior walks alone. An outcast. An outsider. Watching and waiting and forever knowing. He, too, leaves the campfire, walking through the forests of North America with a whistle at his lips. He comes to the Cokori Mage Clan with open arms and progressive ideas. A dangerous man in anytime, but he is welcomed into their homes. To their circles. To their chiefs. He is welcomed, and he takes advantage of the naivety and betrays their secrets to a rival clan.

He walks away, laughing. Children scream. Women cry. Men die.

The clan barely escapes with their lives.

It would seem that Lior is the worst, but he has nothing on the man across time. A politician living as a shadow behind history's finest dictators. He is not a physical man. He does not fight. He merely whispers in the ears of dangerous men and watches the world burn at his feet. To the Mauvais Mage Clan, settled in France, he is a demon. Shubishi, the man with a thousand tales.

And with him, a woman. The youngest. The most beautiful. The one rumored to be able to kill with a single touch: Flora.

Which leaves her. Alone. Sitting by the cackling fire. From the back, she is normal. From the back, her long black hair reaches her waist. From the back, her pale skin marks her as a beauty across the world. From the back, she holds herself erect.

From the front, her eyes speak a story of loss. Of anger. Of hatred. Stained red from her sins.

Their queen.

She lived life watching from the sidelines. Always the last to leave the campfire. But still, her reputation spread far and wide. Never acting, but always aware. Pulling the strings from behind the curtain. She is the one who the mages must stop. She is the one that they must kill.

And they do.

A mage from the Sixiang Mage Clan, a man from Siam, finds a way to end her reign of terror. He kills her. He ends the war.

No one knows how.

No one remembers her name.

But when she disappears, the campfire goes out. The seven disappear into the shadows. And they are never heard from again.

The three teens sat in silence. The story done. The damage incomprehensible. It was so much information that Derek barely knew how to formulate his first question.

The queen wasn't dead.

Somehow, someway, she'd survived.

He closed his eyes and tried to picture the five mage clans Blair mentioned. He'd heard her talk about them before in passing. Hers. Four others. The five major clans of the mage world. This was ingrained in their history, going back thousands of years.

There were eight.

One was stalking him.

But she was supposed to be dead.

"How?" Cody asked, breaking the silence. "If that priest killed her, how is she here, trying to kill Derek?"

Blair gulped, then looked directly at Derek. He didn't need to be an empath to know how she was feeling in that moment. Her eyes said it all. "I have no idea."

She tried to wipe away the tears, but they flowed faster than she was able to. The cold stung at her wet cheeks, but she continued walking. Wandering aimlessly without a goal. Mind replaying the past half hour over and over in her mind.

It'd been terrifying. She'd seen the car before Derek had moved. Her instinct to grab him, to pull him to safety, had overtaken everything. People pointed. Whispered. Stared. Her brother, who'd been taught to look both ways before crossing the street when he was a toddler, had done something so damn *stupid*.

What would she have done if the car had hit him? How would she be able to tell her parents that their son was either injured or gone.

Gone.

The tears flowed faster and she moved her feet at a rate almost dangerous with the falling snow.

She hadn't meant to get so angry. In the bathroom she'd developed a lecture. Maybe something to ease the tension, to calm Derek down, but then it'd gotten out of control. Like something had injected steroids into her moods and taken over her body. Her words.

That wasn't her. Yes, she had something of a temper. She'd had more than one talk with Intira about keeping calm. Breathing exercises. But that was it. This had been out of control. Her heart still raced. Her pulse thudding in her neck. If she could have caught her breath, she would have, but it shuddered like an old massage chair in a dying mall.

What the hell happened?

She halted in her tracks. Little kids screamed from the greenbelt next to her, throwing snow at one another. She glanced at them, thinking back to her first Colorado winter. How frustrated she'd been with the clothes. The ice. The fact that school hadn't closed. Even back then, when her world had become a frayed blanket with too many unfinished threads fighting for dominance, her temper had never gotten *this* out of control.

"It's okay," she muttered to herself. "You're okay. You're okay."

She didn't feel okay.

Her feet moved. The tears eventually dried up, and she realized she didn't know where to go. She had meant to text Steven after helping with Derek's hands to let him know she couldn't help him study, but now that she was out, she found she wanted the distraction.

With a deep breath, she pulled out her phone and dialed his number, hoping to catch him before he left for the library. She didn't want to be around other students. They'd only ask her questions about what happened. They'd want to know that Derek was okay. They'd want to know why she'd been crying.

And she didn't know how to answer them.

"Hello?" He picked up after the first ring.

"Hi," she said. "Sorry, I know this is last minute, but can we study at your place?"

She had no idea what she was doing. Going to a strange boy's house without telling her parents? Without even thinking it through? It was probably one of the stupidest things she'd ever done, but in that moment, she was okay with it. Going back home wasn't an option. Not until she calmed down and thought of an explanation for why she had gotten so angry. Why she'd yelled at Blair. At Cody.

Oh god.

"Um…." Steven's hesitation drove her anxiety into a wall. "I mean, I guess. Are you okay?"

"Yes," she lied.

"You sound like you've been crying."

"I'm okay." She wiped at her face, as if that would reverse time. "Just…I'm okay."

"I heard about Derek," Steven said.

Oh. That was a good excuse for why she was crying. "Yeah. I'm fine. He's fine. Just a little scraped up. Shaken." They were all shaken. "Can I come over? Please?"

There must have been some amount of desperation in her voice because Steven said, "Sure, I'll text you my address."

Her heart fluttered. Relief. Somewhere to go that was out of the cold. Where people wouldn't stop and stare at her. A place to relax. "Thank you."

"See you soon."

He hung up and she clenched the phone to her chest. Maybe there was no explanation for her burst of anger. Maybe she had just been that angry. But whatever it was, whatever had happened, all she could think about was getting to Steven's house, out of the cold, and maybe have a cup of hot tea to calm her down.

It didn't take long for Mia to find Steven's house. He lived a few streets down from Blair in a one-story house that looked like it'd been built a hundred years ago. The house itself was unassuming. Peeled paint, warped siding, with weeds growing up through the porch. If Mia hadn't known better, she would guess that no one lived here. Behind the house, land expanded out for a couple acres. She walked to the side of the house, peeking around the side to get a better idea of what to expect. Horses stood in the snow, coats protecting them from the cold. She spotted three.

Curiosity satisfied, Mia returned to the front of the house. She climbed the creaky stairs, flinching at each squeak. When she got to the front door, she opened the screen, which was quieter than the porch, and raised a hand to knock, then paused.

Maybe it was best to cancel. To tell Steven she was worried about her brother. The image of him running into the street, the absolute terror coursing through her when she reached out to grab him. Her fingers had barely made it. She still wasn't exactly sure how she'd managed to pull him back. She'd always been strong, but that....

She shook her head. It was okay. Derek was okay. Blair and Cody were with him. What she was doing, going to a strange boy's house, was okay.

Her knuckles rapped against the wooden door, heart racing. When the door opened, she sucked in a breath and put on a smile so Steven wouldn't ask her anymore questions about her red eyes. Her shivering body. The fact that she didn't have her books with her.

"Hey." Steven stepped to the side, letting her into the house.

"Hi." As she did, she became aware—very aware—that they were alone. Just the two of them in a house. She swallowed thickly.

"Come in," Steven said. He stepped to the side and she entered, shuddering as her body adjusted to the warmth. Steven took her coat from her and she took off her shoes, placing them on the shoe rack by the door. "You didn't bring your backpack?"

Mia shook her head. She didn't want to answer this question. Her mind raced, trying to come up with an answer for him. Some explanation close enough to the truth to ease her conscience, but far enough away that he didn't know what happened. "Oh. No. I...I... realized I was running late and forgot it."

"Oh."

"Sorry." She reached up and grabbed a lock of her hair, twirling it between her fingers.

"It's fine. We can just use my books."

"Okay."

She followed him, rubbing her arms. The inside of the house was much nicer than the outside. Beautifully furnished living room, and a modern kitchen. Sparse, but beautiful. Mia couldn't believe that they'd done so much for the inside and nothing outdoors. But she kept her mouth shut and continued to examine the house as they walked. The walls were bare. No photographs, no paintings, nothing. Same with the kitchen and the living room. She expected to find pictures of Steven and his parents, but there was nothing.

Figuring it was just the way his family was, she pushed it to the back of her mind and sat down at the table with him. He pulled out his calc textbook and showed her the problem he was struggling with. She went about explaining it to him, but only with the front of her mind. In the back, she took in the aura of the room around them, relaxing with each breath.

It was warm. Sitting with him, she found herself smiling more and more, energy returning to her voice. Everything, from Derek getting sick and almost dying to the woman in the tree, disappeared from her mind, leaving her content and safe. She didn't know how to explain it, but being with Steven was nice. It was uncomplicated.

And she needed that.

With each step, he knew that it was going to end. The jungle floor was soft beneath his feet, his toes sinking into the moist soil. Moss tickled his bare skin like damp feathers sending tingles up his body. Tall trees towered over him, blocking out the inky black sky. Even if he were to look up, even if he were to strain his eyes, he wouldn't be able to view the guiding stars dotted through the heavens. He himself had spent much time as a child laying on the grassy walkways between the rice paddies staring with wide, curious eyes at the dark expanse above him.

The stars fascinated him. They spoke of another world. Of possibilities beyond his own experience.

Just like she did.

Even without the stars to guide him, even with the canopy casting darkness through the jungles, he knew his path. His feet moved without his permission. He glided through the trees, the pulse of life surrounding him, boring a hole into his mind. Into his heart. He breathed in, the musky scent of the previous night's monsoon permeating every inch of his body, and continued to move. His robes, woven from the finest spun hemp and dyed a deep brown with a red sash—the colors of a high mage—restricted his movement ever so slightly, almost as if begging him to turn around. Begging him not to go through with his plans.

But he had to. Her light, her magic, her power, broke through everything, harsh and dark. Broken. Jagged. Crying.

He flinched.

Was she crying?

No.

He couldn't think of that. He couldn't think of her emotions. This wasn't about him. This wasn't about her. This was about what was good for his people. For *all* the people in the world. A world at war with creatures who didn't belong here.

She didn't belong here.

He had to do what was right.

Without warning, his feet came to a stop. His toes sank into the loose earth, pulling him down as if the earth itself didn't want him to continue on his journey. Closing his eyes, he reached into his robes, fingers wrapping around a bamboo handle. The individual strips of bamboo were smooth against his skin.

He shuddered. It passed through his body, shaking his shoulders, extending down to his toes.

Images of the gifter passed through his mind.

Swirling red.

Sky blue.

Menacing pink.

The gifter had promised it would end everything. The gifter had promised the world would be safer without her. Without her, peace would return. Without her, balance would rule the land.

Without her, the war would end.

His chest tightened. He withdrew his shaking hand from his robe. Empty. The warmth of the handle trickled through his skin, dancing along his veins and into his nerves, begging for him to use it. To expel the magic inside and end it all.

He couldn't.

With more steps, more moss, more dirt, and more branches, he continued his journey through the jungle, navigating his way on memory and on her light.

When he came to the edge, when the trees lightened and light from the full moon peered down upon him, he halted. Because she stood there.

Black hair, the color of midnight during a new moon, hung long and loose down her back. It was wild—an abnormal sight—tangled together, unkempt, as though she hadn't groomed in more than a few days. A colorful, as always, *phãnùng* disappeared beneath the dark, murky water. Her pale skin, something he'd never seen before meeting her, seemed to glow in the light of the moon. Or maybe it was her magic. Regardless, the juxtaposition of her dark hair and luminous skin posited her as someone otherworldly.

She didn't belong.

And yet, he couldn't imagine the world without her.

He stepped forward once more. One final time, footprints behind him lost to foliage and the night. Her head, once turned toward the sky, dropped down, and she turned. In the light of the moon, he could see her. Her gentle features. The curve of her cheek, the smoothness of her chin, the wide eyes, all framed by her black hair. They made eye contact, and he sucked in a breath.

Her irises.

Her ruby irises.

They peered at him, devoid of emotion.

Had she given up?

"Do you know why I'm here?" His words came out in a low tremble. Had it been anyone else, he would have questioned their ability to hear him. But she wasn't anyone.

She glanced at the river. The river that had long dictated his life. Food, safety, culture. It all came from the murky waters she stood in.

"You're here to kill me," she said. She spoke louder than him, and yet he could barely hear her. He loved the sound of her language. One unfamiliar to everyone on Earth but her and her friends. It flowed like the river. Each word connected to another as if they always belonged together. Lovers separated by meaning.

And yet, he answered in his own tongue. One as beautiful to her as hers was to him. One he'd rejected for many years in an attempt to distance himself from the life he had never wanted.

"I must." His hand reached for his lapel, for the bamboo handle that called to him. She watched, her dead eyes sparking with something. Curiosity. Possibly…possibly longing.

His hand hesitated.

"What are you waiting for?" she asked. "She's given you a way."

The gifter did give him a way.

A way to kill an immortal.

But he couldn't. He imagined her, long ago, laying by the edge of the river. Giving him a name. A name he didn't know he'd so desperately desired.

"Niran," she'd said. *"Everlasting."*

The warmth of his magic swelled in his fingertips, growing, and growing, until it burned through his skin, raging through his body and consuming every inch of him. He raised one shaking hand. The gifter had handed him a way to end the war. The gifter had given him a way to return his people to peace and tranquility. Kill the queen. End the war.

He couldn't.

He couldn't kill her.

The water at her feet shifted. He focused all of his energy on what he knew he had to do. The water lifted into the air, thick ropes binding around her body. She glanced down, then up at him. A hand extended. A plea for help? Begging him to stop? Something else?

When, focused on his magic, he didn't react to it, she pulled it back against her chest. The water encased her body as her head bowed, eyes closing. It hardened into ice. It hardened into stone.

It hardened until her magic, her light, her soul, disappeared into darkness.

He let go, collapsing to his knees. Drained. The world blurred, ground spinning. He shook his head and forced himself to look at her. To look at what he'd created.

A woman. Frozen in time. A sculpture forever.

The queen.

Chapter Eleven

The locker blurred in and out of focus as Mia struggled to keep her eyes open. She'd stayed at Steven's till after dinner, both to help him with homework and so she wouldn't have to face her brother for as long as possible. At some point, of course, she had to return, and when she'd gotten a text from Derek asking if she was okay, she knew it was time. He hadn't commented on her outburst. She didn't ask him about it. Instead, the two of them went about their evening, which for Mia involved staying up till midnight to do her homework.

But, as exhausted as she was, she knew it was going to be okay. She'd make it through the day. All she needed was a moment to collect herself, grab some coffee, and then run herself ragged with a nice, exhausting practice. One that left her dripping with sweat and breathing so hard she tasted iron.

Her eyes slipped closed again, and she slapped herself on the cheeks to try and keep herself awake. The sting of skin against skin did nothing but leave her cheeks annoyed at her.

Coffee. If she played her cards right, she could pop downtown during lunch and get a cup from Bill's Fabulous Coffee and Pastries and be back in time to pretend like everything was all right. She just hoped they would think everything was normal. Because she wasn't completely sure it was.

"Mia!" Blair's voice carried over the chatter of the other students hurrying off to class. Mia's eyes snapped open and she looked around her locker door in time to see an overly-chipper Blair lean against the locker next to them, grinning.

"You're energetic," Mia muttered.

"No, I'm normal," Blair said. "You're tired."

"I'm not tired." Mia yawned and Blair laughed.

"Uh huh. Sure."

Mia examined Blair for a moment. Her best friend continued to smile, eyes bright and alive like always, as if nothing had happened yesterday. As if Derek hadn't almost died. As if Mia hadn't snapped at everyone and stormed out. As if Mia hadn't been avoiding her friends all day.

Blair was good for that. When you needed to move on from an embarrassing incident, Blair was more than willing to forgive and forget.

"Live in the moment," Blair always said, and that she did.

"I have something for you," Blair said. She glanced around the hall, and Mia did the same, searching for whatever Blair sought. The only people around them were other students, and the occasional teacher heading to their next class. Blair leaned in closer, as if wanting Mia to keep a secret.

Mia had no idea what Blair was doing.

"What?" Mia asked.

Blair grinned and held up an intricately woven, colorful bracelet. A complex pattern of flowers and triangles adorned the center, spreading out into geometric symbols Mia didn't recognize.

"Pretty." Mia wasn't sure exactly what Blair was getting at, or why she had a bracelet for Mia. At least, she didn't, until Blair held up her wrist, revealing a bracelet of similar color and design. Hers, however, had birds instead of flowers. Mia's brow furrowed. "Is this…a friendship bracelet?"

"No," Blair said with a roll of her eyes. "We aren't five. I got bored last night and since I had nothing to do, I decided to make these. I asked my mom for help. No reason. Just bored. But I figured they were pretty and decided to give one to you." She gestured to Mia's right wrist. "Hold out your hand."

Mia did as Blair instructed, waiting quietly while Blair tied the bracelet. The moment she pulled away, a rush of relief shifted through Mia's body. She almost gasped, startled by the lightness of her heart. A dark emotion fleeing from a hoard of torches. Her shoulders relaxed, and she couldn't stop a small smile.

This was what Blair did. She pretended to be nonchalant and aloof, but deep down she had a soft side to her, and it came out like this. In little moments. Trinkets. She was trying to say that everything was okay between her and Mia. Yesterday didn't matter. Through the bracelet, Mia understood Blair's concern for her, and the strength of their friendship itself.

"Thanks," Mia said.

"No problem. Just don't take it off," Blair said. It was obvious from her tone that she meant it to be a friendly joke, but through the outer layer, Mia sensed something. Panic. Fear. Desperation.

Was there an ulterior motive to the bracelet? The weight on her heart stayed absent, but there was something else there. Her own worry and anxiety. Don't take it off? It was a bracelet. Why would Blair care if she took it off or not?

Maybe she's feeling insecure? Blair had been acting odd recently, possibly trying to make up for all the time she was spending with Derek. Mia's best friend had never been great at showing weakness, and Mia had no desire to call her out on it.

"Okay, I won't." Mia gripped her bracelet, still smiling.

The bell rang, signaling the need for them to get to class.

"Oh shit," Blair said. "Gotta go. See you at lunch!"

And then she disappeared down the hall, leaving Mia alone with her bracelet. She stared at it again. It was pretty. A unique design. Bright colors from what looked like hundreds of strands of string. It must have taken Blair all night to make them.

For whatever reason, that made Mia's smile even bigger, and she breathed out, relieved for the first time in a week. With a new spring in her step, she headed down the hall to class, excited for coffee, practice, and the rest of her day.

Derek held the colorful little bag up by its string and tilted his head, eyes narrowing. The moment they'd sat down in the library, Blair had shoved it in his face. There were no words exchanged. No verbal demands. Just a leather bag stitched with thread in distinct patterns smacking his nose. He'd taken it without a word, and then she'd done the same thing to Cody, who'd pushed her hand away. She'd tossed it in his lap.

"What exactly is this?" Derek asked. He glanced around, taking note of who was in the library. It was mostly empty, as most students who had eighth period off left school early. Derek, Cody, and Blair were some of the few who waited till the end of the day since, when it wasn't basketball season, Mia met up with them and they walked home together. Even though she had practice today, they would stay anyway and get homework done.

Well, Cody would get homework done. Blair and Derek usually talked the entire time while Cody tuned them out. This time, though, even Cody kept his books in his bag.

Blair reached out and pushed Derek's hand down. He expected a flush of emotion: annoyance, concern…anything, really. But it was as though someone had placed a layer of thin satin between them. The emotions were there. They tried to push through, to playfully tickle his skin, but something stopped them. He narrowed his eyes.

"Don't show it off," she said. "We don't know who's watching."

From next to her, Cody rolled his eyes. "You didn't answer the question."

Blair scowled. "They're charms. Protection spells. They aren't that strong, since Mom and I don't have the right stuff, but they'll protect you from some basic magic. Mostly passive magic."

"Passive magic?" Derek asked.

"Magic that isn't a physical attack," Blair explained, lowering her voice. "I mean, it has a shield property against physical magic too, but you still have to be careful if someone attacks you."

"And you're giving these to us…why?" Cody asked. He reached into his pocket and pulled out his. It was almost identical to Derek's. The only difference was the design in the center of the leather, mirrored on both sides. Derek's had what he guessed was a wolf, and Cody's had a raccoon.

"Okay, what part of not showing it off don't you understand?" Blair said with a groan.

Derek and Cody exchanged glances before both boys put the charms in their pockets. Derek kept his hand wrapped around it for a moment, running his finger across the delicate thread. Warmth spread up his hand. It was slight, but he noticed it dancing on his skin, as if playing with his own magic. It reminded him of a pleasurable emotion, except it wasn't. It was different. A form of energy, rather than a feeling.

"Look," Blair said. "I don't know if the Gray Spirits are back or not. But if they are, we need to protect ourselves. These creatures know no consequences. You can't kill them. You can't jail them.

You can't punish them. They've been around longer than humans, and they see us as toys to play with. They don't care what happens to humanity, mage or not. Whatever we can do to help, we should."

Derek honestly didn't mind keeping it with him, but it didn't bring him any sort of comfort. Yes, he knew that Blair and Mrs. Arbour had clan secrets, but what good would a charm do against an all-powerful immortal queen?

A thought crossed his mind.

"What about Mia?" he asked.

Blair tugged at the bracelet on her wrist. "Mia thinks it's some kind of friendship bracelet."

"Will it be as effective?" Cody asked.

Derek waited for concern to wash over him, but like with Blair, Cody's emotions were muted. He shifted. At least this time it was just the two of them he couldn't feel. When he reached out, the emotions of everyone else in the room tickled his skin. He breathed out. They grounded him.

"Yes and no," Blair said. "She doesn't have magic, so the chances of her being a target are low. But it'll still protect her from passive magic. Mostly we made her one out of concern. Since you," she pointed at Derek, "seem to be in tune with the queen."

Derek didn't say anything. There was nothing he could say. She was right. Mia was not in this world. There was no reason to believe that she was in any danger. Derek was the one having all the weird issues. The attempts on his life, seeing the strange woman, getting sick in the first place, and the dreams....

He shuddered, thinking of the dream from last night. The dream that haunted him. Blair had said that the priest had killed the queen of the Gray Spirits, but his dream had shown him a different story. Not a murder, but a sealing. Turning a powerful woman into stone. Into a statue. A sculpture. *The Queen.*

"I'm going to go find a book," he said, standing abruptly.

Blair snorted. "You're going to find a book? What book?"

"Just...just...just a book, okay?" Derek snapped. Blair raised her hands by her head, palms open, and Cody raised an eyebrow at him. Derek said nothing, else, taking off from the table.

He didn't really need a book. He needed a break. Last night, Mia had come home before he could fully process what he'd learned in the story, and in the morning, he'd had to rush to get ready for school. He'd had no break from the new information. No respite from the stress and strain of the idea that magical creatures were trying to kill him.

His dreams...they were trying to tell him something. They felt too real. A part of himself that he hadn't realized he was missing. Something nagging at the back of his mind that had finally broken free.

When he got to the bookshelves, he glanced over at the table where his friends sat. Cody had taken out his books, nose buried in one, while Blair was playing a game on her phone. He closed his eyes and reached out his senses, trying to get a grasp on her emotions. Nothing.

And he knew if he stood in front of Mia, she'd be protected too.

He gripped his hands into fists. When had this become his life? Two weeks ago the four of them were hanging around his house, laughing and being stupid teenagers. No charms. No dreams. No woman in black haunting his waking and sleeping worlds. His only concerns in life were not failing math class and keeping his magic a secret from everyone. He didn't even care that his parents were gone all the time. He'd come to expect that. Now it was like no matter what he did, things wouldn't go right.

Exhaustion flooded him. He stopped next to one of the bookshelves and leaned his head against it, breathing in through his nose, out through his mouth. The way his yéyé taught him when he was little and trying to impart the importance of meditation.

Neither he, nor Mia, had taken to it, but they still learned how to relax. To open their minds and let go of their worries.

The world around him seemed to disappear. The metal bookcase, and the books upon it, pressed into his side, holding him up. His only support in the entire world. His eyes slipped closed again and he imagined he was somewhere else. Somewhere green, with trees sprouting up into the sky. The sun, a glowing orange, sank beneath the horizon casting a yellow and pink glow on the clouds hovering in the sky. A gentle breeze rustled his clothes. His hair. It was a moment of peace. Of tranquility.

And then he felt her.

She appeared in his world of zen, a dark figure silhouetted against the setting sun. She stepped forward. Holding up a hand. Her deep emotions brushed against his skin, all feathers, all indecipherable from one another. They mixed together with the emotions of the students in the library.

He opened his eyes, his sunset disappearing into reality. His gaze landed on the full length window at the back of the library. Outside, a field of snow extended back toward their pathetic excuse of a football field.

He took a deep breath, ready to return to his table, when he spotted her. Standing there. Alone. A hand on the glass, watching him. Her black hair hung down to her waist, tamed and smooth, while her ruby eyes watched him. The dress she wore was black, like before, but different. Silky, clinging to her curves, accenting the shape of her body in a way the others hadn't. Elegant. He watched her.

She watched him.

And then, like before, his feet took him toward her. Toward the queen of the Gray Spirits.

She's special, something told him. *She's special.*

She's special.

140

She's free.

He arrived at the window, holding out his hand, when something crashed behind him. A puff of wind pushed against his back, and confusion spread out over his skin. The terror of the other students. He blinked. The woman vanished.

And when he turned, heart racing, he found the bookcase laying on the floor, books scattered all over, and everyone in the room staring at him. Terrified.

Coffee was a miracle drug. From the first sip of the bitter liquid—one cream, two sugars—Mia's energy returned. She managed to answer questions in class, her head didn't dip down in exhaustion, and she could walk through the halls without hating every single person who laughed too loud or said anything.

With raging energy, she hurried to the locker room as the final bell for the day rang, ready for a good practice. Just her, a ball, and some loud music. She wouldn't talk. She wouldn't engage in gossip. She'd save every breath for the game.

The locker room was...loud. As always. Girls changed, some already in their practice outfits, others half naked, and a few struggling to get their sports bras on. Mia smiled at the noise, but looked away from the girls. No socialization today. All she wanted was a good workout to make up for the weirdness. In the gym, there was no blond woman. In the gym, she didn't wake up from dreams she couldn't remember. In the gym, all that mattered was the ball, the game, and victory.

As she grabbed her practice clothes from the locker, the room went quiet, as if the other girls had noticed Mia for the first time. Turning to face them, she prepared a lecture to let them know she wanted to focus today. But when she realized they were all staring at her with furrowed brows and frowns, she hesitated.

"Are you guys okay?" she asked.

The girls exchanged glances before one, Brittany, stepped forward. "You didn't hear?"

She shifted. "Hear what?"

The girls said nothing at first. The air in the locker room turned to ice and Mia shuddered.

No. No. No. This is supposed to be fun.

"What's going on?" Her voice sharpened.

Before anyone could answer her, Coach Smith appeared in the locker room. The girls, who had gathered, dispersed and Mia's heart sank. Her hands trembled as Coach Smith headed over to her wearing the same expression as her teammates.

"The principal needs you," Coach Smith said. "Something happened with Derek."

"Is he okay?" Mia asked the moment Derek's name left Coach Smith's mouth. Her anxiety bubbled. Stomach clenching. Why did stuff keep happening to Derek?

"He's fine," Coach Smith said. She placed a hand on Mia's shoulder. The other girls went about their business, but Mia knew they were listening in. "There was an accident in the library. No one got hurt, but the principal needs you."

An accident? "What kind of accident?"

Coach Smith shook her head. "It's best if you go see the principal. He's expecting you."

She said nothing else before disappearing into her office. Mia, however, couldn't move. Derek was with the principal? What happened in the library?

"Mia...." It was Brittany again. The girls must have elected her to be the spokesperson today. "I was in the library, and it wasn't an accident. Derek pushed over a bookcase."

Mia snorted. "No he didn't."

"But he did. I saw him do it."

"Derek can be hot headed, but he's a pacifist," Mia said. She would never believe that her brother would do something so violent. Brittany wasn't a liar, but that didn't mean her eyes couldn't deceive her. "I'm sure you misunderstood."

Brittany's eyes narrowed. "I didn't, and neither did anyone else. We all saw the same thing."

"All of you?" The entire library had been watching Derek?

"Yeah." Her voice got snippy, but Mia had no time for Brittany's ego.

"Whatever. He would never do something like that." Mia grabbed her backpack and slammed her locker shut. "Now if you'll excuse me, I have to go."

She stormed out of the locker room, all joy from the coffee gone.

Mia entered the principal's office with a light knock. Their principal, Mr. Henderson, sat at the end of the conference table, Derek's guidance counselor, Mrs. York, next to him, while Derek slouched in his chair on the other side and glared at the shining wood. Mia had to resist pulling him aside to ask him what happened.

"Ms. Sòng," Mr. Henderson said, "good of you to join us."

She nodded and settled next to Derek. He didn't look up at her, but she reached out and touched his arm just in case he needed comfort. He didn't pull away, at least. "What's going on? Why am I here?"

Their parents had left early in the morning for Denver, but Mia wanted to hear confirmation from the principal that she was essentially here as a guardian of sorts for Derek. There was no way that they'd hold him for hours until their parents could return. That didn't, however, explain why they hadn't called Mrs. Arbour.

"Your parents have given us permission into release Derek to your custody," Mrs. York explained.

"Why does it sound like you've thrown him in jail?" Mia didn't normally take this tone with adults. But she hated being in rooms like this. It reminded her of when she was a kid and the bullying had gotten so bad that she refused to go to school. She'd sat with the counselor for weeks to figure out how to make it stop.

It hadn't helped.

"We aren't throwing him in jail," Mr. Henderson explained. "But there are several witnesses that said he pushed over a bookcase and that kind of violence causes us to be vigilant."

"I didn't do it," Derek snapped. "I've told you a million times. I was at the window. The bookcase almost fell on *me*."

Mia watched Derek, trying to get a read on his emotional state. He was clearly upset, and shaken. When she looked closer, she saw his hands shake. His brow was furrowed, and his eyes had that stubborn look in them that he got whenever he was in trouble.

"We want to believe you," Mrs. York said, "but everyone in the library says otherwise."

Derek snorted. "Why the hell would I want to push over a bookcase?"

"Démíng." She switched to Chinese. He finally glanced at her. "Don't get mad at them. You're in enough trouble as it is."

"But I didn't do anything. You believe me, right?"

"Of course." Mia didn't hesitate. She didn't care what anyone said, she knew her brother better than anyone. He wouldn't lie to her.

"Kids, we'd really prefer it if you spoke in English," Mr. Henderson said. Mia wanted to glare at him, but her respect for authority made her nod instead. "Derek, we want to believe you. But we've talked to everyone in the library and they all say the same thing. Our hands are tied. If you'll just tell us why you did it—"

"I didn't do anything!" Derek stood, slamming his hands on the table. "I'm the freaking victim here!"

"Derek, please sit down," Mrs. York said.

"But—"

"I think that's enough for now," Mr. Henderson said. "Derek, unfortunately we're going to have to suspend you until Friday. Give you some time to calm down and think about what you did. It'll go on your permanent record, but if you have perfect attendance and impeccable behavior for the remainder of the year, I'll make sure to write to any college you want to attend and explain that you were having a rough few weeks."

Derek groaned. "I didn't do anything."

"Derek...."

"Can I go now?" he asked. "Mia's here to escort me home."

Another exchanged glance, and then Mr. Henderson nodded. "We're going to have a meeting with your parents when they get back to town. We'll have Mia bring you your homework for the rest of the week."

"Whatever." Derek grabbed his backpack and stalked out of the room. Mia watched him for a second, wondering if she should say anything to the adults. But they were whispering to each other, so instead she followed Derek out of the room.

She caught up with him near the front doors of the school. He was grumbling, muttering to himself in Thai.

"Déming," she said when she caught up to him. He stopped grumbling and finally looked at her. There was a hint of fear behind his eyes. "Tell me what happened."

"I was...." His eyes widened. He glanced down at her hands, which made her cock her head before he scowled. "Never mind."

"Seriously?" Mia chased after him. "Just tell me what happened. We can go back there and explain. You said you were at the window? Did someone else push over the shelf?"

Derek spun around to face her. "Just drop it, Méilián. I don't want to talk about it. Let's just go home."

Mia remained quiet while Derek headed off out of the school. She glanced over at her shoulder, at the closed door to the office where Mr. Henderson and Mrs. York were still sitting. She grimaced, and then breathed out heavily through her nose.

Her phone buzzed. A text. She pulled it out and found a message from Steven asking if everything was okay. And the answer was no. Derek had been acting off ever since the night at the museum, and she didn't know how to handle it, especially with her parents so busy.

So, she ignored her phone and headed off after her brother. She wasn't in the mood to divulge this part of her life to her new friend. She wasn't even sure she wanted to chat about it with her old friends. All she knew was that this wasn't at all how she wanted her day to go.

Chapter Twelve

Water spread across the field, expansive and still. The liquid glowed a glorious gold, lit by candles suspended below the surface. There was no discernable pattern. Like splatters of paint on an old canvas, they guided him across the waters. His feet, bare as always, recognized the cool fluid for what it was, but his mind convinced them it was solid ground. An illusion of touch. Ripples danced from his feet as he stepped, yet he never dipped below the surface.

A light breeze rustled his clothes. He closed his eyes and smiled. With it, with the breeze, wafted a scent. A sweet, gentle scent reminding him of the asters of his childhood.

Which childhood, he couldn't tell.

The weight of his heart lifted and he breathed in as deeply as his lungs would let him. They filled with the scent, alive and full of energy, and he stepped forward again. And again. Each time his footsteps grew further apart, pressing into the false ground with urgency and excitement. Before long, he was sprinting, jolting forward, searching, seeking, eager to find her.

Her pedestal rose above the water, just like before. Just like that night. The intricate flowers carved into the sides of the marble shimmered from the light emanating off the water. They rose up, encasing the pedestal, preparing the viewer for the centerpiece. For the thing he was looking for.

And it was her. It was her resting atop the marble. She was waiting for him. Floating centimeters off the smooth, white surface, and he reached out for her, wishing to take her in his hands.

"Who are you?" he asked, though he knew the answer.

Somewhere.

Somehow.

He knew the answer.

His fingers brushed her petals. They were silk against his skin.

"Where are you?" he asked. "Why can't I find you?"

As if to answer him, the sky exploded with thunder. He jolted back, fingers leaving the petals, and he stumbled away. His foot came into contact with the water and slipped through. He yelped and something grabbed his ankle to drag him down.

Further. And further. And further.

Water encased him. The candles extinguished one by one. He tried to breathe, only to find his lungs filling with water. Drowning him. Taking him away.

He reached for the surface as a shadowed figure stood above him. She looked down, her long hair covering her face.

He gasped.

He choked.

Darkness clouded his vision.

Who are you?

Outside his door he heard their footsteps. They paced back and forth, slippers clapping against the ground, voices low and urgent. He, meanwhile, sat on the edge of his bed, elbows on his knees, leg shaking like it always did when he didn't know what was going to happen. His eyes closed. Seeping through the door, his parents' emotions crept along his skin, boring into his pores in an attempt to make a home in his body. He could barely distinguish them from one another. Confusion. Fear.

Guilt.

He knew why they stood outside his door. He knew why they paced. Why their confusion consumed the house. They wanted to ask him about the incident. They hadn't planned on coming home so early, but getting a call that their son had pushed over a bookcase and gotten suspended...well, that would get most parents' attention. He hadn't seen them since they'd arrived. He hadn't seen or spoken to anyone.

Mia had tried.

But he didn't know what to say. He didn't know how to explain to her that the bookcase fell when he was at the window. He'd explained it to them, the staff at school, but they hadn't believed him. They said they had eye witnesses.

His chest tightened, remembering the moment. His heart had been thumping. His body had comprehended what had happened long before his brain. His shoulders had tensed. His hands had shaken. He'd turned, the fear of the others slithering against his skin, expecting...something. A reaction. A shouting of his name.

Because a bookcase had fallen. And if he hadn't been at the window, with the woman, he would have been crushed. Injured. Died. Just like before. With the tea. The car.

Someone was trying to kill him.

And all he wanted was a little sympathy. Instead he turned to find the entire library staring at him and he realized they weren't scared for him.

They were scared of him.

His leg bounced harder and harder until he pulled both of his legs off the ground and clambered to the wall his bed rested against, curled tight into a ball. He didn't want to think of the students blaming him for something he hadn't done. He didn't want to think of his parents discussing what to do with him. He didn't want to think about his sister, who he couldn't read anymore. She'd defended him, but was that out of obligation or belief?

The more she asked, the less he could tell her about the woman in black. About the attempts on his life. About the dreams. Her anger yesterday, the way she'd blown up because of his powers… it was too much. If she found out now what he could do, how would she feel? If he told her what the bracelet really was, would she continue to wear it? Would she be safe from a world she didn't even know existed?

He sighed, leaning his head back. He didn't want to focus on Mia. Instead he thought about the dreams. Of the water. Of the flower. The gentle, quiet room where the only thing wrong was her question. He recalled the last dream. How he'd gotten so close to learning her name. He knew it. Somewhere inside he knew who she was. And the figure who stood above him as he sank into the depths…he knew who she was too.

A knock at his door brought him back to his room. He didn't answer. His eyes traveled to the wooden door. He didn't need to hear her voice to know it was his mom standing outside. Her emotions, never as strong as his father's, pricked at his skin. He rubbed his arms, wanting to scrape it off. A reprieve from all the negativity.

"Derek," she said as she opened the door. She stood in the doorway, dressed in clothes he rarely saw her in anymore. Casual. A pair of tight jeans and a baggy shirt. Even when she worked from home, she dressed up. She always said if she didn't dress for work, she wasn't ready for work.

She wasn't working. His parents weren't working.

Derek and Intira made eye contact. Derek stared into them, and not for the first time, he wished he had his mom's eyes. Mia had gotten them. Mia looked like younger pictures of their aunt, their dad's sister, but she had their mom's eyes. And he...he had green. It pushed him apart from the rest of his family. It cast him as the outsider. The weird one with green eyes.

He curled tighter into a ball. The weird one with green eyes and magic.

His mom stepped into the room. He listened to her footsteps navigate the disaster that was his room and waited for her weight to press into the bed. All the while, he kept his head between his arms, not wanting to look at her. To speak to her.

"Why don't you tell me what happened at the library." Her tone was soft, and soothing, as it always was when she spoke Thai. She didn't speak it much. Even now, her grasp of the language faltered, coming out of the mouth of someone who spoke it so little. Yet it brought comfort to his heart. He loved visiting his grandparents. They spoke little English, forcing the entire family to speak Thai instead. It was when he felt most at home.

He lifted his head. Even though her face was calm, gentle, earnest, he knew her real emotions. The tense confusion tugging at his skin. The fear slithering between his fingertips.

"Derek?" she asked. She reached out and touched his arm.

He yanked it back and turned his back on her, eyes burning as they tried to bring tears he didn't want. He didn't know how to explain it to her. No one believed him. Even Cody and Blair, who had been in the library, said they hadn't seen the incident. The only ones who hadn't seen what happened.

"Are you doing this because we've been gone?" she asked. "Are you acting out for...attention?"

She'd been talking to her shrink friend. Derek had met the

woman a few times, and usually Intira and her friend would debate whether or not psychology was going too far, but every now and then something the friend said stuck, and his mom would use the lingo and analysis to try and understand her children.

"I didn't do anything," he murmured in English. Her emotions shifted, the stab of hurt making him flinch. He never spoke English with her. Not at home. Not since they left Beijing.

She was silent for a moment. The hurt retreated, but nothing replaced it. After a moment, she said, "I want to believe you. I know you. You're my sweet boy. You'd never hurt anyone. You take care of your sister and you love your friends and family. I know that. We all know that. But something happened in that library and everyone is saying you pushed over the bookcase. If you did...we just need to know so we can help you. What can we do?"

"You can't do anything," Derek replied. "You didn't do anything wrong."

"We're never home. We have to leave again. Do you want me to stay? Bà can get a translator in Thailand."

"No. Go. He doesn't trust translators," Derek muttered. "It's fine if you go. You have to work. That's not your fault."

"I don't understand."

"It's fine."

"Derek." She touched his shoulders and turned him. In that moment, when their eyes met, Derek wanted to spill everything. To tell her about his magic. About Cody and Blair. About the dreams, and the murder attempts, and his ability to feel and control emotions. If he'd told her, if he'd let her into his life, she would be able to fix everything. That's what she did. She fixed things.

But he couldn't. He couldn't tell her anything. She wasn't in it. His dad wasn't in it. Mia wasn't in it. He was separate from them. The one with magic. The one with green eyes. He had to keep this part of his life a secret to protect him. To protect Blair's clan. And now, more than ever, he realized he needed to keep this secret to protect them. If someone was after him, why wouldn't they go after his family too?

Once more, he pulled away from her, this time hustling off of his bed. His feet landed on clothes and a video game case. He didn't care.

"Derek?" his mom called.

"I'm going out," he said. He needed to get out of the house. To get away from the people who wanted to fix a problem that didn't exist. The negativity in the house coating his skin dragged everything down and he just needed to get out.

"But–"

"What?" Derek didn't look at her, hand on the doorknob. "Am I grounded? Are you going to lock me in the house and keep me from my friends because someone said I did something I didn't? I'm already suspended, isn't that enough?"

His mom said nothing, and so he left, throwing open the door. Surprise gripped him, and he looked up into the eyes of his father. At this point in his life, Derek stood taller than his dad, but in that moment, flooded with his dad's anger, Derek felt small. Like when he was a child.

"Derek," his dad said, standing at his full height. Derek stared at him for a moment, and then turned toward the front door. He didn't look back, as his dad called out to him, a lecture in Chinese leaving his lips. Derek ignored it all. He pulled on his shoes, grabbed his coat, and left the house, slamming the door on the words of his father.

Mia let out a heavy sigh as she exited the locker room. Her muscles were loose, relaxing for the first time in over two hours.

Coach Smith had destroyed them today. Instead of their normal cardio and drills, she'd forced them all to start weight training too. Mia was athletic. Her entire life, she'd been the one in the family drawn to sports. She practiced Wushu with her father, got into fights with boys at school who didn't want to let her play games with them, and exhausted Derek from the time they were toddlers, wanting to wrestle and play games he just didn't want to play. She craved it.

But weight training? That was an entirely other ballgame. Mia was strong. She could do push-ups and crunches, and lunges. She was not used to adding heavy weights to that.

"You look like death." Blair's voice caught her attention and she looked up from the noodles that were her arms. Blair stood across from the door to the locker room, backpack on the ground next to her, with her hands behind her back.

"Coach Smith is evil," Mia said. She stepped out of the way of the locker room door so the other girls could leave with ease. "What are you doing here?"

Blair shrugged. "I mean, I was gonna go home, then I remembered my little brother is the devil right now, and decided to wait for you."

"Where's Cody?"

"Work."

"Right."

Mia almost asked about Derek, out of habit, but held her tongue. His suspension had barely started, but she already felt his absence. It was a different kind than when he was sick. The whole school talked about him. The whispers rose in the hallways, muted but not gone when Mia walked by. She tried to ignore them. To pretend that nothing had happened, but something had happened.

Derek pushed over a bookcase. Everyone in the library saw him. He insisted he didn't do it, but why would everyone lie?

But...also...why was everyone looking?

Mia clenched her first. No. That was a ridiculous thought. It just happened. There was nothing weird going on. He hadn't done anything. She didn't have a feeling that Derek, Blair, and Cody were keeping secrets from her. There wasn't a woman following her around town.

Normal. It was all normal.

"Do you want to hang out for a bit?" Mia asked.

Blair shrugged. "Sure. I guess. Got nothing else to—"

She fell silent as her phone rang out, echoing in the empty hallway. She pulled it out, face screwing up with annoyance, and then it fell into something like a mix of concern and relief.

"Sorry, I lied, I gotta go," she said. "It's my mom. She wants to spend more time as a family. I was hoping for more time but…." She shrugged. "Let's hang out tomorrow though."

"Sure," Mia said, and she watched Blair take off, throwing her backpack over her shoulder, and answer the phone. Mia frowned. She'd never been as good at reading people as Derek, but even she knew when something weird was going on. It wasn't Blair's mom on the phone. She'd seen the name flash briefly across her vision.

It was her brother.

Her hand went to her wrist, where the bracelet Blair gave her rested heavy on her skin. She didn't get why Blair had lied to her. It wasn't the first time that Blair had lied to her about Derek being on the phone, but in the past it'd always been when the two of them wanted to sneak off and be alone. This time…it felt different.

Mia shook her head, letting out a heavy puff of air. This wasn't the time to be analyzing her friends. She and Blair were still friends. She and Cody were still as close as ever. And she and Derek…they would be fine. They were twins. They would always be fine.

Something was going on with him, and she wasn't going to push. She had in the past. Usually ended with a fight, tears, and a lecture from whichever parent was home that week. This time, though, she had her own worries to focus on. She didn't have time to deal with Derek acting out. Running into the street. Maybe pushing over a shelf. They weren't like him, and she wanted to believe it was nothing. But Blair had lied about him being on the phone. They hadn't invited her to hang out with them.

Frustration raged through her, and she headed out of the school. Externally, she appeared calm. Internally, however, she was a monster tearing down Willow Creek with teeth and flames. Everything pissed her off. The friends talking happily as she cut through downtown. The families together with children holding their parents' hands. She tried to calm herself. In the past, these moments of anger would disappear without her doing much, but right now it wouldn't dissipate.

She didn't want to go home. She didn't want to talk to Derek. To face her parents. To sit and do homework like nothing was wrong in her life. Like her best friend hadn't just lied to get out of spending time with her.

When she was almost home, rage still burning in her heart, something…someone, caught her eye. She stopped, staring straight ahead for a moment as the anger flickered into a new emotion. One she'd felt many times over the past two weeks.

Fear.

She turned her head. Her breath was visible against the cold air, clouding her vision for a moment. When it cleared, Mia knew she was right.

It was her.

The woman.

She stood near the edge of the forest, staring at Mia with a grin. Like before, she was wearing inappropriate clothes for the weather. Mia stood there in a down jacket and gloves, but the woman had on a light sweater and shorts that barely covered any of her pale thighs. Her hair was pulled up into a high ponytail, like the kind you would see on a cheerleader in some teenage sitcom. She stared at Mia, head cocked. Mia stared at her, heart racing.

And then, like her body didn't belong to her, she took off. She didn't look both ways. She didn't pay attention to the black ice. Her feet carried her toward the woman as curiosity and frustration overtook her body.

This woman. This freaking woman.

Mia wanted answers, and she was going to get them.

The woman let out a peal of laughter before dashing into the woods. Mia knew she shouldn't follow. This wasn't smart. It wasn't the right thing to do, following a stranger into the woods with a chance of snow on the way. But she did it anyway. She didn't care. She was going to catch the woman, who might not even be real, and demand to know why she kept appearing. Disappearing. Haunting Mia whenever she got the chance.

Mia followed her deep into the woods. Deeper than anyone was supposed to go alone without proper gear. Mia did a good job keeping up, despite her legs wanting to give out any second, but then, without warning, the woman disappeared. Mia came to a halt, panting, and spun around to find her.

No. No this can't be happening. Just let me catch you!

Mia let out a frustrated scream as she kicked snow off the ground. What was happening?

Why was it happening?

After a moment to let her heart rate return to normal, Mia breathed in deep and shook her head, trying to think of a way to calm herself. Of all those moments in the past when she'd managed to with barely a thought. But she couldn't figure it out. Breathing? Waiting? What had she done?

"I'm going home," she snapped to no one in particular. She looked around, desperate for a landmark. A trail marking. Something to let her know where she was. When she found nothing, she pulled out her phone to at least use the compass app, but found it dead.

She stared at it, blinking. Hadn't it been at 50% when school ended?

Crap.

She shoved it back into her coat pocket. Okay, so no landmarks. No indication of where she was. That was okay. She could follow her footsteps back. She'd grown up in these woods for the past seven years. She knew them as well as any of the natives. Each step back was a drain on her energy. Voices in the back of her mind reminded her that she shouldn't have chased the woman. That she was being stupid. That all of this, the woman, Blair and Derek, Cody, all of it, was in her head.

She was tired.

She was stressed.

She just wanted her parents to make it all better.

She didn't realize it was snowing until thick flakes surrounded her, brushing at her nose. She stopped, staring up at the swirl of snow dancing above her.

Well. That's not good.

Never go into the woods alone. Never go into the woods alone during a snowstorm. Never go into the woods alone without a working phone and a flashlight. Mia had learned these rules, among others, early on after moving to Colorado. Her parents hadn't known. Her dad had grown up in Beijing, and her mom in Los Angeles. Neither were exactly skilled in the art of the wilderness. Mia and Derek had gotten a crash course from Mrs. Arbour, with Blair chiming in with her own facts. Later too, Cody taught her things about the mountains that Mrs. Arbour didn't know. Things he'd learned from his dad.

Yet, despite knowing the rules of the mountains, Mia found herself alone in the middle of an increasing blizzard with no phone, no flashlight, and no idea where she was.

Adrenaline pumped through her. The thought of dying alone on the mountains in the middle of a snow storm was less than pleasing in every aspect. She moved, taking on the blizzard one step at a time as her already exhausted body screamed at her to find a place to sit down. But the winds picked up. The snow dropped thicker and heavier. She could barely see two feet in front of her, much less search for a place to shelter from the storm.

-Right.

Mia jerked back in surprise.

The voice. Was it hers? No. It wasn't…it was…someone's.

-Right.

Mia turned right. Maybe it was her intuition, or maybe she had someone watching out for her. Either way, she had nothing to lose by following the directions in her head. And the directions spoke. They guided her around trees, through the forest, heading down the mountain to her home, until it told her to stop.

-Reach out your hands.

She did, shivering, exhausted. Her gloved hands came into contact with something hard. She pressed forward. A rock. No.

She moved around it, toward the front.

It was a cave.

Relief flooded her and she dashed inside. She expected a normal, simple cave — a place to wait out the storm — but when she looked up from dusting off the snow from her clothes, she found herself facing something…else.

There were many caves in the woods around Willow Creek but none like this. An unnatural warmth wafted from the back of the cave, washing over her. The chill from the blizzard had dug in deep into her body, but it vanished in an instant. She stepped back, shocked. Barely thinking, she dropped her backpack to the cave floor and took off her gloves and coat. They, too, dropped to the ground, landing with a puff.

She barely noticed.

The cave was a narrow hallway, walls lined with glowing blue markings. A calm washed over Mia. All of her anger. Her adrenaline. Her frustration. It all vanished and she stepped toward it, reaching out a hand. She brushed against the smooth wall, fingers taking in the dips and curves of the glowing blue marks. On closer inspection, she realized it was writing. A script. She wasn't exactly the best with languages, written or spoken, but she recognized it. Somehow. It was old. No longer used. But…possibly the origin of something modern.

With one hand on the wall, she continued through the cave, eyes straining in the eerie, blue light. It wound around, twisting and turning, almost like a maze. Mia's hand shook. This…this was a dream, right? She was home. She was asleep.

Or maybe she'd died out in the blizzard?

A shudder passed through her at the thought. She kept going.

Before long, she arrived at a set of stairs. The area in front of her was dark. Almost pitch black. She hesitated. All of this…it was surreal. Unnatural. Strange. Her hand went to the bracelet on her wrist. Her friendship with Blair. Her relationship with her brother. Her connection with Cody.

It's okay.

Was that the voice, or her?

She placed her foot on the first step. Her other on the second. The third. A fourth. The top.

Darkness encased her. A chilling breeze blew the hair out of her face, and she shuddered.

"Hello?" she called out.

Like her voice was the key, a flash of light flooded the room. Mia screamed and covered her eyes. When the light faded, she lowered her arms, breathing heavily. She could see an ambiance of orange light. In front of her, inches from her shoes, a stone path extended out into the cave, dimmed water filling the gap between each stone. Surrounding the path, a pool of lotuses and lily pads glowed from floating candles.

This is a dream, Mia told herself. *This has to be a dream. I'm dead. I'm dying and this is my brain trying to make me comfortable.*

A light breeze, different from the one before, pressed against her back, pushing her forward. She glanced over her shoulder. The cave behind her had gone black. It didn't want her to go back. Her heart raced as she faced the pool again. Standing at the end of the path, rising up above the otherwise flat cave, was a pedestal.

"Is this…what you want me to see?" Mia asked, almost hoping the voice would tell her what to do. It was silent.

Gulping, she stepped forward. One foot in front of the other, almost having to hop from one stone to another. Finally, she made it to the other side. The side with the pedestal. Each step toward it brought a new energy to her. A feeling of completion. Like this… like this would answer all of her questions.

She reached the pedestal and glanced down, shaking.

Sitting there, unassuming and simple, lay a sheathed knife. The handle, made of strips of bamboo, was pristine and untouched, while the leather sheath was worn and torn in places. Mia stared at it. The knife. Strange. Mysterious.

Magic.

She reached out, almost as if a puppet for someone else, wrapped her hand around the handle, and lifted it from its old home.

Chapter Thirteen

Derek's eyes glazed over as he stared out the window of the coffee shop, his mug of steaming tea warming his hands. He couldn't see the other side of the street as the blizzard overtook downtown. Instead, he focused on the flakes of snow assaulting the ground as if they had no will left to live. In the dizzying array, he pictured images, creating a play. He couldn't really see them. But he could. The Gray Spirits.

Sitting with him, Blair and Cody bickered, arguing about something he didn't want to listen to. Something about the situation. About Derek almost dying. About the entire library not having seen the truth. About the two of them not having seen anything at all. Now and then he picked up one or two of their words. Something about magic. About control. The possibility of memory manipulation.

He'd called them here to talk about this. Cody came from home. Blair from school. They'd dropped what they were doing because of him, and yet as they argued about the situation, he found himself drawn away.

Drawn by the snow.

By the thoughts of what this was doing to his family.

His dad rarely yelled. But he'd yelled as Derek left. His mom was often the harsh one in the family, but she'd been so gentle, trying to understand what was going on. To them, he was acting out. In their minds, he'd caused havoc in the library. He could fight with them all day long. He could fight with the school administration until his voice disappeared. But no matter what he did, he couldn't prove his innocence to any of them because none of them knew about the truth.

And if he told them any of it, what would they do? How would they react to learning that magic was real, and this wasn't a case of him "acting out"?

The blizzard continued to dance outside. The rest of the town— those who weren't caught at work—had left long ago, escaping home to wait out the blizzard like good mountain towners did. It was just the three of them, two mages and whatever Cody was, sitting alone in a coffee shop arguing about things most of the world had no idea existed.

"Dammit, Cody, this isn't some video game with stupid power crawls," Blair snapped loud enough that Derek turned his attention back to them. Her face was screwed up, eyes narrowed, an expression he knew to associate with anger and frustration. Yet, the emotions didn't slither across his skin. They weren't even muted, like before in the library. Now, they were gone.

"I'm not saying it is," Cody said with a roll of his eyes. "I'm saying that you don't know everything about magic and there could be something going on here that we don't know."

Cody was always harder to read. Most of the time, Derek knew what Cody was feeling because of his empathic powers, not because of body language or facial expression. His voice tended to stay even and calm, even when his emotions were all over the place. Derek couldn't read him.

Mia always could. She and Cody were like a little clique he could never penetrate. He was the empath, but she could read people without any sort of power. She knew how to talk to people. To get them to like her. He didn't know how to talk to his parents, but she did. She was the favorite, the one who got the best grades, the one who bonded with their dad over martial arts and the philosophical study behind it, the one who loved sitting with their mom when she worked on museum stuff. People at school loved her. Their parents were proud of her.

"I know more about magic than you do," Blair snapped.

Derek sighed.

"It's not hard to know more about magic than I do when you have an entire family who can use magic," Cody retorted. This time, his voice was tense. His expression still calm.

"Only half of my family can use magic." Blair crossed her arms. "Dad's a normal Jewish man from New York."

"You saying Jewish people can't have magic?"

"Yes dipshit, *that's* what I'm saying." Her sarcasm was almost too thick.

"Guys, can we not do this?" Derek asked. At this point, the two of them were arguing just to fight, something he'd hoped they'd grown out of this year. It'd been a while since one of them had started shit with the other, but, he supposed, old habits die hard.

"But he–" Blair started to say when Derek glared at her.

"Seriously," Derek said, glancing between a pissed off Blair and a blank-expressioned Cody, "this is not the time for you two to be fighting. Maybe it's selfish of me to say, but someone's trying to kill me and I'd like for us to talk about that."

"We were talking about that," Cody pointed out. "But you were staring off into the snow."

Derek looked down at his cup of tea. "Okay. Fine. I'm here. I'm paying attention. What are we talking about?"

The table fell silent. The only sound in the empty coffee shop was the barista doing dishes in the back with her music playing through a phone speaker. Blair crossed her arms and turned her head toward the window, while Cody stared at the table, strumming the tips of his fingers across the wooden table.

Finally, after a moment, Blair piped up. "I've been wondering for a while now why the Gray Spirits' queen is after you. Like…what the hell did you do to piss off an immortal queen?"

"Hell if I know," Derek muttered. "I didn't do anything to anyone. I went to the opening. I got sick. Everything fell apart from there."

Blair slammed her hands on the table, making both Derek and Cody jump.

"Uh…Blair?" Cody asked.

"The opening!" Blair exclaimed. Her eyes widened and she glanced at where the barista was doing work before she relaxed and quieted her voice. "The opening. It all started at the opening. Something happened that night."

"Okay, but what?" Derek asked.

Blair sighed and reached over, smacking Derek lightly upside the head.

"Ow! What?" Derek couldn't believe her.

"Think you idiot. What happened at the opening?"

Derek barely had time to think before Cody whispered, "The sculpture broke."

This time, Derek did have time to think. And think he did. His mind exploded with information. The story Blair had told. The woman with red eyes in his dream. The dream of him—of someone—using magic to end the war. To seal her away. He could picture it. Clear as day. A woman in the Mekong River frozen in stone, her captor kneeling in front of her, exhausted, as though she were his queen.

A queen.

Frozen in time for three thousand years. Who'd changed the face of Siamese art history. Who'd baffled his parents. His father, who'd discovered her buried beneath the Mekong River five years ago.

His stomach turned.

"The sculpture was the seal," Derek said. His heart raced. "It wasn't an art sculpture. She was a real queen."

"I think so," Blair said.

"It makes sense," Cody added.

Blair shook her head. "But how did she get out? I mean, did the seal just wear off?"

When he'd collapsed, Derek had had a dream. He'd gone back to the place in the dream later, and…and when he focused, when he thought, he'd been to that place before. A pool of water. A pillar carved with flowers. A lotus atop it, asking to be free.

His words.

If you want, you can be free.

His face went cold. He shook.

"Derek?" Cody asked.

"Shit." Derek said. "Shit, shit, shit, shit, shit."

"You okay?" Blair waved a hand in front of his face.

He ignored it.

"I know how she got free," he said. His heart thudded in his chest. He hadn't known. How could he have known?

"How?" It was unclear who asked louder.

Derek gulped. He looked between his two friends, trying to think of a way to excuse himself from this disaster. It wasn't his fault. It couldn't be his fault. It was a flower in a dream. It'd meant nothing. It had to mean nothing.

Except it had meant something. He'd collapsed. The sculpture had broken. He'd had the dream.

"I did it," Derek said. "I set the queen free."

It was a dream. It had to be a dream. Mia fled through the forest, struggling to run through the freshly fallen snow. Flakes still drifted from the sky, tickling her face and dotting her hair with white. Her breath, visible in the air, strained her already irritated lungs while her muscles screamed at her to stop torturing them already. Weight training, practice, school…they all felt like a million years ago. She wasn't sure how long she'd been in the cave. She wasn't sure the cave was even real.

Glowing walls. A pool with lotus flowers. Candles lighting the path.

It was a dream.

It had to be a dream.

Except it wasn't.

She burst out of the forest, coming to a brief stop in the field before town. Panting, she gripped the straps of her backpack and tried to imagine it without the new weight. Her heart pounded. Her shoulders ached from carrying her newfound mystery. Not just the item, but also the burden of what she'd done.

Why had she done it? Why had she picked it up? Why had she brought it through the cave and placed it in her backpack? Why had she left the cave as if nothing was wrong?

Tears pricked at her eyes. Confused, scared tears. She blinked them away and shook her head. Crying during a snowy night wasn't the smartest thing to do, and she'd already messed up enough today.

Lights from her neighbors' houses flooded the area. It startled her and she bowed her head, trekking through the snow to get out of their line of sight.

If anyone came out to talk to her, she didn't hear them. Her feet brought her between the houses and to the snow-covered sidewalk. With each step, her backpack grew heavier and she struggled not to take off the entire thing and throw it back at the forest. A car or two passed. Each time one did, tires crunching on the fresh snow, she flinched in expectation of a lecture.

Her breath shortened the closer she got home. The cold air squeezed at her lungs. Or maybe it was anxiety. She couldn't tell the difference as she tripped through the snow, trying not to run, but also wanting to get out of the open air as quickly as possible.

It was crazy. All of this was so crazy. She was going mad. She knew it. This entire thing was a massive hallucination. She'd get home and open her bag and it would be gone.

When she rounded the corner of her cul-de-sac, her sight frantically landed on her house at the end of it. Two cars sat in the driveway, both covered in mounds of snow. One higher than the other.

She knew her parents had come home while she was at school, but part of her had hoped it wasn't true. She had a hard time keeping her emotions from them. Especially her dad. If they knew how confused she'd been, there was no telling how they'd react. When her dad had sent her a voice message this morning, saying they were cutting their trip short to come home and deal with Derek's situation, she'd almost wanted to reply and tell him they were doing fine without him. Not because she thought they were, but because she didn't want them to come home before Mia could figure out a way to fix everything.

And now…and now she had a mysterious knife in her backpack that she'd found in a mysterious cave in the middle of a mysterious blizzard with mysterious glowing writing on the walls and a mysterious pool of water hidden in the back.

Shit.

Shaking, she headed up the driveway, up the front walk, and to the front door. She stepped as lightly as she could, flinching at every creak in the wood. Derek always complained she walked up the steps too loud, and so with every step she imagined herself as a feather. She wasn't walking up the stairs to get to her front door. She was sparring with an opponent much faster than her and had to stay light on her feet so her parents wouldn't hear her.

The key in her hands, cold and shaking, slipped into the lock and she gritted her teeth as it clicked. This wasn't what she'd planned for the past two weeks. If it'd been up to her and not whatever universe was trying to destroy her life, she'd be home with her parents, helping her dad cook dinner while her mom sat at the table with a mug of tea telling both of them why they were doing it wrong. Derek would be there too. He wouldn't be acting out, and he wouldn't be behind in school due to the illness. He'd be sitting with their mom, also drinking tea, but on his phone pretending like he wasn't enjoying the family time too.

That's how it should have been.

Instead, when she opened the door, she found the house quiet. The lights were off in the kitchen as well as the hallway, but Mia could hear low voices murmured in the living room. A glance at the shoe rack let her know that her parents were home, but not Derek, and her stomach sunk.

That didn't bode well.

She slipped through the house, desperate to get to her room without her parents noticing her. If she could just get there…if she could get in the room and hide the knife before they spoke to her….

Her hand touched the doorknob to her room when the voices in the living room grew louder.

"Mia?" Her mom's voice rose above her dad's. Mia froze, squeezing her eyes shut for just a moment to collect herself. When she opened them again, she let the false smile spread across her lips and she turned toward the living room. Her parents sat on the couch with its back facing Mia's room, and both of them had twisted in their seats to look at her.

"Māmi," Mia said. "Hi. Welcome home. Bà, when is your trip to Thailand?" Despite her smile and even tone, her heart raced a million miles a minute. She had to keep reminding herself to breathe.

"Where have you been?" Intira asked. She stood and headed over to Mia with crossed arms. "Practice ended two hours ago. We've been trying to call you."

Two hours? Mia bit the inside of her lip. It hadn't felt like two hours. "Um…sorry. I…my phone. It died. I forgot to charge it."

"Well, where have you been?" Her mom tapped her foot, waiting for an answer.

Mia glanced between her two parents. Her stern, brow furrowed, foot tapping, mother, to her concerned father. Where was Derek? How long had he been gone?

"I…." Mia couldn't think straight. The knife dragged her backpack down, growing heavier and heavier as the straps dug into her shoulders.

"Were you at the library?" her dad asked.

The library! Yes. The library.

"Yeah. Because…the blizzard," Mia said. "It got bad and I stayed a bit. I didn't mean to worry you. I'm sorry."

The two adults looked at one another. When Mia and Derek were younger, they'd speak in Thai when they didn't want the kids to know what they were saying. In Beijing, they were only supposed to speak Mandarin and English. House rules. But Derek picked up Thai like he always did with languages and they lost their secret way to communicate. Now it was through looks.

Finally, her mom let out a heavy sigh. "Fine. All right. Don't do it again. Always charge your phone. We're not paying for it so you can let it die."

"I know."

"Dinner will be ready soon. Go put your things down and come help us in the kitchen."

Mia breathed out, heavier than normal, but still as quiet as possible. "Okay. I can do that."

She didn't wait to hear what her parents had to say before she opened her door and all but fell into her room. She closed it, tensing as the door clicked. They would know. If they didn't know already. They would know that she was struggling to stay composed by the way she closed the door. Too hard and they would come knock. Not hard enough, and they would get suspicious. Her heart raced. A fine balance.

The minute it latched she let herself go. No more composure. She struggled to get her backpack off her back. The straps caught on her arms, and she had to twist, straining her arm in the process. Once she got it off, muscles throbbing in her right shoulder, she threw it on the bed, all but hyperventilating. After a moment, she took a step toward the bed. And another. Her backpack lay on the smooth duvet—a rag doll with a dangerous secret.

A shudder ran up her spine, warning her away. To turn away and never look at the contents within her backpack. She ignored it and unzipped her backpack.

It was a dream.

Maybe it was all a dream.

The knife lay there, nestled between her books and the cloth.

Not a dream. It's not a dream. It's not a dream.

She repeated this in her mind the entire time she reached in. Her fingers wrapped around the handle, the ridged strips of bamboo tickling her finger tips. It slid out of the backpack like a dream, heavy in her hands as she examined the strange weapon. Her trembling fingers undid the leather strap holding the sheath onto the blade. Despite its age, the sheath held on tight, and Mia had to physically pull it off to reveal the blade.

Mia knew little about metal. Still, staring at it, she knew there was something off. It was a different color than the knives she normally saw. Not a dull steel but something pure. Bright. Alive. The blade itself curved, almost like a sickle but not quite as steep. And carved, almost delicately, running down the center, ancient Sino-characters. Very ancient. Older than anything Mia had seen before.

She ran a finger along the words. Warmth emanated from them. The knife glowed.

"Mia."

A knock at the door startled Mia into dropping the knife on the bed. She placed her still warmed hand on her heart, feeling it thump over and over.

"Yes?" she called out. She scrambled, grabbing the knife and shoving it back in its sheath before dropping it into her backpack. The door creaked open as she did so, and she spun around, putting on a smile. Behind her, her hands trembled.

Her dad stood in the doorway. She wasn't used to him coming to get her. She wasn't sure he'd actually been in her room in years. Not since he found *The Queen*, at least.

He wasn't a tall man. Liang Sòng had a gentle face. Soft and often smiling. People didn't take him seriously, especially in America, as he—like Mia—struggled with languages and his spoken English was not the best. But through his gentle, smiling demeanor, and through the language barrier, he was a brilliant, ambitious man with eyes for his family and his work.

Yet, he wasn't hands on. He spent time with Mia and Derek, but even during his weeks home, when their mom was in Denver, he holed himself up in his study and let the twins run the house. He cooked dinner, and he taught them things when they asked, but he never came to Mia in her room to see how she was.

He looked her up and down, watching for the tiniest impurity in her actions. She shifted from one leg to another, hoping her clammy hands weren't a sign of another sign of her unraveling anxiety.

"Come to dinner," he said. "I made jīngjiàng ròusī."

"Okay," she said in a quiet voice.

He left the room, but Mia didn't relax. The knife was still there. In her backpack. Her parents could find it at any point.

I have to get rid of it. I have to get rid of it. I have to get rid of it.

Tense and shaking, Mia stepped away from her bed, from her bag, from the knife, and headed out to the kitchen where she was about to have dinner with both of her parents for the first time in months.

Despite the chatter at dinner, mostly between Liang and Intira, Mia couldn't ignore the intense aura hanging over the family. They sat at the table, food sitting in dishes, bowls half empty. During dinner, Mia's parents asked her question after question about school and homework and her friends. They acted like nothing was wrong. Like nothing was missing. But Mia's eyes kept turning to the empty seat where Derek was supposed to be.

They hadn't said where he was. Maybe they didn't know?

She wasn't sure what to think of their actions. She wouldn't put it past them to pretend like everything was fine until it actually was. They'd done it in the past. Their marriage had almost fallen apart but they'd pretended like it wasn't until, without warning, they were all right. They didn't talk about their problems, and they didn't talk about the issue with Derek.

Mia did her best to answer their questions. To keep the peace.

Inside she wanted to scream at them to stop pretending.

When dinner was almost finished, the front door opened, and

the table went quiet. Mia placed her chopsticks on the table, hope fluttering in her stomach. If Derek was home, if he could be here to answer their parents' questions, then she could be off the hook. She could finish dinner in silence as they questioned him, and then she could escape into her room and do something about the knife.

It took a minute, but eventually Derek appeared in the kitchen. He stood in front of them, slowly taking off his scarf, looking at them, but not at them. Through them, almost. His hair was flecked with white, cheeks containing just a bit more color than normal.

"Where have you been?" Liang asked in a tone she only ever heard when Derek got in trouble. Mia ducked her head, expecting Derek to snap back, like he usually did. It was their first night together as a family in so long. So many months. And it'd be another few months before it would happen again.

She didn't want a fight.

"I went downtown," Derek said. Mia detected no challenge in his voice. "Just needed to get out. I won't do it again. Sorry."

She lifted her head and faced him again. His scarf hung from his hand, brushing against the ground. They made eye contact, and for the first time in their lives, Mia didn't feel that thing. That spark. That connection with her twin. It was something they'd always had. How he knew what she was feeling. How she knew when he was about to blow up, or when he was lying to her.

"Well," their mom said, "why don't you join us for the rest of dinner? We made some vegetarian dishes for you in case you made your way home."

"I'm not hungry," Derek said. "I'm just going to go to bed. Night."

He turned without another word and headed to his room.

Don't follow him. Don't follow him. Don't follow him.

"I'll…be right back?" Mia said, smiling to her parents. Her dad furrowed his brow, and her mom clenched her fist, but they didn't say anything, so Mia stood and stumbled to her brother's room. The door was closed and she hesitated. Did she knock? Did she just enter? Normally she just knew which was okay. If he was angry at her, or just annoyed at the world. Tonight, she had no idea.

Taking a chance, she gripped the doorknob and turned it, opening his door. He was at his bed, aware that she was in the room, but ignoring her as he ripped the blankets off his bed.

"You not going to shower?" Mia asked.

"Nope," Derek said. He turned away from the bed and took off his shirt, throwing it onto the pile of…everything he had strewn about the floor.

"But…." Mia searched for something to say for him. He shuffled through the floor before finding his pajama shirt and pulling it over his head.

Mia watched him go about his room, turning off a lamp, grabbing his phone charger, preparing for bed. And as she watched him she felt it. A rift. A rift breaking them apart. He had his secrets. Why he'd dumped the tea. What had made him run out into the street. Why he'd pushed over a bookcase. What he had been doing downtown with Blair and Cody for over two hours that she wasn't invited to.

And she had her secrets.

The woman stalking her.

The knife in her room.

They never used to keep secrets from one another. Well, not big secrets. Where she'd hidden her Valentine's Day chocolate, since he'd already eaten his, sure. The time he got angry with her because she'd beat him at chess when they were seven and he had stolen her stuffed bunny for a month, yeah. Stupid stuff. Stuff they fought over and made up. But these secrets…whatever was going on, it wasn't like them.

Mia didn't want it to be them.

"Hey, Derek?" she called out. He didn't stop fussing. "Can…I talk to you about something?"

He'd think she was crazy. Derek didn't believe in anything spiritual or mystical. He always rolled his eyes when they'd visit Buddhist temples with their nǎinai to light incense and pray. When Mia tried to talk to him about what he believed—if anyone tried to talk to him about what he believed—he'd say some snippy comment about religion and sheep, and then change the subject. Anything that he couldn't touch and feel, he wouldn't believe.

But she had a knife. It was in her room. If she could just persuade him to see it, he would believe her. She wouldn't have to deal with this alone.

When he didn't respond, she called his name again. This time, he looked up and stared directly at her,

"Mia, I really don't want to do this right now. Can it wait until tomorrow?"

"Well, I…I have something—"

"Dammit, Mia, I don't care," he snapped. Her eyes widened. "Whatever happened at school, or at practice, or whatever boy drama is going on in your friend circle that you want me to give you advice on, really isn't important right now. I don't care. Just get out so I can sleep."

The two had experienced their fair share of fights. Mia annoyed Derek. Derek wouldn't do his chores. They disagreed about the rules of a board game. But never, in all of their lives, had Derek ever spoken to Mia like that. For whatever reason, her brother didn't want her near him.

Mia backed away. She closed the door behind her, not saying a word, and leaned her forehead against the door, hands pressed against it with tears pricking at her eyes.

This day.

This damn day.

She had no one to talk to. Her brother didn't care that she was in distress. Her parents were dealing with their own issues and she was not about to add to that. Blair had not only ditched her to hang out with Derek, but she'd lied about it, and Cody...she couldn't involve Cody. He was barely able to handle the stuff going on in his own life, with his crazy mom and his dad who worked twice as hard to pay for everything. Telling him about a glowing cave and a mysterious knife might only stress him out more than he deserved.

This was something she had to do alone. She had no other choice.

Tears streamed down her cheeks and she wiped them away, breathing in and out deeply.

It's going to be okay. It'll all be okay.

She stood up straight. She'd hide the knife. She wouldn't even think about it until things calmed down in the home. She'd have more time to think then. To figure out what she wanted to do and how to handle having a glowing knife from a magical cave in her possession.

She didn't know what would happen, but she knew for now, at least, that she had to deal with it alone. It would be okay. Everyone would figure out what was going wrong in their lives, and they would get fixed.

And she would too.

With one last look at her brother's door, she backed away and headed back to the kitchen where the sound of dishes being piled up brought her mind back to the present moment: she was here with both of her parents.

Chapter Fourteen

Emotions clawed at his skin. He kept his head down, pushing through the halls of the school as whispers rose up around him. About him. Everyone in school knew about the incident at the library. They all had theories. They came up with reasons why he'd pushed over the bookcase.

"He's stressed because he missed all that school."

"He's angry at his parents."

"He's jealous of Mia."

"He's secretly hated all of us."

They didn't know he could hear them. Or…maybe he couldn't hear them. Maybe, as he walked through the halls, hands shoved in his pockets, backpack straps digging into his shoulders, he was imagining the words; personifying the rush of negative emotions overwhelming his senses.

He needed them gone. In his pocket, he rolled the protection charm Blair had given him. It was meant to protect him from attacks. It was meant to keep the magic away and keep him safe from unwanted pain. Well, if that was so, then why wasn't it working? He gripped it, almost crushing it. He climbed the stairs of the building, up to the high school, to his locker, and thought about taking the charm out and burning it. It was a reminder of the library. A reminder of his dulled connection with his sister.

And it didn't take away the emotions.

Theirs, or his.

When he got to his locker, he found writing on it. Small, and erasable, but writing.

Asshole.

He closed his eyes and shook his head. It was fine. Let them believe what they wanted.

Realizing that he'd unsealed a dangerous, immortal queen hadn't helped his sleep. He'd kicked Mia out the other night, pushing her away when she wanted to talk, in hopes of getting some rest. But it hadn't come. The entire night, his brain had exploded with incoherent conversations, voices clamoring over one another to get his attention.

But at least there were no dreams. No red-eyed woman haunting his nightmares. No lotuses floating in rippling water.

No memories that didn't belong to him.

"You look like you haven't slept in days."

Derek blinked for a second too long before his locker came into view. The word, "asshole" stayed in his vision, even as he turned to face Cody, who stood next to him with bags under his eyes.

"You're one to talk," Derek said.

"Yeah. Well…." Cody shrugged. "Are you doing okay?"

A group of girls passed behind them. In seconds, their emotions transformed from a fluttering happiness to sharp fear and anger. Derek shuddered.

"Yup. Dandy."

Cody frowned. Or, he frowned more than usual. "Right…um… well, have you seen Mia today? I haven't seen her and I…well with the charm I can't really...I don't know where she is."

Derek's eyes strayed back to his locker. The word "asshole." He and Mia had come to school together, like they always did. But she hadn't spoken to him. The entire walk to school, she'd remained quiet, as she had during the week. During the weekend. And the moment they had arrived at school, she'd disappeared.

And he hated that he couldn't tell what exactly she was feeling.

He'd thought about saying something. All morning. From the moment she'd entered the kitchen until she'd taken off down the hall. But he didn't need his empathic powers to know that would only piss her off more. She'd come to him, like she did when she was stressed or upset, and he'd pushed her away. Guilt had stabbed at his gut the moment the words left his mouth. He thought about taking them back. About apologizing and sitting with her. But exhaustion had spoken over the guilt and instead he'd watched her leave his room.

He just couldn't do it right now. He couldn't handle her drama.

Not with someone trying to kill him.

The word "asshole" mocked him.

"Derek?" Cody asked, bringing him back to reality. Derek rubbed his eyes to brush away the sleep.

"Sorry," Derek said. "I don't know where she is."

"Oh."

Derek shook his head. They didn't have long before the bell would ring and send them into eight hours of class. He'd been thinking, and he had something to say. "Cody."

"Yeah?"

"I want to look for the queen." He got the words out before he could stop them. He'd been up all night thinking about this. About the dreams. About the woman with red eyes. The lotus. He knew, without a doubt, that he'd unsealed her. And now she wanted to kill him.

But…why?

Cody snorted. A rare sound for him. "You want to *what*? She's trying to kill you."

"I know." Or did he? One thing he didn't understand about the library was that the woman, the queen, had drawn him away from the shelves. She was trying to kill him…so why had she appeared at the window? Why had she placed her hand on the glass, almost beckoning him forward?

She was trying to kill him.

She'd failed to kill him.

Or…maybe she'd succeeded in saving him.

"If she is trying to kill me, then I want to know why," Derek said. "I want to find her. She won't be expecting that. We should try and find her."

"If? I don't understand," Cody said, shaking his head. "What do you mean *if* she's trying to kill you?"

"Uh, yeah, seriously?" Blair's voice caused Derek to jump. Cody flinched too, and the boys turned to face her. She stood with furrowed brows, eyes wild with irritation, arms crossed over a baggy t-shirt with a talking orange on it.

"Morning," Derek said.

"Why are we suddenly questioning if an evil, immortal, non-human queen is trying to kill you?" Blair scoffed. "We know she's here. You've seen her. She's stalking you and your dreams. Of course she's trying to kill you."

"But what if she's not?" Derek didn't want to have this argument where they were. He glanced around. The hall was mostly empty, at least. "All we know is that she shows up sometimes."

"When you almost die," Blair pointed out.

"She has a good point," Cody said.

Derek groaned. "But maybe she's not the one doing it."

"Then who is trying to kill you?" Blair asked.

"I don't know!" Derek groaned. "Look, I'm going to go look for her. You can come with me or not, but I'm going after school. If all three of us are there, maybe she won't try anything."

Cody shrugged. "Or maybe she'll just kill us all."

"Who might kill you?"

Derek's heart leapt into his throat. His lungs failed him for a moment as he turned to find Mia standing away from them, arms crossed. He glanced at the bracelet on her wrist. The damn thing. He wasn't used to this. To not feeling her coming around a corner. Even now, staring at her, he longed to know what she was feeling, as her blank expression gave nothing away.

"Ms. Hensen if we're late to class," Blair blurted out after a moment. Derek thanked whatever supernatural being was out there for Blair's ability to lie on the spot.

"Oh." Mia glanced between Blair and Cody. "Well, I won't keep you from class. But I was wondering if you wanted to hang out after school today? It's been a while."

Derek had to resist exchanging glances with the other two. He didn't want Mia to think that whatever came out was a plot against her.

Cody cleared his throat. "I...I uh...can't. I have...work. Um...I gotta get my homework done before work."

"Well, why don't we work on it together?" Mia asked, confusion creeping into her voice. Derek's chest tightened. They'd never done this before. Left her out when she was right there. He hated doing this. He hated it.

But he needed to protect her.

He needed to protect himself.

Cody shook his head. "I...it's faster if I just do it alone."

A chill fell over the four teens at those words. Derek had to look at the floor, not wanting to see the pain on Mia's face. Cody was her friend first. The two of them had been close long before Cody and

Derek had started speaking. Any other day, Cody would never have said those words to Mia, and Derek clenched his fists.

This was his fault.

"Oh." Mia said. "I...I get it."

"I also can't," Blair said, voice much calmer than Cody's. "Mom's been getting on my case to clean up around the house. My brother's been a brat recently and she doesn't have time with Dad working overtime. Sorry."

Derek glanced up again, ready to give some excuse, but Mia didn't even look at him. She nodded.

"Right. Maybe tomorrow." And before anyone could say anything, she walked away.

The moment she was gone, Blair smacked Cody in the arm.

"Hey!" he yelled. A bell rang throughout the halls, reminding them that class was starting soon.

"You idiot," Blair snapped. "Did you have to hurt her like that?"

"I didn't mean to."

"Oh. Well. That makes it all better."

"We're all shutting her out," Cody said. "You lying about needing to help your mom isn't any better. Mia doesn't fall for lies like that. She knows something is going on."

"So you add fuel to the flame. Okay."

Derek watched them argue, unable to think straight. He was tired. So tired. And Mia was walking away. And the woman in black was haunting him.

And someone, somewhere, for some reason, wanted him dead.

He was so tired.

"If you're coming," Derek said, interrupting Blair and Cody, "then meet me after class outside the front doors." Then, like his sister, he took off without waiting for their replies. He didn't have the energy. He needed to get to class and just try to get through the day.

When she'd seen them in the hall, huddled around Derek's locker, she'd thought that maybe it would be okay. She didn't have to tell them anything. But she could talk to them. Even if they were arguing. Even if voices were raised. Even if they were talking about someone wanting to kill them.

She knew, from the moment Blair answered her first question, that they were all lying to her. Cody's words had stung, nagging at her insecurities, even though she knew he would have never said that on a normal day. She didn't know what was going on there. Blair, too, made no sense. Her dad always worked extra hours. It was part of being an elementary school teacher. This overtime thing was bullshit.

And Derek…well, she hadn't even wanted to hear his excuse.

She went through her day without a word to anyone. She took notes. Turned in homework. Answered questions. And at practice she'd let Coach Smith take charge. All day, she'd floated through life and didn't acknowledge anyone. Her mind was on the knife. The glowing cave. The blond woman. Everything going on in her life that she couldn't explain to anyone.

Even if she could, would anyone listen?

After practice, she pulled her phone out of her bag, expecting… something. Anything from her friends or her brother. But no. She had nothing. She was about to put it away when it buzzed. Her heart leapt and she checked.

It wasn't Blair. Cody. Or Derek.

It was Steven.

<<Want to come study?>>

A smile spread across her face. The strings of frustration

released her heart.

Maybe someone did want her around.

<<Sure.>>

Steven's house hadn't changed. She stood in front of it, staring up at the slanted roof as the sun dipped toward the horizon. A gust of wind blew through the area, sending a chill through her thick coat, and her boots were wet from the sidewalk slush. They'd had a warm spell today. Enough for the snow to melt, but it would get dark soon, and the slush would freeze to ice. She'd have to be careful walking home.

She glanced behind her, at the street leading to Steven's isolated house. It wasn't dark enough for the few street lamps to light up, but it was getting there. Night fall. Evening. She pulled out her phone. A text from her mom reminded her to call when she was on her way home. It didn't tell her when to be home, yet for some reason Mia had a feeling she should turn around and leave. Head back and help her mom prepare dinner.

But she couldn't.

Because she didn't want to see Derek.

Besides, what was one hour with a friend?

With a deep breath, she stepped onto the porch and knocked on the front door, still shivering. The knock sounded hollow. Not like the door was hollow. More like the house was. She stepped back. It hadn't sounded like that last time. Another deep breath. Another knock.

This one was normal.

She waited for a minute until the lock clunked and the door clicked open, revealing a smiling, happy Steven. His blue eyes sparkled with excitement, and seeing him melted the ice off of her shoulders.

"You made it," Steven said with a light laugh. "I was worried you wouldn't."

Mia raised an eyebrow. "It's Willow Creek. I can't exactly get lost."

He stepped to the side to let her in and she rushed in, eager to get out of the cold. Warmth spread across her, and she sighed the cold out of her body.

"I know you can't get lost," Steven said. "But you never know what might happen. I've heard there are mountain lions around here."

"Mountain lions?" Mia laughed as she stripped herself of her coat and boots. "Mountain lions don't come into town."

When Steven handed her a pair of slippers to wear in the house, he smiled. "I know. But weird things happen."

Mia stared at him for a moment, hand half extended to take the slippers. Weird things...did happen. She knew that better than anyone. He said it with such a smile on his face, eyes open and welcoming, alive with happiness and innocence. She thought to Derek. His cold tone. The way he kept brushing her off. How he'd gotten *her* friends to lie to her.

Steven wouldn't lie to her.

The two of them headed into the house. Steven rambled on about what he needed help with, but Mia only half listened. Instead her mind wandered to the past two weeks. All of the events. The statue, her parents leaving, the blond woman, Derek getting sick, him pushing over a shelf, the cave.

The knife.

It was a lot.

Through it all, she managed to look over Steven's homework, understand where he was struggling, and explain the formulas.

Still, other things overtook her mind. The math slipped through her lips, almost second nature to her, but she didn't know what she was saying. There was a disconnect between her mouth and her mind. One said the things she needed it to—explain mathematical formulas to a boy who seemed to be inching a little closer—and the other rambled about the things she didn't want to hear: the world of the unexplainable.

Derek wouldn't listen to her about the knife. Blair and Cody had taken his side. Her parents were leaving, again. Maybe she could put it back?

A shiver ran up her spine. Her chest tightened. She sucked in a surprised breath. One hand shook under the table, but the one holding the pencil somehow managing to stay calm.

So, no.

She wouldn't put it back.

But then…what could she do with it?

"You okay?"

At first the question was quiet, but then it grew louder, echoing between her ears until it was deafening. It consumed all the thoughts. It was the only thing on her mind.

"Huh?" She blinked and jerked her head in Steven's direction. Darkness had overcome them, their only source of light a single overhanging fixture which didn't reach the corners of the room. When had that happened? Mia glanced around the room, trying to get a sense of the time. Shades covered the windows. Had that been like that before? Her eyes landed on the paper in front of her, where she'd been writing, explaining a formula. There was a thick line extending a few inches, out of place, and broken mechanical pencil lead lying next to it.

Her gaze returned to Steven. He cocked his head, watching her with a blank expression, but curious eyes. Eyes that pounded against her soul, wanting it to open up and tell him everything.

"Oh, I'm sorry," she said, shaking her head.

"That's not an answer to my question," Steven said. He uncrossed his arms and reached out, placing his hand on hers. She was too surprised to react. His fingers brushed against her smooth skin, sending tingles through her nerves. Those fingers gripped her hand, stilling it when she hadn't realized it was shaking.

"I…I'm fine," Mia managed to say, trying not to stare at their hands.

"You're shaking." He put on a slight smile. "I…uh…do you need something? Are you hungry? It's getting late. Or something to drink? I completely forgot to offer you something when you got here. Sorry. We have…I dunno. Things. My parents aren't home but they left some money if we want to order some food. Wait… are there delivery places here? Doesn't matter. Do you want tea? Coffee? Water? Soda? Juice?"

Steven's rambling drew Mia back out of her thoughts. Her overactive thoughts. She closed her eyes for a moment, allowing herself time to breathe.

"Water would be great," she said.

Steven nodded and stood. His hand disappeared, leaving hers cold and longing for his touch again. Or maybe it wasn't his touch she longed for. Maybe she longed for someone, somewhere, to give her comfort. To notice her.

To want her.

She watched him grab a cup from the cupboard and fill it with water from the sink. Mia watched him look at it, mutter to himself, dump it out, then go to the fridge and pull out a pitcher of filtered water. He poured some in, then turned around and looked at her, raising it with a confused, questioning smile. She shrugged, and he finished filling the glass. She watched him stare at it. She watched him shake his head, place the pitcher in the fridge, and return with the glass of clear liquid.

She watched him do all this and wondered what he was thinking about when they sat together. He knew nothing about her. She knew nothing about him. They studied together. They didn't talk about their lives. At least, not since he'd opened up about his heritage. What did he think of her? What did he think of her being *here*?

Mia took the water with a small smile and sipped the cool liquid. She imagined Derek rolling his eyes in disgust. She pushed the image out of her mind.

"Feeling better?" Steven asked.

"Yeah, thanks."

He touched her arm, briefly. "Do you want to talk about it? I mean…you seemed angry. Did something happen? I know today was Derek's first day back at school. He's been acting weird?"

"That's putting it mildly," Mia muttered in Chinese.

"Huh?" Steven leaned forward.

Mia shrugged. "I don't know. He and I aren't really talking. He doesn't want to tell me what happened."

"But…there were eyewitnesses. We know what happened. He pushed over a bookcase."

"So everyone keeps saying." Mia sighed. She didn't want to talk about this anymore, but the words tumbled out without her noticing. "But there's something weird going on. I can't explain it. I know when Derek is lying to me. I've always known. And does anyone really believe that he *could* push over a bookcase like that? He doesn't exactly do pushups in his free time." Mia was pretty sure the only reason Derek had ever *done* a pushup was because it was mandatory in gym.

"Okay, but people saw him. So maybe he's a secret gym rat."

"Willow Creek doesn't have a gym."

"The school does."

"That wouldn't be a secret."

"Yeah but–"

"Plus, it's not like weird things aren't happening around here," Mia said, voice growing louder. "The weather has been so off for October. My parents' career is under threat because of some freak accident that shouldn't have happened. My friends aren't being honest with me. My brother is doing stupid shit he *knows* better than to do. Not to mention the crazy woman stalking me and the glowing knife in the cave!"

The moment the words left her mouth she clapped a hand over it.

Shut up. Shut up, shut up, shut up!

She hadn't meant to say any of that. To tell Steven her deepest secret. To convince him that she was crazy. Maybe he'd think it was genetic. The crazy Sòng twins.

Steven stared at her, eyes wide, mouth open just enough. It was like he didn't know how to respond to what just happened, and she didn't blame him. She wouldn't know either.

She bowed her head. "Sorry. I…sorry. That was…I just…ignore that."

And like that, Steven snapped out of his shock. "What? No. Don't apologize. It was just a lot of information. Someone's been stalking you?"

"N-n-no. I…I mean I keep seeing this woman around town, but it's all in my head."

"Uh huh. And a glowing knife?"

"Look, Steven, the interest in my life is flattering," Mia stuttered, trying to form words as her flustered brain tried to switch her back to Chinese, "but really. It's stupid. Let's just get back to the homework okay?"

"Mia," Steven said, voice calm and commanding. She stopped and stared at him. He smiled. "It's not stupid. I want to hear it. You can tell me. You can tell me anything."

And like before, Mia spoke. She didn't know why. Maybe it was frustration. Maybe it was insanity. Or maybe it was the way he said those words. The warmth. The care. The comfort. The interest. He was someone she could talk to who wasn't in her immediate circle. He wasn't her parents, who wouldn't be around in a few days anyway. He wasn't Blair, who was impossible to talk to sometimes. He wasn't Cody, who had enough going on in his life and was pushing her away anyway. And he wasn't Derek, who refused to talk to her because he was tired.

He was Steven.

And he'd asked.

When Mia finished explaining everything, from the night of the opening until the night in the cave, Steven leaned back in his seat, crossing his arms. Mia took a deep breath, waiting for his response. Either he'd think she was crazy and avoid her, or he'd think she was crazy and tell the whole school. And avoid her. She closed her eyes.

"Huh," Steven said after a moment.

"I know it sounds insane," Mia said. "It doesn't make sense. It can't be real. None of this can be real. I know. I'm imagining it all." Except the knife. "You must think I'm crazy."

Steven's laugh caught her off guard. It bounced off the walls, but this time it didn't become deafening. It was a happy sound. A nice sound. Mia's shoulders relaxed.

"You...don't think I'm crazy," Mia said.

Steven shook his head, still laughing. "I'm sorry. I shouldn't laugh. You're definitely in the dark about all this."

"What?" Mia shook her head. "What are you talking about?"

Steven sucked in a deep breath, all laughter gone from him. He glanced around again, almost as if expecting someone to come crashing through one of the shaded windows. Mia waited, patiently, while he did this, until his gaze landed on her again. He let out the air and nodded once before saying, "Okay. I...I'm going to tell you a secret. But you can't tell anyone. Not even Derek."

"Um, what?" Mia tensed, almost ready to leave. She didn't like that Steven was being mysterious. She didn't like the way he had a look on his face that screamed, "nervous". And, more than both of those things, she didn't like that he was asking her to keep this secret from Derek. She told Derek everything. She shared her life with him.

Or…she had.

Now she had secrets. Now *he* had secrets. So…what was one more?

"I need you to promise me you won't tell anyone," Steven repeated. His words came moments—seconds—after her question, but Mia's mind took a different, slower path. Between her inquiry and his request passed a million years.

She blinked, struggling to reorient herself to real time. "O-okay. I won't tell anyone."

"Say the whole thing." He smiled, but his tone was dark. Serious. Confusion overtook her, but she played along.

"I won't tell anyone, not even Derek." Even though she was hesitant to keep whatever the secret was from Derek, she knew that the words were truth the moment they left her lips. She wouldn't tell Derek. She wouldn't tell Blair. She wouldn't tell Cody.

She wouldn't tell anyone.

They locked eyes, his crinkled with worry and hesitance. For a moment, they stared at each other, and Mia fidgeted, wondering if this was all a mistake. Coming here. Staying. Telling him everything. When he lifted a hand from under the table, holding it out, palm up, Mia's worries turned to confusion. Steven sucked in an audible breath, then let it out slowly.

She held hers.

A pressure hit Mia in the chest, and then the light above them flickered, drawing Mia's eyes to it for the briefest second. It stopped, and she returned her gaze to his hand, chest still tight. And when her eyes landed on the glowing orb of white light floating above his hand, she yelped and scrambled to her feet, intense fear encapsulating her. Her heart pounded.

"Hey," Steven said, standing as well. The ball followed his hand as if leashed to it. He stepped toward her, and she stepped away until her back hit the wall.

Images of the cave flashed through her mind. The glowing walls. The mysterious candles. The knife on the pedestal. It was here. It was haunting her. Whatever was going on...it was following her around. Was this a dream? Maybe all of this was a dream.

"No. No, it's not scary." His voice trembled, and he closed his hand into a fist. The ball of light disappeared.

Mia couldn't bring herself to look away from his fist. The orb. She hadn't imagined it. It had been there, floating. Light. Energy? Something. Something mysterious. Something wrong.

"Mia?"

She finally looked him in the eye, hands shaking, unable to breathe properly. His eyes were wide. Concern? Yes. Concern. He held out a hand again, this time as if to take hers. She ignored it.

"*What?*" The word burst out before she could stop it. Steven flinched and dropped his hand, the other gripping the chair next to him. His shoulders shook the slightest bit, but he didn't bow his head, and he didn't break eye contact. Mia pressed against the wall. Words tumbled out. "What was that? What did you just do? What is going on?"

"It's not bad," Steven said. "It's not...it's just...it's magic. I can use magic."

A stark laugh exploded from her lips. "Magic isn't real."

"Says the girl who found a glowing knife in a mysterious cave in a blizzard after being stalked by a blond haired woman for weeks," Steven said with a roll of his eyes.

Mia scowled. "That's not magic. That's me going insane."

"No, it's not you going insane, it's magic."

"*Magic isn't real.*"

Steven groaned and placed his face in his hands before sliding them down and clapping them together with a sigh. "Okay. I knew you didn't know about some things. But I didn't realize you didn't know *anything*."

Mia rolled her eyes. "That doesn't make sense."

"Okay," Steven said again. "Okay. Okay, okay, okay. Uh…how to do this."

Mia finally stepped away from the wall, circumnavigating the table to get her things while staying away from Steven. He didn't pay attention to her, instead muttering in what she guessed was Norwegian.

"I'm going to go," Mia said, grabbing her things.

Steven's head spun around to face her. "Wait! No. No wait. Don't…don't go. Just let me explain."

Mia held her backpack to her chest, still unzipped, but ready in case of the need for a quick departure. Steven looked so pathetic, standing there with his hands trying not to reach out for her, fear dashing across his face. She relaxed for a moment. Her shoulders loosened and she let her backpack slide to the table. It landed with a *thunk*, and both of them flinched.

"Explain what?" Mia asked. She didn't want to believe the ball had existed. It was a trick of the light. All of it was a trick. The knife, the cave, the woman…nothing in her life had been real since the night the sculpture broke.

Steven ran a hand through his hair. "I…okay. Magic."

"Is not—"

"Mia, magic is real and a lot of people have it," Steven said before Mia could finish. She ground her teeth together. He groaned again. "Shit. Okay. I didn't think you'd get scared. Okay. Sorry. Look, that knife, that cave, the weird glowing walls and the water and the candles and everything, is related to magic." He held out his hand again and the ball appeared. This time, Mia stayed quiet, though her stomach clenched.

"Magic isn't scary," he continued. "Well, not on its own. It's just energy. People with magic have a strong energy inside of them that they can manipulate and use to…well, we haven't quite found a limit. Create things, manipulate reality, destroy…. A mage is limited by their imagination, their knowledge of the world, and the amount of energy they have. The more magic you use, the more energy you lose and you can end up weak and sick. You can even die if you lose too much."

Mia listened to him ramble. It all sounded so wrong. So impossible. But she could see the light. She could remember the weight of the knife on her shoulders as it dragged down her backpack. That cave. Had it all not been real? Was this…maybe it was all real.

"You're…a mage?" Mia asked.

"Yeah." So much relief coated those words. A small smile spread across his face and his hands stopped shaking. "Yeah. I'm…I'm a mage."

"I don't understand," Mia said.

"I can use magic. I'm a mage."

"You said there are a lot of mages?" The word didn't sound any less weird the second time. A sharp pain stung her temple as confusion overtook her everything. "How? Where are they? Why don't they run the world? Why don't I know about any of this?"

A moment of silence fell over the two. Steven finally broke their gaze and dropped his head a tad. As he thought, as they stood in silence in his dim kitchen, books scattered across the table, math waiting for them to return to normal, Mia considered her life. Her world. Everything. Besides the past two weeks, had weird things happened? Had magic been all around her and she hadn't noticed? There were odd things. Her parents moving to Willow Creek without warning. Her father's obsession with the sculpture. Tiny things from her childhood she knew happened, but couldn't quite grasp. Dorian, the man who never seemed to age.

But no. No. Those weren't odd. Those weren't magic. Nothing in her life was magic.

Until now.

"Okay," Steven said, drawing out the word with a heavy breath.

Mia rolled her eyes. "Is that your favorite word?"

"Hey, this isn't easy for me to talk about," Steven said. "I'm not supposed to talk about my magic, or the clans, or the issues around it all."

"Clans?"

"Yeah," Steven said, waving his hand. "There are a bunch, and then there are the main ones, but that's super political and I don't wanna get into it. Usually they group up by region, and there are different cultures in different clans but really we're all the same. Magic. Spells. Dying out. My clan is a small one in Scandinavia that keeps shrinking. My parents moved us to America to try and escape the hunters who want to erase magic from the world."

"You're persecuted?"

"Me personally?" Steven asked.

"Yeah."

He laughed. "No. Not really. Kinda. I was young when we left and we're safe here. But my clan, and most people with magic, are. People are scared of magic, especially the ones with the gifts."

The information overwhelmed Mia. She pulled the chair out from the table and sank into it, legs like jello. She didn't want to ask, but she had to. "Gifts?"

"Oh, right. One of the only things different about different clans is the gifts. Everyone can use magic, but sometimes people can do more. Things like seeing the future, persuasion, reality shifts, mind reading…they're special gifts that aren't attached to our energy."

"Oh." Mia didn't know what to say. He sounded confident telling her this. He sat as well, the ball of light still floating, though now higher than his head. She kept glancing to it, then back to him, trying to understand. To wrap her mind around the fact that this world wasn't what she thought it was. "Do…you have a gift?"

Steven's laugh made her jump. "No," he got out through laughter. "God no."

"You don't need to laugh!" Mia said, face heating up. She cross her arms.

"Sorry, sorry," Steven said. "I just…I'm not used to that question. No. I'm not a *begavet*." Mia didn't ask what that meant. "I'm just ordinary. *Begavet* are super rare. Like…once every other generation rare. And I wouldn't want to be one anyway."

"I thought they had incredible powers?"

"They do. Goddamn they do. But because of that they're coveted. I mean, in our stories there are tales of a woman, Hertha, with the power to control the weather, and she used her power one time to create a hurricane to wipe out an invading army." His eyes lit up when he spoke, and Mia couldn't help but smile. It reminded her of the stories her grandparents would tell her. Both her mom's parents, and her dad's. They loved to share old tales that they had heard from their grandparents.

Steven must have heard this from his.

"But, anyway," Steven continued. "My point is, sometimes power isn't all it's cracked up to be. I don't know any *begavet* and I don't think I ever will. Some are so rare we're pretty sure they're just…gone. Like seers. No one's heard of a seer in four generations. But they can change the course of history if they want."

Mia had so many questions. Questions about why the mages are so quiet. Questions about the gifts. Questions about Steven and his family. About where she fit into all of this, and why…why she found that knife. She stared up at the light. It floated there, bright, alive, and warm. Welcoming. It wasn't scary.

Magic wasn't scary.

"Thank you for telling me," Mia said in a quiet voice. The light vanished, and she looked back to Steven smiling. "I…I feel better. Now. After…well…I feel better."

Steven smiled with a light laugh. "I'm glad you're feeling better. And I'm glad you didn't leave. And I'm glad you told me about your issue. You shouldn't have to be going through this alone, and…I guess telling you about magic made me feel less alone too."

Alone. They were both alone. Steven's parents were gone a lot. Her parents were gone a lot. He had no siblings. Her brother was abandoning her. He hadn't seemed to make a lot of friends at school. Her friends…she didn't want to think ill of them. But she could also picture them standing there, lying to her, making excuses to spend time with Derek in secret.

"Well," Mia said, a small weight lifting from her heart, "we can be alone together I guess."

He laughed. "Yeah. And, by the way, if you want me to take the knife and keep it safe here, or whatever, I can. I'll tell my parents about it and I'm sure they'll know what to do."

For a brief moment, excitement overtook Mia. The knife. The stupid goddamn knife. She could get rid of it. It'd be gone from her life, never to be seen again. She wouldn't have to think about it, or worry about someone finding it. The pressure would disappear and she could go back to living a normal life. No magic caves. No knives. And maybe, hopefully, no stalkers.

Then anxiety took over. Questions swam in her head. They drowned everything out, asking why had she found it? Steven was here. His parents. Why had she found it and not them?

The more she considered giving him the knife, the more her heart hurt. Her hands curled into fists, chest tight and angry.

She wanted to give it to him. She couldn't. It was hers. Her knife.

"Thank you," she said, mouth suddenly dry. "But I think I'm going to keep it. Just for now."

Steven's face fell for a fraction of a second. It switched so quickly Mia thought she'd imagined it, but there he was, smiling and nodding like always.

"Okay, sure," he said. "Let me know if you change your mind."

"I will," Mia said. She wasn't sure if she meant it.

"Great," Steven said. "Now, I know this is all crazy and you just learned that magic is real, but I seriously need help with this math homework. Take pity on a poor soul struggling with derivatives?"

Mia laughed. "Fine, fine. I'll help."

They returned to the books, Mia getting hers out again, and like that, light returned to the room, as if a dead bulb came back to life. She thought nothing of it.

Derek stood in front of his house. Darkness had overtaken the town, as it did every night at dinner time this late in the year. Yet, this time felt different. This time, the darkness settled on Willow Creek like a dangerous, foreboding message. Something was wrong. Very, very wrong.

And there was nothing he could do.

His boots sunk into the snow coating the lawn, body shivering uncontrollably as he stayed out in the cold for far longer than any reasonable person would. The cold clawed at his skin: an emotion of its own. It permeated his coat, his pants, and his gloves, sinking deep into his bones. He should go in. He needed to go in, face his parents. Their shadows cast across the second story window, both parents protected from the world by a white shade. He didn't know how to talk to them. What to say. He never did, and now it was all messed up.

And Mia….

They'd abandoned Mia, again, to go searching. But they'd found nothing. All afternoon they'd searched the woods, the town, and even climbed into Cody's truck to see how far they could get out of town. But there was nothing there. No woman. Nothing magical. Nothing mystical.

Derek had wanted to continue. Searching for something that he wasn't even sure existed. Searching for an unidentifiable something. What were they looking for? How were they even supposed to find it?

It was a stupid venture, but he had to. He had to keep going because what else was he going to do?

A light came on in the kitchen. Mia appeared in the window, but she didn't look out of it, head down as she put something in the sink. She disappeared. The light turned off.

Derek slipped off a glove and reached into his pocket, pulling out Blair's charm.

It wouldn't take long to tell Mia. Tell her that they were trying to keep her safe, and that she had to stay protected because this wasn't her world. She didn't have magic. If she didn't know about it, she wouldn't get caught up in whatever disaster was about to befall her. She'd stay safe, and then she'd realize they weren't abandoning her.

Two seconds. That would be all it would take to let her know. The bracelet they gave her would continue to work. His charm would keep working. There was no reason not to tell her.

Except there was. Because they'd lied to her. Not just about this. But their entire lives. Derek had lied to her for their entire lives. And the thought…the idea of telling her that made him want to run away and never return. It'd hurt her less. It'd hurt him less.

He gripped the pouch. He needed it, he knew that, but at the same time…if he threw it away, would everything go back to normal? If he rejected magic altogether, would the woman leave him alone? Would he be able to close his eyes at night and dream of things besides the world of the lotus? The jungles and waters of the Mekong?

Would his assassin stop trying to take his life?

No, he told himself. It wouldn't. It wouldn't do any good. It'd just make things worse. Just like standing here, in the snow, shivering, while his family stayed warm and safe in their home.

He breathed out, watching his breath rise to the sky, the warmth of it tickling his nose, cooling into mist. He wiped it, then put the pouch back in his pocket. He had to go in. The snow crunched beneath his feet. He had to go in. His boots thumped against the porch. He had to go in. His fingers reached for his keys, and he fumbled with them, shaking. He had to go in. The key entered the lock. He hesitated.

He had to go in.

Finally, he unlocked the door. He pushed it open, allowing the warmth of the indoors to encase him, thawing his frozen self. The door closed behind him. He stood in the doorway, scanning the house, listening for someone to greet him. His parents' voices echoed from upstairs. Mia's door was open, but he couldn't see her from where he stood. No one came, and he didn't know if the pit in his stomach was dark acceptance, or disappointment.

He stripped himself of his winter gear. The house was warm, but his bones still shivered. He was in. He was inside.

And he needed to get out.

As quietly as he could, he tripped across the entryway, heading to his room to curl up in a ball under a million blankets and never see the light of day again. He got there. His hand touched the door knob. He hesitated.

He turned to face the living room. It was dim in there, the only light source a reading lamp next to Mia, who sat with her back to him. She must have heard him. She always heard him. His hand went to the pouch. He couldn't tell her things. He couldn't. It wasn't a good idea.

But he also didn't want her to think he was ditching her. He couldn't read her emotions, but he knew her. He knew how much he'd hurt her.

He let go of the doorknob and headed to her, putting on a smile. A good smile. If she saw him as normal, maybe she'd open up to him again. They could hang out. Be normal twins waiting for dinner with their parents. His body ached. His *soul* ached, and he wanted nothing more than to vanish into the pit that was his room.

Still, he sat on the back of the couch, next to Mia, and looked down at her. She glanced up from her book, staring at him with wide, brown eyes. That twinge of jealousy flickered in his stomach, but he pushed it down. This was not the time to think about the color of his eyes.

"Hey," he said. There was nothing from her. No emotions. No indication on how she was reacting to his presence. He didn't want to overdo it. He didn't want to sound too much like normal, otherwise she might think he didn't realize he hadn't been the best brother.

Asshole.

He smiled through the guilt. "Whatcha doing?"

She raised an eyebrow, then jerked her head toward her book.

Derek looked to the pages. It wasn't in English. It must have been a book one of their cousins, maybe an aunt or uncle, had sent her from China, since they hadn't been there in a few years. Scratch marks littered the lines, indicating hanzi she didn't know. She had some writing in the margins—also in Chinese—but it was too small for him to read from this distance.

"Oh. Right." He laughed, struggling to figure out how to handle this situation. He longed for her emotions on his skin. Anything to give an indication on how pissed she was. "Uh…I was gonna hang out in my room until dinner. You can read while I play video games or something."

She looked him up and down, almost as if considering him more than his offer. Then, after an agonizing moment, she looked back to her book and said, "No thanks."

Derek didn't know what to say. How to react. He didn't know what the emotions rushing through his body were. He'd blown her off earlier. Now she was doing the same to him. Was this payback? Was she angry? Did she just want nothing to do with him?

She didn't look at him again, and he knew better than to say anything else.

He pushed away from the couch, heading back to his room.

Exhaustion dragged his eyelids toward his cheeks. His limbs turned to lead, and he trudged to his room. Opened the door. Shuffled inside. Collapsed on the bed. Gripped his pillow. And as the weight of everything, the past few weeks, washed over him, he tried not to cry.

Chapter Fifteen

Sweat dripped from his temple. His body ached as the humidity dug deep into his bones, sucking the life out of each vertebrae running along the center of his back. And when he breathed, his lungs weren't sure if there was more water or oxygen inside each breath. The sun beat down on his black hair, burning the dark brown skin on his neck, and he reached a hand up to protect it. Damp skin met damp skin. He let out a heavy sigh.

Grass tickled his feet. Long and wild, it brushed against his skin as if inviting him to stand there forever, staring out across the murky river. At this time of day, the sun hung high in the sky, boats sailed the waters with their fisherman yelling at each other in incomprehensible slang.

On this side, the fields behind him spoke of farms and villages with superstitious people too frightened to leave their own homes during the times of heightened magic: when the moon filled the sky, when the stars streaked the heavens, when the winds brought summer home. They were his people. His family. His home. They were the ones calling out to him, begging him to join the festivities of a solidified bond of love.

But the other side…the other people…the other world.

It called to him. For twenty-three winters he'd been drawn to the edge, eager—desperate—to cross and understand where he truly came from.

Where his powers came from.

He felt her before he heard her. An energy, deep within her core, resonating with his own in a unique, distinct pattern. It grew closer as his sister said his name. Not the one she'd given him. The one his mother had given him to bring him luck and happiness. The one he'd rejected.

Still, he smiled. He smiled and turned, because no matter what happened, no matter how he longed to cross the river and escape the mundane world dancing in front of his eyes, he could not ignore the voice of his older sister when she called for his attention.

His sister stood in front of him, her handwoven and colored sarong, crafted for celebrations such as this, wrapped around her body in a way indicating her desire to meet someone. Unlike him, sweat didn't drip from her face, though there was an unmistakable sheen on her skin. Her hair, black but with a shimmer of red, was short on the sides, the top long but twisted into an intricate bun with gold flowers decorating the strands.

In another life, he would have said she was the most beautiful woman in the world. Their brothers said it. The other men in the village said it. The women agreed, though some more quietly.

She was beautiful. But he'd met the woman across the river. The woman with red eyes. The woman with skin that glowed in the moonlight and hair as dark as midnight. No one in the world could compare to her.

"Careful using that name," he said, "the spirits may come get me in the middle of the night."

His sister laughed. "You are far too old for the spirits' taste."

"That's what they want us to believe."

She came up next to him, shaking her head. "What would you rather I called you? That strange name you came running back with one day? What was it...Niran?"

"Yes," he said. "That's my name."

No, it's not.

The voice tickled the back of his mind. He closed his eyes and ignored it. It was his name. It was the only name he wanted. It was what defined him. The word that gave him meaning.

No. That's not my name. This isn't my world. I'm a student. I'm in Colorado. I am me.

The voice grew stronger. No longer a tickle. A force pounding against his mind, wanting to take over. He winced, placing a hand against his temple. Colorado? Student? He didn't...he didn't understand.

This isn't me! I don't want to be here. Wherever this is. I want to go home. Why am I having these dreams?

Dreams? These weren't dreams. They were his reality. His life. He belonged here. On the other side of the river. With his family. With those like him.

"Niran?"

He longed for the voice to belong to his sister. But it didn't. There was an accent to it. One he didn't recognize. He didn't understand. It was softer? Confused? As if coming from someone a million miles away.

A thousand years away.

He covered his face.

"Déming?"

I don't want these dreams anymore!

When he removed his hands, everything went dark. He stepped. One. Two. Three. On and on, chasing darkness in search of light. As he did, ripples spread out from his footsteps, each one bringing

206

in a new voice speaking to him. A million words crashing off one another and he continued on, running with fear trailing behind him.

Where was he?

Who was he?

Soft light blossomed in front of him. He ran toward it as the voices drifted into nothingness, and he slowed. His lungs screamed. His chest heaved. He longed for air, even air dripping with water. This wasn't right. This wasn't how it was supposed to be.

And then it was there.

A flower floating above the water.

He closed the distance, the ripples no longer calling out to him. Deafening silence bore down on him as he drew closer to the light. To the flower pulsating with life.

He reached out to touch it. The beautiful, wilting, red aster.

Let me be free.

His fingers brushed the petals. It would only take a second to give in to its demands. To set it free.

To let her be free.

Derek's eyes snapped open as he gasped for air. Energy flooded his system as electric shocks which jolted his heart into an unnatural pattern that left him paralyzed in the darkness of his room. Nothing worked right. His fingers twitched against his will. His breathing sped up, entire body warming to an uncomfortable temperature. For a brief moment, he thought he was going to die.

And then the electricity vanished. The warmth faded. His lungs expanded in desperation, and contracted, satisfied.

He lay in bed, taking in the softness of his pillow and the heavy blankets weighing him down. His hands, now weak, moved to grip the edge of the comforter and pull it up to his chin. He closed his eyes. Despite his struggles to move his body, energy still coursed through him. An energy he'd never felt before. He'd experienced weird sensations after dreams before, but this was different.

While he attempted to block the dream from his mind, something he'd failed to do more than once, it replayed before his eyes. The river. The sister. The conversation. The name. The pond. The voices. The flower.

The aster.

With a burst of energy, he threw the blankets off and scrambled for his phone. It turned on and he flinched at the glaring light. The clock, mocking him, read four AM, making him grumble. In two hours, his alarm would blare under his pillow, startling him awake. And then he'd fall asleep again until his next alarm. Which would lead him to walking with his sister who refused to speak to him. To a school that hated him.

He wasn't sure he could ever get things back to normal. Anything that could explain his actions was so out of this world that people might not even believe him. He couldn't explain that a magical queen was trying to kill him. Which meant he couldn't get the students to stop whispering about him, and he couldn't get Mia to take two seconds to listen to his apology.

What he could do, he decided as he opened his internet app, was search for the significance of asters.

Flowers were not his strong suit. He knew about lotuses, as they were a family favorite and his sister's namesake, but beyond that he was lost. The fact that he even knew the name of the flower in his dream was a miracle in itself. In his dream, it was an aster asking to be free. But why? When for as long as he'd been having these dreams, it'd been a lotus?

Didn't the lotus represent the queen?

He found a site, *The Flower Expert*, and read up on asters. Found mostly in North America, a few species lived across Europe and Asia, but nothing about Thailand. Annoyed, he tried another search, looking for where asters grew, and found the same answer. Another search, this time describing the flower: red petals with a yellow center.

Nothing.

Exhausted, frustrated, and annoyed, he chucked his phone back on the bedside stand and lay down, pulling the blankets over his head again. There was nothing online indicating any connection to his dream. Nothing to Thailand, nothing to the Mekong River, and nothing to a red-eyed queen.

It was pointless. All of this. It was pointless trying to find a meaning in a dream. They were just dreams, not memories.

It was pointless trying to find a woman he was hallucinating. She didn't exist and only connected to Blair's stories because he needed her to.

It was pointless trying to stop himself from being murdered, because who was to say someone actually was behind all the accidents that'd almost taken his life?

Maybe it was all in his head.

There was nothing weird going on. Nothing unique or special. Life just sucked.

Or, that's what he tried to tell himself as he lay there, drifting back to sleep. There was no evil plot to kill him. Nothing strange going on beyond his normal life with his empathy and magic. This Niran person meant nothing. The flowers were nothing. The woman was no one. It was all just a part of his dreams.

The denials didn't stick.

He knew it was all connected. Something was going on. He just didn't know what it was. No one seemed to know what it was. Blair and Cody struggled with Derek's increasing paranoia, and Mia pulled away from them the deeper they got into the mystery. She spent all of her time with Steven, and maybe that was for the best.

She didn't have magic.

She should have someone without magic keeping her company.

If she stayed out of this world, it would all be better. He could keep at least one flower safe.

At least, that's what he told himself as he drifted off to sleep.

Because he needed to believe it was better to lose his sister as a friend then lose her forever. He needed to protect her.

Even if it all felt wrong.

Mia stood in the doorway, letting the light from the hallway lighten the disaster Derek called his room. She leaned against the door frame, crossing her arms to watch the still lump on his bed. His blanket was half off of him, and sometime in the night he'd buried his head under his pillow. Any other day she wouldn't care about having to wake him up. He never slept well. He often turned off his alarm without realizing it. She was used to this.

But today she didn't want to. She wanted to let him lie there asleep and learn the consequences of not going to bed on time.

And if it had been up to her, she would have.

Her parents' voices rose up from the kitchen. She tilted her head a bit to try and listen to their conversation, but it was too muted for her to make out more than a few words here and there. They'd sent her to get him up. They were the reason she was once again helping her brother get to school on time.

With a sigh, she headed into his room, stepping around the mess on the floor. She stopped next to Derek's bed, arms still crossed, face scrunched up in a mixture of annoyance and disgust.

"Derek," she said. The first word she'd said to him in days.

He didn't move.

"Derek!"

Still nothing.

Groaning, she grabbed the pillow from atop his head and yanked it off. He jumped, pushing himself up while somehow managing to roll over at the same time. His eyes were mostly closed, hand over his face as he adjusted to the waking world.

"Wha?" He rubbed the heel of his hand into his eyes, as if that would help them open.

In the past, Mia would lecture him. She'd tell him this was exactly why he needed to go to bed earlier, set more than one alarm, and actually wake up with them. In the past he'd snap back at her that he tried to do all those things and it wasn't working. They'd bicker as he got out of bed and then he'd gently shove her out of the room so he could get dressed and she'd go see if their mom or dad—whoever was home that week—needed help with breakfast.

Instead, she said, "It's seven."

Derek blinked rapidly, glancing around the room. He rubbed his eyes again. "What?"

She sighed. At least it was a full word this time. "It's seven."

It took him a moment. It always took him a moment. Then he grabbed his phone from next to his bed and looked at it. She waited. He stared at the screen. She waited a moment longer. His eyes widened.

"Shit!"

Mia stepped out of the way as he scrambled out of bed, nearly falling flat on his face in the process.

A lecture almost left her lips. She wanted to chastise him. Ask him what was wrong with him that he couldn't get up by himself. It was habit. Their routine. Instead, as she watched him stumble around his room, searching for clothes, she pondered the question by herself. He relied on her. She cooked for him. Helped him get up for school. She always had. He knew how to cook. He knew how to take care of himself. But he didn't.

Instead, he disappeared after school. He came home late. Went to bed late. Spent time with her friends and pushed her out of the picture.

The bracelet on her wrist weighed her hand down. She wondered why she even wore it anymore. She'd barely spoken to Blair outside of lunch in a week, and even then, their conversations were less than warm. Just two girls going through the motions.

"I'm leaving in fifteen," she said.

He didn't acknowledge her. She turned and left the room, closing the door behind her. They were too old for this. It shouldn't be her responsibility to take care of her twin brother. At what point in their life did he start taking care of himself? At what point did she stop giving without anything in return?

"They think Derek might have to redo the year?"

Mia stopped in her tracks right outside the kitchen. Behind the wall, her parents couldn't see her, but she could hear them.

"Yes." Mia's father's voice was dark with disappointment. Or maybe...it was concern? "His school counselor wants a meeting with us to discuss his missing assignments and his failed tests. Teachers have commented that he doesn't pay attention in class and they're uneasy."

Her mother sighed. Mia pictured her pacing back and forth in the kitchen, rubbing her hands together. "What can we do? We're about the leave the country. Again. We're leaving them alone. I could call my sister and have her come stay with them. Maybe some time close to family will be good for Derek."

"I thought your sister was in the middle of a...what did she call it? 'Intense medical trial'?"

"She would come if I asked."

"Derek would know she'd want to be back at her work. He's

always been hyper sensitive to people's moods."

"But–"

"Intira, my dear," her dad said. Mia flinched at the sound of the chair scraping on the floor and moved further from the kitchen. "As much as it pains me to say, I'm not sure there's anything we can do right now. All of this is bad timing. I can try again to explain to the Thai government that we have a family situation, but they insist that it can wait. We'll go to Thailand and be back as soon as we can. After that, we won't have to leave again. The exhibit is open and will go on tour without us. I'm taking a long needed sabbatical, and you can work from home if you please. This summer we will take a trip to Beijing. My parents would love to see their grandchildren."

"I just want him to do well. To be happy again."

"I know."

Mia clenched her fists, staring at the ground. Something akin to guilt picked at her stomach. It reminded her that as frustrated as she was with Derek, something was going on with him. Ever since the opening, ever since he'd fallen ill, he'd been acting weird. This was sudden. It wasn't years of dealing with him being an awful brother. And would it really take that much? Would it take that much for her to suck up her pride and help him until her parents got back from Thailand? She could get him up for school. Sit with him while he did homework. Make sure he went to bed.

This isn't your job.

It wasn't. It wasn't her job, and even if she tried, would he accept it? She'd offered to study with him recently. All of them. They'd brushed her off. They hadn't wanted her around, but Steven did. And Steven needed her help too.

It wasn't her job to mother her brother.

Her fists unclenched and she held her head high, entering the kitchen. Her parents stood close, her father's arms wrapped around her mother with her head on his shoulder. Mia hesitated for a moment, unsure how to react to the sudden show of intimacy, before she cleared her throat. They moved away from each other as if nothing had happened.

"He's awake," Mia said.

"Oh good," Mia's mother said. She sat back at the table, picking up her glasses to read her papers.

"He should be out soon," Mia said.

Sure enough, not even two minutes later Derek stumbled into the kitchen, tripping over himself to his seat where his breakfast waited.

"Sorry," he said. "Alarm. Overslept. Didn't sleep well."

He glanced up at Mia, and the two stared at each other. His face dropped, pain overtaking his expression. She knew that look. He had it when he wanted to say something important. Often an apology.

Her frustration softened.

Until she remembered the lies.

She turned away. Her parents went about their morning, and she went to get ready for school.

They were too old for stupid lies.

Derek leaned his head against the cool locker, begging his eyes to stay open. Students moved behind him, chatting, ignoring his existence. As the days passed, the negative emotions toward him had faded, though now and then they still clawed at his skin, leaving ugly scars on his soul. He wanted to ignore them. To pretend like nothing had happened, or was happening, but he couldn't.

He wasn't sleeping. He was failing classes. His dreams plagued him any time his mind wandered away from the blackboard, which was more often than he wanted to admit.

It didn't matter how much he tried to forget. He couldn't erase them from his mind. The words. The names. The humidity. The river. The flower.

No, the flowers.

He wanted to do research. Needed to. That's what his family did when they didn't understand something. They read scholarly articles and wrote papers. All of his life, he'd been told if he just looked hard enough he would find an answer to anything.

So why the hell couldn't he find an answer to this?

It didn't matter how hard he tried. There were no scholarly articles on magic. He couldn't walk into the dumb little bookstore hidden back behind the coffee shop in downtown and ask for a book on dreams that are actually memories but might actually be dreams that held all the answers, and none at all. The internet was no help either. He'd spent hours trying to search for the meaning of flowers. Looking up the name, "Niran." Trying to at least pinpoint where in history his dreams took place. The clothes, the food, the dances, the music, the boats, the language…anything.

He wanted to spend every waking moment trying to glean something from the world living in his dreams. He needed to understand. To know what it all meant.

But there was nothing. And now he was failing classes. Now his friends, save for the other two with magic, avoided him. Now his parents tiptoed around him as if waiting for him to snap.

Now his sister wouldn't look him in the eye.

She wouldn't speak to him. She avoided being in the same room as him. Even in the classes they shared, she didn't acknowledge his existence. He was too scared to try and text her. And the sad thing was, he didn't know if he was more scared of her ignoring him, or of his teachers catching him texting and making everything that much worse.

The bell rang, and he realized his eyes had slipped closed. They snapped open as the rest of the school flooded out of classrooms, chattering echoing around the halls. A shudder passed through him at the onslaught of emotions. They weren't overwhelmingly negative. The excitement of lunch burned his skin, sucking all of his energy.

He groaned.

"You look like you're about to puke."

Blair's voice cut through it all. He twisted his head, forehead still pressed against the cool metal of his locker. For the first time in a while, he didn't need to feel her emotions to know the look etched onto her face. Furrowed brows. Narrowed eyes. Downturned lips.

Worry.

She was worried.

Yet another person to add to that list.

"Hey," Derek said.

"*Are* you going to puke?" Blair asked. She crossed her arms.

"No."

"You sure?"

"Blair." He meant to snap at her, but found no energy to do so.

She rolled her eyes. "Okay fine. But if you need to, there's a bathroom down the hall."

Derek stood up straight, glaring. She didn't flinch.

"That's not funny," he said.

"I know it's not," she said. "But you seriously look sick and I'm worried. I think your obsession is taking a toll on you. So…I dunno. Maybe laugh a little. It's good for your mood to laugh sometimes."

"I'll laugh when I stop having these dreams."

Blair didn't respond to that at first. The bell indicating the start of lunch rang above them, but neither of them moved. Finally, once the hallways were a bit more clear, Blair asked, "Do you remember them?"

Derek could only shrug. The short answer was yes. The long

answer was no. The longer answer was maybe-kinda-sorta-yes-but also-no. Since they were standing in the hallway of their high school with a time limit on their ability to eat lunch, Derek decided he didn't want to get into it.

Blair must have sensed this, because she dropped the subject. "Come on. We should get to lunch. I think Cody's waiting for us. Maybe Mia too, but god knows what's going through her head."

"Okay," he said. He adjusted his backpack, wanting nothing more than to drop it and pretend like it didn't exist. He didn't need it weighing him down. "We should meet up after school again. I think we're getting closer. We just need to…."

He trailed off when he realized she was staring at the ground. With no one else in the hall, his skin was clear of emotions. For the past week, he'd relished this feeling, but right now he hated it. He hated it because he couldn't read the people he actually wanted to read. Screw everyone else. He wanted to know what Blair was feeling. He wanted to be able to check in on Mia throughout the day, making sure her anxiety didn't get out of hand. He even missed Cody's emotional shift when he spoke to Mia, and when she laughed with him.

His skin was lonely, and he hated it.

"You don't think we should go?" Derek asked when she said nothing.

Blair shrugged. "I…I don't know, okay? I think that you're obsessing, but you're also not sleeping, and school is kicking your ass right now. Maybe we should just take a few days to regroup. We can get some homework done, spend time with Mia, you can take a freaking nap…."

"Someone is trying to kill me," Derek snapped. "Don't you get that? I can't just sit and do my homework. I can't try and make Mia feel included right now. I don't have the time or focus. I need to figure out what these dreams mean and why this queen keeps showing up everywhere."

"Derek–"

"None of this," he said, gesturing around him, "will matter if I'm dead."

Blair shook her head. "At the rate you're going, it's not some supernatural being that's going to get you killed."

Anger flared in Derek's chest. "I'm not asking for a lecture."

"You didn't have to ask," Blair snapped back. "You're being an idiot, Derek."

"I'm trying to survive."

"Survive what? There were a few accidents in a row, and then nothing. Maybe they gave up. Maybe they really were just accidents. Maybe no one is trying to kill you. Did you even think of that?"

"They are, we just don't know how yet!"

Blair groaned. "Oh my god, Derek. *Listen to yourself.*"

Derek hesitated. He and Blair had their moments. Their sarcastic back and forths, her irritated quips at his actions that made him laugh. But she'd never spoken to him like this before. Not with the same tone she used with Cody.

"You aren't sleeping. People talk about you like you should be in a nuthouse. All you can think about is this. When was the last time you talked to your parents? Did your homework? Spoke to Mia?" Blair snorted. "You said that none of this will matter if you're dead, but if you're alive and alone, how is that any better?"

Still, he said nothing. Blair was supposed to be on his side. She was supposed to help him understand what was going on. Magic was her world. All of her brothers had it. Her mom. Her mom's family. She grew up in a house where it wasn't weird to be able to create fire with a flick of the wrist, or lift things from across the room without a thought.

She was supposed to be on his side.

When he stayed silent, Blair groaned.

"Whatever. I'm hungry. Come on. Let's go eat."

She took off, not waiting for him, but expecting him to follow. He thought for a moment.

A brief moment.

He thought about what she said. People hated him. People wanted nothing to do with him at school. No one in the entire town believed that he was a victim here. He was an outcast. He'd gone from relatively popular and a good student to…not that. His parents had given up on him. His teachers were waiting for him to fail.

So what was the point? What was the point of trying to do well and get people to like him? Blair said that being alive and alone was just as bad as being dead, but he was already alone. No one understood what he was going through. They didn't have a supernatural queen trying to off them.

He watched Blair for a second as she walked down the hallway, and then he dropped his backpack to the ground. It landed with a thump. Blair didn't turn around.

But Derek did. He turned his back on her.

There was no point in being here.

No one wanted him here.

Before he could talk himself out of it, he headed down the hallway, down the stairs, picking up speed with each step, and exited the building.

Blair wouldn't help him find the secrets hiding in the mountains. So he would have to do it on his own.

Mia stared at the half filled page of lined paper. The words blurred in and out of focus, as did her attention span. She wanted to do her homework. She really did. Her teachers were really laying on the work as they got ready for the last bit of the semester. She had a paper due in history, four problems for calculus, and some reading for English. All due by Friday. She knew, she really did know, that if she got it done now, she wouldn't have to worry about it at home.

In an ideal world, she would do all of this at Steven's house, but he was behind in some of his classes and needed help. It was easier for her to do her homework before they met up.

She closed her eyes, wanting to stop the growing headache. The noises of the library, however quiet, slipped in and out of her ears, rattling her brain. She placed her face in her hands, breathing in and out. It was always quieter in Mr. Becker's office, where she usually spent this period. Instead of a dozen whispering teenagers, a heater that seemed to enjoy rattling at the worst times, and the thumping of books at the front desk, all Mia had to deal with was his quick fingers tapping at his keyboard.

Her eyes landed on the paper again. The words blurred and she groaned, throwing her pen on the table and leaning back in the uncomfortable wooden chair. Her eyes scanned the room. From her position in the back corner, she had a view of the entire library. The computers on the far side. The librarian's desk in the middle. The reference books clumped together, looking unloved as always. And then the fiction books. Standing tall. Heavy. In front of a large window.

That was it. The bookcase Derek had pushed over.

Mia tried to imagine Derek actually pushing over a bookcase. She didn't want to believe it. Even now, she wasn't convinced that's what had happened. Derek. Her pacifist, vegetarian, couldn't-lift-a-twenty-pound-weight brother. But he had. People had seen it.

Unless all of them had seen the wrong thing.

She tore her eyes away from the bookcase. Derek was the last person she wanted to think about. She was so tired of dealing with him and his inability to get his life together. Her own situation was

a mess, and it was time for him to grow up and start taking care of himself.

As she scanned the library again, attempting to build up the energy to work on her essay, her eyes landed on someone she wasn't expecting to see: Cody.

He glanced around the room until she came into his sight. They locked eyes, and she tensed. He must have too.

They hadn't spoken in a while. Not since he'd insulted her in that awful lie. Mia had wanted to talk to him about it when they were alone, but time had passed, and Steven had become more important in her life. Besides, whenever it seemed they would have a moment, Blair or Derek would show up. Or, sometimes, he'd disappear to hang out with them. Always with some kind of excuse.

Cody shifted. She knew that shift. When he put his hands in his pockets and looked down at the ground, putting pressure on the opposite foot. Cody was always uncomfortable, but this was something else. This was what he did when he felt incapable of handling a situation.

Mia hated seeing him this way.

So, when he looked at her one last time, turning to leave, she waved him over.

At first he didn't move, obviously confused. She rolled her eyes and waved again. He hesitated, but in seconds his feet moved, bringing him across the room to her table. Neither of them spoke at first. She sat in her uncomfortable chair, watching him, and he slowly sank into the chair across from her, keeping his eyes on the table.

"Hi," she said.

He looked up. "Hi."

"Don't you have class?"

His hands were under the table, and she knew he was rubbing them together. It'd been years since Cody had been so nervous around her. She didn't like it. She didn't like any of this. Avoiding Blair. Ignoring her brother. Not speaking to Cody to the point where he was reverted back to his ten-year-old self hiding in a different place every day at recess because all of the kids were mean to him.

"I…we had a test."

"Oh." She glanced at the clock on the wall. Thirty minutes. Longer than normal for him to finish.

"I thought you TA'd for Mr. Becker this period," Cody said in a low voice.

Mia shrugged. "He has a sub. She had nothing for me to do and I didn't want to sit alone with her."

"Oh."

"Yeah."

A moment of silence fell over them. Mia didn't know what else to say. Cody still had his backpack on as if ready to flee at any moment. Mia wasn't sure if she wanted to tell him to take it off or not.

"So–"

"I'm sorry," Cody said before she could get another word out. He still wouldn't look at her.

Mia blinked. "What?"

"For…for lying to you. For saying those things. I didn't mean any of it."

She didn't know how to respond. She hadn't expected an apology. Or maybe she had. Cody didn't like upsetting people. Out of all of them, he was always the first to apologize for anything that went wrong.

Mia grabbed her pencil, needing something to play with. "Why did you say it then?"

"I–" He looked up finally. "It's hard to explain."

She expected to feel irritation. Annoyance. Anger. Something negative in reaction to his dismissive statement. But she didn't.

Because it was nice, sitting here with her best friend.

Maybe it would have been better to press. To get out of him what was going on.

She didn't want that fight.

"Okay," she said.

He finally relaxed, though just a smidge. "Okay?"

"Okay. Thank you for apologizing. It means a lot."

"Oh. Okay."

Mia had to smile at the confused expression on his face. She didn't blame him for having it. She was confused too.

Taking a deep breath, she gestured at her essay. "Turns out I really hate learning about the Revolutionary War."

Cody raised an eyebrow. "Just that one war in particular?"

"Yes. No. Kind of. How many times are we going to go over the same stuff? You have 200 years of history. It doesn't need three separate years to teach it."

"I guess someone somewhere really wants us to learn about all the bad things we've done."

"The US does not teach all the bad things you've done."

"No country teaches all the bad things they've done."

"Okay, true."

Mia laughed and Cody cracked a smile. It'd been so long since she'd laughed. And as the conversation went on, jumping from topic to topic like always, Mia found herself wanting to stay here forever. Just her and Cody joking and laughing, acting like their worlds weren't falling apart in different ways.

Like always.

When the bell rang, disappointment flooded Mia's system. Her homework lay unfinished, forgotten among the conversations about teachers, politics, and the most delicious fruit.

"Guess I should go to class," Mia said. She stood, gathering her papers. Cody didn't move. He had eighth period off, just like Derek and Blair. They would be arriving soon to keep him company, even though it wouldn't take much at all for all three of them to go home.

The three of them would sit. They would talk.

And she would be left out.

"Do you want to meet up when you get out of practice?" Cody asked, startling her out of her thoughts.

"Huh?"

Cody shrugged. "I dunno. I've missed hanging out with you. I thought we could go downtown for a bit. There's nothing to do, and it's cold, but it could be fun."

She almost said yes. The words almost left her lips until she remembered. Her heart sunk.

"I have plans."

Cody frowned.

"With Steven." Mia clenched her backpack. This was ridiculous. Steven was her friend. There was no reason to feel guilty. "Why don't you come with? He needs help with school work and you're better at teaching than I am."

She didn't need to hear his response to know what it was. She didn't even need to see his face fall, eye contact gone, with his hands back together. Before she even asked, she knew that he would say no. Because it was Cody, and Cody didn't talk to new people.

"Okay," she said before he had to turn her down. "I'll uh...I'll see you later then."

He nodded. "Have a good practice."

"Thanks."

She didn't want to leave, but her class called. She walked around the table, past Cody, heart tight. It was right there. Her normalcy. He sat at the table behind her, waiting for the rest of her normal life.

She couldn't be there. She had class. Practice after school.

A knife in her underwear drawer.

Her head pounded. She'd pushed the knife out of her mind, but it was back. Prominent. Wrapped around her thoughts like a piece of saran wrap.

Cody was her normal.

But she couldn't go back to normal, and only Steven understood why.

Chapter Sixteen

Derek didn't care that his cheeks were numb. The bitter cold picked at them like an emotion of its own, but he didn't move from the wire seat placed outside the coffee shop on Main. To be perfectly honest, he wasn't sure that he *could* move. Like the skin on his face, his legs were cold, his jeans clinging to the metal beneath him. But even if he could separate his clothes from the metal, his body had turned to lead after three hours of wandering. The coffee he'd purchased to warm him up sat untouched on the table. Steam rose from the mouth of the lid, almost freezing in the insufferable cold.

Most people wouldn't be outside. As he sat there, watching the normally busy downtown, he wondered if he should go inside. If his parents knew where he was, or what he'd been doing since he ditched school, they would not approve. His mom would fuss that he would catch a cold. His dad would lecture him about going into the woods alone. They'd both be enraged that he'd skipped school in the first place.

But they would never know that he'd spent the past three hours looking, once again, for something that he wasn't even sure existed. They would never know that he'd only come back to town because he'd started to shake from hunger. Or maybe it was the cold. He hadn't been able to tell.

He'd planned to come back to get something to eat and drink and then go back out. But sitting there, frozen to the chair, he wasn't sure it was worth it.

During the warmer months, he and his friends would sit at this same table and people watch. Blair and Mia talked the most. They liked picking people out of the crowd and making up stories about them and their lives. Derek usually made fun of their stories. Cody always sat quietly, his emotions fluctuating between happy and anxious, particularly when a large group of people walked past. There was laughter. Jokes. Mia and Derek arguing in Chinese, with Blair telling them to stop because she couldn't understand. Cody and Derek trying the "tea of the week" every Monday.

They weren't there. His friends. Mia was at basketball practice. Cody either had work or was home. Blair was most likely arguing with her mom about having to babysit her little brother. He hadn't heard from her since she'd told him to come to lunch. That wasn't a great sign, but Derek had no energy to care.

He barely had the mental space to think about them. His thoughts were an entity in themselves: a scramble of voices all vying for attention he didn't want to parcel out. Some of the voices repeated the same things he'd been telling himself over and over. They said he wasn't safe. He needed to figure everything out before the queen killed him. Others said it wasn't the queen. He was missing something. A clue. A piece of a blank puzzle. Others still, and these had become more prominent in the past three hours, screamed that he needed to stop.

"You said that none of this will matter if you're dead, but if you're alive and alone, how is that any better?"

Derek hated how those words echoed in his mind. He wanted them to disappear so he could go back to fixing his problem. The dreams. The accidents. Blair's story. The sculpture breaking. They were all connected and if he just pushed hard enough, if he did more research, searched more, the reason why would reveal itself and maybe then he could get some sleep.

But, like Blair said, would it matter if he'd destroyed his life? If he'd failed out of school, made his parents distrust him…pushed his sister away?

I could tell her. I could tell her everything and it would be okay. We could keep her safe.

He'd wanted to tell her that first night after the sculpture broke. If he had, would things be different now?

His stomach turned, possibly from the terrible muffin he'd broken down and bought, possibly from anxiety. Or maybe it was guilt. Everything was so mixed up in his head and he couldn't tell the difference anymore. Clenching his fists, he observed the few people daring to be outside in this weather. He reached for their emotions, desperate to feel something that wasn't negative. A tickle of excitement. A brush of joy. *Anything* to take away the thick oil coating his skin.

But he didn't feel anything light. Nothing warm. Nothing feathery and beautiful.

His eyes scanned the small crowd of people. People he knew. People he recognized. People who wondered why he was sitting there alone.

And then it slammed him. A feeling. A texture. Something he'd never experienced before. It gripped his skin, nails digging in painlessly before flowing through his veins into his heart. His breath caught in his throat, and he reached up to touch his neck. As if that would help. The hair on his arms stood up, even beneath the clothes he had layered on, accompanied by a million goosebumps.

This.

This wasn't.

An emotion.

It was dark. Cold. Empty. Sad.

Alone. So very alone.

And then, almost as soon as it'd over taken him, it was gone. Warmth returned to every inch of his body, freeing his lungs from their prison. He gasped, leaning over with one arm slamming down on the table, the other clutching at his winter coat.

What the…?

There was no explaining how. There was no explaining why. But in a fraction of a second, as his senses released into normality, he understood what had taken over him. Why it'd been so different. Why it burrowed into his soul. He hadn't felt her emotions. He hadn't felt her sadness or her loneliness. This was different. It was something more. Deeper. Somehow, for some reason, he'd connected with her.

He'd connected with the queen's magic.

He stood. His legs burned with both exhaustion and energy. His heart raced. His eyes darted. Searching. Searching for the woman who had caused all of this misery in his life. The rest of the world didn't matter. Just her. Her and her sadness. Her and her loneliness. Her and the emptiness he wanted to fix.

No.

He shook those thoughts out of his head before searching again. What did she want with him? Why, after all these years of never being able to sense magic, had he been able to sense hers?

He searched. Searched and searched, glued to the spot, desperate to find her here and now. But as he searched, and as the feeling faded into nothing, he realized she wasn't there. No woman standing alone. No woman with black hair and red eyes. No barefoot woman in a black dress.

He'd felt her.

But then she'd vanished.

And he was left alone, standing in the cold on a street in a town where no one noticed the magical world living in their houses, lingering in the streets, and hiding beneath the surface of the earth. People, normal, average, emotion feeling people hurried down the sidewalks on both sides of the street. Not many. But enough. Annoyance from the cold tickled his arms and he shook them, wishing—not for the first time—that his power would go away so he could focus.

The tickle grew stronger, though, and he groaned in frustration, grabbing the coffee before chugging as much of the bitter, lukewarm liquid as he could in one breath. This was pointless. He wasn't going to find anything. He was just going insane.

Once he was done, he shook his head and tossed the cup in the snow covered trash bin nearby. He shoved his hands in his pockets and headed down the sidewalk. Away from the edge of town and toward home. This was it, he'd decided. He was done. No more searching. No more pushing people away. He needed to focus on his real life, not the one in his dreams. Not the elusive woman he kept seeing. Feeling. Wishing to meet.

In his mind, he thought of everything he needed to do. Take a nap. Do his homework—which he realized would prove difficult since he'd left his backpack in the middle of the hallway at school. Nap. Apologize to his parents. Nap. Send Blair a text. Nap. Try to convince the school not to kick him out. Nap.

Tell Mia everything.

As the thought danced through his mind, screaming at him to do it now, a shudder ran through his shoulders, his arms, and his back. The shudder slipped through his body, tingling with electricity until it pricked at his heart. He stopped. Eyes wide. Blood pounding in his ears.

No. No. Stop. Stop this isn't. It's not magic. It's just your imagination. Go home. Go home.

Go home.

He turned his head, eyes scanning the scattered people wandering in and out of shops across the street. Time slowed. Snow drifted from the sky as if it were in a movie playing at half speed. The only thing, person, moving normally was a woman he'd never seen before.

Her hair was long, reaching halfway down her back as her bleached blond waves bounced with each of her purposeful steps. She wore shorts. A long sweater nearly covered them. Tights led down to a pair of heeled, leather boots, like the kind Mia wanted but could never convince their parents to get her. She seemed to float through the people, never moving out of anyone's way, yet never bumping into the slow moving bodies. She was something different. From a foreign world. Separate from the background she walked in front of.

Derek watched her. She didn't hesitate. The fear of black ice with those shoes didn't even seem to cross her mind as she headed toward the end of downtown. Her arms were loose by her side, swinging as if the cold temperatures didn't faze her.

And as he watched her, something pricked at the back of his mind. Something he hadn't thought about. An image out of the corner of his eye. A memory to disappear into his subconscious, only to rear its ugly head in his deepest nightmares. This woman… he had seen her before. He'd seen her many times before.

Out his window when he'd been sick.

Down the street when the car almost hit him.

In the library the day the shelf fell.

Every moment he'd felt unsafe. Every time a gust of wind chilled him to his bones. Whenever he'd woken up from a dream. She was there. Out the window. In the background. Hiding just out of sight.

Go home, part of him said. *Go home and talk to Mia.*

And he wanted to listen. But the woman was still there, disappearing down the street, and his body tingled with the electricity of her magic. It was something. An answer.

His feet took him across the street. A car honked at him but he ignored it and cut through the people as time returned to normal speed. Annoyance lanced at his skin when he almost bumped into a few citizens. One or two recognized him and called him by name, telling him to be careful. He ignored them. All of them. His legs screamed at him to stop. His lungs hated the cold as he ran after her. He needed to catch up and ask a million and ten questions about what was going on.

He was going to get some answers.

Even if his pathetically out of shape body wanted nothing more than to collapse in his bed and sleep until dawn. This was his chance to understand.

He chased her through town. No matter how fast he ran, she always seemed to be a few steps ahead of him, and he wanted to scream. He would have screamed if he could catch his breath for a moment. Instead he stayed focused, following her down the road and out of town. Back into the woods.

Once they were on the edge of the forest, her in the trees, him out, she stopped. He stopped. She turned. Arms behind her back, facing him. His chest heaved, lungs screaming. No words were exchanged. The two of them stood there as time passed. Maybe a moment. Maybe an hour. Derek couldn't tell before she lifted one hand, twisting toward the forest.

She gestured for him to follow.

She took off into the woods.

Even though the wind told him to go home, he didn't. He followed her, snow crunching under his feet, into the woods so he could finally get some answers.

And then maybe he could sleep.

Mia stared up at Steven's house, shivering. The sky above her dimmed as the beginnings of twilight cast a shadow across the town; a stark reminder that she couldn't stay long. As the days drew nearer to winter, it would become more dangerous to be out at night, when the temperatures dropped and darkness masked the black ice.

The clock was ticking. His house loomed above her, paint peeling, roof slathered with half melted snow. Warm light flickered in the windows, inviting her inside, but she found herself rooted to the spot as if she didn't want to enter. She did. Steven knew her situation. He didn't push her away. He didn't think she was crazy. He understood.

But it was more than that. Mia liked spending time with Steven. Someone who didn't belong in this world and struggled to fit in sometimes. Steven, whose parents she'd never met because they were always out working or on trips to Denver. Breckenridge. Anywhere they didn't want to take him. He had a smile on his face when he spoke of them, but she sensed his sadness.

She couldn't imagine what it was like for him. An only child. At least she'd had Derek. Someone to talk to. Someone to lie on the floor with and stare at the ceiling when they were home alone in the evenings, ranting about anything that came to mind.

Steven didn't have that. Yet they'd had so much in common.

So it didn't make sense why she stood outside, staring up at his house, hands in her pockets, feet planted firmly on the ground with no intention of walking up the front porch and ringing the doorbell. Whenever she tried to move, she thought about another lonely boy she'd connected with. She thought of the first time Cody had spoken to her when they were ten. She had hidden under the slide on the playground. He'd appeared. They'd stared at each other, both terrified.

"Um this…is my…spot."

"Oh…sorry."

"It's okay."

"I-I'll go."

"Oh. Um…we…um…we can hide together?"

"…okay."

Her hand, shoved firmly in her pocket, gripped her phone, ready to pull it out and call him. Tell him to meet her downtown and get some coffee together, like he'd asked her to. She'd thought about it all during practice. Coach Smith kept pushing her to work harder. Focus more.

But she couldn't focus on anything but the fact that she had no idea what her life was anymore.

She wanted to ring Steven's doorbell.

She wanted to call Cody.

She wanted to go home and somehow shatter the knife so her life could get back to the way it was before this nightmare began.

Instead she stood there, feet encased in invisible ice, fingers tense around her phone, and tried to get her mind to make a decision.

When the door opened.

Mia blinked, hand releasing her phone. Steven appeared, at first shadowed from the hall light behind him, but gaining features when he leaned against the door frame with crossed arms and a smile.

Mia stared at him, heart pounding with indecision. There was nothing she could do, or say, to explain why she'd been standing outside his house for who knows how long. All thoughts of leaving trickled out of her mind, clinging to the edges with sharp claws before falling into nothingness. Her heart calmed. Her phone weighed in her pocket.

"There a reason you're standing out in the cold?" Steven asked with a light laugh. Mia didn't answer, and he tilted his head. "Come on. I'll make some tea and you can thaw."

Mia's legs, still lead, moved, shattering the invisible ice chaining her to the ground. With each step, the weights around her ankles lightened, becoming nothing but feathers reminding her that they existed. By the time she got to the door, her shoulders had relaxed.

Steven let her in. The door closed behind her, locking out the cold and allowing the warmth of the house to bathe her in comfort.

"How was practice?" Steven asked while she took off her coat and boots.

She shrugged.

"Are you guys ready for the championship game?"

Again, she shrugged.

Steven hesitated for a moment before asking, "Do you think it'll be a fun game?"

Once more, she shrugged and stepped into the house, grabbing a pair of slippers. She waited silently, while Steven watched her with crossed arms and a raised brow. After a moment, Mia's backpack laying on the ground next to her feet, Steven ran a hand through his hair.

"Are you okay?"

She shrugged again but this time he reached out and put his hands on her shoulders, pressing down so she couldn't move them.

"No more shrugging," he said with a heavy sigh. "You normally talk more than this. Did something happen?"

He kept his hands on her shoulders, pressing down, and she didn't fight it. She breathed in deeply, letting it out with a silent, slow, countdown.

"I'm okay," she said. "Just not in the mood to talk."

"Long day?"

She thought of Derek's empty chair in class. About her conversation with Cody. About practice. "Yeah."

"Do you want to just head home?" His question was a lifeline.

Her phone beckoned for her to call Cody. They could sit in her room like they used to, talking about stupid stuff. She could rant to him about Derek and Blair and the growing relationship that they failed miserably to hide from everyone around them. She'd tell him how left out she'd been feeling because of it. How she felt like he was choosing their side. And he'd explain everything. He'd make it better.

But she and Steven made eye contact. His blue eyes were shadowed with concern. Their color, almost unnatural, drew her in. It reminded her of the world she'd somehow found herself a part of. The glowing blue letters on the wall of the cave. The blue on the knife. A lingering color on the edges of her dreams.

Steven had answers.

She smiled. "No. I'll stay for a while. Might finally get you caught up in calculus."

His face brightened. He removed his hands from her shoulders and stuck them in his pockets. Mia's heart leapt into her throat at his smile. He was cute when he got excited.

"Okay," he said, "I'll boil some water for tea. You like black, right?"

"Yeah."

He turned and almost bounded into the house while Mia followed, dragging her backpack along with her. It scraped against the floor, the sound of cloth against wood echoing in the hallway. A cold wind tickled the back of Mia's neck, brushing her hair to the side, and a shudder ran up her spine.

She spun, dropping her backpack. For a moment—a brief second—her eyes caught darkness. But when they adjusted to the new scenery, all she found was a lit hallway leading to the other side of the house. The cold vanished and Mia ran a hand across the back of her neck.

Shaking her head, Mia grabbed her backpack again and hurried away from the front door. When she entered the kitchen, she found Steven filling an electric kettle with water from the sink, two mugs on the counter next to him. She placed her things down and sat at the table, staring around. Like always, the house was barren of anything indicating someone lived here. No photos. No wall hangings or magnets on the fridge. Just wooden walls and older appliances in a dimly lit room.

Mia had only ever been in the kitchen. She'd only seen the living room. The rest of the house was a mystery to her.

As the water boiled, Steven came back to the table, humming something. She watched him open his calculus book and sit across from her, his normal seat, reading over the words with a scrunched brow.

Steven was easy to read. His emotions lived on his face. Mia never had to guess what he was thinking and it was refreshing. Not like Blair, who was always sarcastic. Mia could never tell what she was feeling underneath her shell of false confidence. And Cody was subtle. Quiet. It'd taken her a long time to figure out his tells, and even then she sometimes had to second guess herself because she just didn't know. And Derek…at one point in her life, she thought she knew him better than anyone in the world. He was her twin.

Right now it was like he'd become someone else.

But Steven was easy to read. No lies. No secrets.

The water boiled, and Mia stood.

Steven jumped. "Mia?"

A million thoughts raced through her mind. Questions. Confusion. He'd been honest with her. He'd told her things about magic, bringing her closer to answers about everything. But she didn't know enough. She didn't have the information she needed to come to a decision on what to do about it.

"I want to know more about magic," she said, staring down at him. He stared up at her with wide eyes. The unnatural, blue, eyes.

"Magic?"

The kettle popped, but neither of them moved to pour the water.

"Yeah," she said. "I've had time to think and I want to know more. I want to *see* more."

"See?"

Mia rolled her eyes. Steven was book smart, but apparently slow to catch on. "Yes. See. I...I want to see more magic."

Steven said nothing at first. He sat there, hands still on his textbook, staring at her with a confused expression. Then, after a moment, he looked away, staring around the house with his teeth worrying his bottom lip. His hands bunched into fists and he shoved them under the table.

"I-I mean...I can." He returned his gaze to her. Her stomach turned with excited nerves. When he stood, she breathed in. "Not here, though. I kinda took a risk showing you anything in here last time."

He stepped away from the table, walked around it, toward her, and held out a hand. He wouldn't look at her, and his hand shook the slightest. He was nervous, and she didn't know exactly what the reason was. The magic? Her? Where was he taking her? Heart pounding, she slipped her hand in his, electric tingles going up her arm, and allowed him to lead her out of the kitchen.

Back toward the door.

Back toward the mysterious hallway.

He led her to the other side of the house. Just like the kitchen, no pictures lined the walls. It was as if no one lived here, and Mia wondered if all of Steven's homes looked like this. If they never fully unpacked. Maybe it was to keep them safe. No photos meant no one could learn their secret.

She'd learned their secret.

Eventually, Steven led her to another room. It was at the back of the house. Other doors — rooms — stood closed. Mia wanted to open them, to explore, but Steven opened the one in front of them instead. She followed him into a dark room, and he shut the door behind them. It clicked, almost as if locking, and the two of them stood there for a moment, in the dark. Mia examined the dark bedroom, barely making out blobs of furniture, but she was aware that Steven was watching her.

She faced him.

"Is this your room?" she asked.

"Yeah," he said, voice quiet.

"Oh." She was suddenly nervous. The only boy's room she'd ever been in was Derek's, and that was very much not the same thing.

Mom and Dad are going to kill me.

Steven let go of her hand, heading further into the room. She stayed where she was until he stopped and turned on a lamp next to his bed.

Mia took in the details of his room, wondering how much she could learn about him. His bed was a mess, much like Derek's always was, but across from it was a bookcase filled with so many books, he had them stacked in front of each other. That was different. She stepped into the room, making sure not to walk on anything, and headed to the bookcase to examine what he had on there.

There were books of all kinds. Some she recognized, having read them herself, but many she didn't. And some of the titles, she noticed, were a little odd:

History of the Mauvais Clan
Cultures and Distinctions Among the Sixiang Mages
Passive Magic for the Advanced Learner

And others of that nature. Despite their unique titles, the books themselves were unassuming. If she hadn't been paying attention, she never would have guessed they weren't about the world she knew.

"You can't borrow any of the magic ones," Steven said before she could ask. His hand was back in his hair, eyes trained to the floor. "They uh…they gotta stay here. But you can come over and read them. My parents would get mad if they caught you in here, but they're not home much so it doesn't matter."

"Thank you," Mia said. She moved away from the books, and after a quick scan around the room to see if there were any photos, she faced him again. "Maybe later."

"Oh. Right. You wanted to see magic." Steven nodded. "Uh… yeah. So you should sit." He moved away from his bed and pointed at it.

Mia hesitated. Being in his room was one thing. Being on his bed? She eyed him, trying to gauge the situation. He just wanted her to sit to show her magic, right? Did she just want to sit and see the magic? Did any of it matter?

With a deep breath, she sat on the edge of the bed. Steven stood in front of her, rubbing his hands together as if not sure if this was a good idea. And suddenly, Mia didn't know if it was either. She wanted to see it, really more than anything. But what if seeing more brought her further into his world? What if she got caught up in something she didn't want to because of this?

What if all of this was a mistake?

She opened her mouth to tell him to stop, to wait, but then the lights appeared, and she went silent.

It didn't matter how fast he ran. It didn't matter how many times he stumbled. It didn't matter how hard he panted, how much his legs turned to rubber, or how much his scattered thoughts worked together to tell him to slow down. For each step he took, she took two. Every inch he made, trudging through the snow, brought him no closer to the woman with bleached-blond hair.

But she was real. The woman, laughing, left behind footsteps. Her laughter rang in his ears, mocking him. It was a warning: he shouldn't get too close.

He had to.

Every time they'd gone out looking, him and his friends, or by himself, they'd found nothing. They'd searched and searched, looking for any signs of strangeness. Blair had tried to reach out with her magic. Cody had examined the woods with his ability to see those colored mists. Derek had thought back to his dreams, wanting to make sense of them. To connect the vibrant marshes of ancient Thailand to the dead, snowy woods of Colorado.

Nothing.

They'd found nothing.

No person. No figure. No magic. No strange mists. It was them, angry and cold, searching without a sense of where to go or what to do.

But she was here. The laughing woman with inappropriate winter clothing and bleached blond hair. He had to follow her.

She grew further away. His vision clouded and his legs slowed. It was too much. He hadn't had enough of the coffee. He hadn't had enough sleep. It took all of his willpower to follow her, almost crashing into trees, feet barely lifting above the snow.

This wasn't what he did. He hated exercising. Whenever Mia would go running, he'd roll his eyes at her. When they were kids, and she'd push him to play soccer with her in the garden, he only would to please his grandparents. But he'd hated every minute of it.

He'd let her win one-hundred percent of the time so he could exert as little energy as possible. Mia was the athletic one. He would rather learn languages and read.

His foot caught something. A root. It wrapped around his ankle, and he landed face first in the snow, the icy flakes scratching his face. He wanted to gasp from the pain. From the shock. From anything. He wanted to have a reaction at all, but he was numb. Everything about him was numb as he pushed himself up. His chest heaved. The world spun. He looked around, ready to give up, but found her standing there. Six feet away.

His vision cleared. She had a smile on her face, head cocked, eyes narrowed, but amused.

They stared at each other. So many thoughts ran through his head. Did she want to talk to him? Did she have answers? Was he crazy?

The words wouldn't form on his tongue. Or maybe they would. Maybe it was the fact that he couldn't catch his breath that made it impossible to speak. His body heaved, the only sound in the forest that of his gasping for air. The woman took a step toward him. He pushed himself to his knees. To his feet.

When he looked up, she was closer. Three feet away.

He stepped back.

She was closer. Moving on as if on air.

Derek's heart clenched. His blood turned to ice as fear overtook his everything. Fear he didn't understand. An instinct in his gut. She stepped closer.

A sharp pain shot through Derek's head. He choked on the air forcing itself down his throat as a single thought ran through his mind: *Not safe.*

She gasped.

His vision went white.

She cursed.

His body heated, burning like it did when he used magic.

Then there was nothing. The world returned, but it wasn't the same. He stood there, alone in what had been a forest.

His breath came in short bursts. His hands shook by his side. The setting sun cast an eerie glow across the horizon, and he turned his head slowly, taking in the situation. His feet settled on solid ground, snow melted in a wide circle around him. The root he'd tripped over, and the tree attached to it, were gone. Just…gone. Remembered by a scorch mark in the earth. He stood in the center of a wide, empty circle. The trees at the perimeter, even the conifers, were bare of vegetation, instead singed or decorated with the remaining droplets of flame.

What the…?

He took a step back from the center of the circle. He spun around, trying to understand why he was suddenly in a burned down clearing. The rest of the forest, outside of the circle of char, stood beautiful and untouched, snow reflecting the light.

What have you done?

A voice whispered on the wind, asking a question he couldn't answer. His body chilled. He stumbled back from the new clearing, boots unhappy in the mud, trying to understand.

What had he done?

He squeezed his eyes shut, hoping that when he opened them, he'd be home. He'd be in his room with Mia yelling at him to come help with dinner. Blair would be texting him, complaining about her brother. His homework would be on his desk, waiting for him to finish it. His parents would be back, obsessed with *The Queen* and none of this would be real. No dreams. No Gray Spirits. No red eyed queen stalking him. No laughing woman with the bleached blond hair. It would all go back to the way things were before that night at the opening.

Happy.

Not perfect.

But not this.

When he opened his eyes, he wasn't home. He wasn't in his room. He wasn't even in Colorado anymore. When he opened his eyes, he stood on the edge of the Mekong River, staring out across the murky waters to the other side with longing in his soul.

Where is she?

The voice tickled his ear. He brushed it. He blinked. He wasn't in Thailand any longer. He was at the temple. The rain pounded on his consciousness. His body remained dry. His soul wept.

Where is our queen?

He blinked again. The rice fields.

What have you done, little Niran?

The voice grew louder. Others accompanied it. They whispered, layering on one another until they were a deafening roar, asking the questions, saying that name, switching from language to language. Some he knew. Most he didn't. Some he recognized. Most he didn't.

He covered his ears, wanting to block it out.

"Stop it," he said, voice drowned out by their angry clamoring.

Whatever have you done?

"Shut up!" His voice burst out as a hoarse scream. The voices went silent. In their place, loneliness and sorrow overtook everything. He shuddered and removed his hands from his ears. He wanted to run. To fight. His legs wouldn't move. His body said no.

He had to listen.

When he opened his eyes again, one last time, he found himself in darkness. Standing alone atop the shimmering pool. He glanced down at the water, expecting his reflection, but the man beneath the water wasn't him. It was someone else. A man with long black hair. A man with green eyes. A man wearing colorful robes.

The man looked away.

Derek looked up.

It floated there. An aster. Waiting in a beam of light.

He stepped forward. A bell accompanied each ripple. It rang in the darkness, high and light.

He reached out toward the flower.

And found himself back in the woods.

He looked around. There were no voices. No women. Nothing. Nothing but a scorched forest. His eyes burned. He reached up with a hand and touched the corner, finding wetness.

What is going on?

He sunk to the ground, body done. Mind done. Soul done. Just done. He didn't want any of this to be real. As tears forced their way down his cheeks, he tried again, and again, and again, to convince himself this was nothing. It was a nightmare that he'd wake up from and it'd all go back to normal. He didn't want these dreams. He didn't want to keep seeing strange women in the woods. He didn't want to almost die. He didn't want his magic anymore.

He just wanted to go home.

A low growl interrupted his thoughts. At first he thought he'd imagined it. He'd been in these woods for much of the past seven years and he'd never encountered something that would growl. But then it sounded again. A rumble across the frozen air. Derek looked up.

He didn't have the energy for fear.

When he looked into the glowing gray eyes of a mountain lion, even though he knew that it wasn't normal, that something was going on, he couldn't bring himself to move.

Looks like someone's going to get their wish. His bitter thought disgusted him in every way. The mountain lion crouched. *This sucks. This freaking sucks.*

The mountain lion growled louder and pounced. Derek flinched, closing his eyes in preparation for what he guessed was going to be a very painful death, but there was no pain. A petrified yelp echoed in the forest. There was a thump. Derek opened his eyes in time to see the mountain lion scramble to its feet and hurry away, kicking up dirt, and then snow.

"Derek!"

A voice. A real voice. Her voice.

Derek tore his gaze from where the mountain lion had disappeared off to and found a panting Blair running toward him. At first, he wasn't sure if he was imagining her. If he'd lost his marbles and was hallucinating. Or maybe he'd died, and this was some kind of karmic justice.

Die by mountain lion. Get to be with pretty girl.

"Blair?" he asked.

She reached him and reached down, yanking on his arm until he was on his feet. He stumbled. His legs were jelly, either from exhaustion or fear.

"What the hell happened?" Blair asked, gesturing to the destroyed bit of forest. "What are you doing up here? Why didn't you come to lunch?"

"I-I–" He had no words.

Blair huffed. "Whatever. Come on, let's get out of here before that thing comes back."

"How did you know where I was?" Derek asked.

"Come on," Blair said, tugging at his arm. He didn't move.

"Blair, how did you find me?"

She hesitated. "I…I can't…it's too hard to explain right now. Okay? Let's go."

She pulled again, and he tried to follow, but his body wasn't having it. He had nothing left. "I need to sit down for an hour. Or five."

Blair turned to him. Scowling. Had the situation been different, if he hadn't just been killed by a mountain lion with glowing eyes, he might have laughed. She looked around the woods. At him. Back toward town. At him. To her feet, one of which was tapping, then up at him.

"Oh screw it," she said before she let go of his arm. He thought at first she was going to abandon him, but she grabbed his face instead, hands freezing, and pulled him down into a kiss.

Shock overtook him. He almost jerked back, not sure this was the time, nor the place, to be kissing, but after a fraction of a second, heat flowed from her body into his. Warmth. Magic. Energy. His body, as if craving a drug long after the last dose, relished in every bit of energy, desperate for more. And when Blair pulled away, face redder than usual, Derek had to silence the protest on his tongue.

"What?" he asked.

"There. Now you have energy. Let's *go*."

She grabbed his wrist again and pulled. This time his body did what it was told and followed her away from the scorched trees, down the mountain, and back toward town, leaving the woods, the woman, the voices, and any answer he might have gotten, behind him.

Chapter Seventeen

A million questions ran through Derek's mind. Blair led him through the woods like they were her second home. He may have been exploring them since he was ten, but she'd been doing it since she could walk. He let her pull him, in part because he wasn't sure he could keep going if she didn't, and in part so he could feel her skin against his.

He didn't know what she did to him when she kissed him, but now he was afraid if she let go, the cold might steal away the energy she'd somehow given him, leaving him that panting, exhausted, human being who was too worn down to run from a cursed mountain lion.

As they ran, he tried to understand where that woman had led him. The fact that she had gotten close. The things…the things he did to the forest. The voices. The flashes to his dreams. His reflection.

That man's reflection.

The one that was almost him, but not.

He knew it meant something. Everything that had been

happening to him since the sculpture had broken meant something. But he had no idea. He didn't know who Niran was. He didn't know what these dreams *meant* and why he kept seeing that woman in black.

The Queen.

How did he unseal the queen?

Before long, Blair pulled him back into town, and the two stopped running. Both panting. She gripped his hand and looked up at him, but he couldn't look at her. He just wanted to get home. So they walked, hand in hand, down the streets, toward his house. The sun was hiding behind the horizon, the sky a scarlet twilight, too beautiful for the moment. In his mind, Derek prepared himself for what home would be like.

Was Mia home?

Were his parents?

He expected someone, but when they got home, there were no cars in the driveway. He stared at the empty spots where his parents normally parked, and something boiled in his stomach. They weren't home. Again. Were they ever home?

When they got to the porch, Blair let go of Derek's hand, and he let her in. Warmth washed over him, and he breathed out, body relishing in the heat he'd been denying it for hours. A shudder ran though him. A welcome hug. He almost smiled. This was home. This was safe.

But when he looked at the ground, he realized that Mia's shoes weren't there. Her slippers were.

She wasn't home either.

"Derek?" Blair asked, hesitant.

Finally, he snapped back to life. Mia wasn't home. His parents weren't home. It was just them. That was okay. It was all fine. This way they could talk without risking anyone overhearing them. This was easier. This was the best thing for this moment.

249

He took off his boots, stripped his coat off, and stormed through the house toward his room.

"Derek!"

He threw open the door to his room. His mess of a room. He stared around it, shaking. Then, without thinking, without warning, he bent down and grabbed the clothes off his floor. Clothes. Books. Video games. He scooped them all up and shoved things in places that weren't his floor. Bookcase. Hamper. Desk. He was so focused he didn't realize Blair had arrived, leaning against his doorframe with crossed arms until he turned to leave and grab a broom, only to find her in his path.

"You okay?" she asked.

No. He wasn't okay. But he didn't want to talk about him. There was something more pressing. Something he didn't understand.

"How did you know where I was?" Derek asked.

Blair hesitated. "Derek...."

"I was in the middle of nowhere," he said. "Last time I saw you was during lunch when I ran off the other way. You didn't follow me. Unless you did and you saw the things I saw with that woman."

"You saw the red-eyed woman again?" Blair asked but Derek kept going.

"How the hell did you show up right when I'm about to get killed by a mountain lion?"

Blair said nothing for a moment. They stared at each other, and he could see it in her eyes. Annoyance. Frustration. He would have felt bad, but he needed answers. Any answers. Any kind of answers.

"I saved you," Blair snapped. "Why does it matter how?"

"How. Did. You. Know?" Derek was done playing. Done with the way Blair evaded his questions. How she tried to keep him in the dark about everything in the magical world. He was done with his world falling apart without knowing any reason why it could be.

Blair closed her eyes, breathed in, then out. All leaning against the doorframe. All with crossed arms. When she opened them again, she said in a quiet voice, "I'm a seer."

Derek stared at her, confusion overtaking his anger. "A seer? You can like…see the future?"

"Sometimes," Blair said with a shrug. "Sometimes I see other things. It's…." She groaned. "I don't know how to explain it, okay? Sometimes I see things. Past, present, future, it doesn't matter. Sometimes the things come true, sometimes not."

Derek snorted.

"What?" she asked.

"Are you messing with me?" Derek asked. Blair said nothing. "You can see things. Is there a reason you haven't been using this ability to figure out what's going on?"

"I can't exactly control it."

"Oh well great help you are."

Blair scoffed. "I saved your ass. Don't think I've quite heard a thank you for that."

"Thank you?" The anger rushed back without warning. Not anger. Fury. "You want me to thank you? Whose fault is it that I was alone in those woods in the first place?"

"Yours." Blair's tone tightened and she moved away from the door frame, stalking into his room. "You're the one who ran off. You're the one who spent all afternoon doing god knows what instead of coming to lunch with me."

"I asked you to come with and what did you do? Make jokes? Tell me to slow down? Well I tried to slow down and it nearly got me killed!"

"No, your idiocy nearly got you killed!"

Something licked at Derek's skin. An emotion. Light. But there. Anger. Blair's anger. Her bracelet couldn't contain it.

"Oh, right, I'm just some idiot going around doing idiot things." Derek's voice was louder than he'd let it be in a long time. "It's not like I haven't asked for help every freaking step of the way. But no. First you don't believe me. Then you feed me this story about these immortal beings and their evil queen, but that wasn't easy to get out of you. And god forbid I want anything else about this world I'm apparently part of because you don't tell me shit!"

"I can't just tell you things!" Blair screamed. He'd never heard her scream before.

He rolled his eyes. "No, you just keep it all a nice little secret locked away in your stupid house with your stupid secrets not even thinking for one second that I'm alone and scared and don't know anything about why I was able to destroy a part of the forest without a thought."

"Yeah, like you're Mr. Honesty," Blair said. "You told Mia that you've spent her entire life manipulating her emotions to keep her from feeling anything you've decided is too painful for her?"

Derek's eyes widened, and his fists clenched. "That's not what I do."

"Sure. Definitely isn't. That's why you've told her about it."

"At least I don't keep the fact that I'm a seer a secret from someone who could really use someone with that kind of power!"

Blair threw her hands up in the air. "Yes. Derek. I'm going to tell you about something I have to keep hidden from my own grandmother because…why? You feel butthurt that you aren't part of a secret? Well guess what, Derek. *You aren't privy to everything in my life.* I'll start telling you things about the magical world when you stop being a little *shit*."

That was too much for Derek. The anger welled up inside of him. The warmth built in his stomach. "Someone is trying to kill me. Goddammit Blair, are you ever going to understand that?"

"I do understand!"

"No you DON'T!" The warmth turned white hot and exploded from his body, similarly to in the woods. The walls and ceiling cracked, everything in his room flying up in a fury.

Blair yelped.

Derek's eyes widened, watching everything falling around them. In seconds he moved forward, wrapping his arms around Blair to protect her from the debris. He didn't think about it. He didn't care that they'd just been screaming at each other. He didn't want her to get hurt.

He tensed, waiting for things to fall on him, but there was nothing. Books and clothes and pieces of drywall fell around the two of them, but nothing on them. He pulled away from Blair and looked up. A thin, blue veil of energy surrounded them, protecting them from harm's way.

The blue light flickered, and vanished.

Derek stared down at Blair, arms still around her. She looked up at him, eyes wide. His heart pounded against his chest. He thought to the way she kissed him in the woods. She'd stopped the mountain lion. Three times. This was the third time in less than an hour she'd protected him.

The world stopped.

It was hard to say who kissed who. Maybe it happened at the same time. Maybe someone made the first move. But before Derek realized what was going on, he was kissing her and she was wrapping her arms around his neck to pull him as close to her body as she could.

The lights glittered in the air, floating around the dim room like fairies. Mia stared up at them from her perch on the bed, gripping the blanket, eyes wide. Awe overtook her. There was something so calm. So gentle. She didn't know if she was breathing. Part of her wondered if she was still in Steven's room. The lights danced. The room darkened. An air of peace, of comfort, and of warmth twisted between the little dots of energy.

She smiled.

Her hand left the bed, reaching up to touch the lights. Whenever one moved close to her skin, it darted away, but its warmth tickled her and she let out a series of gentle laughs. She dropped her hand to her lap, gaze coming back down to focus on Steven. He watched her with a smile she'd never seen on him before. It was as though all that nervous energy he had, all that awkwardness he felt when he was with her, was gone.

It was gentle. His smile. And Mia flushed, stomach turning with something she couldn't help but call happiness. Her shoulders loosened, and she realized she couldn't remember the last time that they had. There were moments of reprieve, but this was different. This was like someone had removed every single worry in her life and replaced with gentle euphoria.

"They're pretty," Mia said, breaking the silence that had fallen over the room. Steven lifted a hand and allowed one to land on his hand, where it grew to the size of a tangerine. He held it out to her, and she took it, their hands brushing together. Electricity trickled up her arm, and she shuddered, wondering if it was from the ball of light, or his touch.

The ball glowed, pulsating warmth. It was different. Very, very different. And yet...so familiar. Like something she'd known her entire life.

"I can do other stuff," Steven said, bringing her attention to him. "But you seemed stressed and down. So I thought...I dunno. Maybe something like this would make you smile."

She tilted her hand, letting the large ball of light go. As it fell, it scattered into a million smaller lights which joined their friends in the air. She was smiling. There was no doubt about it.

"They look like fireflies," she said, barely thinking.

"Hm?"

"When we were kids, Derek and I would go out of the city with our parents. There was a place nearby where in the summer there were fireflies everywhere." She closed her eyes, picturing the hot, humid summers of Beijing. Sitting in a field of long grass and tall trees as the little bugs lit up their world. "We liked to try and catch them. My mom would bring these jars and we'd chase the bugs all over, trying not to go too far so we wouldn't get lost. I always caught more than Derek, which would make him pout, and so we'd share a jar and name all of the fireflies until it was time to go. Then my dad would take the jar and tell us that they belonged in the wild, and he'd set them free."

One by one the bugs would fly out of the jar, disappearing into the night. Mia and Derek would fall asleep on the way home. She'd wake up in her bed having dreamt about the fireflies.

"This was here?" Steven asked.

Mia shook her head. "I think there are fireflies in Colorado, but we haven't looked for any. This was something we did before we moved to America."

Pressure appeared on the bed next to her, and Mia sucked in a breath as Steven sat closer than she thought he would. Their arms touched. Their hands close enough that it would only take half a moment to entwine them. Her heart leapt into her throat. But she didn't look at him.

"That sounds like a tradition," he said.

"It was."

"Why don't you look for them here?"

She shrugged. "My parents are busy. I don't think Derek would like doing it anymore."

"Oh." Steven said nothing at first. Mia said nothing either, staring at the lights. Then he touched her hand with his. She didn't look. She didn't pull away. She let him grab it, and she bit her lip. "We could go. You know. When summer comes."

Steven and her exploring Colorado, looking for fireflies. The idea made her too happy. "We could."

"I'll do some research."

"That would help," she said with a laugh. Her gaze returned to the lights and she watched them dip and jump and avoid each other. It was almost unreal. These beautiful lights, something so unnatural, yet so right, floating in Steven's bedroom. Created by Steven.

Magic.

Whenever something odd had happened, with the cave, and the knife, and the woman with bleached blond hair and clothes that did not fit the weather, Mia thought that anything mystical was scary and dangerous. It was going to hurt her. Ruin her life. But this was beautiful. It was warm and safe.

She wanted more of it.

"Why don't you use your magic more?" Mia asked.

Steven stiffened. "It's not really safe. People are scared of it."

"They're scared of this?"

"No. They're scared of what it could be. What it *can* be. Wars have been fought because of magic. People's lives have been ruined. It's not just some amazing thing that is always good. Sometimes the person using it sucks. Sometimes the people who don't have it abuse those who do. Sometimes those people are so scared of being the victims of a crime they can't fight against that they strike first. So we stay hidden. Because people don't understand."

There was so much pain in Steven's voice. It strained, the words barely coming out. She didn't know what to do, so she gripped his hand and leaned her head against his shoulder.

"I don't understand," she said, "but I'm not afraid."

"Anymore," he said with a slight tease to his tone. A sad tease.

Mia nodded. "I didn't know anything. I was scared because there was all of this random stuff going on with no explanation, and I thought I was going crazy. I mean, who finds a knife in a cave in the middle of a blizzard? That's…that's not normal."

Steven stayed quiet. Mia wanted reassurance that she was normal, but he didn't give it, and she pulled away. But when Steven twisted to face her, she did the same, desperate for some kind of reaction from him. He reached out and touched her cheek with a gentle caress. She looked at the bed.

"I'm glad you aren't scared anymore," Steven said.

"I'm glad you were honest with me," Mia muttered. "I don't like lies. I don't like being kept in the dark." She thought of her friends. Her brother. The past few weeks. Their secrets.

Steven lifted her head so she was looking at him again. She didn't fight it. Blood pounded in her ears. Her stomach turned in an uncomfortable, yet pleasurable way.

"I don't ever want to lie to you," Steven said.

Mia's heart thudded. She stared into his eyes, lost in their color. In their sincerity. And then, without thinking, without warning, she leaned in and kissed him.

Blair pushed against him. He stumbled back, emotions running rampant. When his legs hit his bed, he let himself sit, one arm pressing into the bed to keep him upright, the other wrapped around Blair's back to trap her close. She kept pushing against him, ending up on his lap, their lips still connected as they let their passion overtake every decision.

Every one of his senses was heightened. He was hyper aware of her every curve. The smell of her shampoo as he reached up and tugged at the hair ties holding her braids together. The skin on her face was still slightly cold, adjusting to the heat of the house and of the moment. And he craved it all. He craved the mix of floral shampoo, the way her hands tugged at his shirt.

But something was missing. A sense he'd been craving from her since the day she put that bracelet on. He could barely think. He knew it was a bad idea, but he didn't give a damn. He reached, maneuvering while still kissing her, and slipped the bracelet off.

She didn't fight him.

And her emotions gave every reason why.

All of a sudden, the heat and the sexual desire he'd been experiencing intensified as it mixed with hers. He wasn't sure if he was feeling her emotions on his skin, or if they'd consumed every part of him. The electrifying shocks of desire. The warm liquid mercury of lust. The slight tinge of excited nerves.

His actions grew urgent. He pulled away for a brief second, slipping his hands under her shirt so he could remove it before taking his own off. The minute his was over his head, Blair had her hands on his shoulders, shoving him on the bed before kissing him again.

As she did, and as the moment continued on, Derek's mind slipped into a state of relaxed bliss.

Because nothing mattered.

Not the red eyed woman. Not the fact that he'd almost died. Again. Not his dreams. Nor the voices. Nor his magic. Nor his parents. Nor his failing school career. Nor the kids at school.

Not Mia.

Nothing mattered but the beautiful girl he loved—for longer than he'd ever realized—as she kissed him, and he kissed her.

Mia was on fire. She'd never kissed anyone before. She'd never *had* anyone to kiss before. So when her lips touched Steven's, she hadn't known what to expect. She hadn't known about the exhilaration. The way her heart would stop for just a second. A mere fraction of time. It didn't occur to her that her stomach would slip. That for the moment she kissed him, things would seem right with the world.

She didn't realize that when she pulled away, she might feel a little lost. Confused. Empty. It never crossed her mind that she'd get nervous about his reaction. After all, she hadn't asked. She didn't know if he wanted her to kiss him or not. It hadn't occurred to her that she would kiss him at all.

They made eye contact, and she breathed in, opening her mouth to apologize, and she never could have imagined that maybe, just maybe, he might kiss her back.

It was all new territory. Mia didn't know how to react. What to do. Where did she put her hands? Did she touch him? Why was he moving so close? Was this normal? His arm wrapped around her waist in a way she'd never been touched before, and it didn't make sense why it felt so good. Why she wanted him to touch her more.

All of this. The way he kissed her. The warmth of his body. His hand coming up to touch her face, like before. How she hesitantly touched him too. It was so much. So many emotions, so much energy between them, and she didn't understand why her body reacted the way it did, or why her thoughts were only of him.

But she didn't care.

Because the world came to a stop and she was at the center of everything.

And when he pulled away, face still close, their foreheads pressed together, a chill went up her spine.

They didn't say a word. They didn't move for some amount of time. A minute. An hour. Mia couldn't tell. It wasn't until she realized that his hand was shaking that she pulled away.

"Steven?" she asked. He withdrew more. Not far. Still on the bed. But away. He was smiling.

"Sorry," he said. "I uh…got a little caught up in the moment." He laughed with a tremble. Mia frowned. Had she done something wrong?

"Are you okay?" she asked.

She thought she saw something. A pained expression. But it was gone in a second. He leaned in and kissed her again.

"Yeah. Just got nervous," he said. "I uh…never thought you would kiss me."

Mia flushed. "Well. I just…I didn't…."

He laughed, and the tension broke. "I might have been hoping, but I didn't think you felt that way about me."

Mia didn't know how to react. This was the most normal thing that had happened to her since the sculpture broke, which was saying something considering the floating lights in the room, and she didn't know how to handle it. Steven was laughing, teasing her, and she… was a normal girl again.

Laughter bubbled from between her lips. It pealed out, and she and Steven laughed while the floating lights went out one by one.

When they finally calmed down, Mia wiping laughter tears from the corners of her eyes, she glanced around the room again, looking for a clock. What she found instead, on a shelf near his bed, was a photograph. She saw it for barely a second, but it was there: a picture of Steven laughing with two other boys around his age, and a little girl with dark skin and amazingly curly hair.

She wanted to comment on it, but Steven must not have noticed she saw it because he changed the subject.

"It's getting kind of late. Did you want to stay for dinner?" he asked.

Dinner.

Mia wanted to say yes. Steven was here, all alone. But she also knew better. Because her parents were leaving soon and they wanted to have dinner together every night until then. Even if no one spoke. Even if things were awkward. But Mia had to go.

"Maybe another time," she said. She slid off the bed, stretching. "I should get going. Sorry we didn't do any calculus."

Steven shrugged. "This was more fun."

"Yeah." She looked back at the picture, thinking maybe she could ask, but her eyes landed on an empty shelf. She blinked. Had she imagined it?

Deciding not to say anything, she and Steven headed out of the room. Back through the long hallway. To the kitchen. She grabbed her things and prepared to go. But as she was pulling on her coat, Steven walked over to her and touched her wrist. The one with Blair's bracelet.

"You're always wearing this," he said. "I don't think I've seen you without it."

Mia glanced down. Honestly, she'd put it on and forgot it was there. It was like it was invisible. She slept with it. She showered with it. She did everything with it, and sometimes she was unaware she had anything on her wrist at all.

"Oh. Yeah. Blair gave it to me," Mia said. "Some kind of friendship thing."

"Ah." Steven smiled and patted it, like he was petting a dog. Mia frowned. "Well, I think it's cool that you still wear it, since she's been cold recently. Maybe whatever mood she's in will pass soon."

When he pulled away, Mia stared at the bracelet, brow furrowed. "Yeah. I hope so."

Maybe it would be okay. Cody apologized. The two of them were better now. Maybe that was all she needed from Blair. Blair wasn't exactly the most emotionally stable people. She was quick to sarcasm or anger. But at the same time, in all the years they'd known each other, ever since the day Blair punched a girl for calling Mia a racist slur, Blair had never abandoned Mia. She'd been there, Mia's easily angered friend, to keep everyone grounded. Unless of course she was the one off on a random tangent.

She nodded. "Yeah. It'll be okay." But she wasn't sure she believed her words.

She finished getting ready to go, and Steven led her to the front door. She stood in front of it, breathing in deeply as she prepared to go out into the world.

"Thanks for showing me the magic," Mia said to Steven, smiling up at him. Before she knew it, he'd leaned in and kissed her again.

Her breath caught, but he pulled away before she could close her eyes.

"Thanks for not being scared," he said.

Happiness took over her face. "Bye."

"Bye."

Without another word, she opened the door and stepped out into the frigid air. Excitement warmed her. She headed down the steps and into the street, turning around once more to wave at Steven. But as she walked, as the cold overtook her excitement, she found that she didn't want to go home. More than anything, she wanted to return to Steven's house where it was warm.

Where she was wanted.

She didn't want to go to a house where her parents worked and her brother hated her.

Yet she trudged on. One boot in front of the other. Slush jumping up with a *squelch* and staining her pants. She barely noticed, keeping her eyes trained on the ground. With each step, she took a breath. The moment of being with Steven, alone in his room, faded away with each step. It became a distant memory, and she looked up as the street lamps flickered to life above her.

At first, she didn't know what to do. She thought about running back to Steven. She thought about screaming. About pretending like she didn't see the woman with bleached blond hair standing down the street, leaning against a street lamp. She looked different this time. Still wearing inappropriate clothes. One booted foot kicked up and pressed against the pole and she stared at Mia. As Mia stared back.

Her heart raced.

She didn't move.

The woman looked different. Instead of a grin, she wore a scowl. Instead of amusement in her eyes, they were narrowed. And her arms...her face...there were bandages.

Mia opened her mouth, to call out to her, to tell her to leave her alone, but the minute she did, the woman vanished. Mia didn't blink this time. She didn't turn her head away. She didn't look down. Right there, in front of her eyes, the woman vanished into nothingness.

The night darkened. The lamp above Mia flickered and she swallowed thickly. Closing her eyes, her hand went to wrist. The bracelet. It was cold against her skin. She didn't know why she wore it anymore. She didn't know what was the point of anything going on in her life right now. The only thing that made sense was Steven.

But that didn't mean it always had to be that way. Things wouldn't change that much. Blair had still given her this bracelet. An act of friendship she'd never expected from Blair before. It was unlike her. But it was a welcome change.

It could get better.

Things didn't have to keep going down this dark path.

She opened her eyes again. No woman. No magic. Just a dark road with drops of light. Mia breathed in. Things couldn't go back to normal. But maybe she could salvage what little was left. So she stepped again. Moving forward. Letting the slush *squelch* underneath her boots.

Chapter Eighteen

He didn't know what to call the emotion lingering on his skin. He'd felt so many different types over the years. Deciphering them was barely a thought. He didn't question the color blue. He didn't question the tapping of happiness. But this feeling, this light brush of smooth grains—uncooked lentils, possibly rice—shimmering across his body, was foreign. It encased him, soothing his every anxiety. His every worry.

She lay against him. Her head nestled in the crook of his collarbone. Skin against skin. Her back rising and falling as she breathed. He threaded his fingers through her hair, letting the smooth strands mix with the emotion he didn't know. He kept his eyes closed. He enjoyed the gentle smile on his lips.

He couldn't remember the last time he'd felt like this. Relaxed. Every muscle lacking tension as little workers in his mind swept away the dust fogging his every thought. Bit by bit. Second by second. As the two of them lay there, clothes scattered, memories of the moment sinking in, the world became clear. The past few weeks came into focus in a way they hadn't before.

Maybe it was the energy Blair had given him or maybe it was feeling her body against his when he held her close and kissed her.

Maybe it was just a moment to stop and think about something other than the insanity that was his world. All it took was a fraction of time to stop and not *think* to let everything reset. The pieces of the puzzle were no longer floating in an abyss of confusion. They lay on a table. Still scattered. Still unconnected. But stable. Workable.

Blair shifted. He removed his arm from around her back as she sat up, pulling the blanket over her naked chest. He stared up at her, admiring every detail of her face. Her beautiful, dark brown irises, the way her skin seemed to glow from the cascading light from his overhead fixture. Her thick, black hair that was wavy from years of being locked in braids. Though he loved the normal fire in her eyes and when she looked like she was one second away from verbally tearing you to shreds, he found the way her hardened shell had melted into something gentle alluring.

He smiled.

"Why are you staring at me?" Blair asked. The first words they'd exchanged since the fight. Derek reached up and brushed a lock of hair out of her face. It fell back where it had been before, but he didn't care.

"You're pretty," he said.

He wasn't sure what he loved more: watching her face brighten, or the gust of embarrassment slapping his skin.

"You need some more sleep," Blair said. "You're starting to imagine things."

"You're terrible at taking compliments."

"I take compliments that are true."

He sat up, placing a hand on her cheek to pull her in for a kiss. She didn't fight him. A tickle of lust trailed across his body, but he didn't push further. He pulled away and scooted so he was pressed against the wall, still staring at her curled up figure.

"You really should sleep," Blair muttered. "I gave you energy, but not a lot. It'll fade and it's better if you try to sleep before the crash."

The memory of her kissing him in the field came back to him. She'd been soft. Trembling. Thinking back, her hands shook when she'd grabbed him. He'd been so tired and focused on the energy that he hadn't noticed.

"So," Derek said, "if you kiss someone you can give them energy?"

The gentle expression on her face vanished, returning to her normal one. He had to keep from laughing.

"Well, no." She shifted like she always did before she was about to reveal information. "It's just touch. And it's not easy to do, but I needed you to move."

"Just a touch?" Derek asked. "So why did you kiss me?"

Fear overtook him. Hers. His. He couldn't tell. He gasped. It'd been a while since he'd felt Blair's emotions. He wasn't used to them anymore.

"Blair?"

"I…." Her hands gripped the blanket. Sorrow replaced the fear like a bucket of ice water. "I was scared I hadn't gotten there in time. And when you were still alive…." She shook her head. "I wanted to kiss you, okay?"

Derek didn't know what to say. He didn't understand Blair's visions. She was a seer. She saw…things. But he'd been too angry to press more. The way he'd yelled at her…had he really been angry at her? Or was it just all the anger at everything coming out at once? Anger at his parents, at Mia, at the people at school, at himself….

He took a deep breath, not sure he wanted to know the answer to the question he was about to ask. "What exactly did you see?"

Blair shrunk into herself. He'd never seen her like this before. He shifted, as if to go comfort her, but she spoke before he could.

"I saw a few things. Disjointed. I saw a woman with brown eyes, and fire, and a flower, and then Mia, I think, but suddenly it was you in that burning clearing and the mountain lion attacked you and…." She shuddered. "It wasn't good. I didn't know if it was the future, or the past, or if it was happening right then. I just knew where to find you and I ran there as fast as I could."

Derek tried to wrap his mind around what Blair had said. It was a lot of information. For her, and for him. It seemed like a mind-fuck. No wonder she looked like she was having a seizure whenever she had a vision.

"Why did you never tell me about it?" he asked in as gentle of a voice as he could muster.

She let out a heavy sigh. "You don't understand. There are rules. Every clan has them, and mine seems to have more than most. My grandmother is so scared that we're going to die out that she made all these strict rules about everything with our culture and our magic." Blair shook her head. "I want to tell you things. Out of everyone in the world, you're the only person I actually want to answer when you ask me about my life. But you have to understand. It's complicated."

"But you live here," Derek said. He didn't understand. The fact that Blair couldn't talk to anyone about her magic, or her life, even though she didn't live on her clan's land and only visited in the summer for a few weeks, stunned him. "You're part of the clan but you live here. Why do her rules apply so much?"

She wouldn't look at him. She kept her gaze to the blanket, knees pulled up to her chest. "You don't go against Enola Demini."

Derek cocked his head.

"My grandmother," Blair said. "No matter how much I rebel by cutting my hair, and going to a school with people who don't know magic exists, or even…." She looked at him. "Even being with you. When she says something is for the protection of the clan, I listen."

Derek hadn't realized their flirtations were a rebellion. Every time the two ended up alone together. The first time they kissed. His flirting with her. This. Today. Being naked in bed together. He hadn't realized they could get her in trouble.

"What happens if you do break her rules?" Derek asked. "What can she do that's so bad? Why doesn't anyone fight against it?"

"Someone did," Blair said.

"Who?"

"My mom." She shifted into a new position, though kept the blanket up against her chest. Derek's brow furrowed, and Blair continued. "Twenty-five-years ago my mom married my dad, an average guy from New York, and she hasn't stepped foot on our clan's land in twenty-five-years."

Derek hadn't even considered why things were awkward. He knew there was family drama. His own family certainly wasn't lacking it, and he never had to go far to hear some kind of family gossip from his cousins or an auntie. But this didn't feel like the same thing. His mom packing up and leaving China with Mia and Derek when they were ten because of one too many fights with his nǎinai didn't have the same level of complicated as what Blair had described.

"Can't you leave, like your mom?" Derek asked.

She shook her head.

"Why not?"

"Because I'm a seer," she said. "My grandmother doesn't know yet. But she'll find out. And when she does, she's not going to let me leave. I'm a once in a generation occurrence." Her words came out bitter, and a wave of anger pricked at Derek.

He brushed it off, wanting to go back to the gentle emotion from earlier. But that's not how it worked. "So your grandmother is going to keep you locked away like a pet?"

"No."

"I don't understand?"

For the first time since Derek had met Blair, tears pricked her eyes. In a quiet voice, she whispered. "I'll be taking her place."

Derek's jaw dropped. A rush of panic, of confusion, overcame him. Blair would take her grandmother's place? She'd...become the clan leader? She'd be in charge? She'd have to leave Willow Creek and take care of land, of a people, she didn't know well. Would she get to leave? Would he ever see her again?

"But—" he tried to say but Blair shook her head, silencing him.

"Don't you get it, Derek?" She finally made eye contact with him. "This is how it is. There are rules. Boundaries. Magic has always just been this fun side effect of your life. It gives you an edge and makes you feel special and unique. You aren't bound to a clan or their rules. But it's not like that for me. It's ingrained in every part of my life and will dictate every part of my life forever. You've spent the past three weeks struggling with all this new information as magic suddenly isn't that party trick you hold in your back pocket. And I get it. For you, magic has always been fun. And now...now you think you're weird, or special, but you're not. Sometimes magic just sucks."

She moved closer to him, reaching out to grab his hand. The blanket slipped from her body, but he couldn't tear his gaze from hers.

"I never told that I'm a seer because I don't want to be one."

He remained silent, staring at her. When she spoke those words, a rush of fear, excitement, and sadness overtook him, and for a moment he couldn't breathe. She wasn't trying to hide from him. She wasn't restricting her words or keeping her world from him. She was letting him in, for real, for the first time since they'd met in the cafeteria in fourth grade and she told him it wasn't normal for him to have green eyes.

There was no thought process involved. He didn't have to take a moment to consider pushing himself away from the wall. Wrapping his arms around her. Pulling her against him. Her emotions overtook him, and he wanted to make them better. To go back to the happiness. He could do it. He could take away her pain and bring back her smile and laugh. Get a snarky response out of her, like the ones that made him fall in love with her in the first place.

But he didn't. He didn't push positive emotions onto her. He didn't say anything to try and take away the pain or make it better. He couldn't make this better. He didn't understand it. It wasn't his pain or his world. Magic wouldn't fix this.

Instead he hugged her. He hugged her, and he said, "I'm sorry. I won't pry anymore."

He'd been so caught up in himself. He'd never thought that maybe there was something going on with Blair too. With Cody. With his parents. With Mia.

He'd become obsessed. And he'd nearly lost everyone.

Blair pulled out of his hug only to kiss him again. "Thank you."

He smiled, and her emotions lightened. "Guess I should try and figure out why someone wants me dead. And I should probably do it without obsessing and destroying my life."

Blair snorted. "No shit."

He laughed. "There you are."

"What?"

He answered her with a kiss, lost in everything she was, when a sound outside of his door made him freeze. He and Blair separated, staring at each other with wide eyes, both suddenly very aware that they were still naked. The front door closed. Derek's heart raced and he looked toward his door, desperate to know who had just walked in.

He focused. Hard.

And felt nothing.

"Derek, who is it?" Blair asked.

"I can't feel anything," he said, his face going cold.

"Shit," Blair said. She tumbled out of bed, grabbing her clothes and pulling them on. Derek took a moment, panicking internally before he followed suit. It was easier for him, since it was his room, but his shaking hands still made it impossible to pull everything on quickly.

She couldn't find them like this. He wasn't always the most observant when it came to his sister now that he couldn't feel her emotions, but he absolutely knew that she felt abandoned and left out. A situation that was his fault. But he didn't want to add to it. He didn't want Mia to know that he and Blair had slept together. Not right now. Not when things were so fragile with her.

As he searched for a shirt, he spotted something odd in the corner of his room: his backpack. He stared at it, the panic of the moment disorienting his mind.

"Why's my backpack here?" he asked. Last time he'd seen it, it was on the floor of the hallway in front of his locker.

"Are you serious right now?" Blair asked. He straightened up, and she chucked a shirt at his face. "Get dressed."

He did as he was told, yanking the shirt over his head. Blair grabbed the door handle and yanked it open before barreling out of the room. Derek followed her, hoping that Mia was still in the entryway, but Blair had frozen right outside his door.

He couldn't feel her emotions. She'd put the bracelet back on. But he didn't need to, to know she was mortified. He burst out of the room too, trying to keep his cool, but when his eyes landed on his sister, on the way she looked between the two of them with wide eyes, he knew he'd messed up.

Again.

Mia had never seen Blair with her hair down. It was longer than

Mia thought, hanging past her shoulders in cascading, messy waves. She and Mia stared at each other, Mia trying to pretend like she hadn't just seen Blair burst out of her brother's room looking like she'd thrown on the first things to touch her fingers.

They didn't say anything. Blair looked too embarrassed to say anything, and Mia couldn't form the right words. She'd thought… she'd thought that this would be fine. That she'd come home and talk to Derek. That she'd face him and make him listen to her. She wouldn't tell him about Steven, but she could tell him other things.

And when she saw Blair's coat thrown on the ground in the entry way, her shoes—not boots—laying damp on the tile as if ripped off and forgotten about, Mia though that maybe she could talk to Blair too. Her bracelet burned. It was time. She'd decided it was time to talk to them. Even if they didn't believe her, she had to get her secret out to someone other than Steven.

Because she wanted to fix things. She didn't want to end up alone in a house every night with no pictures on the walls.

But there was Blair. Standing in front of her brother's door with wide eyes and messy hair. And there was Derek. Stumbling out of his room with his shirt on backwards. He stopped next to Blair. He didn't touch her, but he didn't need to.

Mia wasn't stupid.

They've been a thing for years, her mind tried to tell her. *This isn't new. This isn't a betrayal. You knew they were going down this road.*

She knew all of that was true. Blair and Derek might have thought they were good at hiding their confusing and uncertain relationship, but Mia knew that they enjoyed each other's company a lot more than the rest of them. Whenever they'd go off together downtown to shop or get more tea and coffee, Mia and Cody would give each other a look, often accompanied by Cody rolling his eyes and Mia laughing.

None of it mattered.

"Mia," Blair finally said, breaking the overhanging silence. "I–" She looked up at Derek as if searching for the right words. An explanation.

Mia's gaze also went to her brother. They made eye contact. She wanted him to say something. To explain. But he stayed silent.

"We were just…." Blair tried to say, bringing Mia's attention back to her. "I just mean that…you…you're home. Hi. Um…."

Blair had never been amazing with words. But for her that meant she always said something snarky and mean. Mia had never seen Blair like this. Incapable of forming a complete, coherent sentence.

"Mia, say something," Blair said. A plea Mia never thought she'd hear come out of Blair's mouth.

Mia glanced between the two of them. During all of this, when Derek was skipping class and messing up and causing problems for their family, ignoring her, telling her that her issues weren't as important as his and then not even bothering to tell her, his twin, what was going on, he'd found support from someone else. Someone who took off her clothes for him. Someone who was supposed to be Mia's friend.

She could have said something. So many angry comments ran through her mind. How they were pushing her away so they could have sex when they thought they wouldn't get caught. How they couldn't even own it when she came home. How it took Blair stumbling over her words to say, "hi". How Derek hadn't even spoken. It was like they'd done something wrong, and not only did they know it, but they knew she knew it too.

It wouldn't take much to yell.

"Mia…."

She didn't want to yell.

She'd kissed a boy today. A boy who cared about her. Who didn't keep secrets from her. Who listened to her problems. Who wanted her around.

273

They didn't want her around. They just wanted each other.

Mia shifted her backpack and moved. Taking steps. Pushing past Blair who didn't try to stop her. She held her head high and ignored them both, instead entering her room. Their voices erupted into whispers. She ignored it, dropped her backpack to the ground, and walked to her dresser. It was in there. The knife. Steven hadn't asked her about it this time, but she remembered his offer when she first told him about it.

He could take it.

She wouldn't have this secret anymore.

If she got rid of it, then she'd stop wanting to tell Derek about it, because it wouldn't matter. He didn't want to know, and every time he showed that it dug deeper into her heart. It was a reminder that they were drifting apart. He didn't want to tell her about Blair. She didn't want to tell him about the knife.

"Méilián."

Mia stayed with her back to the door, underwear drawer open with the knife barely visible from under the cloth. If Derek was using her Chinese name, it meant they were alone. Blair had left. Still, she didn't answer him.

"Will you please look at me?" he asked.

She didn't move.

"Oh come on. I know I've been shitty but I'm trying here. There's just...there's stuff. Okay. I don't know how to explain it. I don't know if I can explain it. And Blair...Blair gets it. And I don't...I don't want to push you away. None of us do. That's not what this is."

Then what is it?

Mia couldn't say the words aloud. She closed the drawer quietly. Hiding the knife. Derek was dealing with something. And now he wanted her to listen? Of course he did. He always wanted to use her to make his life easier, but when she needed him he was too tired.

"Can we talk?" Derek asked.

Mia turned this time. He was near her bed. In her room. Waiting for her. At least he'd bothered to fix his shirt. But she didn't want to deal with him. His face lit up when she faced him, but fell again when she moved. He stepped back. She continued forward. Him back. Her forward. Until he was at her door, and she got close, placing a hand flat on his chest and shoving with more force than he could fight against.

He gasped, stumbling out of her room and tripping, falling on his ass.

She stood over him for a second, hand on her door.

"Mia–"

And then she slammed the door in his face.

At first she stood there, breathing heavily from anger. From her actions. She listened to him get to his feet. He didn't say a word and his footsteps disappeared down the hall. Toward his room. Then she squeezed her eyes shut, and the tears fell.

She placed a hand over her mouth to silence her sobs.

He had wanted to talk. Now, of all times, right after sleeping with her best friend. What could he say? What could he possibly say to make any of this better?

As the tears streamed down her face, heart tight, stomach turning, she noticed Blair's bracelet on her wrist. She pulled her hand away from her mouth and stared at it. Blair had given it to her. Because of their friendship. But were they even friends anymore? What kind of friend abandoned you when the world was falling apart?

Mia gripped it. It was chilled. Ice.

It was too much.

She undid the strings.

Nothing was going right.

The bracelet fell from her wrist.

She didn't need friends who made her feel so awful.

No, you don't.

A chill ran down Mia's spine. Gray settled over her. The tears stopped flowing. The bracelet lay on the ground, dull and lifeless. Mia turned away from it and climbed onto her bed. She grabbed a pillow and hugged it, looking for comfort.

Instead she felt numb.

It'll be okay, she told herself.

It will be, the voice whispered.

She squeezed her eyes shut, wanting the tears to return. To be angry. To shout. To feel. But there was nothing.

It'll all be okay.

Chapter Nineteen

People passed her as a blur. She kept her gaze forward and saw nothing except for the smear of color from the clothes and hair of her classmates. Their chatter rose up around her. If she'd cared at all what they had to say, she might have heard the latest gossip. Questions about Steven who only seemed to talk to Mia. Nasty rumors about why Derek had come to school late again. But she didn't care.

She didn't care about much at all.

It didn't matter to her that Derek had slept in again. She'd left him there.

It didn't matter that her parents were leaving tonight for Thailand. They'd insisted that they'd put it off as long as they could, but some things were out of their control. They'd said they were sorry that they couldn't make it to her big game this weekend, but they would be there next year.

As they'd rambled, getting their things together, suitcases already by the door, Mia had just nodded.

It didn't matter if they were in America or not. They were barely home anyway.

So she didn't care.

As she walked to school, the cold didn't nip at her cheeks. The white flakes fluttering from the sky, a sight she used to gain pleasure from, drifted past her face, landing in her hair and coating the ground in the most mundane fashion. And as she did, the voice spoke to her.

A gentle voice coated with oil.

Of course everything feels dull. High school, this life, is dull.

Mia hadn't acknowledged the voice yet. It whispered to her throughout the night. During dinner with her parents, her mind had gone back and forth between the English whispering in her ear and the Chinese chatter at the table as her parents tried to get her and Derek to engage in conversation. She'd tried to ignore it. It had taken all she had to sit there quietly, picking at her food while her parents asked her and Derek questions.

They both gave one word answers. Neither of them exchanged glances.

And the voice kept going with comments about everything going on at their dinner table. The food being catered to Derek. Her parents leaving again. Her brother acting like a hurt puppy when Mia was the one who'd been injured.

It hadn't gone silent until she'd closed her eyes for the night.

When she woke, it had greeted her. And she'd lain there, as her alarm grew louder on the stand next to her bed, wondering why she didn't care.

Mia climbed the stairs to the second floor. People ran up and down them, having far too much energy for a group of high schoolers this early in the morning. A few people called out to her.

"Hey Sòng."

"You're gonna rock it tomorrow."

"Heard you got a better grade than Elsie on that history essay.

About time someone did."

"Good luck on the test today."

She wasn't sure if she responded or not. She tried to smile, each step draining her of any social energy. The chatter continued, and she slipped down the hall to her locker. When she reached it, hand touching the cool metal, she took a deep breath and closed her eyes.

It'd taken her years to get those kinds of greetings in the hallway. Months of practicing English on her own. Struggling through the homework that Derek had no issues with. Speaking along with audiobooks to work on her accent. Getting into organized sports both because she loved them, and to prove that she was worth being liked.

It didn't make sense. She stood at her locker, listening to the chatter, and couldn't understand why she didn't care.

Why should you? It's all bullshit.

"Mia."

This voice was different. It didn't belong to a classmate she shared friendly chatter with, and it wasn't the one in her head. She turned to find Cody standing there with his hands shoved deep into his pockets. He stared at her with curiosity. They had one class together in the morning and she hadn't said much during it. That wasn't abnormal, especially since everything had gone to hell in their group, but even she had been hoping she'd be back to texting him in class as they both tried hard not to get caught.

"Hi," she said.

Ignore him.

"I was thinking of running to the corner store to grab some caffeine," Cody said. "Wanna come?"

Mia tried to think. It was fourth period. Lunch. She wanted to avoid Derek and Blair. But Cody wasn't them. He…he'd apologized to her. Come to talk. It was all okay with him. She could go get coffee with him at the corner store.

What about Steven?

"I…I don't…." Mia tried to formulate a thought. A way to say yes to him.

No.

A way to reject him.

Cody's brow furrowed and he reached out with a hesitant hand, lightly touching her arm. Her head jerked up until their eyes met. His, gray like the sky before a winter storm, were wide with concern, and she found herself unable to move or think. It all stopped. The moment he touched her, the voice went silent.

"Are you okay?" Cody asked. The only sound.

She didn't like it. Dull, lifeless, noise was exhausting. But in the silence, she floated, unable to control her body or her mind. It collapsed on her. Suffocating.

Her breath caught.

She jerked her arm up, knocking his away.

The world returned, possibly a little brighter. And she breathed out.

Cody backed away, hands up. She brought hers to her chest, wringing them together. The voices in the hallway sharpened. More normal. Color bled through the carpet. The lockers. The ceiling. Not much. But less gray.

She tried to think of something to say. Was she okay? She felt odd. Off. Wrong. But not bad. Just not normal. But that was to be expected. Right?

This is what happens when your friends go behind your back.

Before she could say anything, though, Cody's eyes traveled down to her wrists. His eyes widened, and he gestured at the bare skin.

She looked down.

"You took off Blair's bracelet," he said. "I thought you never wanted to take it off."

Things change.

Finally, for the first time all day, real words formed. "I didn't. But...they...." She recalled what she saw. Blair and Derek coming out of his room, clearly ruffled. Like they'd been in bed for a while. Together. She shook her head. "I don't really want anything to do with Derek and Blair right now. Maybe ever. So. I took it off."

Cody paled. "You know, you never did tell me if you were okay. Has...everything been all right?"

Confusion overtook Mia. Not strong. Dulled. But...there. At least. She didn't want to lie to him, but she also wasn't sure it was a good idea to worry him. His anxiety got the best of him with the smallest things, and she didn't want to add to that with the insanity in her life.

Lying to him is better than telling him the truth. He won't mind. He'll never know.

"I'm okay." The words tumbled out with a mind of their own. She let out a small laugh. Weak. "Why? You look so concerned. It's just a bracelet."

Cody looked like he was having an argument with himself. Something internal. A fight she knew nothing about. Finally, he clenched his fists. Mia's body tensed, not sure why her chest tightened. Cody's face screwed up. He took a small step toward her.

Mia's heart leapt into her throat. Cody...what did he want to say?

"Mia, there's something—"

"Hey, there you are!"

The excited exclamation shattered the moment. Cody's words faltered. Mia jumped, startled, but her body relaxed in the seconds after. Time seemed to return to normal, and Steven appeared next to Mia. She didn't look at him, instead watching Cody. All of his determination faded and he backed away, looking to the ground. His hands clasped together and he wrung them. She wanted to step forward and comfort him, but Steven slipped his arm around her waist, like anyone might do after the way their night ended.

"You...guys okay?" Steven asked, looking between Mia and Cody.

"Yeah, we were just talking about lunch," Mia said. "He asked me to get coffee with him at the corner store."

"Oh. Fun," Steven said. "Why don't we all go?"

Cody looked up from the ground, opening his mouth as if to respond, but he froze again. Mia didn't understand at first. But when Steven shifted from one foot to another, she realized how close he was. How his arm was behind her back. Cody's eyes flickered between the two of them. It occurred to Mia then that she and Cody hadn't spoken much recently. He didn't know about Steven.

She didn't blame him when he stepped away. Cody wasn't good with surprises.

"I'm just...I'll go by myself," Cody said.

Rude.

Mia clenched her teeth. Not rude. Just...Cody.

"Can we talk later?" he asked, looking at Mia.

"Oh." Mia wasn't expecting the question.

Nope. No, no, no.

"Yeah," she said. "Of course. Mr. Becker's out again. If you get out of class early, want to meet up during seventh?"

He nodded. "Yeah. I'll let you know."

"Okay. See you later."

"Bye." He eyed Steven before turning and taking off down the hall a little quicker than he normally would.

Once he was gone, Steven said, "Huh."

She looked up at him, pulling away slightly. "What?"

"Nothing. Just...weird kid."

Mia frowned. "He's not weird. He has trouble with people he doesn't know."

Steven examined her, and she shrank back, feeling like he was doing a physical exam with his eyes. Then, after a moment he asked her the same question that Cody had asked her moments before: "Are you okay?"

No is a good answer.

"I…I don't know," she said. She didn't want to divulge how everything felt gray. Or how she'd lied to Cody. How she would keep having to lie to him. How these secrets she kept inside were eating at her. "I guess I'm just tired of secrets."

Steven nodded slowly. "Is…this about that knife?"

Mia shrugged. "That. Everything."

Steven ran a hand through his hair and looked around. "I…can't fix everything. Or much. But if you're worried that your brother or parents might find the knife, or if you just want to get rid of that, that *is* something I can fix. Might not be much. But it's something off your plate."

Instinct told her to say no. The knife drew her. It felt right hiding in her underwear drawer. But at the same time, it was tempting. Just like last time he asked. Part of her wanted to say yes.

Might as well. He'd know how to handle it better than you do. Leaving it buried underneath underwear.

Mia closed her eyes, wanting the voice to shut up. She didn't need a commentary on every decision in her life. She closed her eyes and thought about what it might mean to have that weight lifted. Knowing that it was gone and would never come back into her life.

She focused. And focused.

And then her stomach growled.

Her eyes snapped open, a hand going to her mouth, embarrassed. Steven's eyes widened as well, and they stared at each other for a moment before he burst into laughter. Mia smiled, though it felt off.

"Let's go eat," Steven said. "Let me know what you decide when you're ready. No pressure."

"Okay," she said. He held out a hand for her and she took it, expecting warmth. But there was no warmth. His hand wasn't cold. It just felt like nothing. And as they walked to the cafeteria, hand-in-hand, she noticed the color slowly fade from the walls.

Derek slouched in the plastic chair, arms crossed, looking anywhere but at the three adults in the room who were staring at him expectantly.

Mr. Henderson, the principal, had been coming up with solutions to their little problem, his irritation crawling up Derek's skin like a thousand centipedes. Derek could have made eye contact, but he didn't want to look at the man's idiotic face this early in the morning.

Mrs. York, his guidance counselor, had a giant grin on her face, pointing out all the great things Derek had done, like getting good grades, and participating in school events. Her voice was high and chipper, but Derek knew the truth. He felt her frustration. Her annoyance. They were sharp reminders that even the people trying to help him had internally given up. They didn't think he was serious about improving his "inherent issues."

As if they had any idea.

And the third person—the woman sitting next to him, emotions a stable, slimy, disappointment—he couldn't look at because he knew that disappointment was aimed at him. His parents were supposed to leave tonight. Drive down to Denver. Wake up in the morning to catch an early flight to a country on the other side of the world. Sitting in Willow Creek High's principal's office was the last thing Intira Sòng wanted to be doing.

"At this point, Derek is going to have trouble catching up in the classes he's falling behind in," Mrs. York said. Gentle tone. Harsh emotions.

"We'll make it work," Intira said. Her tone was not gentle. Her emotions stayed steady.

"With all due respect, Mrs. Sòng–" Mr. Henderson started to say.

"*Doctor* Sòng," Intira corrected, irritation coating the disappointment with fire. Derek shifted, uncomfortable from the new emotion picking at his skin, leaving invisible burns and a sense of dread. The first time Mr. Henderson had gotten it wrong, Derek assumed it was a mistake. But four times was pushing it.

Mr. Henderson smiled, and Derek swore he saw the man's eye twitch. "Dr. Sòng. With all due respect, I'm not sure how he can make up for the class he's missed and the homework he's failed to turn in."

"He'll get it done." Intira pulled out her phone. "Derek's father and I will be out of town for two weeks. In that time, we have family friends who are taking care of Derek and Mia. They'll make sure he gets his work done."

"Yes but–"

"If he does the work, he does the work," Intira continued, interrupting the principal once again. "I don't see why he shouldn't get credit for it. Prior to this, he had exceptional grades, an untainted attendance record, and, as Mrs. York has repeatedly pointed out, a stellar reputation. And you're considering permanently punishing him because he's struggled during these tempestuous few weeks?"

Derek looked between his mother and the principal. Intira stared straight ahead. She'd dressed up for this meeting with her graying hair pulled back into a low bun, her suit pants and jacket a slick black and a blouse Derek had seen on her many times. According to his dad, it was the one she'd been wearing when she'd found out she was pregnant. She considered it lucky.

They needed some luck.

The principal, meanwhile, looked like he couldn't figure out what "tempestuous" meant.

"No one said anything about a permanent punishment," Mrs. York said. "But even if he can catch up, which I do believe he can, there's still the matter of truancy."

"Well, that won't happen again," Intira said. Derek didn't want to look at her, but he knew that she was expecting it, so he took a deep breath and made eye contact.

He didn't want to promise that it wouldn't. Because he didn't know. He didn't know what was going to happen in the next five minutes, much less the rest of the semester. The rest of the year. The rest of high school. Blair was going to talk to her mom, maybe try and figure out what had happened in the forest, but beyond that, they had no leads. Things were going to get worse and worse and there was nothing Derek could do to stop it.

So he didn't want to promise that he'd attend class. Nor that he'd do all of his makeup work. But when he made eye contact with his mom, all he could think was that he didn't want to be the cause of her disappointment anymore.

"I won't ditch again," he said in a quiet voice. "I'll do better."

Her smile was soft and gentle. His lips flickered up in response, and then she turned back Mr. Henderson.

"See?" she said in a sickly sweet voice. A voice Derek recognized. It was the one she always used with his grandmother, and the two women didn't speak much. "Derek isn't a problematic student. The only reason you are focusing on these issues as much as you are is because you're convinced that he pushed over a bookcase. Something you don't actually have any evidence of and his account doesn't match yours. Had I been in town when it happened, I assure you, the fallout would have been very different."

Derek sunk a bit in his seat, eyes darting between the three adults in the room. He hadn't known that his mother felt this way. Or maybe it was a show. Either way, even if he weren't an empath, he would have felt the tension rising between Intira and Mr. Henderson, while Mrs. York had gone very pale. As far as Derek had known, the decision to suspend him had been a discussion with his parents.

Apparently he'd misunderstood something.

Finally, resignation overcame Mr. Henderson. He relaxed back in his chair and took a deep, heavy breath through his nose.

"All right," he said. "I expect one hundred percent attendance from now until the end of the semester. If he's absent, I expect a doctor's note. He has until the end of the semester to get in his missing assignments for full credit."

I'm right here.... Derek didn't dare speak. He'd already done enough damage to his life.

"Excellent," Intira said. She stood, smoothing her jacket. Derek scrambled to his feet as well, keeping his gaze to the table.

"M...Dr. Sòng," Mr. Henderson said. "I think–"

"While I'm sure you have something of vital importance to discuss with me further, I'm afraid I must cut this meeting short. We have a plan for Derek," she placed a hand on his shoulder, an odd gesture, "and we will follow through. As I said, my husband and I will be out of town for two weeks. If you have any further questions, you have my email. I'll reply when I can."

Mrs. York and Mr. Henderson exchanged glances, annoyance and frustration rising from both of them. But you didn't argue with Intira Sòng. When she ended a conversation, it ended. Even if they weren't her colleagues, even if they weren't her children, the finality in her tone made that clear.

"Have a safe trip, Dr. Sòng," Mrs. York said with a faltering smile. This time, her emotions matched her expression. Defeat. Frustrated defeat. Derek scratched at his skin beneath the sleeve of his shirt, wanting the feeling gone.

"Thank you," Intira said before she turned and strode out of the office. Derek glanced between the two adults, who were whispering to each other, and he followed his mom out.

Leaving the stuffy room was a breath of fresh air. It was already time for lunch, and students laughed down the hallway, the tingles of eagerness permeating the air all around him. He wanted to join in. To see his friends and forget all about the fact that he almost got in trouble. Again.

Instead, he stood next to his mom, looking down at her, and wondering when she'd gotten so small. She had her eyes glued to her phone, reading a message from his dad. Derek had never been good at reading upside down, a skill Mia had a particular affinity for, so he wasn't sure what they were talking about, but whatever it was, it was about him. He absolutely recognized the characters that made up his name, even upside down.

After a minute, she put her phone away and looked up at him.

"Well," she said in Chinese, "that could have gone better."

Derek rolled his eyes. "Tempestuous?"

"He got on my nerves." As she put her phone in her purse, she let out a heavy sigh. "I stood up for you in there because you are my son. But they are right to be upset with you."

"I know," he muttered. A few students glanced at the two of them, then broke into whispers. Derek ignored the emotions pouring out of them. They were light enough that he could pretend they didn't exist.

Intira stared at him. Her emotions were a flux of disappointment, concern, and frustration. Once more, he scratched his wrist. Finally, after enough time for Intira to fully examine her son, she glanced at the ground.

"I should stay."

"Huh?"

"Here. In America. I can arrange for a translator for Dad. He's spent months in Thailand without me. He's okay with it."

"What, no," Derek said. He reached out and touched her shoulder, like she had done for him in the principal's office. "Mā, come on. This is your work too. You should go and help him."

She shook her head. "It may be my work, but you are my children. I've failed as a mother. To you and to Mia. The last thing I should be doing is once again putting my work before you two."

The disappointment grew. His skin burned with it as the slime heated and twisted into something similar to guilt. He removed his hand from her shoulder and let it drop to his side as realization came over him. His mom wasn't disappointed in him. She was disappointed in herself.

He glanced at the other students in the hall. Their chatter and laughter resonated up to the low ceilings. In the midst, he spotted Blair leaning against the wall, waiting for him. She was dressed the way she always was in a t-shirt and jeans and her hair was in braids. He thought for a moment back to the previous day. The way it'd felt to kiss her. Running his hands along her bare back. Up into her loose, wavy hair.

A moment of euphoria that he wouldn't have traded for anything. One that seemed to destroy the last pillar of his closeness to his sister. One that happened because his parents were always absent.

His mom was disappointed in herself. She blamed herself for what was going on with Derek and Mia. The fact that Mia barely spoke at home. The way she ignored Derek, even though the two of them used to be so close. Derek failing classes for the first time in his life. His mom had no idea. She didn't know about the magic, or the dreams, or the strange women stalking him, or that Mia was angry at him, not at their parents.

They'd never exactly been close, their family. But it wasn't like they were uncommunicative. His parents worked. He and Mia spent time at home with family and friends to check in with. Yet they always tried to have dinner together and check in. They still tried.

"Mia and I are fine," Derek said. A complete and total lie, but he didn't want his mom's disappointment sludge encasing his body anymore. "You and Bà have things you need to do, and it's not for long, right? Just two weeks?"

Intira didn't say anything. She merely watched Derek for a while, as if wondering what he could be thinking. The sludge shuddered, as if making way for another emotion.

He took a deep breath, and Blair glanced at him. They made eye contact, and his stomach turned when she smiled softly. "You should go. I won't ditch class again. I'll get my homework done, even if it means having Cody tutor me." A solution he did not want to resort to, as Cody was only patient with Mia.

"What about Mia?" Intira asked.

"I'll look out for her," Derek said, forcing a smile. The words were true. But he didn't know how well it would go. "I always look out for her."

"She's mad at you."

Derek's stomach sank and he let out a nervous laugh. "I... uh...."

Intira turned her head until her gaze fell on Blair. Amusement picked at him, and he wondered how much she'd picked up on. "You and Mia have always been close. I hope that you dating her best friend won't change that."

She'd picked up on a lot, apparently. "We're not dating."

She laughed. "That's what I said about your father."

"Mā, seriously."

"I'm being serious." She reached into her purse once more and pulled out her phone. After reading something on the screen, she looked up at him. She had more gray hairs than before, he realized. Despite wearing makeup, he could see the bags under her eyes and the crow's feet aging her. "Do you want me to stay?"

Did he? Did he have an answer? Did he want to spend more time with his mom in the hopes that things would go back to the way they were? Or did he want her gone while he figured out the shitstorm he'd somehow created that night at the opening?

"I…think you should go," he said, voice quiet.

No emotion greeted his statement.

Instead, she nodded and touched his arm. "I'll see you tonight."

"See you tonight."

She turned heel and headed down the mostly empty hallway, heels clacking. Derek watched her go, staring after her until a hand touched his arm. He sighed, running a hand through his hair, and faced Blair, frustration melting away.

"Hey," he said.

"Everything okay?" she asked. Her voice was quiet. He longed to feel her emotions. To know what she was feeling in this moment, as it was the first time they'd spoken since she left the night before. He didn't want to have to ask, or guess. He just wanted to *know*.

He shrugged. "My mom's worried. She asked me if she should stay home."

"Do you want her to?"

"Dunno."

"Oh."

Her hand slid down until it entwined with his. He slipped his fingers in hers, letting the warmth of the moment relax his muscles, calming his nerves and his confusion. He wanted to hug her. More than anything he wanted to wrap his arms around her body and pull it against his. Had they not been at school, he would have. But as it was, he didn't want the other students to spend more time gossiping about his life.

"Did you talk to your mom?" Derek asked in a low voice.

"Yeah," Blair said. "She isn't sure what any of this means, but she wants to talk to you tomorrow."

"Tomorrow works," he said without much thinking. It was Saturday. It was the game. Mia's big game that she'd been excited about for weeks. She'd made all of them promise to go see it. She'd made her parents promise to go see it. Everyone had agreed without question. Except now their parents were leaving. And she hated Derek and Blair. "It has to be early in the day."

Blair nodded. "That's fine."

Derek yawned, and when he opened his eyes again, he noticed Cody walking toward them. No. Not walking. Almost running. Derek nudged Blair's arm and pointed toward Cody, who, as he drew closer, Derek realized had wide eyes and a sense of urgency tensing his body. Derek reached out, looking to make sure those were the emotions, but there was nothing.

"Cody," Derek said once the boy had arrived. But the friendliness in his tone didn't last long when Cody reached out and smacked him, hard, on the arm. "Hey! What the hell?"

"What did you two do?" Cody asked, voice frantic.

Blair and Derek exchanged glances. "What are you talking about?" Blair asked.

"Mia hates you two." Cody hit Derek again, in the exact same spot.

"Stop that," Derek yelped.

Blair's eyes widened.

Cody huffed. "I thought I was hallucinating. Something was so off. But no. Just now. Talking to her. Her mist was off."

Derek furrowed his brow. "What does that even mean?"

"What's wrong with her mist?" Blair asked.

"It's gray."

Derek blinked, recalling back to the day when Cody told him about the mists. Cody had mentioned all of the colors, but Derek couldn't place what they were. Blair must not have known the significance of this either, because she glanced up at Derek with a confused look.

Cody let out an exasperated groan. "Her mist is normally white."

"I thought you said mist colors fluctuate," Blair said.

"Mia's doesn't change like that," Cody snapped. "She was weird. Distant. I touched her arm and her mist lightened, but it's wrong, and then I found out that she's not wearing the bracelet—"

"Whoa, whoa, whoa," Derek said, holding up his hands. Cody fell silent, but with a look of protest on his face. Derek focused on Mia's emotions, trying to find them. When he found nothing, he shook his head. "I can't feel her. She must be wearing it, or have it on her person, or something."

"She doesn't," Cody said. "She told me she doesn't want to wear it anymore because of you two, and then that Steven kid showed up and wrapped his arm around her." He punched Derek's arm this time. Same spot.

Derek jumped away from Cody, grabbing the now quite sore spot on his arm. "Stop hitting me."

"What did you two *do*?" Cody asked.

"We—" Blair started, but then she fell silent, possibly because she didn't want to talk to Cody about their jumping into bed together. But Derek had a darker, sinking feeling about why she'd stopped mid-word. Because when he stopped for a second, rubbing his arm, he realized that something really wasn't adding up. Something none of them wanted.

Derek looked around, frantically trying to reach out and find his sister. Her emotions. Anything to tell him that she was there and okay. That her emotions were in check. Or even if they weren't. Even if she was having a complete breakdown right now, he needed to be feeling it.

His heart slowed as he searched. And when he found nothing, it seemed to stop.

"Why can't I feel my sister?" he asked, barely aware of where he was. When no one responded, he continued. "Mia's bracelet is off. I should be able to feel her. Why can't I feel her?"

"Maybe she's too far," Cody said.

"If she's in town," Derek said, losing all power in his voice, "I should be able to sense her."

It was back. The same feeling as in the mountains. The bone-chilling fear.

All three teens looked at each other, as if sharing a single thought. A single question. A single problem they'd all wanted to avoid.

"Is Mia involved in all this?" Blair asked.

No. No. She can't be.

Derek shook his head. Yes, she'd come to talk to him. Yes, she was acting weird. Yes, things didn't get bad until recently. But that didn't mean she knew anything about what was going on, much less that she was involved in any of it.

But maybe…maybe she was.

"We need to talk to her," Cody said. "She's always with Steven, but she and I are supposed to meet toward the end of seventh."

"We should be there too," Blair said.

Derek wanted to chime in, but he couldn't stop searching for his sister's emotions. He went through every single student, jumping from one to another, focusing in on their emotions even though it was something he sucked at. He would find her if he could.

"You two will scare her," Cody said. "Since she's mad at whatever you did."

"If she's involved I should talk to her," Blair snapped.

"Just let me tell her what's going on."

"No. I'm going to be there."

"You have class. You can't skip."

"Wanna bet?"

Derek snapped back to reality as Cody and Blair bickered. Her emotions really weren't there. She'd removed the bracelet but nothing had changed.

She wouldn't talk to him anymore, or even acknowledge his existence. Derek's stomach curled into the tightest ball he'd ever experienced, and his face went cold as if he were about to puke.

"Derek and I will be there," Blair said. "Right?"

Derek looked at her. He wanted to say right, but he'd literally just told his mom he wouldn't ditch class anymore. And he didn't know what to do. Blair and Cody could talk to Mia. Without him, it might be easier. Blair and Cody were her best friends, and she deserved the support they could give her. If him not being there, if him following the rules and not ditching class, made it easier and better, then he would do that.

"No," he said after a time, voice barely a whisper. "You two do it. I can't miss class."

Blair cocked her head, and Cody crossed his arms, but neither said anything.

Derek gulped. "You two talk to her. I'll try tonight after she gets home from practice. Tomorrow we should talk to Mrs. Arbour and see what she has to say." He didn't like the situation at all. She'd taken off the bracelet. They could get her to put it back on if they just tried. If they told her what was going on.

But he still needed to figure out who was trying to kill him and why. And there were ways to make this all work out. He knew it. It had to be the case.

"So," Cody said, looking at Blair. "Seventh?"

She nodded. "Derek, you'll talk to her tonight?"

Tonight it would just be the two of them. No parents. No Blair. No Cody. If there was any time for him to talk to Mia, this was it. He would tell her what was going on, and he would sit and listen to her. Because he had a strange feeling that the issues she was having all those weeks ago, when she came to him and said she needed to talk, wasn't about school drama like he'd thought.

His stomach continued to tighten as he realized just how much he'd messed up. If those issues she wanted to talk about weren't about who dated who, and it was about why her mist was gray, and why he couldn't feel her emotions, then he was an idiot for not taking the time to listen.

He'd messed up so bad. So he nodded. "Yeah. Tonight. I'll talk to her tonight."

Chapter Twenty

There's no point to any of this.

For the fifth time in the past ten minutes, Mia closed her eyes and breathed in deeply, hoping that if she just focused enough, the voice would shut up. Through the numbness, the gray, a hint of frustration bubbled up to the surface, not quite breaking the tension of the water, but threatening to.

She begged it to. For her body to be overcome with any emotion. The rest of the library bustled with its normal, hushed activity, and if Mia had had anywhere else to go she would have. She didn't want hushed. She wanted loud and explosive; anything to make her feel like she wasn't vanishing into a cloud of mist.

Are you really vanishing? Seems to me like you've been gone from the minds of your friends and family for a long time.

Mia gripped her pencil and continued working on her calculus. She pushed numbers and formulas into her mind, trying to drown out anything in her head that wasn't mathematics. Something. Anything. To get the voice to stop overtaking every inch of brain matter, ringing in her ears, making it impossible to focus on the rest of the world. She couldn't focus on her homework. On her friends. On her family. Her parents were leaving when she got home from practice, and every time she tried to think of what to say to them, the voice shouted over her own words, giving her a million things to say.

Screw em. Don't say anything. They don't care about you. They just care about their work and their own egos. They know nothing about your life, so why should you care about theirs?

And the thing was, sometimes, when the voice was going off, ranting about her parents, about Blair, about Derek, about everything in her life, she wasn't one-hundred percent sure it wasn't her thinking that.

It is you. It's me. It's us. We're not separate from one another.

Mia breathed in again.

I'm not going anywhere. I'm you. All of your anger and pain. Everything you don't want to think.

Don't acknowledge it, don't acknowledge it, don't acknowledge it, Mia chanted. The voice kept prodding her, trying to get her to have a conversation, but she refused to engage. There was no point, she told herself. All she had to do was get through the next two weeks without an issue, and it would be fine. Her parents would be home, basketball would be done, and winter break would be on its way.

Maybe, without school or drama, she could talk to her brother.

No.

YES.

Huh?

Mia looked up from her homework, startled by the new voice. Her eyes scanned the library, searching for the source of the affirmation. It wasn't like the other voice. Familiar, yes, but distinct. Deeper. But...lighter. A gentle whisper of an amused laugh weaving in and out of the gray.

People continued about their business. Students studied. The librarians spoke in whispers. She counted each person. Named them. Ran their voices through her head to match it to the voice. The voices.

But there was no match. The frustration bubbled up again. It didn't break the surface.

She returned to her homework, gripping the pencil tight enough to leave indentations in her skin, but the pain meant nothing to her.

IGNORING PAIN DOESN'T REMOVE ITS MEANING.

Nothing to ignore. It's not there.

YES IT IS.

Shut up. Mia's grip tightened again.

THERE ARE FEW THINGS IN THIS WORLD THAT ARE NONEXISTENT. PAIN IS NOT ONE. IF YOU FEEL IT, IF YOU EXPERIENCE IT, THEN IT IS REAL, AND IT HURTS NO MATTER YOUR LEVEL OF TOLERANCE.

Foolish notion. There is nothing. It's empty. It's gray. Your people have left you and there's no reason for you to stay here.

HAVE THEY LEFT HER, OR HAS SHE LEFT THEM?

Shut up! She pressed down on lead, wanting to write. It snapped and flew across the table. Her thumb went to the eraser and she pressed down, listening to the click as more lead slipped out.

They've left you. Again. And again. It's time to leave them. There's no point to your homework or your friends. No point in falling in love when no one is going to stay with you anyway.

Mia closed her eyes and breathed. And with each inhale, she begged the voices to stop so she could finish her calculus.

IT'S EASY TO GET ANGRY AT ONLY HALF THE PICTURE.

Half the picture is more than enough.

SUCH AN IGNORANT NOTION.

So you would say. Ignorance is what you know best.

"There's my favorite student."

"Shut up!" Mia threw her pencil on the table and gripped her hair. The pencil bounced. Mia squeezed her eyes shut, waiting for more voices to drill insanity into the gaps of her mind. But there was nothing. For a moment, a brief moment, it was silent in her mind. And in that silence, she realized that the last voice, the one that'd made her yell aloud, hadn't been in her head.

She released the clumps of hair from her fingers and looked up. She scanned him as she did. His jeans. His shirt. His crossed arms. They all led up to raised eyebrows. Mr. Becker stared down at her, frowning. Mia didn't see him frown very often.

"Mr. Becker?" Mia asked. Her voice was quiet, almost drowned out by the sounds of the library. "You're back?"

His frown twitched into a crooked smile, and he settled into the seat in front of her. "Don't tell anyone. I'm supposed to be on my trip for another few days, but I got back early."

Mia glanced around them. "You're in the library."

"No one will notice me. How's life? How's school? What's the gossip situation?" he stared at her with his crooked grin and narrowed eyes.

Leave.

STAY.

Mia focused on her teacher. "I don't understand. If you're still on vacation, why are you here?"

Mr. Becker hummed softly. "Here in Willow Creek? Here at school? Here in the library?"

"All three?" Mia wasn't sure how else to respond to that. Mr. Becker wasn't exactly the most normal teacher at Willow Creek High—or possibly any school ever—but this seemed a little odd, even for him.

"Came in to do some…work." His crooked grin evened out into a soft smile. He broke their eye contact to stare at the table, but only for a moment. Then it was back to the previous expression. "Noticed you sitting all alone and decided to see how things were."

You're fine. Leave.

IF SHE'S FINE, WHY SHOULD SHE LEAVE?

It'll just hurt when he abandons you too.

HE'S A TEACHER. THEY DON'T ABANDON THEIR STUDENTS.

Lies.

NOT A BIG FAN OF LYING.

Lies!

"Things are fine," Mia managed to say. With a shaking hand, she picked up her pencil and went back to work.

"Is it? Gossip in the halls is that you and your brother are having a falling out."

Mia grimaced, but didn't look up from her homework.

"How does that even work?" Tapping entered Mia's consciousness. Mr. Becker's fingers clicked against the table one. At. A. Time. "You two live in the same house. You share a birthday. You have the same parents. Can twins even have a falling out?"

"We're not having a falling out," Mia said.

"Gossip says otherwise."

"If you know all the gossip, then why are you asking me about it?" She tried not to think too much about it. Mr. Becker knew things. He always knew things he shouldn't know. He was observant. Patient. He listened, even when no one else seemed able to.

Leave.

"Just curious what your thoughts are," Mr. Becker said with a shrug. "I hear things, but sometimes going to the source is the best."

Mia sighed. Annoyance. Was she feeling annoyance? The gray swirled around her, encasing her mind and dulling every one of her senses. Now and then, it shifted enough for her to feel, but not much. As the two of them sat there, Mia begged for the emotional vibrance she always felt when talking to her favorite teacher.

IT'LL COME BACK.

When you leave.

Leave the library? She hadn't meant for the question to appear in her mind. Don't engage. That was her goal. But it happened.

Leave the library, yes. Then keep going. Leave Willow Creek and never look back.

"Come on," Mr. Becker said. "Give me something. I've been gone from this cesspool of drama for far too long. I miss hearing about it."

"There's nothing to hear about," Mia muttered. Leave Willow Creek? She wanted to, yes. But not now. She had to finish school, and then she'd get out. Go to college. Make a life for herself that wasn't in the middle of the mountains. Make a life for herself that wasn't in America.

"So you're not fighting with Derek?"

"No."

"Nor Blair?"

Mia rolled her eyes. "You must have big ears to be hearing all this."

The moment the words left her mouth, she froze, eyes going wide. Time seemed to slow for a moment as she wracked her mind, trying to understand what the hell made her say something so sarcastic and so rude to her teacher. Yes, she and Mr. Becker had friendly conversations, but she was never rude to him. It was inappropriate.

She slowly looked up at him, making eye contact. It was odd. His eyes. Blue and green. Different colors. She'd always thought so. The entire town always thought so. But today, looking into them, it was like there was something…unique. The colors appeared unnatural. There were no words to describe them. The blue one floating on nothingness. The green burrowed deep beneath the earth and laced with happiness.

Mia blinked. They returned to normal.

"I…I'm sorry," Mia said, flustered. Her phone buzzed on the table next to her. Cody's name appeared, as well as a text letting her know he'd managed to get out of class early. Her chest tightened.

She'd forgotten that she'd promised him they'd talk.

"I don't have big ears." He reached up with one hand and gripped the lobe of his left ear, tugging it down. "They're actually quite small. I just pay attention."

Her phone buzzed again. Cody telling her that he was outside the library.

"Do you need to go?" he asked, gesturing to the phone.

"I…yeah," Mia said. She gathered her things. "It was nice to see you. I'll…Monday." Her hand shook as they shoved her things in her backpack and slung it over her shoulder.

Good riddance.

Mia made to pass Mr. Becker. She didn't want to look at him, to see his disappointment at her talking back. But he spoke again, and his words gave her pause.

"You know, I've lost people."

She glanced at him. The back of his head.

"Fights. Arguments. They all seem meaningless when the other person is gone."

Leave.

SHE WILL.

"A long time ago, I lost a friend," Mr. Becker said. He didn't look at her, but his hands had gone into his pockets. "She was a good friend. Quiet. Awkward. Always tried her best. But something happened. And she went missing. I've been looking for her…well, my friends and I have been looking for her. We got wind that she's resurfaced. But no matter how much we search, and how hard we try, we can't seem to find her."

This time, he did look at her. He tilted his head back with a grin. "But I think we're getting close. And when we do, all of the bullshit will be meaningless."

Incoherent bullshit. Just get out of there.

Mia's thoughts wouldn't focus for her to think about his words.

They swirled around, dancing in the storm of gray clouds that took the color out of the world.

DEFINITELY TIME TO LEAVE. YOU HAVE AN APPOINTMENT TO KEEP.

Mr. Becker's head jerked back to its rightful position. "Not sure I'll make it to the game tomorrow. Good luck."

"Thanks," Mia said. She couldn't think of anything else to say. She'd hoped, just a little bit, that he'd be able to come, since her parents couldn't, but it wasn't realistic of her to expect that of him. It wasn't right to feel disappointment. But she did. Or, she tried to. She wanted to. It danced in the mist.

Her phone buzzed. It vibrated up her hand, tingling her skin until she shuddered. Cody again. Asking her where she was.

BEST NOT KEEP HIM WAITING.

Mia stepped. One foot at a time. Taking her further from her teacher, and closer to her friend. The first friend she'd made in America. The one who always had time for her if she asked.

She loved Blair. Her spontaneity and no-shits-given attitude led to a lot of random adventures and experiences Mia might not have had before. And though Blair kept her emotions and family life close to her chest, often thinking of herself and her needs first, she was oddly caring and tried hard to distract Mia from her family's issues. She cared. Or…used to.

But even with all of that, Cody was the one who seemed to get her.

The two of them sitting under that slide. Him helping her with vocabulary. Her teaching him some Chinese characters. They didn't talk about the bullies or the bruises on his arms. It was months like that before Blair punched a girl in the cafeteria for bullying Mia. Weeks before Derek decided he wanted to hang out with Mia and her friends.

HE'S YOUR BEST FRIEND. MIGHT AS WELL LISTEN TO WHAT HE HAS TO SAY.

Mia stepped. The library passed her by as the gray mist thickened in the corner of her eye. If she turned her head, wanting to see it, it shifted, always staying just in sight. So she decided to ignore it.

Her hand touched the door. It pushed. The door opened. She stepped through it and blinked. The hallway looked normal. Colors their regular saturation. Her mind a blissful, clear, quiet. She didn't dare look behind her.

Instead her gaze trailed down the hallway, where she knew that Cody was waiting for her. Her friend. It could just be the two of them. Maybe Steven. Blair and Derek could go do their own thing.
You don't need them.

She found him, leaning against the wall with his arms crossed, and she wanted the happiness to float to the surface, but it vanished underneath a new emotion. A darker emotion. It shot to the top, clearing the path of any fog keeping her dulled. Her heart dipped into her stomach. Her muscles clenched, hands balling into fists tight enough that her trimmed nails dug into her skin.

Cody wasn't alone. He'd told her they would talk. The two of them. He had something he wanted to tell her. He never once mentioned that Blair would be with him.

The two stood together. Cody against the wall. Blair standing in front of him with crossed arms. Talking. She stepped back.

She didn't understand. What was Cody doing with Blair? The two of them had never gotten along. Even if she or Derek were in the same room, they bickered. If they weren't bickering, they were ignoring each other. They didn't have conversations alone. And Blair had class this period. Was Blair ditching? Mia wouldn't be surprised, but…why? To talk to her?

Was this a plan to get Mia to talk to Blair?
Why can't they just leave well enough alone?
Mia stepped back.
Where's Derek? Did he not decide to join them?

The three of them are plotting together. Just like before. It's no different just because Cody talked to you alone one time. Your brother is still stealing your friends.

He's not even there.

He'll show up.

No.

Just give him time.

Mia shook her head. She stepped back again, terrified.

Why am I terrified?

WELL, THAT'S A QUESTION. WHAT ABOUT THEM BEING TOGETHER SCARES YOU?

You have every reason to be scared. They hate you. They just don't want you to know.

Cody doesn't hate me.

NONE OF THEM HATE YOU.

Leave.

Mia stepped back. Her footsteps were silent against the tile. Cody said something to Blair, and she uncrossed her arms and said something back. He waved a hand and looked away. Not toward Mia. Blair threw her hands up and placed them on her hips. He must have said something else because she threw her head back like she did when she was frustrated.

They were her friends. She should have trusted them. But Blair and Derek were off in their own world, and apparently they were dragging Cody along with them. She couldn't trust them with her secrets. She couldn't trust them with the knife.

They keep lying to you.

Everyone kept lying to her.

You can't trust them.

She could only trust one person.

SEEMS ODD TO ME.

Leave.

Mia turned. She stepped. And stepped. And stepped. Her feet

bringing her further from her two friends. As they did, she unlocked her phone and found the text chain with Steven. Or…maybe friend wasn't the right word for him anymore. The way he'd wrapped his arm around her waist in the hallway earlier indicated something more. As if kissing him didn't.

She typed. Her fingers flew across the screen, making far too many mistakes. Her phone buzzed. Another text from Cody asking if she was okay.

She ignored it and pressed send as she turned a corner. Out of sight of them. She stopped, pressing against the wall and held her phone to her chest, waiting for Steven's reply. She closed her eyes and tried to calm her thumping heart. They wouldn't come after her. They didn't know where she was. There was no way for them to find her, and in a bit, class would start, then practice, then heading home to say goodbye to her parents.

You'll be safe.

She'd be safe.

They can't get to you now.

They couldn't get to her.

They can't hurt you anymore.

Her phone buzzed. Cody or Steven. She took a breath and checked.

<<Sure. I'll see you tonight.>>

Derek wasn't sure he wanted to know why Blair and Cody were waiting for him at the start of eighth period. It wasn't that they were together. It was an abnormal sight, but not unheard of. What got to Derek, as he headed through the halls to meet them, students rushing off to their last class of the day with anxiety stabbing at

Derek's skin, was that the two of them were standing together and not arguing.

He didn't need to feel their emotions to know that something was wrong. A stone dropped in his stomach, dragging him down into the floor. He had to get to them. But he also just wanted to run and not hear the bad news.

"What's going on?" he asked the moment he stepped up to them. Cody looked at the ground, and Blair placed her hands on her hips with a huff. That was enough for him. "She didn't show?"

"No," Blair said. "We have no idea where she is. Probably in class, but it's not like we can just barge in and drag her out."

"Sounds like something you'd do," Cody muttered.

If Blair heard him, she ignored it, focusing instead on Derek. He didn't like the look in her eyes. It tugged at him. Made him feel like she blamed him for all of this. And, no matter how hard he tried, no matter how hard he thought about what Blair might be feeling right now, with her friend possibly in danger because of a world they'd tried to keep her out of, he couldn't tell if *she* blamed him, or if *he* blamed himself. Or if maybe it was a mix of both.

Derek leaned against the wall, pressing his head against the cool brick. His head swam with the events of the day. He'd told his mom he'd look out for her. He always looked out for her. Yelling at the boys who picked on her when she was hiding from everyone. Making sure her anxiety didn't run her life. Watching quietly in case the social status she gained fell apart. It was his job to make sure she was all right. He sucked at cooking and cleaning and getting up on time, but he could make sure she was all right.

And he'd failed.

"Derek?" Blair asked. Her hand touched his shirt, chilling his skin even beneath the fabric. Still, a flutter of enjoyment tickled his gut. One he wanted to disappear. This wasn't the time.

"She's not going to talk to me," he said. He wasn't sure who he was talking to. Himself, or Blair.

"You can at least try," Blair said. "You live with her. What's the worst she can do?"

He wasn't sure, honestly. When she'd shoved him out of her room, it'd been hard. As kids, it wasn't like she was the most gentle person ever. Definitely not like the flower she was named after. Everyone always assumed it was Derek who played rough, but he always had far more bruises than she did. Still, all of that had been in the name of fun. When she shoved him, it wasn't meant to hurt, and if he shoved her back, she laughed. If he got hurt, she bandaged him up and made sure he was okay.

When she was mad, she mostly went silent. But this hadn't been that. She hadn't even cared. It was a side of her he'd never seen before.

While he hoped that it was just a one-time thing, he wasn't sure. He didn't know what was going on in her life, nor in her head. Her emotions. What *would* happen if he tried to talk to her?

"What time are your parents leaving tonight?" Cody asked. "Maybe we can come over and help."

"No," Derek said. "Mia's not going to want to get cornered."

"We need to talk to her," Blair said.

"I know that." Irritation rose in him and he brushed her arm away. He glanced around the now empty hallway. If they weren't careful, some adult would come and scold them for being there during class. But he wasn't sure they should go to the library. While the principal hadn't managed to get him banned, the place still left a bad taste in his mouth.

Cody pulled out his phone, staring at it as if that would make something happen. Derek ignored him and banged his head on the wall slightly.

"Derek what are you going to do?" Blair asked.

Derek groaned and pushed himself away from the wall, heading outdoors. They didn't have to stay on campus during school hours if they didn't have class. He didn't have class. This was not a conversation he wanted to have confined within the walls of high school.

"Derek!"

He ignored Blair's voice and pushed his way through the front doors of the school. And regretted it immediately when the air chilled his bones. He shuddered and wrapped his arms around his body.

"Dammit, Derek," Blair said, appearing next to him. She grabbed his arm, tugging him back toward warmth, but he pulled away from her.

"I don't know what to do, okay?" Derek said. He tried to keep his cool. "I'm not used to this. To not know, or understand. I'm not used to not being able to feel when something is wrong with my sister."

Cody headed over to them, arms crossed. A gust of wind dropped the temperatures, and Derek shuddered.

"We need to figure something out," Cody said. "If Mia's somehow involved in all of this...."

"Okay, but we don't actually know she is," Blair pointed out.

"Her mist is wrong and Derek can't feel her emotions. *Something* is going on."

"Maybe you just misunderstood what you saw."

"I didn't misunderstand."

"I dunno. You're not great at controlling your powers."

Derek watched as Cody's eyes widened, more than confused about the argument the two were having.

Cody, however was not, and before Derek could step in and stop them from arguing, he absolutely snapped.

"You're just going after me because you know it's your fault all of this is happening in the first place."

A chill settled over the three teens, dropping the temperature in the area a good ten degrees. Derek shivered, glancing between his two friends. When Blair stepped forward, hand clenched into a fist, Derek reacted, moving between them, facing Blair.

"Guys, come on, not right now," Derek pleaded.

"No, he needs to take that *back*," Blair growled. Her voice quivered. Derek couldn't tell if her shaking body was from anger, guilt, or the cold.

"I'm just telling the truth. Something you suck at."

"Are you fuc–"

"Stop!" Derek shouted, stopping Blair from bulldozing through him to get at Cody. Blair stepped away from him and crossed her arms, gaze trained to the ground. When Derek looked behind him, he found Cody staring back at the school. Unlike Derek and Blair, he wasn't shivering.

A pang of annoyance lanced Derek's head. He didn't know whose it was, but he continued anyway. "You two can hate each other later. We have other things to worry about right now. Who cares whose fault it is? Something is wrong with Mia, someone's trying to kill me, and it's possible the two are related. So just stop it for two goddamn seconds!"

Neither Blair nor Cody said anything, both refusing to look at the other. Derek had no idea what they'd talked about while they waited for Mia, but whatever it was must have added to this. Any other day, he'd try to figure out what it was, but today he didn't care.

He groaned. "We've all messed up since the sculpture broke and now we have to figure out how to save Mia from whatever is going after her...mist, or whatever it is."

"She's not talking to you guys," Cody said, "and I have a feeling she's going to avoid me now too. She probably saw Blair standing with me."

Derek placed a hand on Blair's shoulder before she could snap at him. She tensed, and another gust of wind encased them.

Cody continued. "How the hell are we going to ask her what's going on when she won't let us? I'm not going to force her to do anything."

He thought. Back to when the tension started. When she'd stopped talking to him. When she'd started spending more time with Steven. But it was all a mess in his head. He'd been so focused on staying alive he'd put everything else aside, and he wasn't even sure if that'd been a mistake. He did know, though, that not including Mia had been.

"My parents are leaving tonight," Derek said. He forced himself to think. "Mia has to be there. I can try–"

"She's not going to talk to you," Cody snapped.

Derek had just about had it with Cody's irritation. "Well, when you think of a better idea, I'm all ears."

Cody went quiet, then turned back toward the school. "Fine. Worst comes to worst, we can talk to Mrs. Arbour tomorrow. She isn't bound by clan laws."

Before Derek could ask how Cody knew that, and what that would even mean, he headed back into the school. Into the warmth. Derek longed to join him. He was practically vibrating he was so cold. Blair too, shook, head bowed. Derek relaxed as much as he could, and hesitantly reached out to touch her cheek. It was wet.

"Blair?" he asked.

"It's not my fault," she said.

He didn't know how to respond. It was all of their faults. They'd all made mistakes.

"I didn't cause this." It wasn't clear if she was convincing him, or herself.

Derek pulled her into a hug, relishing in the warmth of her body, but hating how she clung to him. "We should go inside."

She pushed him away after a minute and wiped her eyes. "Yeah."

The two hurried back toward the front doors as another gust of wind smacked him from behind. He paused and turned, as wind didn't usually shift direction like that. What he found, when he turned, standing away from him, black wind, black dress, dancing in the wind, was the woman with red eyes. She stared at him, and he stared at her. She cocked her head, as if inviting him to chase her.

His heart tugged at his chest. It begged him to go to her. To get the answers he desired.

He couldn't.

Instead he faced the school again and headed into the warm building where Blair waited for him. Despite his soul calling for him to find her, and despite the cold, alone, and empty energy mixing with his own, acting as a beacon, she didn't matter as much as his sister.

The queen needed him, but so did Mia, and he cared more about his sister than a fairytale.

Mia refused to look at him. Derek leaned against the couch as his parents checked over and over that they had everything they needed for their trip. They bickered, switching between Chinese and Thai as if they couldn't decide which language they wanted to be annoyed in. But he didn't care about them. They were leaving. They'd be back. Nothing he could do or say would change any of that. His sister, however, he was dying inside to know about.

He kept glancing at her. She sat in one of the kitchen chairs with a smile on her face. Without being able to feel her emotions, Derek had no idea which smile it was. She had many. Happy. Sad. Irritated. Disappointed. He'd never had to pay attention to which one it was before. He'd always been able to read what was going on in her soul, not what she put on her face.

Regardless, she smiled at their parents, and he watched her. A million words floated in and out of his mind. Ways to confront her. What he could say. How blunt he needed to be. What to say first. What to say last. When to apologize for pushing her away, and why he didn't come to her before he realized that she was having the same kinds of issues. After all, she'd come to him.

What did he say to that?

"Okay," his mom said. She stood, staring at the suitcases. "I think we have everything."

"Finally," his dad said with a groan. He sat on the floor, his T-shirt and jeans an odd sight considering how well he dressed on a normal day.

"Are you two going to be safe driving?" Mia asked. They weren't the first words she'd said, but it was the longest sentence she'd uttered since coming home. "I heard there was a blizzard coming."

Intira walked over to Mia and placed her hand on her shoulders. "We'll be fine. The blizzard is coming tomorrow night. We'll be somewhere over the Pacific ocean by then."

"Okay," Mia said. Her tone was even. Derek clenched his teeth as irritation bubbled in his stomach.

Intira glanced between Mia and Derek for a moment, and she frowned. "Are you two sure you'll be okay? I can call Aunt Malee and she'll come look after you."

"She's doing a medical study, right?" Mia asked.

"Well, yes...."

Mia let out a small laugh, but Derek shuddered at the sound. It didn't sound like her. But, if anyone else noticed, they didn't have time to speak before she said, "We know Aunt Malee doesn't like to be disturbed when she's busy. We'll be okay. Coach Smith and Mrs. Arbour are going to check in on us, right?"

Intira gripped her right wrist, rubbing it like she always did when she was uncertain or nervous. "I can stay."

The way her voice jumped caught Derek's attention. His mom's emotions fluctuated, jumping from nervous to conflicted. The ants on his skin made him want to strip off his clothes and jump into a bath of ice water to kill them all. It took all he had not to have a physical reaction to the sensation of her indecision. And while this wasn't the most abnormal thing in the world, it was odd because he'd never felt so much jumping around from his mom. His dad, yes, but his mom was steady. She made a decision and she stuck to it. But all day she'd been off.

In a normal situation, he'd push it off on the fact that she was leaving her two seventeen-year-old kids alone for two weeks with no constant adult supervision while she was across an ocean. Despite their parents being pretty absent much of the time, that had *never* happened before.

On an average day, he wouldn't think twice about a mom being hesitant and scared. But nothing about this situation was normal. His mom would have decided weeks ago that she wasn't going. She wouldn't ask her kids what they wanted. She'd say it wasn't fair to have them make that decision for her. And even if for some reason she did change her entire personality for this one situation, if Mia was somehow involved in the magic thing....

Were his parents?

"Māmi, go," Mia said. "We've been alone before, we can handle two weeks." When Intira didn't look convinced, Mia took a deep breath. Derek's skin stilled, and he rubbed his arm. "If something goes really wrong, we'll call Aunt Malee, okay?"

Intira's emotions swirled, but lighter. More relaxed. Liang stepped forward, placing a hand on her shoulder, and the emotions solidified back into decision.

"Okay," she said, voice stable again. Derek wondered if Mia really would make them call their aunt if things went wrong. Intira turned to the suitcases. "Okay. We'll go. But if something goes wrong before our flight, call me. Okay?"

"We will," Mia said.

Intira looked at Derek. "Derek?"

"Yeah," he said.

"Darling, we should go," Liang said. She nodded and he turned to Mia. "Next year we'll come to your final game. As for tomorrow, you will be amazing."

Mia smiled, and again, Derek couldn't tell which kind it was. She went off with Intira to move the suitcases to the front, but Liang hung back. Derek wanted to help, but it was clear his dad wanted to talk to him.

"Um...have a safe trip," Derek said. He found he couldn't look his dad in the eye. Whenever he tried, all he could think about was the realization that he was the reason his father's work got destroyed. He didn't know exactly what he'd done, or how, but he was the reason everything fell apart.

"I am not home as much as I would like to be," Liang said slowly. "I've missed much when it comes to you and your sister. But I'm concerned that the two of you are falling apart."

"We're fine," Derek said. A lie, and everyone knew it. But he'd needed to say it or else he might believe that Mia would never speak to him again.

Liang shook his head. "Twins are a blessing. And you two have always been closer than most. You rely on each other, maybe a little more than is healthy, but I'd rather see you two close than not speaking, as I did with my sister for many years."

Derek's brow furrowed. Aunt Lilan, his gūgū, always seemed to have a great relationship with Derek's dad. She even got along with his mom, which wasn't the most common thing on that side of his family.

"I—"

"Whatever you two are fighting about, I'm sure you'll resolve it without conflict," Liang said. He placed a hand on Derek's shoulder.

"Why are you telling me this?" Derek asked. "Mia's the one who's angry."

Liang laughed. "What makes you think I haven't spoken to her too?"

Before Derek could reply, Liang went to help the women with the suitcases. This time Derek didn't move to help, not because he didn't want to, but because he didn't know what he could do. Once they got everything set up, they said goodbye. His mom reiterated that they should call her sister if they change their minds about being alone, and he wondered if she secretly wished they would.

Eventually, though, the two walked out the door. Intira hugged both Mia and Derek. She told them she loved them, and her emotions fluctuated like before. Then, like that, they were gone. They closed the door and left Mia and Derek alone—not for the first time—to take care of things with help from family friends.

For a moment, the two of them stood alone in silence. It was the longest Mia had been in the same room as him without some external force keeping them together. Like class, or their parents. At first, he thought that maybe whatever their dad had said to her had changed her mind about hating him. He reached out, desperate, and tried to feel her emotions. It wasn't like with the bracelet, he realized. There was a difference.

The bracelet muted her emotions. If he tried hard enough, he could sense some of what she was feeling. It was like they were a bird in a glass jar screaming for help. Now, standing only a few feet away, close enough for him to get some sense of her emotions, it was gone. This wasn't like with the jar, this was like when he'd fallen ill and couldn't feel a thing.

Cody said he'd touched her and her mist lightened. Derek wondered if maybe he could push away the barrier around her emotions if he did the same thing. He could manipulate them. Coax them into something happier. Why not this too?

He reached out, to touch her shoulder, a brotherly gesture, maybe, like he did when he was calming her anxiety, but before he could, she spun around, startling him, and headed toward her room.

He huffed. This wasn't going to work, but he figured he might as well try.

"Méilián," he called out to her.

She didn't say a word, instead disappearing into her room and slamming the door.

I gotta do this. I gotta do this. I gotta talk to her. Derek shook his head, preparing himself, and opened the door, something he never would have normally done.

She looked up at him, startled, with her backpack open.

"Hi," he said. "Can we talk?"

"Go away," she said before grabbing clothes from her drawers and shoving them in her backpack. When he didn't move, she glared at him. "Get out. I don't want you in here."

"Come on, at least hear me out."

"No." Her voice was firm.

Derek groaned. He didn't want to explain any of this to her while she was running around her room packing.

"Where are you going?" he asked. He couldn't stop the concern in his voice.

"Away from you," Mia said.

"Oh. Yeah. That's specific." Derek rolled his eyes. "Look, I want to talk to you about what's going on."

"I said no." She stopped what she was doing and glared at him. "You don't care what's going on in my life, right? No drama, no stupid shit?" He bit his lip. Those words were not his finest moment. When he stayed quiet, she snorted and continued packing. "You keep on hiding your secrets and screwing Blair. Leave me alone."

She threw the backpack over her shoulder, then glanced behind her, at her dresser, before storming past him. He let her go without a fight. He knew this wouldn't work.

Just shout it at her. Stop being scared and tell her that you have magic. That you all do. That someone's been out for your neck. That you want to know what's going on in her life.

Derek glanced around her room, wondering if there was anything he could glean about her. There was nothing out of place. Nothing odd. Except when his eyes passed her dresser.

A tingle passed through his body, catching his breath. His mind twisted, squeezing his eyes and his heart. He closed his eyes. An image appeared in his mind's eyes. A flower. No, a man. No a knife. A flower. A woman. The river.

He shook his head, and the images mixed together with a single voice bouncing in his ears. She said:

"It's time."

His eyes snapped open, and the world returned to normal. The images danced with one another, slowly fading as if on an ever dimming screen. Before long, he couldn't recall what they were, or why his heart was thundering in his chest. He scanned the room, disoriented, blinking rapidly. But there was nothing. He placed a hand over his heart, breathing in deeply, before remembering that his sister was running off somewhere with an overnight bag and she hadn't told him where. He needed to talk to her.

Just one more time.

He took a deep breath and ran out of Mia's room, hoping to catch her, but found the house empty. Dark. He halted, looking around in confusion. It hadn't exactly been light when his parents left, but dusk, at least. And he'd been in Mia's room for only a few minutes. Hesitant, he stepped out in the dark house.

"Mia?" he called out. No answer. Her shoes were gone. Her coat. It normally took her longer than that to get ready.

He stopped in front of the kitchen when his phone buzzed in his pocket. He jumped and grabbed it. Blair.

"Hello?" he said when he answered.

"Oh my god, Derek!"

He jumped at her anger. "What? Why are you yelling at me?"

She snorted. "You serious? I've called you like ten times."

"You have not," he said, but when he pulled the phone away from his ear, Blair angrily ranting, he realized that she had indeed called him that many times. And sent him texts. And those notifications were right underneath the time, and the numbers mocked Derek.

They read 8:00 pm. His parents had left at seven.

Shaking, he placed the phone back to his ear, where Blair was still ranting.

"–you can't go disappearing like that, especially not with all the shit going on, okay?"

"Blair," he said.

"What?"

"Did you…*see* anything?"

"What? No. Why?"

Derek didn't know how to explain. He glanced around his empty, dark house, and in that moment he longed for his sister. "What time am I talking to your mom tomorrow?"

"Come over whenever. How'd it go with Mia?"

"It didn't. I'll let you know when I'm headed over."

"Wait, what? Derek what's–"

He hadn't meant to hang up on her. Or maybe he did. All he knew is that something was off. His home, at least, had been normal. Just a regular place. But the shadowed ceilings, the creaking floorboards, and the only light coming from Mia's room, changed everything.

He backed into his room and closed the door. All he could hear was his heart thumping in his chest. And when he closed his eyes, trying to understand, the only image on his mind was a curved, glowing knife.

A mug of tea sat steaming in front of Mia. She didn't touch it. The gray had thickened the moment she'd left her front door. Derek hadn't even come after her, which might have surprised her if any emotions would come to the forefront.

Doesn't surprise me at all. He's selfish. Always relying on you for everything.

Her mind was too exhausted to form words in response. In favor, or against. Instead, she stared at the mug in front of her. It was large. Larger than the mugs her parents kept in their house. And well loved. A pattern of flowers were painted on the side, faded from years of being washed. Mia tried to picture what it looked like. Steven's mom washing each mug in the cupboard with care. Maybe she used magic, or maybe she decided it wasn't worth getting caught and used her hands.

Regardless, the mug had a story, and she was a part of it, and holding on to that grounded her for reasons she didn't understand.

"You doing okay?" Steven asked. He was across the table from her. No mug. Just watching her.

She nodded. Then shook her head. "I don't know."

Steven wrung his hands together. "I…I'm sorry. Do…you want to go home?"

NO!

She flinched at the scream in her mind. "It's fine. This is better. I can't handle being alone in that house with him right now." Her mind wandered to her aunt's phone number. She'd texted Mia to say that the twins could contact her whenever they needed. Mia had told her mom not to bother her aunt, but maybe it was the right thing to do.

No. If she's here then it'll be harder to get away when you need it. She'll make you talk to Derek.

OH NO. THE HORROR.

Mia scowled.

"Do you like chocolate?" Steven asked. "I have some."

She finally looked up from her mug. He was leaning forward just a bit, brow creased, eyes wide with worry. He'd been so understanding when she'd asked him if she could stay at his house for a few nights. She didn't want to worry him. But the gray took it all.

If you don't like the world of magic, you should leave it. Give it all up.

Give up what? The only thing she had was....

The knife. Was that her connection to all of this? The stalking had started before, but things just got worse once she found that cave in the blizzard. She had meant to bring it. If Derek hadn't burst into her room, she would have.

You know what to do with it.

CARVE A TURKEY. IT'S ALMOST THAT TIME.

"Steven?" she asked.

"Do you want chocolate?"

A light laugh escaped her lips at the eagerness in his voice. For a moment, the fog lifted, only to slam down twice as hard.

"No," she said. "I...do you still want the knife?"

He blinked a few times, then glanced around the kitchen. "I... uh....."

"Oh," she said. A rock of disappointment dropped in her stomach.

"What? No." He waved his hands. "I just meant I don't *want* it. I just think it'd be safer with me. And you won't have to deal with it. I can give it to my parents and we can figure out what to do with it. Why?"

Mia crossed her arms across her stomach and breathed in. "I don't want it. It's made everything worse. I was hoping you'd take it."

A good idea. That's a first.

Mia dug her nails into her arm as if trying to punish the voice for that rude comment. All it did was hurt her.

"I can take it," he said. "Do you have it?"

She shook her head. "No. But I can get it."

"Okay, cool. Just let me know whe–"

"Tomorrow," Mia said. "I'll get it tomorrow. I'll give it to you after the game."

Steven nodded. "Okay. Sounds good to me."

"Yeah." Mia reached out and finally took her mug of tea. It burned her chilled hands, yet she didn't flinch from the pain. She barely felt it at all. And as she drank her tea, Steven rattled off about school and things he was excited about this weekend, but Mia didn't listen. Instead she stared at the faded flowers on the mug and tried to block out the two voices arguing in her mind.

Everything will be better once you do this. Things will go back to normal.

NORMAL CAN NEVER COME AGAIN. BUT TOMORROW WILL CHANGE EVERYTHING YOU KNOW. I JUST HOPE YOU'RE READY.

Chapter Twenty-One

Soft grass tickled his toes, creeping up around the bamboo sandals protecting his feet from the stones buried in the mud. But he knew it wasn't real.

A warm, thick breeze rustled his clothes, his hair. It caressed his face in a gentle embrace, like a mother holding her child for the first time.

He breathed it in. The musky scent of a lazy river floating on every tendril of air dancing around him. But he knew it wasn't real.

Water stretched out before him. Boats drifted along the currents as men and women in large hats woven from bamboo and ola palm leaves moved with their guide, preparing the nets for the daily catch. Reeds peeked above the water, swaying in time with his robes. They called out to him. A gentle whistle among green encouraging him to sink his toes into liquid mud and disappear into a world that wasn't his.

But he knew it wasn't real.

His gaze drifted from the water. It traveled down scanning his hands. The long, calloused fingers. His skin wasn't quite so dark in real life. Outside of this fantasy, this dream, they were softer. They didn't belong to the hands of a farmer. They belonged to a spoiled kid who spent his days in a classroom. Even the callouses from when he was young, when his parents made him play violin until he protested at fifteen, had mostly faded over the past two years.

These weren't his hands. They had the same shape. The same size, though in real life they were thinner. But they belonged to someone who lived long ago. Who lived the life at the edge of the murky river with boats and reeds and a mysterious land on the other side.

Except there was something different.

Because when Derek returned his gaze to the scenery, he realized that this wasn't the same cliff as before. The view in front of him had changed. Morphed. Grown into something else.

A smile spread across Derek's face, and he laughed, letting the sound explode into the silence of the day. Because this man, the man whose body he inhabited, had made it. Niran had made it to the other side of the river.

His laugh grew in volume. It consumed him. He lifted his hands. Those hands. The hands of the man who wasn't him. A heat spread down his arms and into his hands.

Light swirled from his finger tips, dancing into the air and bursting into tendrils of fire like a ballet. It was simple. So simple. But that simple act would have gotten him executed on the other side. On this side he could be free. He could be him. Even if he wasn't really him.

The fire died, as did his laughter. He stared at the orange and gold sky and once more breathed in the thick air.

"Niran."

A voice. A voice he knew. Derek. Niran. They knew. It was unlike anything else in this world. Soft and warm. Sharp and cold. Distant, but longing for closeness. No matter where he was, in a thousand lifetimes, over a million years, Niran would know that voice.

He turned. Back to the river. Facing the jungle rising into the sky. She stood back, blanketed by the trees' shadows. At the sight of her long, midnight hair and her ruby irises, skin pale as the moon, Derek wanted to run. His legs burned with the desire to flee. Instead, the stepped forward. A smile spread across Niran's face, and he spoke to her. A language he knew. A language he didn't.

And then…and then another. A new figure. A man.

He hesitated.

The man came to stand next to her. He stood taller, hair as black as hers, skin darker than Niran's. He whispered to her, and she smiled.

The man looked up at Derek. Unlike her eyes, his were perfectly normal. Brown, like the dark chocolate he would get for Blair when she having bad cramps, and deep set. They looked so different, the two of them, but Niran knew that they were the same.

And Derek found he knew the man. Somewhere, deep in his subconscious, a face he'd seen before but couldn't place, as if someone had taken an eraser to just that part of his memory. Still, the slow, calculated, deep voice coming from the man nagged at his brain. He tried to reach for the words to ask.

When the woman gasped and stepped away from him.

His hand grew heavy. His eyes dropped from the terrified woman to his calloused fingers. They were curled. Wrapped. Encasing a handle of ridged bamboo strips. His eyes widened. The handle extended down, seamlessly transitioning to the pure and bright curved blade. Characters he knew—he didn't know—were etched into the living metal.

They glowed.

Energy slammed Derek in the chest. He gasped and looked up again. The woman had backed away more, a delicate hand covering her mouth, while the distorted man cocked his head. Then smiled.

Meanwhile, a voice in the wind tickled his ear, begging him in a sultry tone to end the war.

Derek's eyes snapped open. Darkness flooded his vision. Chest tight, he gasped for air, body burning as a bead of sweat dripped down his temple, inching toward his neck. He wiped it away and sat up. Just like the other nights, after the other dreams, his heart pounded against his ribs as if wanting to burst out. He closed his eyes for a second, but her expression returned, so he snapped them open, not wanting to even blink.

Instead he glanced around his room, eyes adjusting to the dark. It was clean. He rarely cleaned his room, but after last night he'd needed *something* concrete to do. His parents were gone. Mia had disappeared to god knows where. He couldn't feel her. Couldn't find her. Even if he wanted to start, he couldn't because he had no idea what was going on in her life, or even how long she'd been gone. Besides, what was he going to do if he did find her? She wanted nothing to do with him.

Pulling his legs to his chest, he rested his head on his knees and continued to work on calming his breath. His heart. They were erratic, no matter what he did.

He blinked. He couldn't stop it. He blinked and the eyes of the woman flashed before him. Again. This time, the man. Again.

This time, a knife.

The knife.

He'd seen ones like it. A kukri knife, thought to be used by the Gurkhas in the Indian subcontinent. Back before Liang found the sculpture and this deep dive into Southeast Asian art began, he and Intira had been studying ancient cultures in Nepal, and Intira would show Derek some of the artifacts on loan to them.

Derek gripped his hair as frustration overcame him. All of his dreams took place in Thailand. Geography wasn't exactly his strong point, but he wasn't sure how the national weapon of Nepal somehow ended up in Ancient Siam. Or why it seemed to glow with life. Or why it had ancient Sino-characters etched into the side. Very ancient. So ancient he didn't even recognize them. It was a mishmash of culture and magic and he didn't understand it.

It was a dream. Dreams don't make sense.

He tried to tell himself this, but the words refused to imprint in his mind. They were dreams. He had them while he was asleep.

Except in the woods. And Mia's room.

Derek smacked his forehead with the heel of his hand to shut his brain up. Because if he let the thoughts run rampant, if he gave up convincing himself that these were dreams and nothing more, that meant that they *were* something more.

Something like memories.

He'd toyed with the idea before. He wasn't just dreaming he was a man named Niran, he was somehow living in his memories. Walking through scenes of his life as the events tried to tell him something he didn't want to hear. After all, why would he be having these memories?

Unless….

An idea popped into his mind. A stupid one, he was sure, but he needed confirmation. He scrambled for his phone, looking for it under his blankets and pillows before eventually discovering it on the floor. It lit up, heavy in his hand like the knife had been, and he had to squint to find the right name.

When he clicked Blair's picture, the phone rang and he waited, hoping she'd wake up.

Right when it was about to go to voicemail, there was a click.

"It's three in the morning. What?"

Derek couldn't stop his smile. Even angry as hell, Blair's voice relaxed him. It grounded him, and he breathed in, then out, his heart finally calming.

"How did you know you were a seer?" he asked.

Silence.

"Blair?"

"Why?" Annoyed exasperation filled her voice.

He didn't know if there was a good way to explain. Maybe there wasn't at all. So he just went for it. "I think my dreams are memories."

"We've talked—"

"And I think that they're trying to explain what's going on right now. The reason the red eyed woman wants me dead."

"Why would she want you dead?"

"Does the name, Niran, mean anything to you?"

She groaned, and there was rustling. "What part of three in the morning do you not get? I'm barely able to think, much less try to recall a name in some language I don't know."

"It's Thai." Derek rolled his eyes. There was no way for Blair to know that, but he thought after years of hearing him speak it she might at least recognize what part of the world it was from.

"Don't roll your eyes at me. It's three in the morning, I don't know languages," Blair snapped.

Derek pulled the phone away from his ear and stared at it for a second before shaking his head. "Whatever. I think he and I are connected. Like, maybe I bonded with his soul when I got sick. What if this guy is regretting not killing her and is trying to give me clues to stop."

"Stop her?"

"With a knife. I saw it tonight, in my dream. What if that's the thing I've been looking for but haven't been able to find? You said that he had a way to kill her. What if this is what he used?"

He knew it was the one Niran was supposed to use. The dreams had told him so.

After another moment of silence, Blair said, "You sound crazy."

Derek squeezed his eyes shut. "Which part?"

"All of it."

"A little elaboration please?"

"No, it's three in the morning!"

Derek flinched at her yell. "Look I–"

"You are overthinking this," Blair said. "Look, our lore says he killed her and your dreams say he sealed her away. Both could be wrong. They're just dreams, and lore gets mixed up constantly. If this guy, Neeran or whatever, regretted his decision now, why the hell would he *attach* to your soul? You're just a teenager."

She had a point, but he wasn't sure it was the right point. "I still think I'm right."

"Well, fine. Ask Cody tomorrow."

"Huh?"

"He calls them mists." Blair yawned. "My mom says he sees souls, so ask him. Can I sleep now?"

Derek glanced around his room again. His eyes landed on the door, which led out into the empty house. He'd never been in the house alone this late at night. There'd always been someone else. And with the losing time, and the dream, he really didn't want to be alone.

"You didn't answer my question, you know."

"What question?"

"About how you knew you were a seer."

Blair fell silent, and this time it was for so long he figured she'd fallen asleep. But as he opened his mouth to make sure she was still there, she spoke in a low, dark tone.

"You aren't a seer, Derek."

The words both soothed him, and sent his mind into a scramble. He wasn't a seer. These weren't visions, like what Blair had. He had no idea how her gift worked still, but she did, and he wasn't about to question that. So, at least he had an answer to *that* burning question.

If only it hadn't left a million more in its place.

"I'm going to sleep now," Blair said through another yawn. "Come over in the afternoon, yeah?"

The conversation was over. He resigned himself to letting her sleep. There were no answers to be found at three in the morning. "Yeah. I'll make sure Cody knows what time to come."

She groaned. "He'd better not lecture us again."

He snorted. "You know he's protective of her."

"Yeah, well he can tone it down before I shove his–"

"I'll see you tomorrow," Derek cut in before Blair could go on a hateful tangent.

He could imagine her rolling her eyes as she said, "Whatever. Night."

"Night."

The line beeped, then went dead. The phone slipped from his hand, bouncing on the bed, before he lay next to it and stared at the ceiling. Above him was his parents' room. Next to him, his sister's. Both empty.

He thought about the knife. When he closed his eyes, he didn't see the woman or the man anymore. Instead he saw the knife as if it were a high definition, 3-D image floating in an abyss of darkness. It sat there, close to him, but just out of reach.

As he faded, darkness like gas overtaking the knife, he told himself that Mrs. Arbour would have all the answers. They'd explain everything to Mia, and she'd forgive them. They'd find the knife. They'd kill the queen. And everything would go back to normal.

The house stood empty. Mia looked around the darkened building, trying to wrap her mind about what she was about to do, and about what had happened last night. For reasons she couldn't understand, she couldn't bring herself to enter. Instead she stood in the entryway, backpack hanging in a puddle of dirty, grimy snow melt, and stared into the hollow place she called home.

She remembered the first time she'd set foot in the house. Ten-years-old. Exhausted from traveling.

It'd all started with a trip to see her grandparents. She'd only been to America twice before, but those had been different. Vacation. No one had expected her to speak English. They hadn't made her learn how to order by herself. They hadn't taken her shopping for new clothes to fit the trends of her new country of residence. Her mom hadn't looked for a school for the twins. There weren't whispers among the adults about divorce.

She hadn't known the word in Thai before then. It wasn't one she'd ever forget.

This had gone on for three weeks until one day her mom packed up all their things again and said they were going to go see Dad. A two hour flight and three hour car ride through a mysterious and new terrain later, Intira had pulled them into the driveway of this house where her dad waited for them.

Mia and Derek had been too happy to see him to care that they'd moved to a strange place. And while Derek got excited about their new house, running inside the open door to explore, Mia had clung to her father. He made joking comments about how she'd make him trip, but kept his hand on her back as he led her inside. She'd stared around it, to the room that would soon be hers, up the stairs to where her parents' bedroom and office were already forming, around to the kitchen with boxes of dishes half unpacked, as her parents told her and Derek that they'd have so many new memories here.

It was a fresh start for everyone. A way to start anew.

Seven years later she wondered if this is how her parents imagined life in America. Them, off in Thailand trying to explain away the destruction of a treasured national artifact, Derek keeping secrets and pushing her out of his life, and Mia…and Mia running away to spend the night with a boy she hardly knew. And why? To avoid a conversation she'd never wanted to have in the first place?

You don't have to avoid it. What is it people always say? Communication is key?

You tried. It didn't work. There's no reason to keep trying.

Mia ignored the voices. They'd been bickering all day. All of last night. They were a constant stream of questions and declarations. Besides, she didn't need to listen to them. She and Steven had a plan.

Get in. Get the knife. Give it to him.

Then you'll be free to do whatever you want.

Yes. Though I have to wonder, what do you want?

Mia's eyes narrowed and she stepped inside the house, boots on. They squeaked against the hardwood, leaving water in the shape of a footprint, but she ignored them and hurried to her room. Steven had used an old fortune telling technique from his clan to predict when Derek would leave, but he said it wasn't always accurate. She was racing against two clocks: when Derek might show up, and when the basketball final game began.

After the game, things would be okay again.

Her room remained the same as last night. Bed covered in clothes she decided not to bring. All but one drawer ajar.

Get it.

A shudder spread through Mia's limbs, but she did as the voice commanded. Her hands touched the cool metal of the drawer handle and she slid it open.

It was there. Half revealed from her scrambling the night before. The leather sheath mocked her. A reminder of all the strange going on in her life.

We don't have time for this.

YOU NEVER DID ANSWER MY QUESTION.

Shut up.

WHAT DO YOU WANT, MIA?

What did she want? Her hand trembled, half outstretched toward the knife. In short, the answer was she didn't know. Three weeks ago she'd known exactly what she wanted. Good grades, exhausting practices, her family in the place they were supposed to call home with no distractions, and no more trips abroad.

Now, standing in front of her secret, none of those things mattered. It wouldn't matter if her parents never came home. It wouldn't matter if she and Derek fixed their problems. The results of the game didn't matter.

None of it matters.

She reached for the knife.

Her phone rang.

Her hand stopped, withdrawing as she turned toward the ringing phone on her bed. The buzzing was muted, but still distinct, marking it a call from her favorites list.

With a deep breath, and a quick glance back at the knife, she snatched the phone from the bed to take a look at the name on the screen.

Confusion overtook her. Her heart all but stilled as her brother's name enticed her back into his world.

Don't answer it. He's just going to lie to you.

HE SEEMS DETERMINED TO TALK. MIGHT AS WELL GIVE HIM A MINUTE.

A minute is all it takes to hurt someone.

A MINUTE IS ALL IT TAKES TO UNDERSTAND.

"Shut up!" Mia screamed. She clicked the button on the side of her phone, sending the call to voicemail, then threw it on the bed.

Placing her head in her hands, she backed up until the small of her back hit the dresser. It was too much. The voices. The calling. Derek wanted to talk to her, but she couldn't do it. She couldn't talk to him after all the lies. The hurt he'd caused her.

IT'S OKAY IF YOU'RE HURT. BUT HE IS YOUR BROTHER. DO YOU REALLY WANT TO LOSE HIM?

Her phone beeped. A voicemail. Mia stared at the phone as the confusion continued to build inside of her. It mixed with the gray, the empty, and tore it to shreds bit by bit. Her heart thudded in her chest. It wasn't like Derek to leave voicemails. He said they were the worst thing ever. He'd rather text or just talk on the phone. This wasn't like him at all.

Manipulative.

DESPERATE.

Mia grabbed the phone again. It weighed her hands down, dragging her toward the floor like a ball and chain desperate to remove her from the situation.

Still, she hit the message, and on speaker it played, the sound of her brother's tired, out of breath, voice reminding her of the world she was about to throw away.

"Hey. Um. So, still don't want to talk. Okay. I…uh…ugh. Sorry. Hate this." There was a pause. Rustling. Mia shifted and sat on the bed.

He continued, words shaking. "I don't know what's happened the past three weeks. Or I do. I dunno. But I'm standing outside Blair's house so I can talk to her mom about the insanity that's been going on, and all I can think is that I haven't told you anything. Fuck. I don't know how to do any of this, okay? It's just…I'm sorry. Okay? I'm…sorry."

Something wet trickled down Mia's face. She reached up with one hand and wiped away the tear, but it was replaced by another soon after.

"Maybe you'll get this in time. Maybe not. But we're at Blair's, and you should come. I don't know how to explain to you what's been going on, but maybe…maybe I can start by saying that I–"

A loud ring interrupted the message. Derek's voice vanished, and Mia jumped, nearly dropping her phone in the process. It vibrated in her hand, and she stared down at the name on the screen.

Steven.

She'd forgotten about him. About the knife. Listening to her brother's jumbled message and awkward apology had pulled her away from her mission. He'd mentioned insanity. An invitation to go to Blair's. With them.

He'd apologized.

He'll say whatever he wants to get you to stay. He doesn't care. He's desperate.

I FAIL TO SEE WHAT'S WRONG WITH FAMILY WANTING TO STAY TOGETHER.

False apologies mean nothing.

Mia knew her brother. The small tremors in his voice. The hesitations. When he'd throw in an English word because he was so frustrated or flustered that he couldn't recall the right word in Chinese. She knew when he was lying to her. And she knew when he meant an apology.

The phone continued to buzz in her hand. It'd go to voicemail soon. She could listen to the rest of what her brother had to say.

The knife.

Mia wiped the rest of the tears from her cheeks and answered the phone.

"Hello?" She tried to keep her voice level.

"Hey, did it go okay?" Steven asked. "I hadn't heard from you and got worried."

Mia sniffed before turning toward the drawer. The knife. Her knife. Someone's knife. It didn't belong with her. She wasn't part of the magical world. Steven was part of it. He could take it from her, and things could go back to normal. Maybe it could start with her talking to her friends.

Weren't you going to leave?

WHERE WOULD YOU EVEN GO?

"Mia?"

"I just…got distracted. I'm getting the knife now." She checked the time. She had fifteen minutes before she had to be at school for the game. Enough time to get to school. Not enough time to stop by Blair's, even if she'd wanted to.

DON'T YOU WANT TO?

No.

"I'll see you at school," she said.

"Okay. I can't wait to see you play."

"Yeah." Mia didn't say anything else. She hung up and stood. Phone to her chest, she stared down at the knife. She hadn't finished Derek's message. There wasn't much time left on it.

Later. Listen later. Finish your mission first.

Mia lifted the knife.

WHAT IS YOUR MISSION?

Get the knife to Steve, Mia answered without hesitation. *Get everything back to normal.*

BUT WHY?

She didn't want to answer that. She didn't know *how* to answer that.

With the knife in hand, she grabbed her things and hurried out of her room. Through the empty house. Out the front door into the chilled day. The door closed behind her, latching, and she breathed in. The world remained gray. Her emotions dimmed. But it would be over soon.

She examined the knife and her chest tightened.

It'd be over very soon.

None of them had spent much time at Blair's house. It took a moment for Derek to remember where it even was, since she always insisted that they hang out somewhere else. Downtown in the summer, Derek and Mia's house in the winter. Never Cody's house, and never Blair's. Derek found it odd, sitting in her kitchen. It was very different from his. Dried plants hung from the ceiling with dishes piling up in the sink and boxes of food on the counters. The table, big enough to sit the family of six, had scratch marks in it, some stains, and what looked like a faded cuss word originally written in permanent ink.

Even outside of the kitchen, the house couldn't have been more different than Derek's. Photographs lined the walls, showing Blair and her brothers growing up. In the living room, where Blair's youngest brother, James, played, toys and video games were strewn across the floor. Blair had insisted, when they came in, that they'd cleaned, but apparently seven-year-olds had vendettas against clean houses. But honestly, Derek didn't mind.

Blair's house was messier than his. But it was lived in. It was clear that there were human beings living beneath the roof, just doing their best to get through their day. It was warm. Full. And after sleeping alone in the house last night, this was a very welcome change.

They sat at the table. Derek, Cody, and Blair. When they'd arrived, Mrs. Arbour had insisted she'd be ready in a few minutes and suggested they wait for her in the kitchen so she could gather what she needed to answer their questions. So they sat. Quietly. As James yelled about something from the living room.

Antsy, Derek pulled out his phone and checked to see if Mia had called him back. Or texted him. Or showed any sign of life. He'd figured leaving her a message was a long shot. If Mia didn't want to talk to him, she wasn't going to listen to a message either. Yet, he'd known he needed to try. Standing outside Blair's unassuming house—a house that contained more magic than anything else in Willow Creek—it'd felt so wrong not to try at least one more time today.

And for the first time in their lives, he'd told her he had magic.

Focusing on his apology clawed at his soul. A constant reminder that he should have told her that night in the hospital. When he'd wanted to. Before any of this began.

Instead, he focused on the house. On the warmth of the wooden walls, and the dim lights hanging from the ceiling. They provided little light, but the sunlight streaming in through the frosted windows supplemented them. He shuddered, remembering the chill of the outdoors, and crossed his arms as if trying to melt the ice encasing his bones. The house was warm. Safe. Welcome. But he…he wasn't sure he'd ever get warm again as long as his sister hated him.

"Are you okay?" Blair asked.

Derek blinked, drawn back to the situation at hand. "What?"

He found Blair and Cody staring at him. Cody hadn't said much since arriving. It didn't take a genius to understand that he was still pissed at them. Though, Derek had to wonder if he was pissed, or scared. Derek and Blair had friends outside of the group. Not many. And not as close. But they existed. Mia, too, had a circle of friends from sports. But for Cody…this was it. Was he scared that if Mia didn't speak to him, no one would?

"You're acting weird," Blair said with a roll of her eyes. She'd been cold to him today. He'd hung up on her. Then he'd called her at three in the morning. He could imagine that had displeased her. And he had no excuse.

"I…." He didn't want to admit that he'd told Mia to come over, in part because he didn't believe she'd show. There was no need to risk getting into a fight about acting on his own if he wasn't sure she'd ever listen to his message.

"So sorry." Mrs. Arbour's voice broke through the silence. All three teens looked at her as she hurried into the kitchen, wiping what looked like glitter off her hands. "Turns out you shouldn't start cleaning your husband's office right before an important visit. You never know what you're going to find on a first grader teacher's desk."

She smiled at all of them, but no one laughed or commented. Derek didn't know what he could say to the woman, honestly. But if she minded, she said nothing and sat at the table with them, placing a wooden box in front of her. It was beautifully carved, marked with symbols Derek had never seen before. He tried to make out any sort of pattern, and wondered if it was the written language of Blair's clan. Like everything else in her life, Blair didn't talk much about what language her clan spoke, or even if they had one, but he'd heard her speak it on the phone sometimes when she thought no one was listening.

Besides the writing, the box had carved and dyed shapes, creating an intricate, geometric patterns that exuded magic. A warmth, similar to the one that Derek had felt when Blair gave him energy, floated off the box and tapped against his skin. He shuddered and look away.

This home was definitely not like his own.

"Blair tells me you've been having dreams," Mrs. Arbour said. Her eyes were gentle and kind. Like a mother speaking to her crying child.

Derek shifted. "Yeah. Weird dreams. They're like memories."

"Can you describe them to me?"

Could he? Were there enough words in the world to describe them? But...he had to try. So, he did. He opened his mouth, and

340

words tumbled out, describing everything in so much detail it was like they were reality. As he spoke, Mrs. Arbour opened the box and dancing light clambered out, expanding through the kitchen. Derek faltered for a moment, watching it, but before long, the words began again.

So many words to describe so many dreams he'd almost forgotten.

And when he finished, when there were no more words, Mrs. Arbour closed the box and placed a hand on it. The writing lit with a golden glow, shining for a brief moment before going dark.

The room went silent. Derek stared at the box, confused. He wanted to speak, to ask what was going on, but found he had nothing to say. No more words to speak.

"Mom?" Blair asked, voice jumping in pitch. She had her eyebrows raised, arms crossed and was leaning away from the box. Cody too, appeared apprehensive, eyeing the box with a furrowed brow and a frown.

Mrs. Arbour moved the box to the side, still smiling. "A cleansing ritual. Dreams can weigh us down, darkening our souls, and through our souls, our magic. If our magic is darkened, then everything darkens."

"Like…depression?" Cody asked with a little too much curiosity in his voice.

She shook her head. "No. But it mimics depression. From the moment Derek entered my home, I knew there was something eating away at his energy. I needed to hear the dreams, and I wanted to release his soul from the darkness." She looked at Cody. "Can't you tell a difference?"

Cody's eyes widened and he shrunk into his chair. Then, after a tense moment, he glanced at Derek and relaxed.

"Yeah. It's…brighter."

Mrs. Arbour nodded. "The box will cleanse the dreams, turning them back into energy. Derek, you should feel lighter now."

Lighter? Derek didn't feel any different. He shook his head. "I...feel the same."

Right?

She nodded. "I learned something about your dreams, in any case."

"What?" Blair asked before Derek could.

Mrs. Arbour's expression darkened for a moment. She breathed in, and then out again. "It would seem...that you've bonded with someone from the past. Someone with extraordinary magic in your bloodline."

Derek slapped the table, excitement coursing through him like fire. "I was right!"

Mrs. Arbour looked between them. "Right about what?"

Derek turned to Blair amped in a way he hadn't been in weeks. *Maybe I do feel lighter.*

"Remember? This morning when I called you? I thought that maybe this Niran guy attached to my soul? That he was showing me something? When you told me I sounded crazy?"

"You do sound crazy," Blair snapped.

"Your mom agrees with me?"

"I'm going to have to go with Blair here," Cody said. "All of this sounds crazy."

Derek groaned. "I'm not crazy."

"Kids," Mrs. Arbour said. The three of them fell silent, but Derek knew that he'd been right. Something was going on. And it had to do with the red-eyed woman. It had to do with the knife. Mrs. Arbour continued once they were quiet. "Nothing is crazy when it comes to magic. The clans have been keeping records of their experiences for thousands of years and we still run into new things every day. Magic is alive. Just like everything else, it evolves and changes. It's not a set of static rules. Soul bonding is uncommon, but not unheard of."

Derek relaxed, mind piecing everything together. The puzzle pieces were still separate, but closer, waiting for the right hand to put them in their place.

"So…this…guy," Blair said, rather than trying to say his name. "He's a relative of Derek's who had tons of magic and is trying to tell him something?"

"It would seem that way," Mrs. Arbour said.

"What is he trying to say?" Cody asked.

Derek realized that Cody had no idea about his revelation this morning. He'd meant to tell him, just like he'd told Blair, but he'd gotten so distracted by his call to Mia that it'd slipped his mind. But while telling Cody had been overlooked, what he'd dreamed about hadn't. The river, always by the river, and the woman with red-eyes, and the peculiar man.

And the knife.

"I think he wants me to fix his mistakes," Derek said, repeating his thoughts from this morning. "He…he had this knife. I've…I keep seeing it. On and off. And the woman with red-eyes…."

"The queen?" Mrs. Arbour asked.

"Yeah. She's afraid of it. And he didn't use it on her and…." Derek squeezed his eyes shut. An image of the knife was carved on his eyelids. "I need to find that knife."

Once more, silence fell over the group. Derek realized, after the words had left his mouth, that it sounded impossible. It was a knife from his dreams. Dreams that took place thousands of years ago and halfway across the world. He was the only person who had seen it, who knew what it looked like. What it felt like. The knife was real to him, but to the others it was nothing more than words out of his mouth.

Mrs. Arbour stood and disappeared again. Derek watched her go, feeling like an idiot. This wasn't helpful, and Mia still hadn't called him back. But he knew she wouldn't. The game was starting.

"Derek." Blair touched his hand. He didn't look at her. "We knew...I mean no one has all the answers. But we figured out what your dreams are."

"And how's that going to fix anything?" Cody asked.

"God, not now," Blair snapped at him.

"When, then?" Cody frowned. "Mia is acting weird. We should be at the game to talk to her, not sitting here getting no information. Find a knife...how are we going to do that? It's not like we have a map."

"No, but we have a seer."

Mrs. Arbour's voice appeared without warning, and all three teens jumped. She glided to her chair again, carrying a black stone, smooth as if the ocean had washed it for a million years. She placed it in the center of the table, like she had with the box, and held out her hand for Derek and Blair to take.

The two of them exchanged a glance, while Cody's brow furrowed. Derek wondered if he knew about Blair's ability. He had no time to ask.

"Uh...Mom?" Blair said. "What are you doing?"

"Finding the knife," Mrs. Arbour said. Derek didn't appreciate her "no duh" tone.

Blair crossed her arms. "How?"

"It's a magical artifact. Derek's bonded with it. You're a seer." She smiled. "This shouldn't be difficult."

Derek had no idea if he believed that or not. Or how any of this was going to work. Mrs. Arbour spoke as if all of them had decades of experience with magic, and while he wanted to point that out, she nudged his hand, and nodded at Blair, and the two had little choice but to do as she wanted. Cody sat back, watching with crossed arms.

At first, there was nothing. Derek closed his eyes, imagining once more the knife on his eyelids, and it came without question. His hands tingled as the bamboo handle brushed against his skin, the leather sheath rough on his palm. And then, after a second, a trickle of warmth spread up his limbs. On his left, from the hand connected with Blair's, the energy was familiar. On his right, with Mrs. Arbour, it was new. Each energy pulsed at a different rate, shooting through his body with dissonance. They met in the middle, a battleground, and the image of the knife grew brighter. He flinched.

The energy swirled in his chest, mixing together and drawing at his own, before shooting back down his arms, pulse even.

Derek couldn't breathe. He couldn't think. He didn't know what was going on, or how this was working, or why the stone in front of him rattled, but it all was. And then, as soon as it had started, it ended with a scream.

His eyes snapped open, left hand going cold. The chair to his right clattered. Mrs. Arbour flew across the room, grabbing her daughter's shoulders as Blair placed her head in her hands, curling into a ball. Cody stood as well, but Derek remained frozen to the spot.

"Shh, it's okay," Mrs. Arbour said, wrapping her arms around Blair. "You're safe."

Blair's words from the other day lingered in the back of his mind. He'd seen her have a vision before. When they were twelve. She'd called it a seizure and no one had questioned it. And since her revelation, he hadn't put much thought into what her visions were like. But this...she was in pain. Rocking, cocooned in her mother's arms. Derek wanted to go to her. To help. But he wasn't sure he could.

"I saw it," Blair said. She removed her hands from her face, and Mrs. Arbour pulled away.

"Where is it?" Mrs. Arbour asked.

Blair looked up, directly at Derek, and he knew. He didn't need to hear the words. Because it all made sense. Why she'd been acting weird. The thing she wanted to tell him. The feeling he'd gotten in her room the night before. The loss of time. His dream of the knife right after.

He didn't need Blair to say it.

But she did.

"Mia has it."

Chapter Twenty-Two

Coach Smith spoke, and the rest of the girls cheered. Called and responded. Their normal game routine. All of them participated, and excitement flooded the locker room as they prepared to finish off a season Mia had led them through. A strong season. Only two losses. Better than any other school they'd gone up against.

If this had been last year, Mia would have joined them. This is what she loved to do. To feel the sweat drip down her temple. To pant as her lungs tried to keep up with her thumping heart. The adrenaline of the game. The fight to win. The desire not to lose. It brought out her competitive side. It took all of her anger and frustration, and gave it an outlet that elicited cheers from anyone watching.

She'd needed this. From the time she was young, she'd needed this stimulation.

But tonight, surrounded by her excited teammates, none of that was true. Maybe it was the gray settling on her, weighing down her shoulders and squeezing her chest. Or maybe it was the knowledge that there was a magical knife sitting in her locker. And possibly, when she thought about it, the disconnect came from the fact that she knew none of this really mattered.

Magic existed. It had wrapped its hands around her neck, holding her hostage and acting as a constant reminder that there was so much out there she didn't understand. Why did a stupid basketball game matter?

Why does anything matter in this godforsaken place?

As Coach Smith spoke, Mia glanced toward her locker. The knife sat in there. In her backpack. Waiting for her to hand it off to Steven and move on from this part of her life. But she also couldn't stop thinking about the other piece of the puzzle sitting in there. While she had no plans to listen to the rest of Derek's message yet, it still waited for her. Whatever he wanted to say, whatever he wanted to tell her, it had to be important.

But she didn't have time.

Unless....

"All right, ladies!" Coach Smith clapped her hands and Mia jumped, turning her attention back to the moment at hand.

It's best to let it go. Play the game. Get rid of the knife. Get out of this life. It's not worth the pain anymore.

"It's time to get out there and warm up. You ready to play?"

"Yes, coach!" the girls choruses. Mia chimed in, half a beat behind.

"You ready to *win*?"

"Yes, coach!" They were louder this time, and Mia mumbled the words. A beat behind.

"Let's go then!"

All of the girls stood, pumped up and excited. Some of the excitement came from adrenaline. Some came from nerves. The perfect mix of emotions for a game that would either get them a trophy, or leave them talking about a rematch next year.

Doesn't matter. You won't be here next year anyway.

She stood as well, following the girls out of the locker room. The knife, behind her, her phone, behind her, called out, begging her to return. But she kept her gaze forward, wanting to get this over with. Her parents weren't here. Her brother wouldn't come. Her friends had abandoned her. She was going through the motions because her team expected it of her, but she didn't care.

"Mia."

She halted at the sound of her name. Coach Smith stood behind her, arms crossed, smiling. Her dirty blond hair, curly and pulled high, gave her such a youthful look. Likewise, her gray eyes showed a strange mix of energy and wisdom. It was odd. Looking at her. Mia had never noticed it before, but the way Coach Smith stood in front of her, it was like…there was something different.

But when she blinked, the image was gone.

"Yeah?" she asked.

"You seem distracted." Coach Smith stepped toward her, heading toward the exit. "You doing okay tonight?"

Mia nodded, but didn't speak. It wasn't a full lie if she just nodded, right?

"That's good," Coach Smith said. She reached out and touched Mia's shoulder. It was a simple touch. Innocent. Like any coach would do to her student before a big game.

Except it wasn't.

A shot of electricity sank into Mia's muscles, into her bones, and she gasped, body tensing. It spread through her body, traveling along her nervous system as if wanting her to spasm, but also trapping her in stillness. She couldn't breathe. She couldn't blink. She could do nothing but stand there, in shock.

"Regardless of what happens tonight, tomorrow will still come. Don't be too worried."

Coach Smith's hand left Mia's shoulder, drawing all the electricity out of her. Breath returned to her lungs. Her body relaxed, and everything returned to normal.

She stared around the locker room, trying to understand what had just happened. She waited for the voice—either voice—to show up and talk to her. Tell her what to think and feel. What to do. But they were strangely quiet. Her mind was strangely quiet.

"You coming?" Coach Smith asked, drawing Mia's attention back toward the locker room exit.

Mia breathed in. Her eyes scanned the colorful walls before she nodded and followed her coach. Down the hall. Into the gym. All the while, examining the world around her as her mind remained silent. She lifted her hands, staring at them. They were…warm.

Noise greeted her. She examined each person's color and warmth for a fraction of a second each until her eyes landed on Steven, sitting up front in the stands. He smiled at the sight of her and waved, but she found she couldn't wave back. Her limbs wouldn't listen to her. It was like someone had threaded wire into her veins, turning her into a puppet.

Steven's expression faltered.

She wanted to go to him, and to tell him she had the knife and she'd give it to him, but her attention moved elsewhere. Down the line. Up into the pathetic set of bleachers that looked like they'd fall apart at any moment. By the time she'd made it to her team, she'd seen every single face in the crowd. She recognized almost everyone, and those she didn't she assumed were here for the opposing team: a group of girls dressed head to toe in crimson and white. Their colors seemed to dance. Vibrant. Alive. Like fire.

And though she knew they weren't coming, her heart still clenched when she found her brother and friends weren't among the sea of people.

A whistle blew, startling Mia back to the game. The ref stood in the center of the gym, holding the game ball, and one of the opposing girls walked up to it, stretching her arms. Mia didn't move at first. Not until the other starters jogged out to their places, and she realized that she was up.

She headed to the center of the gym as well, facing a much taller, much broader teenage girl who had that competition grin on her face. She held out a hand for Mia to take. A welcome to the game. Mia hesitated, as if something was drawing her away from the game. Away from this life. But then her arm moved on her own. A puppet on a string. Their hands connected, then released, and the game began.

Chapter Twenty-Three

Shouting. Lights. Cheers. The pounding of her heart. Of the ball. It touched her hand, the rough skin glued to the pads of her fingertips for a fraction of a second before descending. The crack of the ball against the linoleum floor grated on her ears. Another sound. Another distraction.

A girl crouched in front of her. Tensed. Ready for whatever move Mia was going to make next. And Mia did the same. It was a game of chicken, one that could only last a few moments before someone acted. The girl stepped forward a tad, her blond ponytail swaying, sweat dripping down her temple. Mia meant to step back. But in that second, the girl was someone else. Her blond hair bleached, determined face morphing into one of sneering contempt.

Mia hesitated, a shot of fear icing her heart.

The girl moved again, jerking forward to take the ball. It left Mia's control, and the girl laughed as she passed by, the sound gripping all of Mia's concentration and tearing it to shreds, bit by bit.

"Mia, seriously?"

A shout caught her attention. Kaylee. Mia blinked. The girl's features returned to normal.

Shit.

She shook her head and tore down the court. Her legs had turned to lead. Moving one was excruciating. Both was torture.

The girl cleared the court, Mia too far behind her, her team too far away, and scored with no interference. A whistle blew, and Mia slowed to a halt, panting. She leaned over, coughing as her throat burned with the taste of blood.

It was ridiculous. This entire game was ridiculous. She glanced at the clock on the wall. Two seconds to halftime. That wasn't enough time to do anything, especially not to catch up to the other team's ridiculous lead.

She coughed again. This shouldn't have been so difficult. It was a game. But she couldn't keep her focus. The world twisted as she ran. People transformed into someone else. And her head…it was quiet. So quiet. Everything was falling apart around her but the voices remained silent.

"What the hell, Mia?" Miranda appeared by her side.

Mia straightened, hand going to her sore shoulder. It twinged, and she flinched. All she could think to say was, "Sorry."

Miranda looked her over. She and Mia had been on the team together for three years. She had no idea how many games they'd played together, and Miranda knew that this wasn't like her.

"Are you okay?" she asked. "You…don't look great."

She wasn't great. Her shoulder twinged again. She gripped it, face screwing up as she tried to focus on reality. The world in front of her. Her eyes scanned the crowds. There were college recruiters here. It wasn't often they came to games up in the mountains, but for some reason they'd come today, and girls like Miranda, who were hoping for a basketball scholarship, relied on this game.

A game Mia kept royally screwing up.

"I…." Mia didn't know what to say, and she didn't have time to say much either when the whistle blew. They had to get back to the game. The two seconds left.

Mia waved goodbye to Miranda and went to her position. Everyone knew it was pointless. A formality. And when it started, Mia didn't move at all until the buzzer rang, announcing the end of the second quarter.

The pre-game energy had vanished. No one was feeling the moment anymore. Defeat had wormed its way over their heads. In the back of her mind, Mia prepared a speech to pump them back up. They were behind, but it wasn't an impossible lead. They could catch up. It wouldn't be difficult.

But the words wouldn't come.

Instead, she let Coach Smith talk the girls up, not listening to a single word she said. Instead, her attention returned to the stand, looking over all of the people. They were a blur. Faceless shapes chatting and cheering. One stood out.

Steven.

"Mia."

Coach Smith's voice caught her attention. She focused on the group again, only to find the girls walking with a little more pep in their step to cool down in the locker room. Get some water. Take a seat.

"Oh," she said. "Sorry."

She made to leave, but Coach Smith stopped her, touching the same shoulder as before. Mia tensed, waiting for the electricity, but it didn't come.

"You seem distracted," Coach Smith said. "I think it'll do you some good to sit out the next quarter. Go on a walk. Get some fresh air."

"But–" Mia cut herself off. She didn't even know what she was protesting for. She didn't want to be here. There was only one thing she wanted to do. She glanced at Steven again. He noticed her, and smiled, cocking his head in a question. She nodded at him. "Okay. I'll…I'll do that."

Coach Smith smiled. "Great. Make sure to dress warm. Might be light out, but I heard snow is coming our way. Can't be too careful."

She let go of Mia's shoulder, and walked off to join the girls in the locker room. Mia waited for a moment, uncertain, then went off as well. When she entered the hall, she found Steven waiting for her, leaning against the wall.

He smiled at her, and opened his mouth to talk but her words tumbled out.

"I'm going to get the knife," she said.

His eyes widened, and he closed his mouth.

She continued. "I don't…I don't want to do it here. There are too many people. But…can I give it to you outside? In the woods? I'm…supposed to go on a walk anyway."

They stared at each other, and Mia's heart raced remembering the night before. They hadn't said much. Just the two of them. Alone. Mia had felt…something close to safe. But like now, like the past couple of days, everything had been just off. A movie not synced with the sound.

Steven nodded, but his face betrayed his emotions. Concern. Uncertainty. "I…okay."

"Yeah." She looked down the hall, toward the locker room. Before she could move, his arm jerked out, wrapping around her and pulling her into a tight, warm, hug.

Startled, she didn't move. His grip tightened and his arms shook around her.

"Steven?" she asked.

"I just…don't want you to feel like this anymore," he said.

"What?" Mia pulled away from him, but he didn't let her go far, leaning in to kiss her. The world seemed to stop for a moment. Everything stilled. The sound caught up to the picture. She closed her eyes as the warmth of his lips, his hand on her cheek, grounded her.

And when he pulled away, she wanted to pull him back. She didn't want to let that feeling go. To spiral back into the disorienting world that had descended on her. But she didn't. Something else pulled her back. A puppet on a string.

A pained look overcame Steven's face. He brushed his thumb under her eye, wiping away a tear she hadn't realized she'd shed.

"Go get the knife," he said. "I'll meet you in the woods behind the school. And…everything will be better after this. I promise."

Mia nodded. He moved away, heading to the school entrance, and she made her way to the locker room, ready and eager to get rid of the knife. For her life to go back to normal. For things to get better. She knew they would. They had to. After all,

Steven doesn't lie.

Derek burst into the gym, panting. Searching. Cody and Blair followed close behind. Blair told him to calm down and Cody insisted that everything would be all right. He ignored both of them and had been since he'd bolted from Blair's house.

He didn't know how Mia had gotten the knife. None of them did. Mrs. Arbour had had no answers as to how Mia had gotten a knife last seen in ancient Thailand. In Derek's dreams. He'd thought that maybe she had magic too. He'd hidden his powers from her, why not the other way around? But Mrs. Arbour insisted that Mia's energy levels were too low for magic.

It didn't make sense. How long had she had it? Where had she kept it? How many nights had Derek slept in the room next door to it without realizing a part of his dreams was right there?

The gym was loud. Derek stormed forward, prepared to find a game going on, to find Mia out on the court, but it was empty. Everyone in the gym huddled around the bleachers, chatting, exchanging stories, having a good time. But there were no girls in uniforms chucking a ball at each other to throw it in a hoop.

Derek didn't understand, and he cursed himself for not coming to more of Mia's games. Or…any of them, really. He'd tried when she first made the team. He went to one with their mom and tried so hard to pay attention, but sports were not his thing. Mia'd told him he didn't have to come to any others after that. So he hadn't.

Stupid. Stupid. Stupid.

"Where is she?" Derek asked, spinning around to face Blair and Cody. "I thought she was at the game."

"Hell if I know," Blair said.

Cody sighed. "Do you two never pay attention? It's half time. She's probably in the locker room."

Derek groaned. "Well, we can't go in there. Coach Smith will kill us." They could wait outside for her. It wouldn't be weird. Right? He was her brother. Blair and Cody were her friends. They were there to show her support. Make sure she was safe and get the dangerous ancient knife from her, yes, but also show her support.

He made the suggestion, but Cody didn't look convinced.

"Mia's not going to talk to us just because we're right there," he pointed out. "If she's coming out, it's because it's time to get back to the game. She won't have time to say anything."

"Okay, but then what do we do?" Derek's frustration grew. He needed to talk to his sister. He needed to feel her emotions and figure out what he could do to make them better. When it was just the bracelet, he could understand. That was Blair and Mrs. Arbour keeping Mia protected. Now it was something else. Some*one* else, and he didn't like it. If they had control over her emotions, what else were they manipulating?

"We're just going to have to wait till the game is over," Cody said.

At this point, Blair butted in. Literally. She placed her hands on Cody and Derek's chests and pushed them apart so she could step between them with a roll of her eyes.

"Goddamn," she said. "You two are idiots."

"Excuse me?" Cody snapped.

Blair flat out ignored him. "You two can't go into the girl's locker room, but I can. Why don't I just go in and get her?"

She was right. He was an idiot. But would Mia even talk to Blair? Would she talk to any of them? There was no way out of this mess that didn't involve testing at least one of those options.

He wanted to tear his hair out.

"I'm gonna go now," Blair said. "You two...." She looked the boys up and down, then shook her head. "I don't even know."

Then she took off toward the locker room. Emotions licked at Derek's skin, stronger than the past two weeks. He thought back to what Mrs. Arbour had said, about the dreams weighing him down. He did feel...different. He hadn't realized how heavy the weight on his shoulders had been until she'd removed it, and he wondered how long it had been there. The way he felt now...he hadn't experienced such lightness in years.

How long had I been having those dreams?

"Let's wait in the hall," Cody muttered.

Derek glanced at him, then back at the crowd of people waiting for the game to resume. Their emotions, bright and alive, would have overwhelmed him if he hadn't had years of practice shutting out this many people, but Cody was different. Derek didn't know exactly how the mist thing related to his anxiety, but regardless, this was not the kind of place he wanted to be. Even now, as he backed toward the door, he looked to the floor, hands clenched, shoulders hunched.

He didn't give Derek a chance to say no to his request, and even if he had, Derek wouldn't have fought him on this. Instead, he followed Cody back out of the gym into the quieter hallway. People were out there too, standing with bottles of water, laughing and joking in the fresher air.

Cody wouldn't look at them, and Derek's brow furrowed. His foot tapped, waiting for Blair to return with his sister, but he needed something to take his mind off the situation.

"How have you gone to all of Mia's games if you hate crowds that much?" Derek asked.

Cody spared him a glance before returning his gaze away from the people. "She helps."

Derek rolled his eyes. "Crowds paralyze you. The power of love isn't that strong."

When Cody flinched, Derek realized that the two of them had never exactly discussed how Cody felt about Mia.

"Never mind," he said, but to his surprise, Cody spoke.

"It's not...that. Her mist...it's...different. It always has been. There's a warmth to it, and I can't explain what it is. When she's around, I'm calmer."

Derek wasn't sure how to respond to this revelation. Cody and Mia had always had a kind of special bond, but he'd never understood it. "Is that why you got so pissed at us when her mist was the wrong color?"

He shrugged. "I dunno. Maybe. It scared me. All of this scares me. It always has."

Derek crossed his arms, watching Cody carefully. "What always has?"

"What I can do," he said. "What others can do. It's hasn't exactly brought me fortune."

Glancing down the hall toward the locker room, and then back at Cody, Derek tried to make sense of what he was saying. Was it like with Blair and her clan? The rules and secrets and complications? Or was there something going on? Something he wasn't saying? Blair had known about his powers. Mrs. Arbour knew what he could do, what he could see, without even having to ask.

A thought occurred to Derek. "Is your magic the reason why Blair hates you?"

Cody tensed, then shrugged. "It's complicated."

"But—"

"Blair." Cody nodded in the direction of the locker room, and Derek dropped his line of questioning. Blair stormed toward them. Alone.

The first thought that crossed Derek's mind was that she'd gotten in a fight with Mia, and was now storming toward them to rant about how there was nothing they could do and Mia was being unreasonable. Not exactly what Derek wanted to hear, but he could work with that. It meant she was around and at least willing to acknowledge Blair.

Except, when Blair made it to them, her emotions bled through the bracelet. Just a trickle. A tickle against his arms. It wasn't anger. There was no fire, no nails on a chalkboard. The emotion leaking through was liquid mercury sinking into his skin. Light, and yet it made him shudder.

"She's not in there," Blair said. Even if he hadn't been able to feel the anxiety, Blair's voice was shaking with it.

"What do you mean?" Cody asked.

"Exactly what I said." Blair glared at him. "She's not in there. Kaylee said she got changed and left."

Derek placed his face in his hands and groaned. This wasn't going well. It'd barely started and it was already falling to shit. They lived in small freaking town with a population of less than a thousand people. How difficult could it be for three people with magic to find a teenage girl with a mystical knife?

"Okay, so we have to find her," Cody said. "I…I can try and find her mist. I…I…I don't know if I can, but I can try."

"Not sure we have time for trying," Blair snapped at him.

"Well if you have any better ideas, I'm all ears."

Derek was not in the mood for another one of their arguments. They didn't have time to try things out, but they also needed to do *something*. He thought. If Mia had left, then she probably wasn't in the school anymore. It wasn't dark out. She could have disappeared into the woods and no one would notice. Or she was downtown. But why had she left in the first place?

Then there was something.

A feeling.

It clawed at his chest. It sent shudders through his limbs. A darkness like no other. He stared down the hallway, blinking as it seemed to twist. As the world around him changed and morphed into the river. It rushed away from him and toward the outdoors, guiding him. In the dreams, the river had always been a barrier. It kept him away from the other side. An obstacle in his path that he needed to tear down to achieve his goal. But…it wasn't just that. He thought to the fishermen. The boats floating down the river.

The river wasn't an obstacle. It was a path. He didn't know where this path would lead him, or what it meant, but he needed to follow it.

He didn't say anything to Blair or Cody. They were arguing, and he didn't want anything to do with it. Instead he moved. The water splashed up over his feet, but they remained perfectly dry. Blair called out to him, but he ignored her. The river glowed, and pulled him out of the school. Away from the gym. Toward the woods.

Cool air greeted him when he left the building. The river continued on, twisting down the field where most of the outdoor sports were played before disappearing into the woods. He followed it. His feet crunched against the snow as new flakes drifted from

361

the sky.

"Derek, where are you going?" Blair called from behind him.

He spared them a glance. They were following him, but neither looked pleased about it. "I'm finding Mia."

The two of them looked at each other, their expressions the exact same mixture of confusion and annoyance. On a normal day, when Derek didn't need to find his sister, he would have laughed at them actually getting along, even if it was because he was making no sense.

"How are you finding her?" Cody asked as the three continued on, following a river that two of them didn't know existed.

Derek just shrugged and kept going. Before long, they were surrounded by tall, dark pines, and the river narrowed. Derek gritted his teeth. If the river disappeared and they hadn't found Mia, then this meant nothing. It was nothing.

The river came to an end, deep into the woods.

Derek halted, panting. He examined the woods, trying to find any sort of clue about where his sister was. If not his sister, maybe the knife. She must have had it. He had no idea what she could possibly want to do with it, nor what it all meant, but it was here. She was here. Something in him said it was the case.

"Derek, what are we doing out here?" Blair asked.

"I think she's here," he said.

Blair glanced around. "I don't see her."

He didn't either. And he couldn't feel her. This was getting to be enough. He'd never gone a day in his life without being able to sense her somewhere.

"This is stupid," Blair said. "We're wasting time."

"I know that," Derek muttered. He wanted her to stop talking so he could think.

"Derek–"

"Guys." Cody's voice cut Blair off in an instant. It was tense.

Pitch higher than normal. Derek spun around and found him pointing into the woods. He didn't move. Derek's eyes widened. Not fifty feet away, with her back to them, stood Mia.

Her hair was pulled up into the high ponytail she wore for games, but she had on her street clothes. A winter coat, jeans, and a pair of boots. Without thinking, Derek ran toward her, feet crunching in the snow, breath visible in the chilled air.

"Mia!" he called out.

She jumped, and turned. He was so pleased to see her safe and all right, that it took him a moment to realize she was clutching something to her chest. But when he did, and when he looked down, he realized that the knife, the one in his dreams, the one on the back of his eye lids when he tried to sleep, was, in fact, real, and that his sister was holding it like everything in her world depending on what happened to it next.

Chapter Twenty-Four

Mia gripped the knife tighter to her chest. Snow drifted from the sky, as gentle as a mother with her newborn baby. Her eyes wanted to focus on the flakes fluttering in front of her nose as if keeping her from paying attention to the situation at hand.

She blinked and forced herself to look in front of her. The three people standing in the snow. Every time her eyes landed on one, the world twisted and her gaze fell to the ground. She squeezed her eyes shut and shook her head to clear it from the fog. The dense, angry, gray fog.

The further into the woods she'd walked, the thicker it'd become, and with the thickening fog arrived the dark voice at full volume, screaming in her imagination's ears like an eagle desperately looking for her first meal.

"Mia."

She opened her eyes, and this time managed to focus on Derek. He stood there, panting, eyes flickering to the knife. She clenched it tighter. Behind him, Blair and Cody waited with exchanged glances.

Mia's brow furrowed. Her vision attempted to divert again, back to the snow, but she blinked to get them back on track. Confusion coursed through her. They were here. Her brother. Her friends. They'd…followed her? Had they come to her game? She hadn't seen them.

They stayed back. Hesitant, as if they were afraid of something. **They're scared of you.**

Mia bit her lip. *Why are they afraid of me?*
They can't handle that you want to leave.

They don't know I want to leave.
Do you want to leave?

"What are you…doing here?" Mia asked. She clenched the knife. The leather, normally soft, dug into her skin like a million pins. It shot through her hands, up her arms and down to her feet, locking her in place. Forcing her to confront the people she'd been running from.

Derek's stance relaxed, shoulders dropping as he took a step forward. Then stopped.

"We came looking for you," Derek said, switching to Chinese.

Mia's brow furrowed. Derek only spoke to her in Chinese around their friends when he wanted a private conversation. But what could be so private right now?

Run.

But Mia hesitated. Or, maybe, she couldn't move. Her feet remained planted firmly in the snow, nailed down with jolts of electricity. When she spoke, she replied to him in Chinese, though she wasn't sure why.

"You've spent weeks pushing me away," she said. "Weeks. Lying to me, spending time together behind my back, ignoring me when I came to you for help."

"I know," Derek said. "I…I know. And I want to talk to you about that, but there's a ton of shit going on and I don't know how to explain it. There's not a lot of time."

"Derek, what did she say?" Blair probably meant to keep her voice low, but in the silence of the afternoon, every sound was amplified. The words carried over on the non-existent wind and wrapped Mia in chills. She hadn't heard Blair's voice since that night.

Derek turned to wave Blair off. The girl scowled, but the scowl vanished when she and Mia made eye contact. Instead, concern replaced it.

Concern.

All of them were concerned.

Why are they concerned?

You TELL ME.

Mia's feet moved. An inch. Away. Shuffling through the layer of snow with a crunch.

"What's going on?" Mia asked in English. She couldn't stop the tremble in her voice. With every second, the gray settled in deeper. The voice, the dark voice, grew louder, telling her to flee so she could be free.

FREE FROM WHAT?

Derek struggled, and confusion mixed in with the gray. He always had a quip. He knew how to use his words to get what he wanted. To get his point across. Derek didn't struggle with words.

When Derek didn't speak, Cody stepped forward, placing a hand on Derek's shoulder as if letting him know that he was taking over.

Mia stepped back.

"You feel off, right?" Cody asked.

Mia took another step back, clenching the knife. Off. He meant…did he meant the gray? The voices? How could he know that she felt off?

"Cody, stop," Derek said, grabbing his arm. But Cody yanked it out of his grasp.

"You're not saying anything and she deserves to know."

Mia's eyes widened. She'd never heard Cody snap at Derek like that. In fact, the only time Mia ever saw Cody get angry was when Blair got on his nerves.

"What is going on?" she asked again. Her voice trembled. "Why do you think I feel off?"

"Because–"

Before he could finish, Derek pushed him out of the way.

"Did you hear my message?" he asked.

Mia froze, and both Cody and Blair turned to face Derek. Blair's hand touched Derek's shoulder, and words left her mouth, but Mia couldn't hear them. All she could do was stare at her brother. He'd been trying to tell her something in the message. Something that Steven had interrupted.

"I…." Her body loosened. Arms fell from her chest. Knife still in hand. "I heard…some of it."

Don't answer him. Leave.

But her feet wouldn't move.

Derek clenched his fists. "Mia, we know…I know there's something off because I can't feel your emotions anymore."

An unsettling silence fell over the woods. The snow drifted from the sky. Just a little more. Just a little faster. Mia stared at her brother, trying to process his words. Trying to understand what he meant.

Trying to comprehend the addition of the word, "anymore."

A whirlwind of thoughts swirled in her brain. Memories of her and Derek as children. The way she was always calmer with him. How he always seemed to know what she was feeling.

She couldn't stop them. They battered her mind, forcing their way in. Moments from when they had lived in Beijing. A moment when a boy at school had stolen her notebook and she was angry. When their mom had told them they were moving to America. On the playground when the girls had bullied her. At home when she was stressed about an assignment. How he always knew when to make her a cup of tea when she was on the verge of tears. He was always quick to understand. To empathize. She never needed to explain how she was feeling to him.

He knew.

He always knew.

A gasp left her lips. Her eyes widened. Her grip loosened on the knife and it fell to the snow with a soft *thud*.

Two weeks ago she wouldn't have understood. Two weeks ago she might have asked him what he meant, but she knew. She knew the words that he was going to tell her on the call:

"I have magic."

She looked between them. Cody, paler than normal. Blair, half ready to run. Derek, stubborn. On the verge of tears.

"All…of you…?" she asked.

Derek stepped forward, body shaking.

"Yeah." He screwed up his face. "All of us."

"I…." Mia had no words.

Even if she did, though, Derek kept going, urgency rising in his tone. "I know it's confusing. And it's hard to explain. We…we'll explain later. Right now there's a lot going on. I don't know how much you know, or have seen. But that knife?"

Mia looked down at the glowing weapon. She crouched, picking it up again.

"What about it?" she asked. What did they want with the knife? She was supposed to get rid of it. Steven was on his way and would be expecting it. She couldn't just give it to her brother. That wouldn't get it out of her life.

Derek grimaced. "I…I don't know. But I need it. It's been in my dreams."

"What?" Mia asked.

"We don't have time to explain," Blair said, butting in. Mia's head snapped to look at her, startled that Blair had spoken up at all. Blair continued. "I know you're pissed at us, but my mom is waiting for us with whatever hot drink you want and I think a chocolate cake so we can explain. Here? Kinda cold."

"Smooth," Cody said.

"Shut up."

Mia relaxed. Explain. They were going to….

No. Stop it. They're lying.

They have been lying a lot. All her life, in fact. Their entire friendship. *So?*

Mia's head swam with a sudden onslaught of voices. The world tilted. They'd been lying to her about the same thing she'd been lying to them about. How long had this been going on? When did this insanity start?

You KNOW WHEN.

"Mia," Derek said. His voice broke through it all.

She opened her mouth to speak.

"There you are!"

The voice came from behind her, and when she turned, feet crunching in the snow, knife tight against her chest, she found Steven standing a ways off, the same distance as her brother and friends, with a hesitant smile on his face.

A chill ran down Derek's spine. He hadn't seen him. The teenager standing across from them. On the other side of Mia. She faced him, back to Derek, so he couldn't see her reaction to the sudden appearance of her friend. Derek tried to recall a name. Mia had mentioned it, and she'd been spending a lot of time with him, but he hadn't paid much attention to names. He'd figured he'd learn it later.

"What the hell is Steven doing here?" Blair asked.

Steven. That's what it was.

Derek shrugged. "I...don't know."

The air around them shifted. He felt it. It wasn't an emotion. When he focused on Steven, he couldn't feel his emotions. It wasn't like with Mia, who was just gone. For Steven, it was more like someone had put him in a plastic ball bouncing around in a forcefield that Derek couldn't penetrate.

No, it wasn't emotions. There was something else weighing down on his shoulders. Similar. But not the same. His body remembered what his mind had forgotten and transported him back to that afternoon he'd ditched class. The woman with blond hair. It was like her magic.

Derek's chest tightened. Behind him, Blair gasped.

"Oh my god," she said.

Derek wanted to turn to her, ask her what was going on, but he couldn't take his eyes off his sister. A dark sense of dread overcame him, one he couldn't place, and all he wanted to do was run up to her and drag her away from the situation. Nothing about this felt right. The way his blood tingled almost seemed to stop his heart from fear and concern for his, and for Mia's, life.

But he couldn't move. No matter what he did, his feet refused to move from their spot, like a forcefield holding him back. It made him want to scream, but even that he could not manage to do.

"Derek," Blair said, grabbing at his arm.

Finally, he tore his gaze from the scene in front of him to look at his wide eyed friend. Her hand shook, clinging to his jacket. "Blair?"

"I couldn't see it before," she said. "I...I must have been distracted or diverted or something, but–"

Steven's voice cut Blair off, drawing both of their attention back to him and Mia: "I'm glad to see you brought the knife."

Steven...wanted the knife?

OF COURSE HE DOES. IT'S QUITE THE ARTIFACT.

Derek jerked back, snapping his head from side to side to search for the source of the voice. But it was just the five of them, standing alone in the woods with snow drifting from the sky with increasing intensity. The sky—or, what he could see of it—had gained a hint of cool tones to it, indicating the beginnings of dusk.

Blair pushed past him, halting the same distance from Mia that Derek had been unable to push past. As she struggled to move forward, she shouted, "You stay away from her!"

Mia's head swung between her friends and Steven. He looked tense. Maybe as stuck as they were?

Derek extended his hands, barely thinking, and where Blair was frozen, his hands found resistance. He didn't understand. His sister, his terrified, confused, sister, was somehow stopping them.

But Mia didn't have magic.

So....

IT'S QUITE THE ARTIFACT.

"I'm just trying to help," Steven said, and Derek blinked. It must have been a fraction of a second between Blair's angry shout and Steven's retort, but Derek's mind had almost slowed the world down.

"Help?" Blair's voice bounced between the trees like a ball racking up points in pinball. "You're not helping her you piece of shit!"

The entire group went silent as Blair's words vanished into the afternoon air. All eyes were on her as Derek tried to understand what had set her off like this. She was tense, but it wasn't like when she and Cody got into it, or when she and Derek had screamed at each other. This was different. A side of Blair he'd never seen.

"What the hell?" Cody asked, breaking the silence.

Derek glanced at him. The boy was guarded, looking Blair up and down, and Derek wondered if something about her mist had changed. There was a step behind him. A crunch of snow. He spun around. Mia faced them, but she'd stepped away. Just one foot. Just a little. His eyes flickered to Steven, and then back to her.

The feeling, deep in his bones, returned. The dark, pulsating energy. Like the blond haired woman's. But...different.

"For weeks something's been off," Blair said, voice raised but not quite a yell. "This town, our lives...*something* has been off, and here we are thinking it's the Gray Spirits, but no. It's been *him*!'

No. Derek shook his head, knowing that Blair couldn't see him. No, it wasn't Steven. He'd already figured out who it was. It was that woman with the blond hair.

PIECE BY PIECE. PUT THEM TOGETHER. STOP SEEING THINGS AS SEPARATE.

The voice again. Derek groaned and put his head in his hands when his sister's trembling voice called out.

"Why are you attacking Steven?" she asked. "He's right. He's trying to help me. He's going to make all this insanity stop."

"No, he's not," Blair said. She tried to step forward again, but couldn't.

It's quite the artifact.

Derek looked to Steven, also stuck in his spot, remaining strangely quiet. Mia didn't have magic. But...Steven did. Steven had magic. It's why he couldn't move. Like the rest of them. They were all stuck away from Mia as she held a knife that didn't want to leave her possession.

"Mia, he's not trying to help you." A hint of desperation leaked into Blair's words.

"Hang on!" Steven called out. "You guys don't even know me. Just stay out of this."

"Like hell we will," Blair snapped.

Derek had no words. He was confused. There was a piece of the puzzle missing. Steven was just a kid. He had magic. Derek could feel it pricking at his skin, but what if he really was trying to help Mia? The enemy here wasn't Steven, right? It was the queen?

He caught Mia's gaze. They stared at each other, snow falling between them. Blair shouted something next to him, but he didn't hear it. A hand touched his shoulder. Cody.

He barely felt it.

Steven's words echoed through the air: "Mia, come on. Just give me the knife and we can go. Everything will be over soon."

She didn't react. She stared at Derek, and he stared back, and he tried to understand what was going through her head. What she would do next. How this would all play out. But most of all, he wanted to know what she was feeling.

Fear.

Confusion.

Anger.

Frustration.

They bubbled inside of her, each one fighting to take over and make a decision on her actions.

Did she give the knife to Steven?

Did she give it to her brother?

WHY GIVE IT AWAY AT ALL?

She wanted her life to go back to normal. To return to the days when everything was simple. But could it even go back there? She didn't really understand. Not yet. There were too many questions to be had. But magic. Her friends. Her brother. All of them had magic. This world she didn't know existed until two weeks ago…it was their life.

So many things made sense.

So many answers to questions she hadn't wanted answers to.

They knew things that could have explained everything. About the knife. Derek said he'd been having dreams about the knife. Did they know other things too? About where she found it? The woman who had been stalking her?

Steven?

Blair screamed at Steven and called him a piece of shit. And Mia didn't get it. She didn't understand why, if all of them had magic, and if all of them cared about her, they weren't rejoicing in discovering one another. Hadn't Steven said that the magical community was small?

Mia's body shook. Fear. Maybe. Was it dominating?

And her brother. Derek. Standing there quietly, looking like he had when he'd thought she wasn't watching seven years ago in the Beijing airport. Exhausted. Scared. Resigned. She gripped the knife.

Give it to Steven and be done with this world. They don't care about you.

Then why are they here?

They want to hurt you. Steven is the only one who has ever been honest with you. They hate that.

"Mia?" Steven asked.

She twisted, looking over at him. Then back to her friends.

"Mia." Cody, who had been silent for a while now, stepped forward, in line with Derek and Blair. The three of them stayed away from her. And on the other side, so did Steven. A hint of comfort broke through the negative emotions. At least they weren't trying to take the knife from her.

It was her choice.

A HARSH BURDEN TO BEAR.

Choose wisely.

"Why are you guys doing this to me?" Mia asked. She didn't know who she was talking to: the voices, or her friends.

Derek remained silent, as did Blair, as did Steven. Instead, it was Cody who answered her, speaking in a low, calming tone. The one he often used when she was anxious.

"We aren't doing anything to you." He struggled to move, but eventually managed to force himself forward one step. Mia shrunk away. "We're trying to help. All this magic stuff is just…it's just something that is. We want things to go back to the way they were before too."

Where they keep you in the dark about their world.

"You all *lied* to me!" Mia said. "You lied about everything. How long have all of you known? Huh?" She glanced between them, desperate to read their faces. Blair's furrowed brow. Cody's panic. Derek, unmoved, unchanged, still resigned. "Did none of you notice that something was going on with me? If you all have magic, why could you tell there was a woman stalking me? That I had a magical knife in my drawer for weeks?"

Tears welled at her eyes as they remained silent.

"How did you not know?"

Finally, Derek spoke, "Because shit's been going on for us too."

"Then why didn't you tell me?" Mia's voice cracked. "Why did you never tell me?" Her words slipped into Chinese as she continued. "Why have you lied to me all of our lives, Démíng? Why didn't you tell me that you're an…an…." She struggled to fine the right word. "An empath? Don't you trust me?"

If he did, then he would have told you.

Derek took a deep breath. "I…I wanted to tell you. But I didn't know how."

He's lying.

She wanted to believe him.

Lying.

He was her brother. He didn't want to hurt her.

Lies.

But she couldn't do it. She couldn't believe him. With a shake of her head, she backed away. One step. Two.

"Méilián," Derek said.

"No." Her resolve grew. She knew she had to be done with him. With his lies. Tears pricked her eyes. "I can't do it. I can't trust you."

She turned, taking a deep breath as her friends exploded behind her, shouting her name. Steven smiled, eyes soft.

"I'm sorry they've been lying to you. I can't imagine what it's been like living with an empath without knowing it."

Ice flooded her veins. Her breath caught. She stopped. Her foot came down on the snow with a loud crunch, eyes never leaving him. She watched him. His face. The way it went from relief to confusion.

"Mia?" he asked.

She stepped away. "How did you know he was an empath?"

She hadn't said the word in English.

Any color Steven might have had in his face vanished like an octopus blending in with the snow. His jaw dropped. His eyes darted around. Maybe looking for an answer. Maybe looking for an excuse.

Behind her, the others had fallen silent again. Listening. She didn't want to know what they were thinking, or what they would do now. They'd still lied to her. But now...had Steven lied to her too?

Had anyone been honest with her?

Define honest.

Mia backed away again.

"Wait, Mia," Steven said. He held out a hand, moving toward her. But just like with her brother and friends, something held Steven back, and eventually he gave up.

"You said...." Mia struggled to get the words out. "You promised me you wouldn't lie to me."

"I didn't...." Steven's head spun around, his search now desperate. "Mia, I didn't want to. I'm sorry. I just.... We need to go. Okay?"

"Why do you all keep lying to me?" Mia screamed.

She didn't want a response. Yet, for some reason, she got one from a new voice. A woman's voice. A silky, chilled voice. One that sent shivers through every vein in Mia's body. One that froze her lungs. Stopped her heart.

One that said, "Because you're weak."

Steven's eyes widened. He turned. Behind Mia, Derek gasped and muttered, "It's her."

But that confused Mia even more. Because the woman floating out of the woods, wearing inappropriate clothing for the snow, was the bleached-blond woman that had been stalking Mia for three weeks.

Every bone in Mia's body begged her to run. As the woman came to a stop next to Steven, Mia's heart exploded in her chest. Adrenaline pumped it. It warmed her body, grabbing her muscles to get them to flee.

She couldn't.

As the woman, towering over Steven, placed her arm on his shoulder, Mia found herself rooted to the spot, chest fluttering like a hummingbird as she tried to catch her breath.

"See," the woman continued, "you're fragile. A flower too easy to crush. So we had to lie to you. Your friends didn't think you were strong enough. Your brother decided he had to protect you from your own emotions. And Steven here?" Steven flinched when she said his name, and Mia's eyes widened. "Well, Steven was following orders."

Orders? Mia stepped away from them. The rest of the world didn't matter. It didn't make sense. She expected Steven to brush off the woman's arm. To say it was all a lie. To make everything better. To bring back the beautiful lights and gentle moments.

"What orders?" Mia asked.

"Mia it's not–" Steven started to say, only to fall silent when the woman a hand over his mouth.

"Irrelevant right now," she said. She glanced over Mia's head at

Derek, Cody, and Blair. Then she smirked. "Man, you really screwed this all up, Steven. Hope it was worth it to chase some tail."

Steven ripped the woman's hand off his mouth and turned, anger scrunching up his face.

"Kathleen, that's not what happened–"

Her name. A name. Mia's eyes widened at the sound. It was… so normal. It was normal, and Steven knew it. He knew her. The woman who had been stalking her.

"Be quiet and do your job," Kathleen said. She focused on Mia, smiling. "Now then. Miss Mia. I think you owe us a knife."

The knife. Mia's hands had grown so numb she'd almost forgotten she was still clenching it to her chest. Her grip on it tightened, and she glanced over her shoulder at her brother and friends. They looked as dumbfounded as she felt.

Give us the knife. Get this over with. It'll be over soon.

Mia clenched her teeth.

Do it.

But….

DO IT.

Mia couldn't think straight. The voice grew louder, blocking out all the other sounds in the clearing. Kathleen, asking her again for the knife. Steven, saying something. Blair, shouting. A tiny voice in her ear, whispering quietly.

RUN.

The chains trapping her to the ground shattered. Her feet moved on their own. Turning from Steven and Kathleen. Ignoring her brother and friends. Facing the woods, away from the school. They moved. She bolted. And dusk continued to fall.

Chapter Twenty-Five

She ran, disappearing into the woods, and Derek's first instinct was to go after her. With her, and the knife, moving further away, he was finally able to push past the magic that had kept him barricaded from his sister. But he'd barely taken three steps when the ground beneath him erupted into flames. The snow melted with a loud *hiss*, and he stumbled back, nearly tripping over his own feet.

His heart raced. On the other side of where Mia had stood a few seconds ago, Steven tried to run after Mia, but instead of fire stopping him, it was Kathleen's long, pale fingers. She leaned in toward Steven's ear, whispering something, and all the while keeping eye contact with Derek.

Her eyes.

He knew them. They weren't from his dreams. They were from his nightmares. The ones that he hadn't wanted to remember. His body turned to ice, recalling that moment in the woods when she'd come after him.

After a fraction of a second, her lips left Steven's ears and she glided through the woods after Mia. Panic crushed his rib cage, squeezing his lungs until he could barely breathe.

He tensed to run after them, but more fire appeared at his feet.

"Dammit!" he cried out, stumbling away from the growing inferno. He jerked his head back in the direction of Steven. The boy had always been pale. But now it was like he'd become the snow itself.

Derek felt out for Steven's emotions. He found nothing.

"I can't let you go," Steven said. His voice was low. It trembled. All of him trembled. Derek didn't know how to respond. He needed to go after Mia.

But he also knew, despite Steven's angry exchange with Kathleen, that he would do as she said. She called the shots and he was powerless to fight against her. But not to fight against Derek.

He needed to protect Mia, but Steven wasn't about to let him go without a fight.

Blair grabbed his arm. He glanced at her, and out of the corner of his eye he spotted Cody slink off, back into the woods after Mia and Kathleen. And it seemed that Steven had no idea.

Thank god.

"What do you want from us?" Blair snapped with a tone Derek had never even heard her take with Cody.

Steven stepped toward them without an answer. Derek retreated. The feeling from before, the weight boring down on his shoulders, grew more powerful. It consumed the entire clearing, as if attempting to flatten the forest into a prairie. Derek shuddered. This magic—and he had to guess it was Steven's magic—was unlike anything he'd ever felt before. It wasn't like Kathleen. It wasn't like The Queen. It wasn't like Blair. Or Cody. Or Mrs. Arbour.

It was different. It fought against itself, tearing. But like a muscle, the more it tore, the stronger it grew back.

"Blair, we need to go," Derek said.

"I'm not sure we'll be able to. Not with magic like his." Blair's words came out laced in terror. The way she'd screamed at Steven earlier had been a clue, but this guy...what was he?

Had Derek's voice not already dropped, he would have squeaked. "Fucking hell."

Steven held up a hand and a fire encased it, running along his fingers until forming into a vortex of flame.

"I'm sorry," he said before he jerked out his hand and a firestorm of towering flames spread along the ground, separating Derek and Blair.

Derek yelped and jumped to the side, landing face first in the snow. Warmth licked at his feet. He scrambled away from what had to be a fire hazard and pushed himself to his feet

"Blair?" He coughed, the heat from the flames violating his throat.

No answer.

He reached out, wanting to feel her emotions, desperate for any sign that she was okay, but the damn bracelet kept her from him. His eyes darted, desperate to find a way to get to her, when he noticed Steven on his side of the flames.

Of course.

Derek tensed. Steven stayed back, hands in his pockets, watching Derek.

Derek tried to recall the years of wushu lessons his father had forced on him when he was a kid, but that was so long ago. Even if it hadn't been, he'd never been any good at any of it, much less hand to hand combat. That was, of course, Mia's specialty. Still, he had to imagine that somewhere he could channel his father. Or his sister.

"Why are you doing this?" Derek called out.

"You wouldn't get it," Steven said. "None of you get it. You want the knife but you don't even know what it is."

"I don't need to know what it is to know that I can't let someone who messed with my sister have it," Derek snapped.

Steven's eyes widened. And there it was. A hint. Something. A small touch of self-loathing on Derek's skin.

It was gone in seconds, leaving Derek confused. Steven had used Mia. That much was clear. He and Kathleen were working for the queen. That had to be it. Why else would they want a knife that Mia was so frightened of?

But if that was the case, and if Steven really had just been using Mia, then why had Steven felt self-loathing at Derek's accusation?

He'd barely had the thought when Steven moved. Fast. Derek jerked back to attention and spun to the side to avoid Steven's fist. Steven, unlike Derek, must have paid attention when he was taught martial arts, because he twisted. This time, Steven's fist connected with Derek's face.

Pain exploded in his nose. He tasted blood and gasped, stumbling back against a tree. With some luck, he managed to look up in time to see Steven back in front of him.

He yelped and let his legs turn to jelly, sending him to the ground. A crack echoed in the woods, then a hum, and finally, an explosion of wood and snow as the tree fractured into a million pieces above Derek's head.

Derek scrambled to his feet and ran as fast as he could from the monster going after him.

Shit, shit, shit, shit, shit, shit.

As explosions kicked up fire and snow at his feet, he darted around the woods, looking for Mia. For Blair. For a way out. But the woods never seemed to end, getting longer until he had to stop to relieve his heaving lungs. Iron coated his throat as he panted.

A shiver ran up the back of his neck. That feeling. Steven's magic.

He spun around. Steven stood there, sparking energy around his fingers. Derek stepped back, but it was too late. The lightning death shot out toward him.

He cringed, covering his face with his arms as warmth seeped out from his skin. It peeled off like glue from a child's fingers and left him chilled.

Chilled, but not electrocuted.

It crackled in front of him, above him, behind him. Trying to break through. He glanced up, and a thin bubble of his own energy surrounded him.

Gold.

Hadn't Cody said his mist was gold? That'd felt like a lifetime ago. Derek sick. Cody revealing his secret. That was the moment Mia truly became an outsider in their group. When they'd decided not to tell her.

The electricity crackled into nonexistence, and drops of golden energy fell around Derek, mixing with the snow.

And just like that, Derek's mind connected two dots he couldn't believe he hadn't thought about before: Derek had magic too. He didn't have to just run.

YOU CAN'T HEAR IT, BUT I'M APPLAUDING.

Derek gritted his teeth. Steven stepped forward and Derek held up a hand, drawing the warmth into it. The magic. The sweet sensation of energy pulsed through his veins. And when Steven took another step, Derek ran over what he knew about magic.

It was energy

It was versatile.

He had an abnormal amount of it.

Nothing is crazy when it comes to magic.

And all he wanted to do was survive.

The warmth turned white hot and he gasped as light swirled in the circle of his palm. Steven hesitated, eyes going wide, before he charged forward.

I can do this.

He'd created balls of light before. Tried small little things. But this was different. Because it wasn't for fun. It wasn't an accident.

When the ball left his hand, shooting out with flames trailing behind it, mimicking Steven, Derek felt the energy rip from his limb. It jerked him forward, and he stumbled through the snow to catch his footing.

When he looked up, this time it was Steven on the ground, head swinging between Derek and the trail of trees lit with smoldering flames.

Derek let out the air in his lungs, a small laugh accompanying it. *I did it.*

He had no time to celebrate, though. Steven jumped back to his feet, moving at an almost inhuman speed, and charged at Derek. Derek jerked back. He tried to summon more magic but Steven was faster, reaching out with one hand and clenching a fist. The tree next to Derek exploded, showering him with shards of wood.

He brushed them off him, fingers wet with the fresh welling of blood on his face.

Steven was there.

Derek dodged a punch. Only to get slammed in the stomach with an invisible force.

He gasped. Steven punched him again, this time in the jaw. Derek crashed into a nearby tree and tried to summon his magic, but Steven was too fast for him.

Again and again. A dance that Derek didn't know the steps to. Until finally he lay on the ground, hurting.

Steven stopped.

Derek pushed himself off the ground. A bruise was forming on Steven's jaw where Derek had managed to get him with magic. But that was it. Nothing like Derek himself. He thought briefly how he was going to explain this to his parents.

I think they'll wonder more why I'm dead.

"You know nothing," Steven said. "I don't...I don't get it. You know nothing about magic. You can barely fight. He told me you were a powerful mage, but you can't even wake up on time. I'm pretty sure he got it wrong."

Derek groaned. "What are you talking about?"

Steven snorted. "You don't even know? You're off trying to find the queen, chasing Kathleen into the woods, trying to find the knife, and you don't even know who you are." Another snort. "God. This is so stupid. Mia deserves so much more than to have you as a brother."

Anger coated the pain like ice. "Shut up! You don't know anything."

"I know more than you," Steven snapped. "I actually care about my mage heritage. I looked it up. I found books. Searched the internet. I sought out everything about my life and who I am so that I could understand! And what about you? Hoping your girlfriend will tell you the basics?"

"No," Derek said, shaking his head. He didn't want to have this conversation, but he couldn't move. "It's not like that."

"No?" Steven asked. "Then tell me, who do you think you are?"

"I–" Derek tried to say who he was. His name. Derek.

I am Derek.

But he wasn't entirely Derek. A piece of the puzzle fell into place.

The dreams.

The Queen.

The knife.

The grassy cliff on the edge of the Mekong River.

A priest who sealed away The Queen.

I am Derek.

Yes. And no.

"Niran," Derek said. "I…." He hadn't bonded with the man in his dreams.

He *was* the man in his dreams.

Nothing is crazy when it comes to magic.

"Took you long enough," Steven said.

Derek gritted his teeth, trying to wrap his mind around this revelation. "Shut up."

Steven rolled his eyes. "Yeah. Sure. I'll do that. If you can make me." Derek shifted, wincing from the pain, and managed to get to his feet. But he couldn't move, and Steven waved a hand. "Like I said. You can barely use all this magic that you have, much less use it to fight."

"Then kill me already," Derek snapped. He leaned against the nearest tree, panting, sweating. Or maybe that was blood. All he knew is that he really should have paid more attention to his dad.

Steven hesitated. An emotion bled through whatever mask he had up. Conflicted. Confused. Scared. Derek couldn't tell which, or if it was all three.

Regardless, a hint of relief pushed its way forward. Derek straightened, ignoring the cracking of his joints. "You don't want to."

Steven said nothing.

Derek scoffed. "Why are you doing this then?"

"Because it's what needs to be done," Steven said. But he shook. Maybe he didn't believe that.

"Because I'm...what?" Derek asked. He searched for the right word. "A...a...a reincarnation of an ancient priest?"

Steven shook his head.

"Then what?"

He shook his head again. "You told me to shut up."

"Are you kidding me?" Derek exclaimed but didn't continue as Steven held up a glowing hand.

Okay. So he is going to do it. He's going to kill me. I'm going to die. My sister's crazy sixteen-year-old boyfriend is going to kill me. Great.

Steven moved forward, and Derek tensed, when a burst of blue light fractured the sound barrier. Derek heard it. The high pitched scream. But he didn't hear it. It was in his mind, but not his ears, and he stood untouched as Steven collapsed to the ground, covering his ears with his hands.

A hand grabbed Derek's arm from behind, firm and pressing painfully into some of his bruises. He gasped and pulled away, tensed for another attack, but found Blair panting, also beat up, grabbing at him again.

"Why do you suck so bad at running?" Her hair was down.

"What the hell happened to you?"

"I couldn't explain it if I tried. Now come on!"

She tugged and Derek struggled to move. The sound vanished, and Steven stood, anger unmistakable.

"You bitch," he snarled. The change in attitude caught Derek off guard.

Blair continued to try and tug Derek, but his limbs weren't listening.

"Derek didn't grow up with magic, but I did," Blair snapped at Steven. "You want to fight someone? Then fight me."

Derek's jaw dropped. "What?"

Steven shrugged. "Fine."

He held up a hand and the world around them seemed to twist, but Blair let go of Derek and pushed past him, holding up her own hands in a strange formation. The twisting stopped, and Steven once more dropped to his knees.

Derek realized, standing there, watching Blair and Steven, that he'd never really seen Blair use her magic. He'd always seen it as limited. Small things. Her magic, and his own. But watching the blue energy spring from her fingers, manipulating the world around them, he realized that she was quite powerful.

If the situation had been different, he might have smiled like the love struck fool he was.

Gotta help, he told himself, trying to get his broken body to do what he wanted. He probably had at least one broken rib. Maybe two. Everything was stiff, both from the injuries and from the cold.

Before he could move though, Blair missed a step and Steven hit her with the same invisible force he'd been beating Derek up with earlier. She flew backward, crashing into Derek. He caught her and managed to keep them both from landing on their backs. But that was about as much as he could do, and both of them crumbled to the ground, him holding her as she moaned in shock.

Steven, panting, clenched his fists.

"Mages aren't good enough to fight me!" he exclaimed. "You all think you're so great but you are nothing compared to us."

Derek's brow furrowed. "What are you talking about? You're not a mage?"

Blair stirred and sat up. Before Steven could answer, she said, "No."

Derek glanced between Blair and Steven, trying to understand.

"I'm half mage," Steven said. "Like Blair."

"We're nothing alike," Blair snapped. Derek grimaced and gripped her to keep her from attacking Steven.

"You're right," Steven said. "I'm not half *human*. I'm something more powerful than a mage could ever be."

Derek was so confused he stayed quiet and listened to Blair speak.

"The Natara are not more powerful than mages," she said. "And just because you're half one doesn't make you more powerful than me!"

"Natara?" Derek asked.

"They're related to the Gray Spirits," Blair said.

Steven cocked his head. "The who?"

But Derek ignored his question, because the reason he wanted him dead made sense. He'd refused to reveal earlier, but it all made sense. How the woman with the red eyes was always there when he almost died. Kathleen's appearance. Their desperation for the knife. How they knew that Derek was Niran.

"Why did the queen ask you to kill me?" he asked.

A spark of realization crossed Steven's face. He smirked, a slight laugh coming out. "Oh. You two are talking about the Iravata."

The word washed over Derek like he'd known it his entire life. And in a way, he had. Because that word, Iravata, immortals, was one he'd known in another life. Three thousand years ago when he lived as a mage named Niran.

"Yes," he said. Blair whipped her head around. He ignored her.

Steven took in a deep breath, then shook his head. "You two have it all wrong. I'm surprised they didn't tell you."

"What?" Blair asked.

"We're not working for the Iravata," Steven said. "We want to kill their queen."

Chapter Twenty-Six

She flew through the forest. Confused tears pricked at her eyes as she tried to erase the image of Kathleen with a hand on Steven's shoulder. He'd lied. He'd lied to her about who he was. She'd told him about Kathleen and he hadn't said a word. He'd lied about not knowing her brother had magic. And about knowing that he was an empath.

He'd just lied.

What else was he lying about?

The knife grew heavy in her hands. The more she thought about Steven, the more weight it gained, dragging soul down to the depth of the Earth. Her legs screamed at her to stop. Her lungs expelled iron along with carbon dioxide. Her feet were soaking wet from the snow.

Deciding to listen to her body, at least for a moment, she came to a stop and leaned her back against a tree, clutching the knife to her chest.

More tears streamed down her face, chilling in the cold air. It was too much. She couldn't understand why everyone kept lying to her. Steven, her brother, her friends…hell, even her parents lied, and had lied, her entire life. Just one more trip. Just one more dig. Just one more month of this and everything will go back to normal.

Mia squeezed her eyes shut. She wasn't even sure what normal was anymore. Everything she'd clung to was gone.

And, when all of her safety nets had shriveled and turned to ash, the thing she had grabbed onto like her life depended on it morphed into a vicious snake ready to consume her.

With one hand still gripping the knife, the other went to her mouth, covering a sob while tears dripped onto her glove. There was nothing left for her. She couldn't keep her friendships alive. She couldn't trust anyone in her life.

She expected the voice, the dark voice, to tell her to just leave. But it stayed silent. And even if it had, where would she go? Steven had been her only out. She couldn't go live with her grandparents. They'd tell her she needed to stay with her parents and brother. That family was the most important thing.

A stark laugh escaped through the sobs. Family. Important. She wasn't sure her parents or brother knew the meaning of either word.

Her friends had been her family for a long time now. But even they had lied to her. Blair and Cody. Both of them with magic.

Magic. Magic. Magic.

She found she hated the sound of that word. Twenty minutes ago it'd been something amazing and mysterious, but now it was the source of everything. Steven had tried to show her how beautiful it was while simultaneously working with the woman who had caused Mia nightmares for the past three weeks. It'd been a party trick.

And Mia had fallen for it.

YOU HAVE TO ADMIT, IT WAS QUITE THE CONVINCING TRICK.

The lighter voice caught her off guard, as it'd been more or less silent for a while. She searched for the will to tell it to be quiet, but instead found that without the dark voice, she didn't hate the words whispering in her mind.

"I'm an idiot," Mia muttered. She should have known better than to trust Steven. Someone so new. Someone with so many secrets. Someone who was interested in her.

AN IDIOT? NO. IGNORANT IS A BETTER WORD.

That isn't better.

YOU CAN'T FIX BEING AN IDIOT. YOU CAN FIX BEING IGNORANT. ALL YOU HAVE TO DO IS LEARN.

How can I learn when no one tells me the truth?

YOUR BROTHER DID.

Years too late.

BUT HE STILL DID.

Snow crunching caught Mia's attention. She grabbed the knife with both hands and held it against her chest, her back to the tree. A quick scan of the area revealed no one. But the snow crunched again, and Mia tensed. She could run again soon. When her lungs calmed down and her legs stopped shaking from exhaustion.

The crunching stopped, and Mia relaxed. The knife in her hands continued to grow heavier, and she stared at it.

Magic.

She hated magic. Everything having to do with magic. And this knife…this knife was part of that. It was part of the world that she hated so much. It brought her so much pain. So much confusion. And, she realized, it was the whole reason Steven had taken an interest in her in the first place.

He tried to get her to give it to him. He'd promised her that he could take care of it. Deal with it. And even though it'd felt wrong, she'd decided to.

Only now she wasn't sure why. But she also wasn't sure why not. She could give it to Steven. She could give it to Derek. What did it matter to her?

MAYBE THIS ISN'T ABOUT YOU.

Mia ignored the voice and held the knife out to examine it. It was stupid. She hated clinging to it. She could give it to one of them.

Or, if they wanted it so badly, they could fight over it themselves.

DON'T.

Mia lifted the knife by her shoulder, twisting.

MIA, STOP.

She stepped. Her arm extended.

No.

And the knife flew far away. It was the knife they wanted. She was nothing. No one. No magic, no special powers. If they wanted the knife, they could have it. She would head back into town and pretend like none of this had ever happened.

"Well that was a silly thing to do."

The hairs on the backs of Mia's neck stood up at the sound of the voice right behind her. She spun around, backing up, and came face to face with Kathleen and the grin that had haunted Mia.

"You—"

Kathleen grabbed the collar of Mia's coat, yanking her forward.

Fear and adrenaline mixed together, returning with a vengeance. Mia barely thought. Her body moved without warning, a reaction to the assault. Her left hand shot up and gripped Kathleen's, trapping her, while the other arm jerked up into Kathleen's elbow. The woman cried out, possibly from pain, possibly from surprise, and Mia's arm snaked around Kathleen's, gripping her forearm before pulling the woman's body into a knee.

Kathleen gasped and crumpled to the ground. Mia backed away, body in a loose bow stance, hands tense.

Mia breathed out. Kathleen remained on the ground, and Mia realized what she'd done. One thought ran through her mind:

Oh god, did I just do that?

She'd sparred before, but that involved a judge, a ring, an audience, points, and, often, protective gear. Despite all of her years of martial arts, even her years in sports, Mia had never been purposefully violent.

"You...bitch," Kathleen spat, pushing herself to her feet. Her eyes were wild with anger.

Mia tensed. "Don't come closer."

Kathleen rolled her eyes and brushed a lock of hair out of her face. "You really think you can stop me if I wanted to do something to you? I have powers your stupid human self will never understand."

"Steven showed me his magic," Mia snapped at her. But beneath the strong words, her body trembled. "I've seen what mages can do."

"Oh?" Kathleen raised an eyebrow and crossed her arms. "Really?"

"Yeah."

"Well, that's great. But I'm not a mage."

Mia's hands dropped, her stance relaxing. Not a mage? But... that didn't make sense. "What do you mean, you're not a mage? Steven...Steven said that he was one. And you...you're working with him."

Kathleen merely shrugged. "Steven lies."

Mia backed away. Steven wasn't a mage, which meant...had anything he said been true? Had his words last night meant anything? The things he'd said to her when he kissed her? Did he actually care about her? Or had he just been, as Kathleen had put it, chasing tail?

Steven may lie, but not about everything, poppet.

She wanted to cry, but her body was out of water to spare. Instead, she backed up a little more, shaking her head. Kathleen followed her.

"Now come on, Mia. Give me the knife, and we can leave."

Mia's brow furrowed. "It's over there. Take it if you want it. Leave me alone."

There was a moment of silence as Mia's words hung in the air, dangling, waiting for a response to ground them. Then, Kathleen let out a laugh. One that Mia had only imagined before this. One that made her want to run home and never crawl out from under her blankets.

"There are two things you don't seem to be understanding," Kathleen said. "First, I can't pick up the knife. It chose you as its bearer. Only you can touch it until you hand it to someone."

Mia thought back. The others…her brother…Steven…they'd wanted the knife. They could have taken it. Mia couldn't fight them if she tried, not if they had magic. And Kathleen hadn't grabbed her until she threw away the knife. The knife was protected. When Mia held the knife, she too, was protected.

GO GET THE KNIFE.

"And second–" Kathleen stepped closer. Mia stumbled away, unable to take her eyes off the woman's glaring, hazel eyes.

GET IT NOW.

"–when I say, 'we'? That includes you."

Now!

Mia didn't even think about ignoring the voice this time. She bolted, back toward the knife, away from Kathleen.

Stupid, stupid, stupid, stupid. She couldn't stop the word from repeating as she ran. It didn't make sense why Kathleen wanted her, but she wasn't about to question it until she was safe.

But before she could get near it, the world shifted. Tilted. Mia slowed, blinking rapidly to gain her bearings. It didn't work and she had to come to a stop as a splitting headache overtook her every thought.

A hand grabbed the back of her coat and yanked her off her feet. She was powerless, flying backwards and skidding across the snow.

The world twisted back to normal, but Mia continued to lay there, dazed. Confused. Terrified.

Her emotions, she realized. They were back. The gray fog that had clouded her mind had lifted, inch by inch, slow enough that Mia hadn't realized it was happening.

"What's wrong, Mia?" Kathleen asked. "I thought you wanted to leave this place. Are you telling me you don't want to come?"

Mia sat up, shaking her head.

"Well, I'm hurt." Kathleen shrugged. "And here I thought you liked Steven."

She had. She did. She bit the inside of her lip. There was nothing about this that was easy. As she pushed herself to her feet, she realized that while she wanted nothing more than to get out of here, that didn't make sense.

Because she was seventeen.

Because she had nowhere to go.

And because even if her parents were absent, and even if Derek had lied to her their entire lives, they were still family, and they hadn't meant to hurt her.

But Steven had meant to hurt her. And so did Kathleen. If Mia got to choose who got the knife, then she sure as hell wasn't about to give it to the woman who had stalked her and the guy who'd manipulated her into believing she was special. Even if she wasn't.

HOW WOULD YOU DEFINE SPECIAL?

Magical. Worth something.

I SEE.

Mia straightened and made eye contact with Kathleen who stood, waiting. Maybe for an answer. Her grin said all Mia needed to know: Kathleen thought that Mia was going to come with her because of Steven.

Instead, Mia darted around Kathleen, aiming for the knife again. Kathleen grabbed at her. Mia sidestepped and twisted, facing Kathleen. When the woman reached for her again, Mia was ready. She moved one foot forward and grabbing Kathleen's wrist in the same movement. Kathleen yanked against Mia's grip. But, while Kathleen had magic, Mia was stronger. Using both of their momentums, Mia rammed her elbow into Kathleen's sternum.

The woman gasped and fell back, wrist slipping out of Mia's hand. Mia let her fall and bolted again, toward the knife. Toward safety.

She reached it. She bent down to grab it. Her fingers were inches away.

And the world tilted. Her mind went to war against itself.

Grab the knife.

No.

Get it.

No.

Come on, Mia. You can do this.

No.

Her hand shook. Color drained from the world. The glittering white snow dulled. The blue-green needles on the spruces turned gray. The leaves on the deciduous trees fluttered to the ground. Dead.

Her heart hardened into a heavy stone, and she collapsed to her knees.

You won't do what I want. So I'll do what I want.

A hand grabbed the back of her shirt. Dragging her. She couldn't move. The world continued to contort more and more into a forgotten van Gogh painting.

Kathleen dropped Mia to the ground. She lay there, unable to move. Unable to properly think.

"Fuck," Kathleen said. "He's gonna kill me." She crouched in front of Mia. The twisting stopped, and Mia's eyes trained on her, cheek pressed firmly into the snow. "Not supposed to use my full powers on you. Whatever. This works."

Get up.

She tried to convince herself to move. To stand. To fight. She was physically stronger than Kathleen. If she could just get up, she could find a way to incapacitate the woman. If she could just get up, she could defend herself and grab the knife. If she could just get up....

Her body wouldn't move.

Come on, Mia.

Kathleen gripped Mia's upper arm and tugged. Mia's body responded, but not to Mia. To Kathleen's powers. She stood, a zombie, and a few thoughts returned.

The way she'd been feeling. The voice in her head. The confusion. It'd all been Kathleen. Somehow Kathleen had done all of it, like she could manipulate reality. But she didn't go after the knife. She didn't use this magic to take the knife.

Which either meant she wasn't that strong, or the knife really was.

What the hell did I find?

IT'S ONE HELL OF AN ARTIFACT.

Kathleen glanced at the knife, hands on Mia's shoulders. "Well, guess we can come back for it. Not like anyone can pick it up."

Oh no. Oh god. Oh no, oh no, oh no.

Kathleen smiled at Mia. A different smile. More...genuine. "Sorry it had to happen like this."

The world twisted. Morphed. The scenery blended together with another that Mia didn't recognize. Something green. Some place warm.

And then it untwisted.

Kathleen's eyes widened, then narrowed. The world twisted again, but only a fraction before undoing itself.

"What the hell?" Kathleen asked. She let out a gasp, dropping Mia, and then flew backwards square into a tree. It shuddered. Snow dumped from the branches, landing on Kathleen who lay stunned underneath it.

Mia blinked. Startled. Confused. Unable to fully process the scene with the gray screen.

"Mia!"

She heard the voice. She knew who it was. But her mind refused to register it. All it could experience was the gray. The gray and the dark voice.

That is, until his hand touched her shoulder. Until he turned her. Until he grabbed both of her shoulders with shaking, warm hands.

Warm. How were they warm? She was wearing a coat.

She looked up, into the sea-gray eyes of her best friend. But these weren't gray because of Kathleen. They were always gray. A hint of blue. A hint of green. Mia had always liked those eyes. They were different. A color that made him stand out.

And other colors stood out. His cheeks were red from the cold. His hair a chestnut brown. Jacket mostly black, but with a silver lining. A coat her mom had given to him one winter when he tried to sew a tear in his old one.

"Mia," Cody said again, gripping her shoulders tighter.

"Cody?" she asked. "You...why are you here?"

He smiled, breathing out as if the weight of the world had been lifted from his shoulders. "Oh thank god. I was worried. Your mist was almost completely gray."

"My what?" Mia asked. Her mind jumped back into gear. Her body twitched. Cheek cold. Side sore from when she'd been dragged and dropped. The sensations were almost too much to handle at once, and Mia shuddered. She rubbed her hands up and down her arms as shaky breaths left her lungs.

Cody examined her, then did something so unexpected it seemed to make the world stop: he reached out and pulled her into a rib cracking hug. With her arms pinned, Mia couldn't do much but stand there, the tightness of his arms around her almost as surprising as his hand on the back of her head.

"Cody?" she asked.

"I'm sorry," he said. "For not telling you. I—"

Mia managed to place her hands on his chest and push him away. He fell silent. She wanted to hear what he had to say. God she wanted to hear it.

"Probably not the best time," Mia said.

Cody nodded. "Right. Sorry." He looked her up and down. "Are you okay?"

"No." Mia wasn't in the mood to lie. "I'm not okay. We should go before she wakes up. We have to make sure that Blair and Derek are okay."

She hadn't expected those words to come out of her mouth, but she decided to just roll with it. There was no point in trying to pretend like she didn't care about them all. Even if they had hurt her. Even if they had lied to her. There were so many other things about them. And she'd forgotten that.

SHE'D MADE YOU FORGET THAT.

"Okay," Cody said. But he hesitated.

"What?" Mia asked.

"I...the knife?" he asked.

Mia gasped. She'd forgotten. "Shit." She turned to face the place where she'd left it. It wasn't far. But this would be the third time she'd gone after it, and it hadn't worked in the past. Still, she had to try.

Before she could move, though, the voice of her nightmares spoke.

"Well aren't you two cozy."

Mia froze, a jolt of fear stunning her heart. Under her tree, Kathleen stood, hair wild and dotted with snow.

DON'T FEAR HER. GET THE KNIFE.

"Leave her alone," Cody said. His voice was loud, though it

trembled. He moved in front of Mia, holding out an arm to protect her.

"Cody," she tried to say but he shook his head.

"Go get it."

Mia nodded. Energy, the kind she hadn't had in a week, flooded through her, and she tried to understand what had just happened to her. What Cody had done to fix an issue she'd thought was because of her anger at her brother.

"You shouldn't have shown up," Kathleen said. Mia snuck from behind Cody's arm, paying attention in her attempt to get the knife. "You aren't even supposed to be part of this. None of us are interested in killing one of our own."

One of their own? Mia glanced back at Cody, who looked to her with a furrowed brow. Cody was...like them? Like Steven and Kathleen? Not mages?

Cody mouthed at her to go, then turned back to Kathleen. "Then don't. Leave."

Mia nodded and hurried toward the knife with Kathleen distracted by Cody. The knife lay there, right where she'd left it, glowing a bright blue. Mia hesitated. It'd been a while since it glowed like this. Or maybe she'd just been unable to see it. Maybe the gray had dulled the knife as well.

Either way, she ran toward it.

"Can't leave. Need the knife. Need Mia. And I'll kill you if that's what it takes to get them both," Kathleen said.

Mia reached the knife and snatched it off the ground. Pulsating electricity shot through her body. Warm. Terrifying. Beautiful. Magical. Just like the night she found it in the cave. She smiled. She was safe.

She spun, to show Kathleen that it was over and stop her from hurting Cody, but when she turned, she found that she was already too late. Kathleen was after Cody, had his hand out, a film of shimmering purple surrounding his body. But it shattered, and she smacked him to the side.

Mia couldn't protect Cody. She could barely protect herself.

There was nothing she could do.

OF COURSE THERE IS.

She sank to her knees, trembling. Cody stood back up, and tried to fight but Mia knew it'd be worthless. He wasn't athletic. None of her friends were. And unless they'd all been training in magical combat for years, she had a feeling this wasn't going to end well.

She closed her eyes.

Please, someone help.

"Well, if it isn't my favorite student."

Mia's eyes snapped open, expecting to find the scene before her, but it wasn't there. The trees, the snow, Kathleen and Cody fighting. All gone and replaced instead by an empty background swirling in the color of a rainbow. Like the inside of a very large bubble.

And standing above her, a gentle smile reaching up to his ears. Jeans. A leather jacket. Blond hair cut almost too short. One eye green. One eye blue.

Time slowed. The world around them danced. And Mia ignored it all. She could only focus on him. The teacher who always made her feel so safe.

"Mr. Becker?" she asked.

Mr. Becker nodded, then crouched, an arm on each leg. She was reminded of the way the men in her dad's family would sit when there was no chair to perch on. It would have made her laugh, had her confusion not taken over every facet of her being.

"Can't keep having you call me that, now can I?" he said. He reached out and with a long, pale finger, brushed away a lingering tear from her cheek. Or…possibly a new one.

"I…don't understand," Mia said. "You…why are you…here?"

"I know it's a lot to take in," Mr. Becker said. "You've already learned so many secrets today. But I don't have much time. Adelia doesn't like to do this for very long. Says it gives her a headache, and I'm not about to argue with her."

"Who?" Mia asked.

"Ah, yes." Mr. Becker shook his head. "Coach Smith. Her real name is Adelia. I think she wanted to tell you herself, but she put a restraint on how long I have."

Her coach...had a real name?

"You two...." Mia tried to comprehend. "Are you...mages too?"

Is everyone a mage?

No, POPPET. BUT WE'RE SOMETHING SIMILAR.

She blinked. The voice. His voice. The two of them. They spoke as one. The same.

He smiled again. "I know it's confusing. I wanted you to have someone in your corner, but I couldn't come to you sooner. So I used my gift."

"But—"

He shushed her, and she clamped her mouth shut. "I don't have time. First, my name is Lior. I'm what humans of all sorts call an Iravata. So are Adelia and Eran, her husband. We're immortal, and the knife you're holding is something we need."

Mia shook her head. Immortal? That wasn't even possible. "Why do you need the knife? What do you want from me?"

He breathed out then looked to the sky. "Sorry Addy." Back to Mia. "We've been looking out for you for years. Making sure you're safe. Keeping you out of harm's way. Until three weeks ago when your brother unsealed our queen."

Queen. *The Queen.* Mia hadn't thought about the sculpture in weeks. But...he was right. Everything started when Derek collapsed in front of *The Queen*. When she'd broken to pieces and ruined all of Mia's hopes for normality.

The Queen had always seemed like a real person.

Guess she was.

"I need the knife," Lior continued, "because right now Derek and Blair are in danger. And if I can't get the knife to Derek, there's a good chance he's going to die."

Mia clutched the knife closer to her. "Why should I trust you? You've lied to me too."

He chuckled. "Mia, I'm not your brother. Or your friend. My life is none of your business. I lied to you. All of us have. But I'm not lying now. And I will tell you everything when we have time."

Time. Mia's eyes widened and she twisted to try and find where Cody was.

"It's okay," Lior said. "He's fine for now. Once Adelia releases the hold, time will start again."

"If I give you the knife, I'll be powerless," Mia said.

Lior shook his head. "You need to have more faith in yourself." He grinned. "I don't call powerless people my favorite student."

She stared at him. This was so much. The information was overwhelming. But she knew, somewhere deep down, that this was how it needed to be. He'd lied about who he was, but he was right. It wasn't any of her business. He'd tried to protect her. The voice in her head. He'd wanted to save her.

Help. Not save. You don't need to be saved.

He smirked. The less serious side of her favorite teacher.

She let out a deep breath. Her hands seemed to move on their own, lifting the knife. He reached out. Took it. Disappeared.

And the world snapped back to normal, the colorful rainbow of colors replaced with the scene of Cody trying to fight against the wild-eyed Kathleen.

Chapter Twenty-Seven

Derek had never run like this before. He didn't know where he was, or how he'd gotten there. Blair was missing again. And somewhere, Steven was out to kill him.

Everything hurt. He didn't know how he was moving. Adrenaline. He knew that it would eventually wear off, and then where would he be? Lost in the woods with the sun setting ever lower in the sky? Already the shadows made it difficult to see the ground, and considering Derek's swollen eye, that was saying something.

But he had to get out of here. He'd survived being poisoned. An attempted hit and run. The magical pushing over of a bookcase. A goddamn mountain lion. This couldn't be where he died. He had to believe his luck hadn't run out yet.

Except the adrenaline wore off. His legs tired, believing there was no longer any threat. Maybe Steven was fighting Blair. Derek hoped she would knock Steven out and the two of them could escape to find help.

Derek would have given anything to have Mrs. Arbour show up. Panting, he came to a stop and leaned against a tree with one arm, then with his back. He sunk to the ground, pain leeching the energy out of his veins.

He was pathetic. A pathetic pile of nothing. Who had he been kidding these past few weeks? Months? Years? He may have had magic, but Blair was right when she'd told him it had always just been a fun side effect of his life. He hadn't understood the real consequences.

He'd believed himself to be something special, but really, he was just pathetic. So pathetic that it'd taken him seventeen years to tell his twin sister that he had magic. He'd thought she wouldn't understand, and that she'd hate him.

But that was stupid. Because Mia wasn't like that. She'd spent so much of her life being bullied and judged, she never would have done that to him. She was stubborn and intense, but caring. And if he'd told her about his magic when he first learned about it, then she would have taken the time to try and understand it.

He shouldn't have lied to her.

They wouldn't be in this position right now.

He closed his eyes, breathing deep. The pain was getting to be too much as the adrenaline evaporated.

Then there was none.

At first he thought that maybe he'd died. But when he focused, he realized there was a soft, warm hand on his cheek. The warmth spread through his body, chasing away the pain like a child running after ducks. It grew hotter, and hotter, until it almost burned his body worse than Steven had beat him.

Then, it was gone.

All of it.

Derek opened his eyes. A woman crouched in front of him, staring at him with a concerned expression. Derek blinked.

She was absolutely beautiful. Gorgeous, even. Like a super model. Perfectly smooth olive skin with honey brown hair and irises a shade of green Derek hadn't realized eyes could be. Every feature on her face was perfectly shaped, perfectly proportioned, and perfectly symmetrical.

He blinked again.

"What?"

The woman's expression relaxed and she stood. She smoothed out the navy peacoat she wore and clasped her hands together, smiling.

"I'm glad you're okay," she said. "I was worried."

Derek shook his head. "*What?*"

The woman said nothing more before vanishing into thin air. Derek jerked his head around, trying to understand what just happened. He reached up with his hand and touched his face and found it smooth. Even a slight scar he'd gotten as a kid after losing a fight with a broken window was gone.

Am I dead?

He pushed himself to his feet and flexed his fingers. His lungs expanded and collapsed like normal, no pain from the broken ribs, and when he pressed his hand against his body he found that pressure didn't make him want to die.

Healed. She'd…healed him?

"Who the hell…?" Derek asked.

He hadn't expected a response, so when he got one, he jumped almost a mile.

"That was Flora, Derek. Next time you should thank her."

Derek spun until he found the man who spoke standing nearby. The man was not tall. He wore a black cloak and his brown hair was long, pulled back into a ponytail. Derek's jaw dropped. Not because yet another new person had shown up in the middle of the woods for no discernable reason.

No.

His jaw dropped because he knew this man.

"Dorian?" he asked.

The man, who had been a part of Derek and Mia's lives for as long as they'd lived in America, closed his eyes and shook his head with a light chuckle.

"I'm afraid that clever little nickname you and your sister came up with isn't my real name. Nor is it accurate. There's no painting in my attic."

Derek ignored that. "Why are you here? Aren't you some kind of philanthropist? What are you doing in the woods near Willow Creek? My parents aren't even here!"

Dorian, or whatever his name was, shrugged, then reached into his cloak. Derek tensed, not even sure what to expect, and then his stomach dropped a mile when Dorian pulled out a curved knife sheathed in leather, handle that of smooth bamboo.

"My name is not Dorian," the man said. "It's Shubishi. And I'm here to deliver a present from your dearest sister."

He held out the knife.

Maybe he should have hesitated. He didn't know this man. But the knife, the glowing, beautiful knife, called to him in a way that nothing ever had before. Or maybe it wasn't him that it was calling to. Maybe it was Niran. Who was him.

But he didn't care.

Because he darted out and snatched the knife from Shubishi.

The moment he made contact with it, a surge of energy coursed through him. His eyes went wide, and he almost dropped the knife, but his hands refused to let it go. He'd been waiting for this. For years. Thousands of years. To hold the knife again and be complete.

Shubishi laughed. "Ah yes, little Niran. Good to see you still cling to power."

Derek's eyes widened. He stepped away from Shubishi. "What did you just call me?"

"Niran." Shubishi raised an eyebrow. "I was under the impression you knew who you were."

"How do you know who he is?" Derek asked.

Shubishi smirked. "Think. To what your brain doesn't want you to remember."

Derek had no idea what that meant, and he really wanted to explain this to Shubishi with a few choice words, but before he could something nagged at him. A memory. A dream. The figure who he couldn't remember, no matter how hard he tried. The dream of him standing at the river on the other side with The Queen. And a man appearing from the jungle.

Shubishi appearing from the jungle.

Derek shook his head and continued to back away. "You're one of the Iravata."

"Yes." Shubishi didn't even try to deny it.

"You!" Steven's voice echoed in the woods.

Derek paled. He'd gotten so caught up in the appearance of Shubishi and the woman who healed him that he'd forgotten about Steven. Shubishi didn't bother turning around. He kept his focus on Derek instead, but Steven stormed toward them, flames encasing his arms.

"You're one of them," Steven shouted. "You're one of the reasons our lives are hell!"

Derek thought, for a moment, that Steven would actually attack Shubishi, but the boy stopped in his tracks. Perfectly still. Perfectly silent. The flames vanished, and he remained perfectly. Still.

A shudder ran through Derek's spine.

"That's better," Shubishi said.

"What did you do to him?" Derek asked.

"It's not important." Shubishi waved the question away.

Derek brought it back. "*Tell me.*"

His grin widened. "Same temper, I see. Shouldn't be too surprised. You're the same person, after all."

"*Who are you?*" Derek didn't want to yell, but the words were out of his mouth before he could stop them.

"I told you." Shubishi remained calm.

"No, you–"

"You have the knife now," Shubishi interrupted. "Use it. End this."

Derek scoffed in a mixture of disbelief and confusion. "Why don't you end this? You can stop him without moving."

"Because you need to fight," Shubishi said.

Derek flinched. He hated fighting. He didn't want to fight or hurt anyone. He just wanted to disappear under his covers and get some freaking sleep. "I don't know how."

Shubishi stepped closer to him, moving like a lazy cloud in the sky. He came to a stop right in front of Derek and leaned in. Derek couldn't move.

"It's time to learn then, Derek," he said. "You've restarted a very old, very violent, war, and now you and your friends are in the middle of it."

He moved away, and Derek's body relaxed into his control again.

"Learn to fight or die. It's your choice."

Then, like the woman, he vanished.

His words echoed in Derek's mind. He stood in silence, staring into space. He barely registered Steven moving. He barely heard the scream of anger that Steven shouted at him. All he could think about were the last words that Shubishi said.

There was a war. He was part of it. And if he didn't learn to fight, he would die.

PAY ATTENTION.

That voice again. Derek snapped back to reality and found Steven charging him, flames back.

Learn to fight or die.

He had to do this. He had to learn to fight.

He gripped the knife and a calm overcame him. Steven ran. He pulled the sheath off the knife, revealing the blade with markings that glowed blue. The light brightened, and Derek breathed in.

He ran forward, meeting Steven.

At first he wasn't sure what was happening. Steven attacked him, and he barely had to think to deflect the magic. The warmth guided him. All he had to do was imagine something, and it happened. He wanted energy to knock Steven back.

It happened.

He wanted to create a forcefield around himself to deflect an attack.

It happened.

Steven grew angrier. And the calm around Derek began to shatter, revealing the absolute fear underneath. Derek tried to control his magic, but the smoothness wavered, and Steven got in a hit. Derek fell to his knees. He looked up.

Steven hovered over him, face screwed up, anger clawing at Derek's skin. Derek gasped. Magic welled in his arms and he lifted the knife, stabbing upwards into Steven's chest.

A moment of silence fell over the two. Steven's eyes widened. Confusion and fear bled off of him. His actual blood dripped into Derek's hand.

Derek's stomach rolled and he jumped to his feet, pulling out the knife in the process. A wave of energy exploded from the knife, from Steven, and obliterated the closest trees.

Steven fell to the snowy ground, eyes still open.

Lifeless.

Dead.

Derek stared at him for a moment. Then at the bloody knife in his hand. Then back to Steven.

For the first time since Shubishi gave him the knife, he released it. It thumped into the snow, and Derek backed away as panic overcame him. Dead. Steven was dead. Derek had killed him.

His limbs shook. He could barely control them. His breathing quickened and he gripped his hair.

I just killed someone.

Something caught his attention. A set of emotions he'd gotten used to not feeling, even though he longed to. His head jerked up. Blair stood on the other side of the new clearing, looking around at the damage, and then to Steven's lifeless body, then to Derek.

Fear. Confusion. Disgust. Concern.

"Derek!" she exclaimed. She ran—well, more limped—to him, nursing her arm with bruises all over her face. Whoever had visited Derek had not given Blair the same courtesy. "What happened? Why's your face fine? Are you okay?"

Derek looked her up and down before answering her with, "Are you okay?"

There was a moment where no one said anything. And then the concern was tossed to the side and replaced with terrified anger.

"*Fuck no,*" she said. "No, I am not okay! My arm's probably broken, I'm all beaten up, I've seen things I don't know how to explain today, my best friend is missing, my boyfriend is freaked out, and there's a dead kid at my feet!"

She continued on, and Derek focused on the fact that she called him her boyfriend. His eyes warmed, preparing for tears, and all he could think was that she was safe. Okay. Able to rant like always.

He couldn't stop himself from hugging her. She yelped, possibly from her arm, but didn't push him away.

Together, they stood like that for some time Derek. She was warm and soft in his arms, and he whispered how sorry he was for dragging her into this mess. She didn't respond. Instead, she pushed him away before kissing him.

He kissed her back.

Then, he pulled away and closed his eyes, trying to wrap his mind around what had just happened, when Blair tugged at his arm. He opened his eyes, and to his shock, Steven's body had shriveled. A gust of wind picked up the pieces and carried them away like ash until there was nothing left on the ground but the glowing knife.

They stared at the place where Steven had been.

Then, Derek asked, "What the fuck is that knife?"

And Blair replied, "I have no idea."

Derek tried to think of something else to say. But he couldn't. Instead, he walked over and picked up the knife. He wasn't sure he wanted it, but he knew that he had to. It was his now. It had always been his.

Something pricked at the back of his neck. An emotion. New. They didn't belong to anyone he knew.

He turned, and standing in the trees was the young woman who had healed him before. She stood, looking as beautiful as ever, with clasped hands and a smile.

"Blair, Derek?" she asked. "Will you please come with me?"

Mia blinked and the world returned. But when she blinked again, it was different. Because Cody and Kathleen were missing.

Everything fell down on her at once. Her brother was in danger. Her teacher and coach were immortal beings. The knife was gone. Cody was gone.

Cody was gone.

Mia jumped to her feet, all focused on the fact that her best friend was missing with a crazy woman who'd threatened to kill him. Cody didn't know how to fight. Cody could barely stand up to people who picked on him. She had to find him and protect him. Even if she didn't have magic, even if she wasn't special, she could at least try.

So she ran, energy returned. She dashed through the trees, trying to follow the set of foot prints left by Cody and Kathleen. It was getting dark. Difficult to see. Mia panted as she ran, searching.

"Mia!" Cody appeared in front of her, coming out of the shadows.

Her heart fluttered at the sight of him. Safe. He was safe.

"Cody!" she ran up to him and threw her arms around his neck, so pleased that he was all right.

He caught her, stumbling back, before hesitantly squeezing her back. She pulled away, smiling.

"You're okay," she said. "I thought…you guys were gone…."

"Kathleen's missing," Cody said. "I think we should get out of here. Find Blair and Derek and then get to Blair's house."

Mia frowned. "Why Blair's house?"

"Her mom knows everything. We can ask her questions and get her help."

That made sense, though Mia wasn't sure exactly what was going on. The only thing she could cling to was the fact that Cody knew more about all of this than she did.

"Okay," she said. "Let's go."

But they didn't go anywhere. Cody froze, body tense, shaking, mouth half open, before he flew across the forest and slammed into a tree. He collapsed in the snow. Mia stared at him, unable to move at first, when Kathleen appeared in the corner of Mia's eye.

She stalked toward Mia, ignoring Cody's lifeless body, with rage flaring her nose and widening her eyes. Mia trembled. This was different. Kathleen wasn't playing around anymore. She was done with the games.

Mia turned to run toward Cody. Kathleen appeared in front of her and grabbed her wrist. Mia countered and brought Kathleen to her knees before bolting off to Cody's side. Her heart thumped.

Tingles of anxiety and fear crushed her ribcage as she collapsed next to him.

"Cody," she called out. She wrapped her arms around him and pulled him into her lap, shaking him. He breathed deeply, but didn't stir.

"Goddammit!" Kathleen screamed. She stood and headed toward Mia. Mia couldn't move. If she left Cody, he would die alone in the snow, and Kathleen would probably get her anyway. There was nothing she could do but sit there and let her nemesis stalk her yet again.

Mia gulped.

"I am so sick of you," Kathleen continued, getting closer. "You just sit there with your victimhood and pretend like your life is so awful. But you have two parents who love you, a brother who tries to protect you, and friends who would die for you. Why the hell he wants you makes no sense to me."

Mia tensed. "Wants me? Who wants me?"

Kathleen waved her off. "Whatever. We're leaving."

Mia clutched Cody closer to her. Kathleen would separate them. That much was clear. But she had to try something. She squeezed her eyes shut and waited for the moment when Kathleen grabbed her and won.

But there was nothing.

Except the warm spatter of liquid on Mia's face.

Her eyes snapped open and she looked up. Kathleen stood swaying. Her legs tilted. Her torso twisted. Her arms cooked noodles.

Her head gone.

Kathleen's body fell to the ground. Her head rolled through the snow.

Mia's stomach clenched. Her hand shot to her mouth, and something wet touched her fingers. She pulled them away.

Blood.

Oh my god. What just…what…?

Mia looked at the body. The dead body of the bleached blond woman who'd tormented her. And then she looked.

To the woman.

Standing behind the lifeless body.

And the rest of the world faded.

The woman's long, black hair swayed in a gentle breeze, dotted with flakes of snow. She wore a sleeveless, knee length, black dress. Simple. Elegant. Contrasting with her pale skin with an almost ethereal glow.

The woman stared down at her hands, glancing between each of them and whispering to herself.

Mia shrunk back and the woman looked up and they locked eyes.

Ruby red.

A calm washed over Mia. Her shoulders relaxed. The million thoughts in her mind quieted. The woman said something in a language Mia didn't know, or even recognize.

The woman moved. She stepped over the body and came to a halt in front of Mia and Cody. She said something again. A prompt. Wanting something from Mia. But Mia had no idea what she was saying.

The woman nodded slowly. Extended her arm. Palm up.

And even though her every instinct screamed at Mia to run away, she lifted her own hand and placed it gently in the woman's grasp.

Chapter Twenty-Eight

Derek had no words. The beautiful woman, who'd introduced herself in soft, gentle words as Flora before healing a stunned Blair, led them through the trees. It wasn't until Derek's lungs screamed for oxygen that he realized they were climbing in elevation, and quite steeply, despite having no indicators of an uphill trudge. The forest around them changed. Still pines and spruces, but a mixture of aspen trees, their leaves at the end of their glorious fall yellow lives, popped up one by one.

Blair's hand brushed against his, and he took it, gripping tightly with their fingers intertwined.

"Where are we going?" she whispered.

Derek stared at her. Even now, with things calmer and no Steven chasing after him, he was still convinced the woman was a model. She was beautiful, but almost too perfect. Untouchable. Unattainable. The kind of women in magazines that made Mia dislike herself, even only for a few moments.

Mia. Derek realized he had no idea if Mia was okay. He'd been trying not to think about it. There was so much going on, but he knew that wasn't okay of him to do. Him focusing on his own issues is what caused these problems in the first place.

But, there was nothing he could do now. Mia was somewhere, and he didn't even know where to begin. He just hoped that whoever this woman was, and whatever the Iravata had planned for them, they were going to protect his sister from Kathleen.

"I…don't know," Derek whispered in response to Blair's question. "Do you think that this isn't going to end well?"

Blair shrugged. "No idea. I'm so confused. You said one of the Gray Spirits gave you the knife?"

"Yeah." Derek was so confused. "I think the right term is Iravata, though."

"Whatever. Do you think Mia is okay?"

"Dunno." He focused, breathing in, but nothing. He could feel Blair's emotions, as she'd lost the bracelet at some point fighting with Steven, and maybe a hint of something from Flora, but no Mia. And no Cody.

The two fell silent, and before long they came to a clearing with a two story cabin. Derek had no idea what to say. He'd been all over these woods, but had never been in a place like this before. It was beautiful, lights from inside the large windows brightening up the massive deck and revealing light wood and paint. The roof was slanted, and made of a dark material.

And while he noticed all of that, and while he realized that this was going to be really weird, there was one thing he also noticed.

A set of emotions he hadn't felt in so long it was like they were brand new to him. Like the day he first realized that when Mia cried, something pricked at his skin. The first conscious understanding of his powers.

Derek let go of Blair's hand and ran, despite her calling out to him. He pushed past Flora, who said nothing, and continued up the steps onto the porch. Through the large windows, he saw her sitting there on a couch. Alone. Staring at a fire. He knocked on the window, and Mia looked up. When she saw him, her eyes widened, and it was like having a bucket of water heated to the perfect temperature dumped all over him.

Mia scrambled to her feet.

Derek ran to the front door. He unlocked it with his magic and opened it in the same motion. Mia greeted him.

It was hard to tell who hugged who. And Derek didn't care. All that mattered was his sister, his shaking, crying sister, was safe and alive. Her happiness washed away everything. His exhaustion, his fear, his shame at what he'd done, all vanished. They'd be back. But at that moment all he could think about was clinging to his twin. Who was alive. And clinging right back.

Eventually, they let go of each other, and Mia's joy turned to anger. Her face screwed up and she smacked him on the shoulder.

"Hey!" Derek exclaimed, backing up.

"You dick!" she screamed. Tears pricked her eyes, and Derek's first instinct was to help her calm down.

But a thought occurred to him.

Maybe…she needed to be angry at him.

"You're a dick!" She hit him again, and this time he didn't fight it. "You couldn't just tell me? I'm not some random person on the street. I'm your *twin sister!*"

"I know," he said. Footsteps on the porch caught his attention. Blair and Flora stood together, watching the scene. Flora wrung her hands together, and a hint of nerves tickled the back of his neck. Blair crossed her arms, waiting. Maybe for the show. Maybe for her turn.

Derek had no idea.

"Why didn't you just tell me?" Mia asked. She pushed him and he had to step to stop from falling. "Are you really that stupid? Because you must be if you think that I wouldn't be able to understand this…." She gestured to him then gave up with a sigh. "You lied to me."

"I know."

"For our whole lives."

"I know." He had no excuses.

The tears streamed down her face, and she wiped them away. "I hate you."

He laughed. "I hate me too."

"You don't get to hate yourself," she snapped.

His laughter grew stronger.

"Stop laughing at me!"

"I'm sorry," he said. He reached out and pulled her into another hug. This was Mia. The annoyed, strong willed, sister who stood up for herself. Not the shadow of a person she'd become. "I'm sorry. I'm sorry."

Mia relaxed, and then hugged him back. After an agonizingly long moment, she muttered, "I forgive you."

Derek had no idea what he'd done to get that level, but he wasn't about to look a gift horse in the mouth. He doubted they were entirely okay. There was way too much to talk about, too much anger. Even now, he could feel hers biting his skin. But it was soft. Gentle. Mixed with relief.

"Excuse me?"

Flora's voice distracted Derek. He let his sister go and turned. Flora stood closer now, Blair behind her, and smiled.

"Oh. Uh…." Derek shrugged. "Mia, this is Flora."

"Flora?" Mia asked. She pushed Derek out of the way, causing him to hit the door frame. "You…they said you can heal. Are you here to help Cody?"

Derek's eyes widened. What had happened to Cody?

Flora nodded. "This is my home. But, yes. I'll go help him." She touched Mia's cheek. Mia breathed in deep, eyes wide, standing like that even when Flora moved into the house and disappeared down a warm hallway.

Derek didn't speak until he heard Mia step further onto the porch, and he remembered that Blair was there, and neither Blair nor Mia were great at talking about this kind of thing. So he faced them, watching the two girls look each other down as snow continued to drift from the sky.

There were so many emotions running through Mia's heart as she stared at her friend. So much had happened. The woman with red eyes had brought her and Cody here, though Mia hadn't quite figured out how, and they'd met Lior and Adelia. They'd taken Cody away, saying Flora would heal him, and told Mia to wait in the living room.

She had done as they said because there was nothing else she could do. The entire time she'd sat there, she'd thought about her brother and her friends. This...she had no idea why they were keeping secrets from her, but maybe after today she understood. It was dangerous. They'd almost died.

Kathleen had almost taken her away.

So when she saw her brother, and the relief had taken over every ounce of her being, she'd decided she wouldn't hate him forever. She'd decided to forgive him.

But Blair...she didn't know what to do with Blair. Already her friend had that defiant look on her face, arms crossed. Mia had no idea about Blair's story, just that her mom also had magic. Was her whole life magic?

"Why didn't you tell me?" Mia asked. A question she'd been asking a lot recently.

Blair shrugged. "Cuz there are rules."

"Did you want to?"

Blair's defiance softened and she nodded. "I almost did. After Derek found out. When we were hanging out. A few sleepovers. I just wanted you to know because…well, you're my best friend, and if anyone outside of the world should know, it's you."

"So…?" Mia asked.

"I don't know how to explain it," Blair said. "Not right now. Maybe when it's not five degrees outside."

Mia hadn't even noticed the cold. "Oh. Right."

The three teens headed inside. Once the door was closed, Mia breathed in the warmth and turned back to face Blair and Derek, and found him brushing a strand of Blair's loose hair away from her face, brushing his knuckles on her cheek.

Mia wrapped her arms around her body and squeezed. There was no pain. Flora must have healed her when she'd touched her. It was so different seeing an intimate moment between Blair and Derek. She knew they'd slept together, and that they were more of a couple now than ever, which was saying something, but they'd always kept it a secret. A poorly kept secret, but a secret nonetheless. Just something between them.

Derek's head jerked up and he looked to her. He always did that when she was feeling something strong, and now she understood why. He wasn't just good at reading people. He could *actually* read people.

Derek's hand dropped from Blair's cheek.

"Uh," he tried to say, running the same hand through his hair. Blair and Mia made eye contact, but the girl didn't say anything.

Mia sighed quietly. This was how it was going to be. And it wasn't their fault. "Just don't make out in front of me."

Derek's jaw dropped, and Blair snorted.

Mia continued, changing the subject. "Look, I don't know what's going on. I'm not sure I understand anything right now. And who knows what these people…things….” She groaned. “Who knows what they want from us or what they're going to say. But can we promise we won't keep secrets like this again?”

She knew it was a lot to ask, but she was in this now. They had no reason not to tell her everything.

Both Derek and Blair nodded.

“I can do that,” Blair said. “And if Derek and Cody can't, I'll tell you for them.”

“What?” Derek stared down at Blair who ignored him.

Mia smiled. This…was what she wanted.

“You can come see him now.” That gentle voice. Mia spun around, toward the hallway, and found Flora standing there with a smile. “He's okay. Hasn't woken up yet, but he will.” She gestured toward the back of the house and Mia wasted no time.

She all but ran through to the open door near the end of the hall. The room was dim. Two lamps gave all the light, and blinds covered the large windows on the other side of the king sized bed where Cody lay asleep.

Lior and Adelia stood near each other with Mr. Smith, who Mia recalled was actually called Eran. It was odd, calling these people she'd grown up with as neighbors and teachers and coaches by new names, knowing they weren't human and that they could never die.

It raised a million questions.

And explained so much.

But she ignored them and went to Cody's side, settling in one of the three chairs that someone had surrounded him with.

He looked small, lying there. He wasn't small. Thin, yes, but not small. She gripped his hand. He'd gotten hurt protecting her. Kathleen had said he shouldn't have gotten involved, but he did.

Blair and Derek sat in the other two chairs, and the three adults—if Mia could call them that—faced them.

"Wait," Derek said. "*They're* Iravata?"

But his question fell to the wayside when Adelia spoke.

"So," she said, looking between them. "That didn't go too badly."

None of them responded.

She laughed, nervous. "Okay. Guess my definition of bad is different from yours. But it went okay, at least."

"Yeah, no," Blair said. "You don't get to do that. You need to explain to us what's going on, right now."

Mia was startled by the harshness in Blair's tone. These people had saved them.

"Blair?" she asked in a small whisper.

"Oh, Blair just hates us because the mage clans made up these false stories of us and tell them like fact," Adelia said with a smile.

"We did not make them up! Not to mention what you just made us go through!" Blair stood, knocking back her chair. Mia flinched and looked at Cody, but he remained asleep. "You all have incredible power and yet for some reason you made us deal with this shit. Derek almost died how many times because of this shit? And then what just happened in the woods? You gave the knife to Derek? Why? I don't get it? Why'd you make him kill Steven?"

Mia gasped, hand flying to her mouth.

Both Blair and Derek stared at her, and she looked between them. Steven was…dead? Derek had killed him? Derek had killed a person? Steven….

Her heart fluttered a million miles a minute and she tried her best not to cry. Derek stood and was by her side in an instant. She didn't know if she wanted him to be there, but she didn't move.

He held up a hand. "Can I?"

She didn't understand at first, but then she realized he was asking to help her calm down. While she wanted to do it on her own, her body fought against her mind, and eventually she nodded. His hand came down on her shoulder, gentle, and a familiar feeling washed through her. One she'd felt so many times in her life and hadn't quite put together.

He was calming her.

"I'm sorry," he muttered. "I…it…."

She didn't know what to say. Steven had attacked them. She doubted Derek murdered him. But still, Steven was dead. Gone.

Mia looked back to Cody and tried not to think about it.

"This is such a cozy little scene," a voice said. One that Mia recognized. She spun around to face the door. A man she'd known for years stood there, staring back at them. Her heart raced again, only to calm with the wash of Derek's influence.

"Yeah," Derek said. "It's Dorian."

The man rolled his eyes. "Shubishi, please. Call me by my name."

Mia groaned. "Is there anyone in our lives who's not an Iravata?"

The question settled over the room, and all of the Iravata exchanged glances. Then, Shubishi spoke.

"There are only eight of us, Mia. But most of us have been in your life at some point."

"Why?" she asked.

"Because your brother is the reincarnation of the priest who sealed away our queen," Shubishi continued. Mia didn't know how to respond to that, so she stayed quiet. Shubishi smirked. "We knew, when you two were born, that things were going to change. So we've watched over you to protect you. And as for Blair's questions, we could have interfered, but there will come a time when we can't save you. So why start now?"

"But–" Blair tried to say, but Shubishi held up a hand.

"We are fighting a war here, there is no time for questions tonight." Then, he turned. "Our queen, Shion, has retired for the night, but at some point, sometime, in the future, you will meet her. She's eager to get to know you all."

And then he was gone, leaving Mia even more confused than

before. Next to her, Derek shuddered and whispered, "Aster?"

Another thing she didn't understand.

Adelia, meanwhile, scowled. "Well. He's as friendly as always."

Eran and Lior both chuckled, and then Eran moved forward. "We'll be around," he said. "We don't know what else will happen, or when, so we're sticking around to make sure you're all safe. We can answer questions as time goes on. For now, it might be best if you stay here for the night."

Mia looked at her teacher. They made eye contact, and a little voice in the back of her mind said:

WE'RE HERE TO HELP YOU. GET SOME REST.

Mia nodded, and on the bed, Cody stirred. She jumped up as he moaned and helped him sit. Relief spread through her. Derek moved to help as well, while Blair stood at the foot of the bed with crossed arms.

Cody looked around. Blinking. Staring at the Iravata. His teacher and coach and the friendly neighborhood Mr. Smith.

He looked at his friends, mouth opened just a touch.

Then, in a small voice, he said, "What did I miss?"

Mia and Derek sat up alone. They'd moved the chairs to stare out the window while Blair slept on the couch and Cody continued to rest on the bed. Mia didn't know how to feel. She'd gotten answers, but not enough. Not enough about The Queen, about why this was happening, or what to do.

All she knew is that she and her brother seemed to be okay now. He'd told her as much as he could about his powers. And she'd told him about the past three weeks.

But she also knew that things couldn't go on like this. They'd both promised their parents they were going to be okay, and then this happened.

"Derek?" she said.

"Hm?"

"I think we should call Aunt Malee."

Derek was silent for a moment, then he laughed and said, "Yeah. We need an adult."

And the two sat in silence again, Mia leaning to rest her head on his shoulder as the weight of the past three weeks crashed down on her.

Epilogue

Blair breathed in the warm spring air. Birds twittered in the air, and along all the shops downtown, flowers bloomed in planters, while trees turned green as the warmth of April welcomed them back out of dormancy. Blair loved spring. Her magic was alive, dancing along her nerves as if begging her to use it. But, and she looked around to check, there were too many people walking downtown during the Saturday afternoon. While insanity had occurred less than a mile from where Blair sat at the coffee shop, only a handful of people knew what had gone down.

Blair was one of them.

Derek, her boyfriend, another.

Cody, who she had to admit had been pretty heroic when he tried to help Mia, another.

And of course, Mia herself. The one person Blair had always wanted to tell about her magic and had been too afraid to. But this worked. Because she hadn't told Mia. No, a half-Natara half-mage had done that for her.

Blair twirled the coffee cup she had gotten while waiting for her friends to show. Things hadn't been quite right since that night. Mia tried not to talk about Steven, but all of them could tell that she was torn up about him, and Derek tried not to talk about the fact that he had killed him. It kept him up at night. He kept saying it was his normal insomnia. The dreams about Niran.

Blair knew better.

Blair could see better.

She hadn't told anyone yet about the newfound ability she had, in part because she wasn't sure it was a newfound ability. It might have been a fluke that she could focus her visions on one person. On Derek. And until she knew that she was getting stronger, she didn't want to tell anyone, lest she worry her mother who already fretted over the fact that Blair was a seer.

Blair scowled.

There were only a few things in this world she actually hated, and her powers topped the list every time it got an update.

"Your face is going to freeze like that."

Blair jumped. Cody, looking far healthier than she'd ever seen him in their entire lives, stood in front of the table, holding a cup of what she guessed was tea.

She continued to scowl.

"Why are you always here first?" she asked.

Cody sat. "Because Derek is incapable of getting up on time and Mia refuses to leave him alone so he learns."

He wasn't wrong. Which only annoyed Blair even more. The two fell silent, and Blair tried her best not to think of some fight to get into, just to see Cody react. He was normally so stoic. He smiled with Mia, but other than that it was hard to read him. Not that Blair wanted to read him. Or, maybe she did. The two of them had so much history, but they were trying to move past it.

It wasn't Cody's fault, after all, that he was like Steven.

A rarity, for sure. Blair's mom had mentioned that Natara

children rarely come from a mage mother because the magic of each side was too much for a fetus to survive, but they did exist. And even though he refused to acknowledge it, and Blair was still convinced his mom was just a normal human, Cody sat there with ever growing magic, and a fear to keep him from exploring it.

And the twins knew none of this. They knew Cody was a Natara. But they didn't know about the mage part. Blair didn't feel it was her place to say, and Cody wished it wasn't true. The four of them had promised no secrets, but Blair knew that none of them stuck to it fully.

Blair opened her mouth to speak, to ask Cody any kind of question about how he was doing, but two arguing voices came into her earshot. Cody looked up, and she turned.

Derek and Mia came up the sidewalk, arguing in Chinese too fast for Blair to pick up any of the words. Not that she would have normally anyway. Derek had tried to teach her, but it'd gone over her head.

"Well, this is going to be fun," Cody said.

"Oh yeah," Blair replied with a roll of her eyes.

When the twins got close enough, Derek sat angrily in his usual seat, arms crossed. Blair nudged him, wanting to comfort him, but he refused to respond.

"What's going on?" Cody asked.

Mia, phone in hand, was ready. "You know how we're going to Beijing for a month in July?"

Know? Blair was hating every minute of that trip as they planned it. She was going to be in Wyoming with her clan for much of that time, and she'd been hoping that Mia and Derek would be able to keep her company through text. Time zones made that difficult.

"Yeah?" Cody replied when Blair said nothing.

"Well," Mia continued. "Our Aunt Lilan has asked both of us to accompany her for two weeks to a bunch of other countries, and

Derek is refusing to even think about it."

"No one said you can't go," Derek snapped. Blair nudged him again. Things never went well when he got snappy with Mia. He waved her off. "But I am not spending two weeks with the two of you. I want to come home and have a somewhat normal August. Okay?"

"But–"

"I'm not arguing about this anymore."

"Won't the Iravata be annoyed about this?" Cody asked.

Blair rolled her eyes. Of course Cody would bring them up. "Who cares what the Iravata think?"

"You should," Cody replied. "They could mess with you if they wanted."

"Yeah, well they're not going to," Blair muttered, and then, as Cody said something else, starting both Mia and Derek on another argument, Blair's world froze. Lifted. Floated. Lost.

Everything swam, and she floated on the wind.

She blinked. A pair of eyes flashed through her mind. Blue gray. At first she thought they might be Cody's, but they were missing the green.

She blinked again, and the world returned to normal.

"You go and have fun, I'm coming back to hang out with my girlfriend," Derek said. A clear conversation ender.

But Mia wasn't looking at him. She touched Blair's arm, drawing her attention to her friend.

"Blair?" Mia asked. And suddenly the boys' attention was on her too. "Are you okay?"

Okay? Yeah. She had to be okay, because she had no idea what just happened to her. Every vision was different, but usually they had something more concrete.

"I...." Blair decided the specifics weren't worth mentioning yet. Not until she'd had more visions like that. "Yeah. Weird vision.

431

Think it means nothing. Will let you guys know."

Mia nodded, and the conversation returned to normal, though this time Derek held out his hand for Blair to take. And as they chatted, laughing, relaxing from school and the insanity that was the Iravata, Blair couldn't shake the feeling that someone was watching them.

To Be Continued in...

AN
IMMINENT
DREAM

Acknowledgements

One night, late October, I was sitting with Chika and Rachelle and I told them this idea I had about a group of kids who get adopted by a demon queen. The two of them helped me foster this story. A week later, I had a first draft. Ten years later, I'm finally able to publish. So, to Chika and Rachelle, who have dealt with the changes for the past ten years, thank you.

On the same note, to Jen and Nani. Thank you for sticking with me and giving this book another chance, even though you've read the first chapter more times than probably anyone else. Good thing for you, this time is the last.

To my critique partners who helped me prepare this book and point out all the things they hated until I cried (I didn't really cry. Much), thank you. Karen, you are a saint for dealing with me sending you scene ideas and freaking out. Kathleen, I know you hate Derek, but thanks for sticking with him anyway. He appreciates your support with sarcasm and tea. Ashley, you helped me think outside of the box when I didn't want to. And of course, to all of the people in the Critique Circle discord. You're all weirdos and I appreciate you.

Thank you as well to Cas and all of her help with me and my struggles learning Photoshop and InDesign which I used to design my initial cover and format the book. It has been a real help and I don't think I'd be where I am right now if you hadn't pushed me to make a website, make a cover, and work on all of the things I needed to make this beautiful.

To Jules, who worked so hard to bring this beautiful new cover into the world and managed to shift through my complicated explanations and moods and timelines to create something so freaking beautiful!

To Jessica, who has spent hours listening to me go back and forth on whether or not I was ready to publish, if I should traditionally publish, or if I should self-publish, thank you so much for not abandoning me.

And lastly, to Aunt Lorin and my sister, Rachel. Aunt Lorin for her excellent eye and constant pushing for me to read classics to expand my knowledge, hone my prose, and show me a new night. And Rachel for introducing me to writing when I was seven years old and could barely write my own name. You are the reason I'm here today. I love you all.

About the Author

A Colorado native, Linn Coldiron spends her time reading, writing, and studying languages. Her love of language and culture has led her to live a peripatetic life filled with inspiration from all over the world.